By the hour

RONI LOREN

By the hour/Roni Loren - First edition: April 2017

ISBN (paperback): 978-0-9985213-1-2

Edited by Kelli Collins

Cover Design by Sara Eirew

Cover Photo: © NejroN Photo/BigStock Photo

Interior formatting: Indie Formatting Services

This is a work of fiction. Names, characters, places, and incidents either are the product of the author's imagination or are used fictitiously, and any resemblance to actual persons, living or dead, business establishments, events, or locales is entirely coincidental.

also by roni loren

*To my readers, thank you for continuing to buy, read,
and ask for more of my books. Lane and Elle's story wouldn't
have happened if not for you. *hugs**

Love your enemies, for they tell you your faults.
—BENJAMIN FRANKLIN

chapter one

Maybe she was a masochist after all. God knows what else could've compelled her to attend someone else's party on her birthday.

Dr. Elle McCray shifted against the worn wooden chair and traced her fingertip over the smooth-with-time initials that had been gouged into the table of Parrain's PoBoys. *D + R = 4Ever*

Forever. Sure. That's a realistic plan, D and R. Good luck with that. She flattened her palm over the stranger's engraving and tried not to look as if she were about to jump out of her skin.

She should've never come. The food was good and the music all right, but the festive atmosphere was grating against her mood and drawing blood. Dr. Marin Rush had gotten a permanent position at The Grove, the elite mental health institute where they all worked, and everyone was celebrating. Yay for Marin. She'd also gotten the guy. Donovan West, former resident of Elle's bed, was currently wrapped up in an embrace with Marin, smiling like a love-drunk idiot. *Radiating*, for God's sake.

The deep-fried shrimp Elle had eaten a few minutes ago

turned in her stomach. *Ugh.* She hated the knee-jerk reaction seeing the two of them caused. Why should she care one way or the other? She didn't even *like* Donovan West. Personality-wise, they'd always been incompatible. But he'd been a convenient solution to her no-dating policy. Donovan had seemed as uninterested in a relationship as she was and was fine keeping it strictly physical. It had worked.

But somehow, a new, younger psychologist had strolled onto the scene and had woken up a part of Donovan that Elle hadn't even known existed. Elle had been discarded like yesterday's takeout. And that—that feeling of *losing*—had stirred up old crap and turned her into some embarrassing version of herself. The jealous shrew.

God. She'd tried to get Marin *fired*, all because Elle's pride had been dinged—and her feelings hurt. The thought was enough to make her want to gag. She was not that type. She was not that woman who fought over a guy. When she'd caught her husband cheating, she'd walked away without fighting for him, without letting him see her flinch. She couldn't hold on to much dignity with what had happened in her marriage, but she'd held on to that. Until now.

So every time she looked at Marin and Donovan together, that was all she could think about. *I've become that woman. I screwed up and let myself feel something for a man.* Once again, the man had reminded her exactly why she couldn't let her guard down. He'd bailed, leaving her looking pathetic and petty. Runner-up to some other woman. Again.

Second place. First loser.

It was her own fault. She'd broken her rules. Lesson learned. Never again. That was the main reason she'd forced herself to this party—to show that she wasn't bothered, that she was a grown-up. That, and the fact that it was her birthday and it felt a little too pathetic staying home alone for it. Not that anyone knew her calendar had clicked over to a new year today. The only birthday card in her mailbox had been from her mother. The inscription had been the same as the one on the Christmas card she'd received from her a few weeks ago. *Best wishes. Love, Mom.*

There'd been an expensive bottle of Pinot Noir delivered with it. Elle had brought it to the party as a gift, an olive branch of sorts. She'd even managed to congratulate Marin and mostly mean it. At the end of the day, it wasn't Marin she was angry with. The situation with Donovan had been fucked up before the woman had ever arrived on campus.

As if hearing her name from Elle's thoughts, Marin glanced her way, a wrinkle in her brow. The woman was probably wondering why Elle had shown up. They'd managed to forge a professional working relationship in the last month or so, but they were not friends who hung out after work and would never be. But before Elle could attempt to give some sort of polite, nothing-to-see-here nod, Marin walked with purpose over to one of the other guests. The man she singled out turned and offered Marin a smile full of warmth and affection, the expression lighting his already too handsome face.

An unwelcome ripple of awareness went through Elle.

Great. With all her ruminating, she hadn't noticed him walk in.

Lane Cannon. Resident sex surrogate for The Grove's sex therapy wing—or the X-wing, as most of the staff had dubbed it. Big. Blond. And way too cocky for his own good. Though, he probably should be, considering he'd figured out how to make a legitimate living sleeping with their wealthy, often famous clients. *Therapeutic assistant.* That was his official title. But in her opinion, getting some certificate in California didn't make what he did much different than being a prostitute who happened to be a good listener.

She'd said as much to a colleague one day when he'd suggested one of the patients may benefit from Lane's services. Of course, Lane had walked up and overheard her calling him a hooker. He hadn't said a word, but the dimpled smirk he'd given her had held a big dose of *go fuck yourself.*

Then, he'd proceeded to talk to her colleague about the patient and ignore Elle completely.

First, it had pissed her off. It was her wing, dammit. Her patients. She'd started to interrupt, but then he'd sent her a look of simmering challenge, brow cocked, eyes daring her. For some reason, it had sent a rush of wildfire through Elle, heating her from the inside out, and it'd had nothing to do with anger.

She was so used to people deferring to her, being exceedingly polite, being professional because she was a doctor, because she was a boss, because she was in charge. Because she could be a scary bitch and didn't apologize for it. But with that one look, Lane had thrown down the challenge. *You don't intimidate me, doctor. You don't impress me. Just try and play those games and see what happens.*

It had been further proof that her wires were tangled now when it came to sex and men. Other women wanted romance, sweetness, love. She'd been that way once upon a time. Her ex-husband had promptly burned that fantasy to the ground, exposing it for the sham it was. Window dressing on lies. Now, she got turned on by the thought of a good hate fuck. Those were honest. Those were real. Pure physical release.

And everything in that look that day had said that Lane was more than capable of hating her right into a screaming, begging-for-more orgasm.

Dangerous.

So when Marin handed Lane a fresh glass of wine and nudged him Elle's way, Elle should've known that it was time to get up and leave. She didn't like Lane. He didn't like her. And she certainly didn't need Marin sending him over because she pitied Elle sitting alone. Screw that.

But Elle couldn't seem to make herself get up and bail. With Lane eating up the space between them with those long, powerful legs, his green eyes locking with hers, she couldn't seem to do anything at all. His lips curled at the corner, as if he knew the effect he had on her. To others, the expression probably appeared friendly. After all, he was the laid-back, good-time guy in everyone else's eyes. The guy you'd call when you got a flat tire or if you drank too much and needed a ride. But she saw the wicked glint beneath. The one that said he liked to stir up trouble, that he liked to put people off balance. That he could put *her* off balance.

And damn, it didn't help that he was nice to look at. Dark blue henley stretching over broad shoulders, jeans soft and worn in the right places, and thick-soled boots that made a heavy sound against the wood floor. Nothing pretentious or overdone. He looked like a guy who drank domestic beer and worked with his hands.

Hands. The thought snapped her back into reality. The guy *did* work with his hands. On other women. *Hell.* This is why she needed to steer clear of Lane Cannon. He scrambled her goddamned brain, especially after so many months of abstinence.

She sat up straighter in her chair and crossed her arms, sending the *go away* signal with a bullhorn. That always worked. She had a Ph.D. in that signal.

Lane ignored it. He grabbed the chair next to her, slid into it, and then plunked the glass of wine he'd been carrying onto the table in front of her. When she didn't reach for it or acknowledge him, he draped his arm over the back of her chair as if she'd invited him there. He didn't touch her, but his body heat warmed her neck as he stared out at the group like she'd been doing.

"You know, I've heard you can't really kill someone with a look. But good on you for continuing to test the theory."

She didn't look his way and tried to keep her expression smooth as he did the man-spread next to her—knees wide, big body taking up too much space. He smelled like laundry soap and dark, rich beer. And when the side of his knee bumped against hers, soft jeans brushing bare skin, an uninvited spark of awareness shot straight upward, announcing his presence to her renegade lady parts.

She cleared her throat. "Brave of you to be a test subject."

His lips quirked in her periphery. "I saw you give the death ray to Donovan earlier. Figured if he survived, I was safe."

She frowned, hating that any of her emotions about Donovan had slipped through, hating that she even *had* emotions about Donovan. "Don't be too confident. If you're coming over here to tell me to smile or join the party, I may dial the look up to eleven."

"Ouch, *Spinal Tap* level." He took a drag off his beer. "But no. You do your thing. I don't need you to smile and fake it to make me comfortable. I'm good."

"Because you're comfortable anywhere," she said, not hiding the wryness in her tone.

He shrugged. "Pretty much."

She grabbed the wine and sipped, enjoying the smooth warmth of it and hoping it would settle the jumpy feeling Lane's presence was causing. "Must be nice."

"It is." He peered her way. "So why are you so *un*comfortable?"

"Never said I was." She took another long gulp of wine.

"Right. So you're totally chill with watching the guy you used to hook up with fawn all over his new woman?"

The wine caught in her throat, making it burn and forcing her to cough. No one except Marin was supposed to know about her and Donovan's history. They'd been so careful. "He's not—we weren't."

"Calm down. Not judging. Just observant." He glanced back at Donovan and Marin as the two goofed around and danced to some upbeat country song drifting from the jukebox. "If it helps, she turned me down for him. So that just proves that fate had a plan for them."

She snorted. "Fate?"

"Absolutely. Because, let's face it, I'm really hard to turn down. I mean, look at me."

Elle turned automatically and he grinned.

"Made you look."

She groaned. "Can you go away now?"

He swigged his beer. "Nope. This is fun. We should do this more often. Or are you afraid my hooker cooties are going to get on you?"

She sniffed. "If you're expecting me to apologize for stating an opinion, don't hold your breath. You get paid to get off. I call it like I see it."

"Is that right?" He cocked his head. "Always so sure you know it all, huh? Must be a nice view from that glass tower."

Her teeth pressed against each other.

He leaned in, getting way too close, and lowered his voice. "Truth is, you don't see me at all, doc. You don't try to see. Not me or anyone else at this party."

She glared.

He tipped his beer back, finishing it off and holding her gaze, then plunked it down on the table. He turned to face her fully, arm still on the back of her chair.

"But they don't see you either," he said. "Because you don't want them to. And because they're not willing to look hard enough." His gaze traced over her face, down her throat, and then back up to her eyes, challenge there. "But I see more than you think, and that freaks you out."

The assuredness of the statement cut right through her, made her muscles go tense, her defenses heighten, but something else charged along with them to the surface. Awareness. Deep, visceral awareness of this man who was now so close.

"I know this game," he continued, his voice like a rough caress. "Get them before they get you. I can play it better than anyone. Believe me. But nobody wins that game. It's a miserable fucking existence. You came to a party with people who aren't your friends to do what? Sit here in judgment? To prove a point? To show him that you moved on? What? It's certainly not to try to make friends because I'm the first person to really talk to you tonight, and you've done everything you can to chase me off."

She wet her lips, defiantly holding his stare. "I don't need a friend. If you're here for that, this is the wrong tree to bark up."

Something flickered in his gaze at her tone and his jaw flexed. "What do you need then?"

The question hung between them, taunting her. *What do you need? What do you want?*

The silence stretched on until she could hear her heartbeat in her ears.

"Tell me," he said, quiet command in his voice. "And maybe you'll get it."

That was what she was afraid of. She knew what she needed, but he was the last person she should get it from. This was why she should've walked out when he sat down next to her. "I need to forget."

The words slipped out as his thumb moved along the back of her chair, giving an inadvertent, barely there brush to her shoulder. It set her on fire.

"Forget what?

All of it. Her failed marriage. Her screw up with Donovan. That she was almost forty and alone on her birthday. That she was—So. Fucking. Angry. All the goddamned time.

She needed oblivion and to get out of her head and to just *be* for a little while. She needed to leave, go to some other bar, find some other man in some other place. Escape the knowing gaze of Lane Cannon. But that was not what came out of her mouth. "I need to forget that you're you and I'm me and that we don't like each other."

A half-smile touched his lips, a slow lift, but there was no humor in his eyes. His gaze was intent, searching…soul-stripping. "I like you just fine, Elle McCray. In fact, I'm liking you more and more each second that you look at me like that." His thumb traced along the spot where her neck met her shoulder—hardly a touch but most definitely on purpose this time. "Tell me what would make you forget."

She swallowed, trying to ease the sudden dryness in her throat and ignore the gathering warmth between her thighs, the brush of her hardening nipples against her bra. She was losing control of this fast and wasn't sure if she was happy about that or panicked. "Do I have to spell it out? Or are four-letter words too long for you?"

The smile became a full one now. A predatory one. Her insult seemed to only egg him on. "Bold suggestion from a woman who was trying to scare me off a minute ago. You don't even like me."

"No. I don't." She closed her eyes for a second, trying to regain her breath, and whispered. "That's the best part."

The confession slipped out and he tipped his head as if he were processing her words, assessing her. But then his thumb pressed against her spine. "I promise you. That definitely won't be the best part."

Her neck felt hot, the air in the room thick. "No?"

He bent close to her ear, his scent drifting over her. "No. The best part will be when I'm deep inside you and you're riding your edge, begging for this guy you hate to give you exactly what you need, to drive you so out of your mind that you have no choice but to forget everything except the way I'm fucking you and how good it feels and how much you want it."

She closed her eyes again, the words rushing over her like open palms on naked skin. *Fuck.* "We can't...I don't..."

Lane sat back. "Tell me to go away again, Elle. Lie and tell me you want me to go away and I will."

Her eyes fluttered open and she wet her lips, nerves and good sense trying to take hold. She shifted her gaze to the party. It felt like spotlights were burning down on her and Lane, exposing all their secret whispered words. But no one was paying attention to them. And even if someone looked over, all anyone would see were two people talking. No one would be able to see how fast her heart was beating or how damp her panties had gotten. No one would see that the man who spent his days patiently guiding people in intimacy training had just offered to fuck her until she was begging.

She needed to say no. To end this. "We can't leave together."

His smile went smug. "Don't want to be seen slumming it with someone who doesn't have a doctorate?"

She shot him a look.

"Give me your address. I know you live on campus. You can leave first. I'll wait a few minutes and then head over."

Before she could think too hard about it, she nodded. "I'm the only house on the northwest side of the pond. My name's on the mailbox." She took a breath. "No one can ever know about this. I don't want to talk when you get there. You will use protection. And if I say *no* to something, you stop."

"Wow, a checklist. No romantic wooing for you, McCray? No drinks by the fireplace while we get to know each other?"

"If that's what you're looking for, you're looking at the wrong woman. And let's not pretend you actually want to get to know me. We have nothing in common."

He narrowed his eyes, considering her. "Leave your door unlocked. Keep the lights low so no one sees me coming in.

And don't change out of this dress." He let his gaze slide down over her with slow deliberation. "I want to have the pleasure of ripping it off of you."

A shimmer of anticipation went through her at that image. Maybe this was exactly what she needed tonight. An ill-advised, forbidden night with a guy who looked like he could keep a dirty promise. She drained her wine and then picked up her handbag, rising on tingling legs. "'Til then."

He stayed in his seat but grabbed her wrist before she could leave. "One more thing."

She tugged her arm free of his loose grip in case anyone looked their way. "Yes?"

"If you lock your door, I'll walk away and never come back. You can dislike me all you want, but you won't play games with me. At least not that kind."

She nodded, the undercurrent of authority in his voice doing more to her than it should. Mr. Happy-Go-Lucky had a darkness to him, things lurking in his tone that scared her a little. She wished seeing that didn't make her want him ten times more. "Nothing will be locked. You'll have full access."

The look he gave her promised filthy, tawdry things. "Full access."

"Yes."

To everything her body had to give.

And nothing her heart did.

She left him sitting there and walked out of the party without saying good-bye. She hadn't found any friends tonight, but maybe she'd found exactly what she needed for her birthday.

A way to forget.

And someone to forget with.

chapter two

Lane forced himself to stall at the party after Elle had strode out of the restaurant without looking back, hips swinging with the kind of sass that said she knew Lane was watching. He made small talk, joined in on a toast to Marin's promotion, and generally acted like he had nowhere to be. But after a while, impatience edged in, and he headed over to Marin and Donovan to tell them good-bye.

"Leaving already?" Marin asked, giving him a tight hug. "We haven't gotten to the bread pudding yet."

He released her and patted his stomach. "None for me. Gotta watch my figure."

She snorted. "Right. I think all the single women at The Grove like watching your figure. When you walk down the halls, it's like watching a tennis match with all the turning heads."

Donovan smirked at her. "Hey, I'm right here."

Marin rolled her eyes and bumped her shoulder into Donovan's. "I said *single* women. But seriously, is everything okay? Did the goodwill mission I sent you on with McCray ruin your night? Because if it did, I'm really sorry. She looked kind of pissed when she left."

Ha. If Marin only knew. "She didn't stab me with her fork, so I figure that's a win. But no, I just have to get up early in the morning. It's been fun though. Congrats again."

Marin smiled and Donovan shook Lane's hand before he headed out, saying good-byes to the others on his way. It seemed to take forever, but he didn't want to look like he was in a rush. Plus, he wanted Elle to wait a bit.

When she'd left the party, he'd fought hard not to head out right behind her, haul her up against a wall somewhere, and kiss her until she forgot how much she disliked him. Their little chat had left him fighting a hard-on and ready to conquer Dr. Ice (the moniker he'd given her in his head a few months back), but he'd held himself in check. Elle was used to people following after her like loyal subjects—employees, patients, interns. He wasn't going to be another minion. That was the last thing she needed. That wasn't what had turned her on tonight. What had tripped her wires had been the very fact that he didn't cower when she shot her poison arrows at him. It definitely wasn't because she liked him.

Elle was being honest about that part. She'd slapped a *prostitute* label on him and believed it. Of course, she had no clue how spot-on accurate she was. He wasn't an escort anymore, but he'd spent more years in that role than in his current one. And the insult still poked at old, raw things. When he'd heard her call him a hooker that day to another doctor, he'd seen red. He was used to that shit outside of the therapy community but not from within it. He'd worked hard to get to where he was now—legitimately helping people—and didn't need anyone knocking him back down into the gutter.

But not until tonight had he realized that her aversion to him wasn't simply because of his job. She was scared of letting him near her because she *wanted* him. Tonight, she hadn't been able to hide her physical reaction to him. He'd caught her off guard. And for a moment, he'd seen how shockingly human she was. Had seen it in her eyes when she'd looked at everyone having a good time. She was fucking lonely. An outsider. She'd created that for herself, but he also got the sense that she had no clue how to fix it. He remembered what that was like—always feeling as if there were a thick glass wall between you and everyone else. Like you were watching a movie and hadn't even gotten hired as an extra.

It'd made him want to ask questions, to get to know her. But that was not what she'd needed tonight. She wouldn't have allowed it anyway. *Nice* scared her. She didn't trust it. She didn't want nice-guy Lane. She didn't want to like him.

That's the best part. She'd whispered the words but he'd heard the honesty in them. She needed the ire between them. That made it safe for her. She was turned on by their combative words, their insults. He'd been a dominant long enough that he'd seen a lot of different kinks, and God knows he'd seen a dose of most everything in his former career, but he'd never slept with someone who openly disliked him. The thought probably shouldn't turn his crank, but it had nudged something inside him.

He'd had an exceptionally shitty day, had gotten bad news and had been in a terrible mood on the way to the party. He'd hoped being with friends would help him forget, but instead he'd found something much more interesting by sparring with the beautiful doctor. She owned her role as ice queen, not hiding the fact that she thought she was above him. And man, after the day he'd had, he'd wanted to knock her down a notch.

He'd just never expected her to want the same thing, and he definitely hadn't expected her to want it in bed. But when she'd put the idea out there and looked at him as if she wanted to take a bite, he hadn't been able to hold back the onslaught of desire it'd set off. Those pale blond locks of hers wrapped in his fist, those pursed lips begging for his cock, that ever-simmering judgment in her eyes fading into the haze of orgasm.

Yes. All that.

She wanted a hate fuck? He was ready to deliver.

Elle paced her floors and shook out her hands, trying to get rid of the nerves that had insisted on stalking her as soon as she walked into her house. She never got nervous about things like this. It was only sex. Since her divorce, she'd had her fair share of it with a number of men. Some better than others. This would just be another hookup. A one-night stand.

So what if she'd have to see Lane again at The Grove? He didn't work on the rehab wing, her domain. He was easily avoided. Plus, she was a grown woman who could separate business and pleasure. She'd compartmentalized the hell out of Donovan. Compartmentalizing was a long-practiced art of hers. This would be no different.

If she were really that worried, she would lock her door. Shut down the possibility for good. Because she knew Lane would hold true to his threat. If she locked it, he'd never look her way again. She put her hand on the lock briefly, but she couldn't bring herself to turn it, not with her blood pumping this hard and the silky panties she'd changed into already clinging to her.

She wanted this.

But after twenty minutes of pacing, her focus switched from worrying about the possibility that this would happen to worrying that Lane wouldn't go through with it, that it had been a tease. A joke.

So when she heard the back door click open, she had to bite her lip to keep from making a sound of relief. He was here. This was happening.

She halted in the spot where she was in the living room, waiting in the hazy gray moonlight that filtered through the curtains. She wouldn't go to him, wouldn't reveal how eager she really felt.

Heavy footsteps sounded on the wooden floorboards, the one in the hallway creaking beneath his shoe, and then he stepped into the doorway of the living room. Somehow he looked even bigger here in her house. Over six feet of man filling up the unevenly framed antique doorway. The stained-glass pane above the door showered pale, colored light onto his shoulders and left his face half in shadow.

Her throat went tight, bone dry. "It took you long enough. Decided to stay for dessert?"

His mouth curved as he stepped forward, absorbing her sharp tone like she'd said something sweet. "No. I'm having you instead. Hope you're worth skipping bread pudding." He eyed her. "Frankly, I have my doubts."

The jab made her pull up short. But instead of it pissing her off, a breath she hadn't realized she'd been holding released, the insult somehow softening the edge of her nerves. "Screw you, Cannon."

Amusement crossed his face. He was close now, almost

within arm's reach, making her step back. "That's the idea, sunshine."

She licked her lips and her back pressed against the wall. "No one knows you came here?"

His hands planted against the wall on each side of her shoulders, caging her in and enveloping her with his scent, his... bigness. "No, don't worry. No one knows you're slumming it. That you're horny and hot for the institute's *hooker*. Your dirty secret's safe."

She winced. "I didn't mean—"

"Yeah, you did," he said. "But it's all right. I wouldn't want anyone to know I'm here either. I've got my own reputation to keep."

She narrowed her eyes. "What? For only fucking people who pay you?"

He smiled, a wickedness to it. "Oh, people don't pay me for this, sweetheart. This isn't for sale."

Before she could register what was happening, he spun her around, pinned her against the wall, and pressed his body along her back. His erection pushed hard and heavy against her and a hot shudder of need chased down her spine. She had to fight not to whimper.

"Give me a safe word, McCray," he said, his voice low and serious against her ear. "Because I'm about to give you what I know you want, but I'm not gonna do it without one of those. Your attitude's got me wanting to do bad things to you."

She closed her eyes, heat flooding her sex and making every part of her prickle with awareness. She said the first word that came to her head. "Birthday."

He pressed his nose to her hair, inhaling. "Good girl."

"No." She tensed, the endearment scraping across her psyche and making her stomach clench.

He stilled. "No, what?"

"Don't call me that. Ever."

He was quiet for a second, and then his hand coasted down her bare arm in a soothing touch, like he was trying to calm a skittish horse. "Got it. That's all you have to say to me, all right? Anything that's out of bounds for you, just tell me and I'll respect it."

She took a deep breath, hating that she'd reacted so strongly, that the demons floated so close to the surface. That her ex-husband's old endearment would get to her. She was off her game tonight. *He* was putting her off her game. "I don't need your therapy mode, Lane."

"This isn't therapy mode. This is me being a responsible dominant and human being."

A dominant? Great. Of course he was. "I'm not submissive."

"Yeah, I got that."

"And if you ask me to call you sir, I will fucking punch you."

He chuckled behind her, his breath tickling her neck. "I'd like to see you try."

He grabbed the hem of her favorite black dress and dragged it up her hips, exposing the pale blue silk panties she'd changed into. He grunted and cupped her ass with a hot palm. But unlike the guys she was normally with, he didn't fawn over the sight of her expensive lingerie or throw any compliments her way.

"No way you wore these to the party. Are you trying to impress me, McCray? Or did your other ones get too wet from talking to me?"

"God, you're an asshole." She meant the words as an insult,

but they came out more as a sigh with an undertone of *please for the love of God, touch me* instead.

He squeezed her ass in his big palm and then smacked it hard. She gasped.

"And you fucking love it. I don't care what you call me. Bitch at me all you want, but your body gives you away." His boot insinuated itself between her feet as he forced her stance wider. His hand slid between her legs. When his fingers grazed the soaking-wet fabric, he made a low sound of victory in the back of his throat. He pushed the panties aside and grazed roughened fingertips over her slick flesh, sending pleasure snaking up her spine and out to her limbs.

She held in the moan that threatened. She wouldn't give him the satisfaction.

His soft laugh brushed against her ear as he found her swollen clit. "Now, now, that's not a game you can win, so don't bother trying. You won't be quiet for me."

She squeezed her eyes shut and gritted her teeth as he made skilled circles around the sensitive bud, slicking her skin with her arousal and driving up her need. It was just the right pressure to send her heart galloping and her breaths quickening. It'd been a while, and her body wanted to tip over, take that release, but she couldn't let it. Not this easily. Not yet. She pressed her forehead to the wall and rocked her hips, trying to adjust the touch, make it less potent. But he was too agile, too aware of her every move.

He shifted his hand and slid a thick finger inside her. She couldn't stop her reaction then. Her moan came from the back of her throat and filled the quiet living room. *Fuuuuck.*

"That's it," he said, slowly pumping his finger inside her and then going back to her clit in a maddening dance. "It's okay that you enjoy it. It doesn't mean you lose. It means we both win."

He was right. She knew that. But it was so hard to give in, to accept that this was happening with Lane and that she wanted it this badly.

He found her most secret hot spot, right of center and just where she liked to touch herself when she was on a solo tour. The precision of the stroke was too much. Her fingers curled against the wall and she breathed through her teeth. "I can't... not yet..."

Lane kissed the back of her neck. "I've got all night, doc. And I'm patient as fuck. This won't be the last one. I promise. Stop fighting."

She panted. Orgasm was beating down the doors, but she couldn't give in. She had no idea why she was resisting still, but she found herself staving it off. Counting in her head. Doing anything and everything to lead away from what she knew would be full-on pleasure.

Stop. She tried to push away the resistance, tried to let herself feel it, but her brain slammed the door shut again. Her fingers balled into a fist and tapped the wall. "Can't..."

He continued for a few seconds more but then paused as if her words had finally sunk in. "You're not lying, are you? You really can't give in."

The stillness of his fingers was torture. She rocked her forehead against the wall. She wanted to come, needed that release, but her brain and her body were battling.

Before she could form any words to explain, Lane was backing up, the loss of his heat startling. He dragged her dress over her head, leaving her in her wrecked panties and lacy bra.

"Remember your safe word, doc."

"What?"

He lifted her off her feet without warning, cradling her against his chest. She gasped and blinked her eyes open, the sudden shift making her head spin. She peered up at him but he wasn't looking at her. He was staring straight ahead as he carried her into the hallway, a determined set to his jaw.

"What are you doing?" The question popped out of her.

He bumped open the door to her bedroom and set her down on the bed. He pointed a finger her way. "Don't move."

Her lips parted, but he was out of the door in a flash. Her heartbeat picked up speed and her body throbbed with ultimate frustration, but for some reason, she didn't get off the bed. A minute later, he came back with an armful of mint-green sheets—the ones from her guest room. "What the hell?"

"Lay down," he said as he knotted the fitted sheet to the top sheet. "I don't have what I need but this should work."

"Work for what? And it's *lie* not *lay*."

He looked up, smirking. "Are you really giving me a goddamned grammar lesson while you *lie* there with a soaked cunt and a *fuck me* look on your face?"

The words were rude. Harsh. True as shit. And for some reason, sexy as hell. She let her gaze travel over him as he continued to tie the sheets and then lingered on the impressive outline in his pants. "You're not exactly the vision of restraint either. Your dick's about to shred the denim."

He gripped his erection and smiled. "Offering to make it better, doc? You can't correct my grammar with a full mouth."

She leaned back on her elbows, following his earlier command. "I don't give head. Not my thing."

His eyebrow lifted. "Beneath you, huh?"

No, I stopped when I tasted someone else on my husband. "Something like that."

"Lucky for you, I have something else in mind." He walked over to the bed, put his hands on her shoulders, and guided her down. Before she could protest, he draped the sheet over her chest and tucked one side under the mattress.

She had no idea what he was doing but found herself lying there and watching. He dragged the tied sheet fully beneath the mattress then yanked the other half out the other side. He grabbed the unsecured side of the sheet over her and knotted it to its partner, cinching it tight. The tug stretched the flat of the sheet over her shoulders, breasts, and stomach, pinning her arms at her sides and her body to the bed but leaving her bottom half exposed.

Her breathing stuttered. "Lane?"

"Take a deep breath for me."

She inhaled through her nose, filling her lungs and making the sheet pull tighter.

He nodded. "See. You can breathe. Anything hurt?"

"No, but—"

"I didn't ask for additional commentary. Your safe word or quiet from you, doc. Earlier you said you can't come. But you really meant you won't—not for me. Now you don't have a choice."

Her muscles tensed as he stepped around to the end of the bed and stared down at her like a victor of war. He climbed onto the mattress and grabbed the thin fabric of her panties, dragging them down her legs and exposing exactly how he was affecting her. Her scent filled the air.

He inhaled deeply and smiled, tracing his fingers over her sensitive flesh. "Let's see if you taste as bitter as your attitude."

Oh, God. She didn't have a moment to prepare herself before Lane was pressing his big hands on the backs of her thighs and opening her wide, exposing every private inch of her. Then, he lowered his head. His hot tongue swept over her like sweet, blessed fire, and she tried to bow up. But the sheets held fast, trapping her in place and not giving her any reprieve.

Lane let out a soft grunt of pleasure. "Hmm. Not bitter at all. At least one part of you is very, very sweet."

And that was the last he spoke before he put his lips and tongue against her and made her goddamned world explode. He didn't just tease her or lap at her like an eager dog. She'd found men tended to fall into one camp or the other. He did neither. He *kissed* her, open mouthed and sensual, sucking her flesh between his lips and circling her clit with his tongue as he slid two fingers inside her. It was slow and tortuous and downright worshipful. Like she was an instrument and only he knew the notes to the song.

Her head tipped back and heat tracked up her body. The pressure of the sheet against her breasts only added to it, the restriction making the lace of her bra drag over her sensitive nipples. Everything was lit up, aware, needy. She tried to reach out to grab his hair to regain some control, but her arms were pinned. The effect only ratcheted her arousal higher. He required surrender.

She hadn't come for him, so he was going to force it out of her. It was a game. And suddenly, she wanted to play it.

"You think that's going to work?" she said between panted breaths and fingernails digging into the mattress. "You think you have some sort of magical talent for—"

That was the last word she got out before he curled his fingers right against her G-spot and enveloped her clit with a circle of his tongue.

Every resistant cell in her body flopped over in abject surrender, white flags going up, and release rumbled through her without warning, making her jerk and quiver against the bindings and cry out against her will.

He didn't stop. He didn't soften his assault. He continued the magic dance of his fingers and tongue, and somehow, she found herself climbing to the next level of orgasm. The kind that made her sound as if she'd been stabbed with something sharp.

Later, she'd probably be embarrassed about the noises she was making, but right now, she couldn't think to care. She was tied down and a beautiful, supremely annoying man was going down her like he was giving a master lesson in how to make a woman scream. Maybe he was. She was a mere example in his imaginary seminar. *Look how subject A writhes when I rub my fingers against her G-spot. And listen to how she cries out when I massage her clit with my tongue. Observe how her back arches and her pussy clenches when I lick her juices off her like I'm starved for her taste. I am starved for her taste.*

The last thought had her cresting, and when her cries turned to wordless gasps and she didn't think she could take any more, Lane finally eased back. The loss of his warmth almost made her call out for him, but she bit back the urge and panted through the end of her release.

Breathe. Breathe. Breathe.

She had to get herself back together, find her thoughts so she could deal with him again. Keep the game going.

But he didn't give her time. The sound of a zipper dragging open had her eyelids lifting. Lane stood at the edge of the bed as he unfastened his pants, forearms working, his gaze hot on her, almost mean. Like he was annoyed he wasn't inside her yet. Like it was her fault. Like he was going to make her pay for it.

That look did things to her it shouldn't.

But she couldn't let her focus get hung up in those eyes of his. That was too much. Plus, he was pulling off his shirt and, *Christ*, the man was something to behold. Broad-shouldered and muscular, more bulked up than she typically was drawn to, but goddamn, did it work on him. Her gaze tracked over the dusky trail of hair that led down to his waistband. The waistband he was opening.

Her tongue pressed to the roof of her mouth as he tucked his hand in to adjust his erection before sliding his jeans and boxer briefs down his hips. His long fingers wrapped around the shaft of his thick cock and stroked, causing everything inside her to clench. A bead of moisture gathered at the tip and he deftly rolled his thumb over the head, making it glossy. There was something unbearably erotic about the way this man handled his body—so confident and without shame. It was a promise. *I know what to do with this. How to make myself feel good. How to make you feel even better.*

She could watch him stroke himself like that and never get tired of the show, but she tried to pull her expression into one of boredom. "You just going to jerk off all night or are you going to use that thing?"

He smirked as he continued the slow strokes, spreading more fluid gathering on the head down his shaft. "Maybe I'll just stand over you and make you watch. Get your sheets all messy. You'd look pretty covered in my come."

On a different guy, the words would've sounded straight out of porn but coming from him, it raised goose bumps. She could picture him doing just that, could imagine how it would feel to have his hot release sliding over her bare skin.

His sly smile went crooked in a deliciously evil way. "And someone likes that idea. You've got layers of filthy thoughts in that head of yours, don't you?"

"Maybe I figure that would be easier, seeing as I've already come and gotten what I need."

He stepped to the edge of the bed and grabbed the condom he'd tossed onto the sheets. He rolled it on while keeping his eyes on her. "Oh, no, I promise, you haven't gotten near what you need tonight."

Before she could respond, he released the knot on the sheet and grabbed her ankles. He tugged, dragging her body out from under the bindings until her ass was at the edge of the bed and he was looming over her. All her breath had left the minute he'd pulled on her, and now she had no chance at regaining it. Not with him standing between her knees, cock in hand and gloriously naked. But now that she was free, she tried to lift herself up and flip over.

Two big hands captured her and pushed her onto her back again. "Not so fast, doc. I didn't tell you to turn over."

His palms pressing against her shoulders made her squirm, but the fight was making her burn hot again even though she'd just had an orgasm. "I come easier if I'm on my hands and knees."

Truth. Sort of. Turning her back always made it easier to

focus on the sensations. To block her partner out.

"Well, good news, this portion of the festivities isn't for you. It's for me. And I want to watch your face when I fuck you."

He kept his hands on her shoulders but lifted a brow, as if asking a question, and she realized he was giving her a chance to tell him no, to use her safe word. But that would be a version of losing, and she didn't want this to end right now. She wanted it on her terms, but not enough to pull the parachute cord. She'd just close her eyes. "You're a selfish bastard. I thought you were supposed to be the sensitive, giving surrogate."

He rubbed his cock along her crease, teasing her. "Only with people I like."

"Only with people who pay you."

His jaw clenched and he angled forward, entering her without warning and burying deep.

Her body was so slick, it welcomed the invasion, but the surprise of it and the delicious fullness of his cock had her gasping. Her head tipped back and she tried not to look so affected, but it was useless. Her muscles flexed around him and her fingers curled into the sheets.

Lane let out a quiet groan, a little break in his own cool facade, and he braced a hand alongside her as he pulled almost all the way out and then sank home again. The glide of his heat against hers was like scratching the deepest, most satisfying itch. Goddamn, she hadn't realized how much she needed this, that feeling of being joined, of having a gorgeous man filling her. He put a hand behind her knee, opening her farther, and pumped into her with long, slow strokes that made her nerve endings sing with pleasure. She closed her eyes, letting herself fall into the oblivion of it.

"Look at me," he said, the words a low rumble.

"Hmm?" Her voice had taken on a dreamy quality.

A hand slipped behind her neck and squeezed. The sudden change caused her eyes to pop open. Lane's face was inches from hers, his eyes ablaze. "Look. At. Me."

Elle licked her lips, her heart pounding high in her throat. He was so close that she could see flecks of gold in his green eyes and the intensity burning there. The eye contact had her anxiety surfacing. She didn't do the intimacy thing. She didn't fuck face to face, much less eye to eye. But he pumped into her again and held her gaze. Somehow, she couldn't look away. He was *daring* her not to look away.

"That's right," he said, his voice barely above a whisper. "It's me, Elle. That's who's making you feel good. The *hooker* from the X-wing. Ask me to make you come again."

She swallowed hard, her pride and the need in her body having a throwdown. "I don't beg, Cannon. I'm not one of your submissives."

"You used the word *beg*, not me. Are you feeling tempted to beg?" He shifted his hips, angling right against that sensitive spot inside her and tucking his hand between them to provide maddening friction to her clit. "Because, boy, would that be a feather in my cap."

She took a shuddering breath, trying to breathe through the need. "Fuck you."

"Already doing that. Effectively, based on the look on your face."

She closed her eyes, but he tapped his forehead to hers. "Look at me, McCray. Look at me or I'm going to kiss you, and I know you don't want that."

Her eyelids flew open. She'd never had anything against kissing. She'd done it with other guys, had kissed Donovan. Could keep it separate and label it just another physical act. But the thought of kissing Lane sent fear through her. "Don't. Please."

His lip curled. "And that, you beg for."

There was something wrapped up in those words, but before she could process them, he picked up his pace and, despite his demands on her, he closed his eyes. There was no stopping her reactions now. His fingers and the rhythm of his body pumping into hers were driving her past the point of control. But despite her railroading hormones, she couldn't keep her gaze off his face. Now that he wasn't looking at her, she could take in the view. The glisten of sweat on his brow, the hard jaw, the way his hair was curling at his temple. He was beautiful and lost to the moment. Lost to her.

Suddenly, she missed his eyes on her, missed seeing that ferocity. She lifted her hand to move his hair away from his brow, but then caught herself. This wasn't a time for tenderness. Not here. Not with him.

So she let her head fall back, sank into the pleasure of their bodies joining and his adept fingers working her, and let it all go. The cry that came out of her sounded distant to her ears and light tracked behind her eyelids as she came. He wasn't far behind, his composure falling away as he grunted and groaned. He grabbed her hard and sank as deep inside her as he could get, roaring with his release.

Her body shook with the force of their orgasms, everything trembling like a tuning fork until all the tension left her and she melted into a puddle on the bed. He pressed his forehead to hers for a moment, their eyes still closed, their breathing heavy, and bodies quietly joined.

The moment felt unbearably intimate and for some reason, she wanted to cry.

The urge had her planting her hands on his chest and easing him away. He went without resistance and slipped out of her. She rolled onto her side, putting her back to him.

A hand touched her hip. "You okay, doc?"

The concern in his tone and the gentle touch only made the anxiety welling in her worse. "I'm fine. The bathroom has fresh towels if you need to shower."

He didn't say anything for a long moment, and she worried she'd have some sort of panic attack if he didn't go away. Right. Now. But finally, he moved his hand from her. "Thanks. I'll be right back."

She swallowed past her parched throat. "No rush."

Take all the time you need. Please.

Because she needed to be alone to get herself back together. And then she needed to get him the hell out of her house.

chapter three

Lane toweled off in the small, pristine bathroom and tried to get his head together. He'd started the day at school, facing yet another failing grade and having a spectacularly shitty meeting with his professor, and then had somehow ended the day in bed with Dr. Elle McCray. Not just in bed with her—but hate-fucking and playing kinky games and enjoying himself way too much. There was a twist he hadn't anticipated.

Much to his shock, the normally frosty doctor had been into it, too. She'd tried to fight it, had tried to pretend like it wasn't doing it for her, but she wasn't that good of an actress. And man, when she came, she really didn't hold back. He loved when a woman dropped all self-consciousness and just owned the pleasure of it all, not caring how wild she sounded or how unraveled she looked. He wouldn't have guessed Elle would be the type to let go like that. The woman was sexy as fuck.

But mean as hell.

He hated to admit it, but her obvious aversion to kissing him had stung. Knowing her, she'd probably thought of all the potential places his mouth had been and deemed it unworthy of touching hers. Maybe she had a right to think that. His rap sheet in that department was long. But it had brought back the old days, when he was the hired help and women were happy to have their bodies kissed by him but not their lips.

He rubbed a hand over his face and tried to shake off the feeling. *Get over yourself, Cannon.* She had probably only been playing the game. She was supposed to hate him. She wouldn't kiss someone she hates.

But now that the game was done, he'd find out.

Lane tugged on his jeans and draped his shirt over his shoulder. He didn't want to leave Elle on her own too long. She'd seemed off at the end. She'd resisted his attempt at making sure she was okay, but that wasn't going to fly. As a dominant, it was ingrained in him to check in with his partner, to provide that aftercare. He relished that phase himself—those quiet moments after the intensity of a scene when the world came back into focus.

But when he walked back into the bedroom, Elle wasn't tucked under the covers waiting for him. The bed was neatly made, the sheets he'd stolen from the other room were gone, and only a lamp had been left on. It looked like a tidy hotel room instead of a personal space where he'd just had some of the best sex of his life.

He frowned and dragged his shirt over his head. Clearly, he wasn't going to be invited to spend the night. He wasn't surprised, but her absence made tension gather in his neck.

He headed out of the bedroom and toward the living room. The low sound of a late-night talk show drifted his way, and TV light flickered on the wall of the hallway. When he stepped inside, Elle was on the couch, drinking something from a mug and watching the screen. But it wasn't a cozy picture. This wasn't, *Hey, we just had great sex. I made us some decaf. Let's hang out and get to know each other a little.*

Her back was as stiff as stone and her knuckles were white around the mug. Her expression revealed nothing. He cleared his throat.

"Hey," he said, when she didn't look his way.

She glanced over but didn't meet his eyes. "Hey. Found the towels?"

"Yeah, and your shower gel. Now I smell like peach blossoms and girl."

"Sorry. I should've grabbed you a bar from the guest bathroom."

He'd meant for his comment to lighten the mood, but her deadpan response put a chill in the room. He took a breath, trying to find his patience. "I wanted to make sure you're okay. You seem—"

"I'm good. Thanks for tonight," she said, the words clipped. *The doctor voice.* "I trust you'll be discreet about what happened. Your keys are on the table by the door."

His fingers flexed at his sides. He was so used to being in charge that he had to fight the urge to walk over and put her on her knees for the disrespect. But she wasn't his submissive. She wasn't his anything. "So, I'm dismissed. That's how it is?"

She glanced over at him, expression smooth as glass. A porcelain doll back on the shelf, flat blue eyes revealing nothing. "We both got what we wanted tonight. I have rounds early in the morning."

He stared at her until she looked away. He wanted to call her out, to figure out what this bullshit was. The budding therapist in him wanted to untangle it all. But what could he say? She hadn't promised anything more than what had happened. They'd had an attraction and acted on it. Fine. Done. She wasn't acting any differently than how a lot of single dudes he knew acted. They may put on a better show, but this was one-night-stand protocol without the window dressing of, *I'll call you.*

"Yeah. Well, see you around."

When she didn't respond, he headed to the door. He didn't need this shit. Yeah, he'd had a great time with her and the sex had been top shelf, but he had no interest in hanging around where he wasn't wanted.

For a little while, he'd thought maybe there was more to her than the ice queen she portrayed herself to be. But if there was, clearly she wasn't interested in showing him that side. And he definitely had no interest in being involved with someone so damn cold. If this was how she wanted things, that made it easy for him. He was the king of walking away. That was part of his job.

But when he grabbed his keys, there was an envelope lying next to it with his name on it. Wary, he picked it up and peeked inside. There were three crisp one-hundred dollar bills inside.

"What the fuck is this?" The sharp edge in his voice cut through the laughter on the television.

She stared at the screen. "I don't know what your fee is, but I figured that would cover it. That's all the cash I had on hand."

"*My fee?*" Oh, screw that noise. Anger sparked bright and his voice boomed as he stepped closer to her. "Are you fucking kidding me right now?"

She turned his way, the haughty, above-it-all expression back in place. "Do you charge more?"

He scoffed, amazed at the gall of this woman. "This was a hookup, McCray, not a job, and you know it. What are you trying to do here? Is this part of your game?"

"What I'm doing here is making things clear. This isn't an anything. I wanted sex. You were available and provided. This keeps it neat and doesn't leave any questions going forward. And I know you have no qualms about charging for your services. You do it every day."

He shook his head in disgust. "Unbelievable. You're screwed up, doc. You know that?"

She looked away.

"You want to label me a whore because it's easy to dismiss me. You can box me up neatly instead of treating me like a person—or God forbid, a colleague. You think this is what I do with clients?" When she didn't answer, he charged on. "Yeah, you probably do. Better to assume instead of asking and finding out that I don't even get off with clients, that I help them work through anxiety or trauma or self-esteem issues and the focus is one-hundred percent on them. That it's not sexy. Or fun. Or a paid fuck. It's work. It's therapy. But instead of asking, you just let yourself believe the stereotype. You don't want to know because then you might actually have to consider that I'm not an enemy and that you liked what happened tonight. That I'm just a guy you talked with at a party, who had kind of a shitty day himself and who tried to make small talk with a co-worker so that she didn't have to sit there alone on a night that was probably kind of difficult for her. And that it turned into more. And that you wanted it to."

The words made her posture stiffen, but she didn't turn his way.

"Stop bombing allies, McCray. There'll be nothing left but wasteland." Exhaustion washed over him, his bad day sinking in deep now. If he thought he was getting through to her, he was fooling himself. And he'd been made a fool of enough for one day. "Enjoy your night, doctor." He leaned down close, bracing his hands on the arm of the couch. "And for what it's worth, I charge a hell of a lot more. And what I just did to you in there? Sweetheart, you wouldn't be able to afford that even on *your* fancy salary. It's not for sale. Now you can go to sleep knowing you'll never get it again."

She glared at the TV so hard, he was surprised the screen didn't melt.

He tossed the money onto the floor in front of her and walked out.

What a fantastic fucking day.

Elle rose from the couch and watched through a slit in the blinds as Lane strode down her walk to his black sports car, his anger still crackling in the air of her living room.

His words echoed in her ears, and her body still thrummed from his touch, but she stayed glued to the spot. Maybe she should be the type of person who would go after him, apologize, try to get to know him and make a friend. But what then?

Yes, sex with him had been explosive and more intense than she'd bargained for. But that was all there was. She wasn't equipped for more than that, and she definitely couldn't date someone who slept with other people for a living—therapeutic or not.

No way.

Plus, he was a world-class, egotistical jackass.

She stepped away from the window, feeling a rush of self-righteousness, and collected the dollar bills that were strewn across the floor. But before she'd gotten all three of them, she felt wet warmth tracking down her cheeks.

Goddammit.

All the air sagged out of her and she sank down to the carpet, letting the money fall from her fingertips and the despair she'd been fighting take over.

He'd asked her if she knew how screwed up she was.

She hadn't responded.

They both knew the answer.

chapter four

"**S**he needs to be naked in front of you and learn how to be comfortable with you touching her body."

Lane hooked his ankle over his knee, considering Marin's words while relaxing on the couch in her office. "But she doesn't have issues with intercourse?"

Marin set her steno pad aside and turned fully toward him. "No. Do you need something to take notes on, by the way?"

He shook his head and tapped his temple. "I've got a good memory. I'll just lose a notebook."

She smiled. "If I didn't have my notepads, I'd lose my mind. I'll email you the case file. But sex isn't the issue for Carlotta as long as it's done in the dark. The issue is more about being observed and feeling confident in her body when a man is looking at her."

"What triggered that?" he asked, already formulating some preliminary sessions in his head.

Marin sighed, the move ruffling the bangs of her short dark hair and making her look more college student than psychologist. "She started acting when she was really young.

She had a gig on a long-running kids' show, and there was all this pressure to stay looking like a child in order to keep the job because she was supporting her entire family. So when her body started to change as a young teen, she tried to keep the curves away by restricting her food and it morphed into an eating disorder."

Lane frowned, empathy brewing. He knew what that kind of pressure was like, to need money so badly that you would do anything to stay afloat. He rubbed the back of his neck. "That's a lot to put on a kid."

"Yes, it's not surprising that things went downhill. Thankfully, she moved past the food issues with some pretty extensive therapy and got to a healthy weight in her early twenties, but she still has trouble believing that her body is good enough. The upcoming role she's landed is the biggest of her life and she's committed to making it work, but she'll be playing a spy that has to go undercover as a stripper. There will also be love scenes that require nudity with Bradley Chastain. The first time they tried to do a topless scene, she had a massive panic attack. They're shifting those scenes in the production schedule to give her a chance, but she only has a few weeks to get over the fear. If she can't get past it, she could lose the role."

"More pressure on her."

"Yes, but I think she wants to move past this for more than just the role." Marin tapped her pen on her pad. "She sees this as her last hurdle. She's motivated to do what it takes, which is why I think she's a good candidate for sessions with you."

He nodded, pleased to hear the client was ready to work. That was vital, especially with the kind of therapy he did. Gray areas weren't acceptable. People were either one-hundred percent on board or he didn't take them on as clients. "When would she be able to start?"

Marin checked her notes. "How quickly do you have room in your schedule? Are you taking a lot of classes this semester?"

Marin was one of the few people he'd told that he was back in school, trying to get his degree so that he could become a clinical social worker. But he hadn't shared with her that he was struggling with his classes. He thought he'd figured out ways around the issues he'd fought with in high school. He'd done fine with the first two years of courses because he was good at retaining information he'd heard in lectures. But now that the classes were getting more intense and specialized, the amount of required reading and term papers was drowning him. He was a breath away from flunking out and had already dropped one class. He was beginning to think it was a pipe dream. "I have room. I could see her as soon as tomorrow afternoon, if needed."

Marin smiled. "Awesome. That's perfect because she's on a deadline. I'd suggest letting her get comfortable with you but not too comfortable. She needs to be able to replicate the behavior on set with Bradley, who is only a casual acquaintance."

"So don't make it too warm and fuzzy."

"Exactly." She jotted down a note and then turned back to him. "You have a natural talent for putting people at ease, and I want her to feel safe in therapy, obviously. But she's going to be doing scenes in front of a crew, and she's not going to have the chance to get comfortable with each person. She has to be confident enough to be that vulnerable in front of strangers. Confident enough to do those stripping scenes on stage with other actors catcalling her."

"Does she understand what she's getting into?" Lane asked, a thorn of worry poking at him. "I don't want to do anything to trigger a relapse with the eating disorder."

Marin's brow wrinkled and her lips pursed, her thinking face on full throttle. "I dug into a lot of that with her. No role is worth risking a relapse, but she's determined and she's been on track with her health for over four years now. I believe that she's moved past it, but I need you to pay close attention. Any hints that things are going south and you come to me."

Lane sat forward, feeling the weight of that settle over him. "You trust me to be able to recognize that? I don't have that Ph.D. in my pocket like you do."

Marin tilted her head and smiled. "Don't sell yourself short. You've had training for what you do, and you're very observant with your clients. Plus, you've been doing this a while now. I have no doubt you'd recognize warnings signs. I'll be seeing her weekly to continue that portion of her therapy, so I'll be monitoring her closely as well. But trust your instincts and if you have any questions, call me."

Lane rolled his shoulders, trying to shake off that kick of insecurity. He could do this. Of course he could. Understanding people and reading in between the lines had always come easily to him. It's what made him a good dominant and why he wanted to be a therapist. It was goddamned school that was making him doubt himself.

Some things never changed. He should probably give it up and stick to what he was good at.

He thanked Marin and headed out of her office, mentally recording all the information he'd gathered about Carlotta and arranging his schedule for the week. He was supposed to go to an afternoon statistics class, but he needed to grab some lunch first.

He headed toward one of the employee lounges to see what he could snag out of the vending machine. The Grove had a vast dining hall with lots of gourmet choices for employees. Everything was top notch here since they catered to celebrities and the wealthy. But he wasn't in the mood to socialize, and really, he always felt a bit like an imposter. He was a contractor here, not a full-fledged employee, not a doctor. And though he wasn't ashamed of what he did for a living, he knew a lot of the staff had their own opinions about his line of work.

Like one Dr. Elle McCray.

He hadn't seen her in over a week, but he'd thought about her more than he'd wanted to. Half the time he got hot over those thoughts, remembering exactly how she'd looked pinned down by those sheets and tossing challenges at him. The other half of the time, he got pissed all over again, thinking of the money she'd tried to give him. No sex was great enough to make it worth putting up with that kind of bullshit.

Last night, he'd gone to the kink club he belonged to in an attempt to exorcise thoughts about her, but he hadn't found anyone he was interested in spending the evening with. A few of the women he casually played with had offered, but they all seemed too...submissive. Which was just a fucked-up thought because that was what he was normally drawn to. That was what had turned his crank since getting out of the escort business— all that control. But last night, the prospect of scening with one of them had seemed...too easy. Boring.

He groaned under his breath as he pulled open the door to the lounge.

Fucking Elle McCray. Now he had another reason to be pissed at her. She'd screwed with his head on top of everything else. She'd tainted what he normally enjoyed.

When he stepped inside the lounge, he found Oriana Wallace, a social worker who worked with Elle on the rehab wing, and a nurse—Joleen, if he remembered right—deep in conversation. A platter of frosted pink cupcakes sat between them. He lifted his hand in silent greeting.

Ori smiled his way, her halo of curly black hair backlit by the window behind her. "Hey, Lane. How's it going?"

Joleen peeked at him and gave a shy smile. He'd caught her openly checking him out one day in the hallway when he'd helped her with some supplies she'd dropped. Joleen had blushed to her red roots when she'd realized he'd noticed her ogling him. She'd tried to play it off at first, and then had attempted to flirt a little, but he'd kept it polite. She was pretty and seemed nice enough, but she was young and had that tang of innocence about her.

Innocence wasn't his thing. He dealt with that type a lot with his job—women who lacked experience for one reason or another. But that was therapy. In his personal life, he liked women who'd lived some life already and weren't afraid to own their needs and their sexuality. Plus, his job and what he craved in bed were too much for the innocent.

Lane returned Ori's smile. "Can't complain, and don't let me interrupt. I'm just hunting down snack food."

Ori shook her head and sighed, eyeballing the cupcakes as if they were going to blow up. "You're not interrupting. We're just stalling."

He lifted a brow as he dug his wallet out to get a few dollar bills. "Stalling? Over cupcakes?"

"The *delivery* of the cupcakes," Joleen clarified.

"They're for Dr. McCray," Oriana explained, glancing at the offending baked goods again. "On my wing, I'm in charge of cupcakes. We get them for every employee's birthday. But I got sidetracked with planning Marin's party and kinda sorta missed McCray's big day."

Lane instantly abandoned what he'd come in here for and turned to fully face them. "What?"

"I whiffed my boss's birthday. Aren't I so smart?" Ori groaned and adjusted the headband keeping her hair away from her face. "Apparently, it was the same day as the party. So not only did I forget, but I threw a party for someone else." She cringed. "So these are already guilt-ridden, I-screwed-up cupcakes, and then they made them *pink* when I asked for white. Dr. McCray doesn't seem like a pink kind of person. And now I'm wondering if forgetting altogether would be better than after-the-fact, fluorescent-pink cupcakes."

Lane processed the words, lining things up in his head. Birthday. The party. Her safeword. The night he'd spent with Elle had been her *birthday*? She'd been at a party for someone else and no one had acknowledged her. Goddamn. No wonder she'd been in such a shit mood. It didn't give her an excuse for the way she'd treated him, but it explained a lot.

"So what do you think?" Ori asked, holding up a cupcake. "Bring them with a big fat apology or just forget it altogether?"

"Is she on the unit right now?" he asked.

Ori glanced at the clock above the door. "Should be. She takes an early lunch and is usually back by now."

"How about I take them over for you?" The words were out

before he could evaluate them.

Ori's brows went up as if he'd just volunteered to jump in a pit of snakes. "Why would you do that?"

Good fucking question. But he forced a shrug. "I'm heading out, and it's on my way. I'll tell her the dates got screwed up and the cupcakes were delivered to the wrong department. She doesn't have to know it was your oversight. If you go over there right now, the guilt on your face is going to show. You look like you killed her dog."

She blew out a breath. "I know. In sessions, I can keep a poker face but for stuff like this, I'm hopeless. You wouldn't mind?"

"It's not a problem."

"Lord, I feel like a chickenshit for passing this off to you, but McCray's been in a seriously bad mood lately. Now I get why, but man, I'm not sure I have the energy for it today. Two of my patients got into a fistfight, and I spent all morning dealing with their lawyers."

"No worries," Lane said, walking over to the table and closing the lid on the box of cupcakes. "I've got it. She already doesn't like me, so I'm immune to the bad mood."

Joleen lifted her head, surprise on her face. "How can she not like you? I mean"—she looked away—"what'd you ever do to her?"

Sexy, filthy things that I can't stop thinking about. He shrugged. "Some personalities just clash."

"I think a lot of personalities clash with hers," muttered Joleen.

Ori smiled. "She's not as bad as all that. She's great with the patients and smart as hell. I've learned a lot from her. But I've also learned that when she's in a mood, to steer clear. I'd like to stay on her good side." She pushed the box toward him. "Which is why I'm smart enough to accept a gift of mercy when one comes along. Thanks, Lane."

"You're welcome. I *am* going to take a cupcake for payment though."

She handed him the one she'd been holding. "All yours."

He took a big bite, the icing getting on his nose, and lifted the box.

Ori laughed. "Now you have pink all over."

He polished off the rest of the cupcake and swiped at the rogue icing. "They're Pepto-Bismol colored but at least they taste good."

"Well, there's that. Let's hope it's enough." Ori gave a little wave as he headed out the door.

But just as he stepped into the hallway, he heard Joleen groan. "God, he even looks hot eating a cupcake."

He shook his head and smirked. He'd hold on to that. *Some* women liked him. He'd remind himself of that when he walked into Dr. Ice's office without an invitation and with an armful of everyone-forgot-your-birthday cupcakes.

Why had he signed up for this again?

chapter five

Elle swallowed down two aspirin before returning to her case file and typing up her notes. This Monday was turning out to be full of Monday-ness. The whole rehab unit was on edge after a fight had broken out in morning group between a reality star and a Tony award-winning actor. Neither guy knew how to throw a proper punch, but both had put on quite a show, and she hadn't had a chance to get some quiet time in her office until now.

Everyone had wanted to process their feelings about what had happened. Normally, she would encourage the patients to talk things out. But she hadn't slept well for over a week, and after two separate processing sessions, she got the feeling that the residents just wanted to gossip. It was always easier to talk about other peoples' issues rather than deal with your own.

Speculation was that the two guys were fighting over a woman—an actress who was checking in early next week. Both had denied it, but things would probably only get more complicated when the actress in question got here. Sometimes Elle felt like she was running a co-ed dorm at a boarding school instead of a substance abuse program. She'd learned quickly once she'd gotten into this field that people trapped together in places for too long tended to dissolve into sophomoric behavior, with most of them fighting or screwing or both.

Fighting and screwing. She shook her head as she typed. She'd resorted to that kind of behavior the night of the party, and she'd only been trapped at a table with Lane for half an hour. So maybe she shouldn't judge. She could be just as immature. And just as hormonal.

Lord knows she hadn't been able to get that night out of her head since. It had ended in a mess, but the journey to get there had been one hell of a good time. She hadn't had sex light her up like that…maybe ever. Had it been anyone but Lane, she would've already invited the guy over again. With all the day-to-day stress at her job, she could use a big serving of that brand of relaxation in the evening. But the cost wasn't worth it. Dealing with Lane Cannon wasn't worth it. Not that it mattered anyway. She'd effectively burned that option to the ground and then stomped all over it. He'd outright told her she'd never have a night like that again.

As if he were the only man who could do that to her.

She sniffed. Well, screw him and his ego. He was just a guy. Not a superhero. Now that she'd analyzed what specifically turned her on about that night with Lane, she simply needed to find someone who was willing to play those kinds of games without all the baggage that came from sleeping with a guy like him. Someone who wouldn't ask questions afterward. Someone who had no interest in getting into her head.

Her cell phone buzzed against the stack of papers she'd set it on, breaking her from her thoughts. The screen lit with her mother's name.

She grimaced. Since when did her mother call when it wasn't a holiday? It's not like she'd bothered on Elle's birthday. Elle hit the button to send it to voicemail. She definitely didn't have the mental energy to deal with her mother today. She'd rather be back out on the unit, separating big, angry men with swinging fists than having a conversation with Cassandra McCray, which really was never a conversation as much as her mother subtly trying to pry into her personal life or why she never visited. As if why she never visited was a mystery.

Even before her mother had let her down in such a soul-crushing way, Cassandra had never had a particularly warm and fuzzy relationship with Elle. Her mom had been married to her career and hadn't been that interested in motherhood. But since Elle's divorce, things had gotten even more distant and strained. When they spoke, they talked about everything except what really needed to be talked about. It took too much goddamned energy—not talking about things. So Elle had learned to avoid interactions for the most part.

The phone rang again almost immediately. Same number. Her mom didn't like to leave a voicemail, but that wasn't Elle's problem. "Give it up, Mom."

She picked up the phone with intentions of turning the ringer off, but before she could silence it, there was a sharp knock on her door. The interruption startled her and made her drop the still ringing phone onto the rug beneath her desk.

"Dammit." Distracted, Elle called out for whoever it was to come in and then bent down to grab the phone and silence it. "If you want to talk to me, leave a freaking voicemail. I do have a job, you know."

"I'm aware."

The deep rumble of a voice had her head snapping up, and she promptly banged it on the underside of her desk. "Son of a *bitch.*"

The ringing that had stopped with the phone started in her head. She rubbed the sore spot, and sat up to find Lane standing in her doorway with a white box in his hands and an unreadable expression.

"You okay?"

The spot on her head was throbbing but she gave a curt nod, not wanting to give him the satisfaction. "I'm fine. Why are you here?"

His signature smugness touched his lips. "Always such a warm welcome from you, McCray. I bet you worked your way through college as a greeter at Disney World. Am I right?"

"Yep. Wore the ears and everything," she said, not missing a beat. "Now answer the question."

Because the sooner he did that, the sooner she could get him out of here. Just seeing him leaning against her doorframe with that lazy, self-satisfied way of his had her mind replaying the scene from that night in her head. Only the highlight reel, of course. Not the ugly parts. Not the part where she ended up alone on her living room floor having a freak out. Her dirty mind was fantastic at editing out the stuff she was supposed to be focusing on.

He lifted the box. "I come bearing cupcakes."

At first, all she heard was *I come.* Boy, did he. With sexy grunts and brute force. She shook the images from her head. God, she turned into a horny teenager when she was around this guy. *Pack the hormones away, Elle.* She cleared her throat. "Cupcakes?"

He opened the box and revealed eleven cupcakes with hideous bright pink frosting. "These got delivered to the wrong building on the wrong date, and I'm guessing with the wrong color, because no one who wasn't having a pretty, pretty princess birthday party would choose these. But they were supposed to go to you for your birthday. Happy late birthday, Elle."

She kept her expression smooth, even though hearing someone finally wish her happy birthday had her throat tightening. She swallowed past the unexpected and unwelcome emotion. "What happened to the twelfth one?"

He set the box on her desk and the door closed behind him. "I did a poison test for you. They're safe but turn your tongue and teeth colors."

He stuck out his fluorescent tongue and then grinned a toothy, pink smile to demonstrate.

She couldn't stop the snort that escaped. She pressed her fingers over her mouth, trying not to show any break in her stone wall.

He waved a hand. "No, go ahead. I know. So many jokes that can be made. Don't let your head explode from not saying one."

"You should get that checked."

He gave another encouraging flick of his hand. "I know there's more."

"Did Miss Piggy at least buy you a drink before you went down on her?"

He grinned wide.

"Did she taste like bacon?"

He laughed at that one, a warm, open sound that he'd never made in her presence. "I knew there was a sense of humor in there somewhere." He lifted an eyebrow. "And Miss Piggy bought me a whole meal, which is more than I can say for the last woman I slept with."

She stiffened at that, and the smile that had slipped out fell away. "Thanks for bringing them by but—"

"You're busy. Yeah, I'm sure you are. And I got that we're not supposed to talk about it. But look, here's the deal. I have a very low tolerance for drama in my life these days. This"—he pointed a finger back and forth between the two of them—"is drama neither of us needs. So consider what happened done. I do. Both of us should've known better. We didn't get along to begin with. A hot night in bed isn't going to change that."

She tipped her chin up, trying to maintain her cool composure. "No, it's not."

He smiled. "Got you to admit that it was hot."

"Lane."

He lifted his hands. "Just messing with you. You make it too easy. And for what it's worth, I'm sorry that it was your birthday and that no one knew. That sucks."

She shrugged, though the move felt tight. "I wasn't interested in celebrating."

"Oh, come on. Everyone should celebrate their big twenty-one."

She straightened the file in front of her, needing to do something with her hands and searching for a way to get him out of her office before she did something embarrassing—like let him see exactly how much this conversation was getting to her. "Don't mock me, Lane. I'm well aware that we're in different age brackets. I'd rather not remind myself of the cliché of the older woman taking a younger guy to bed on her birthday."

He crossed his arms like a bouncer about to eject her from the building and gave her a bored look. "Oh, don't be so dramatic, doc. You didn't seduce some college student. Well, technically you did, but—"

She stilled. "What?"

He smirked. "I'm taking classes, so technically a student, but I'm thirty. I can't imagine we're that far apart in age, and you didn't take *me* to bed. That was the other way around. The taking, that is."

"Lane," she warned again.

"You're blushing, McCray."

She pushed the box of cupcakes to the edge of the desk, ignoring the heat running over her skin, and turned on her terse doctor tone. "Thanks for bringing these by, but I don't want them. Put them in the break room for the staff. I need to get back to work."

He glanced down at the box and his affable expression fell away at her brusque dismissal. "So that's how it's going to be? I'm just another worker to do your bidding?"

She stared at him, not offering a response.

"Right. Well, save your directives and bring the doughnuts yourself. I'm not your employee. Not right now. And not that night." He flattened his hands on the edge of her desk, his green eyes calm but holding her gaze without reprieve. "Hear me, Elle. You can't control me with your money or intimidate me with your position, so stop trying."

"I didn't mean—"

He pushed off the desk and straightened. "Yes, you did. It's your way. But I'm sticking to my no-drama clause and am going to let it go this time. Here, let's practice treating someone like a normal co-worker. Dr. McCray, I have brought you a treat from your dedicated staff with belated birthday wishes."

His tone was breezy, the words painfully polite.

She hated that version of him, the falseness of it all. But what else could she do? He was right. They needed to bury this so they could work together. If they kept arguing every time they saw each other, she'd just end up pissed off, frustrated…and completely turned on. Something about their clashing did it for her. So the best defense was treating him as if he were a benign colleague. "Thank you, Lane. I appreciate you walking them over."

"You're welcome."

"Have a great day."

"Right." A little smile touched his lips, and he tucked his hands in his pockets. "Polite looks so wrong on you, doc. But I appreciate the effort." He turned for the door. "Enjoy the cupcakes."

He strode out without looking back, giving her an unimpeded view of his wide shoulders and well-sculpted backside. The door clicked shut behind him before she'd gotten her fill.

Elle sagged back in her chair, all the breath whooshing out of her. God, she hated that guy.

And still wanted the hell out of him.

She sighed. What else was new? The scoreboard was only getting worse. *Poor taste in men: three. Elle: zero.* Story of her life.

She reached out and grabbed a cupcake from the box, pink teeth, calories, and sharing with the break room be damned.

That night, Elle picked at a kale salad, trying to offset the four cupcakes she'd managed to polish off at work, as she flipped through movie stations. But she wasn't really hungry and she was looking through the TV instead of at it. Maybe she was tired.

No. She stabbed a slice of tomato. She was restless and annoyed and…lonely.

Lonely. The word rattled around inside of her and made her stomach turn.

She set aside her salad and reached for her glass of wine instead. Usually she was one-hundred percent fine with being alone. Growing up, she'd gotten accustomed to it. Her parents had both worked long hours, and she was always left home and responsible for her younger sister, Nina, when the housekeeper left for the day. Then once Nina hit her preteens, Elle didn't even have that on her plate. Nina was always out at a friend's house or a sleepover. The girl had popularity as a part of her DNA and had never been short on invitations. Elle had been less outgoing and had spent most of those nights reading, studying, or working on some hobby or another. So flying solo was her default setting.

But lately, after Donovan, and particularly since her night with Lane, her evenings had felt vaguely empty and… depressing. She took a measured sip from her glass and turned that word over in her head. *Depression.* It was an ugly, scary word. One she was far too familiar with. After her marriage had fallen apart, she'd been walloped with a bout of it that had lasted for months and had left her feeling dangerously hollow.

She'd confided in a friend from med school when things had gotten bad enough that she was finding it hard to get out of bed and do her job. She hadn't wanted to die. But she just didn't care about…anything. She'd overslept. She'd barely eaten or had eaten everything in sight. She'd only put in the bare minimum effort at work. Being cheated on by her husband was bad enough. She hadn't wanted to add unemployed to her list. And she certainly hadn't wanted to give her ex the satisfaction of knowing he'd broken her. She hated knowing that she *could* be broken by someone. That she'd allowed herself to be that vulnerable. So she'd decided to do what she could to try to fix it.

Ainsley, the friend she'd told her secret to, had suggested therapy and meds. Elle had sucked at talk therapy. Doctors were notoriously bad patients, and she had been beyond difficult. She'd quit a few weeks in. But the prescription had helped, and once she was able to get some of her energy back, she'd forced herself to start eating right and exercising again, and had thrown herself into her work and research. Eventually, it'd gotten her out of the hole, and all that hard work had afforded her an opportunity to interview here at The Grove—a job she'd wanted for a long time.

Since then, she'd been hypervigilant about not letting herself sink into that quicksand again. She stayed busy, focused on her health, and had kept her attachments to others in check so she didn't put herself at risk again. But at the same time, she hadn't let herself become a monk. Having a sex life was important to her. She knew herself well enough to know that she needed that physical connection on a regular basis. It kept her feeling feminine and sexy and alive. She'd simply chosen to go about it like a young single guy would instead of how a thirty-nine-year-old woman was expected to. It worked for her.

Or at least it *had* been working.

But now that tendril of unease was growing in her, sprouting vines and spreading. Donovan had started it. He'd put a wrinkle in her neatly ironed-out life. He'd shown her how things could be when you stuck with the same person instead of stringing together one-night stands. How the experience became richer, more satisfying.

Things hadn't been romantic with her and Donovan. Neither of them had had any interest in committing to an actual relationship—well, he hadn't until he'd met Marin. He and Elle had barely talked outside of bed unless it was work-related. But it had filled a need for something steady that she could count on and was strictly physical. Safe and satisfying. And without the stress of having to manage a relationship.

For a while the other night, she'd thought that maybe she had found something similar in Lane—only a hundred times more intense. Their physical connection had been electric and amped up to a level she'd never had with Donovan. There was something more there—darker, dirtier. Lane had been fully present and into it. Donovan had never been like that. Donovan had only slept with her after he had a few drinks in him, and he had always kept an emotional distance between them. He didn't try to get in her head. Lane, on the other hand, left nothing standing between them. He'd wanted her eyes on him. He'd wanted her stripped. Naked in every way.

It'd freaked her the hell out.

But it had also left her craving more. Had made her realize how wholly unsatisfying it'd be to go pick up some guy at a bar and have perfectly adequate vanilla sex where the guy would tell her she was smart and pretty and sexy, whether he meant it or not. Where the guy would try to impress her with his job or his car or his timeshare in Mexico.

Snore.

That was what had her restless. She'd finally figured out what she needed and now she couldn't have it. Not with Lane at least. Even if she hadn't insulted him and he was open to some kind of arrangement, he was too dangerous. He saw too much too easily. He expected emotional openness. He would require things she couldn't give.

She just wanted the hot time in bed, not that guy who had recognized how lonely she was at the party. But she didn't have the faintest idea of how to find that with someone elsewhere. Donovan had once suggested she go to a kink club and find a dom. She'd visited one a few weeks afterward—out of curiosity or as a last resort, she wasn't sure. The staff had been welcoming and the place upscale. But after spending the evening observing, she'd only confirmed what she'd known in her bones already. She wasn't submissive—or dominant, for that matter. She wouldn't be what those guys wanted and vice versa. Everyone would be left disappointed.

Elle sighed, polished off the rest of her wine, and idly flipped through stations. When a young and very naked Richard Gere filled the screen, she stopped the aimless clicking. *Ah, the eighties.* When full-frontal male nudity in movies was somehow less scandalous than it was today. The thought only made her feel old, but she didn't change the station because…Gere. Naked.

She hadn't seen *American Gigolo* in at least a decade, and an old movie with a good-looking guy seemed like a better way to spend the evening than flipping over to the news or catching up on emails. Richard could be her date tonight. Tomorrow, she'd figure out a more realistic solution to her nonexistent dating life. She wouldn't let that melancholy feeling linger too long. Depression had an insidious way of sneaking back into people's lives, especially when it'd made a home there before. She'd seen it with her patients and she refused to let it happen to her.

She poured herself another glass of wine and grabbed a blanket off the back of the couch to curl up for the movie. Richard the gigolo—or his character, Julian, rather—was standing naked by a window and talking to Lauren Hutton about how he had a client who couldn't orgasm and that it'd taken him three hours to get her off. *Who else would take the time?* That was what he asked Lauren.

But Elle found herself answering him with a derisive snort. *No one.* Not unless the guy was getting paid to do it.

Paid.

Of course, that thought had Elle's mind wandering again. That was what Lane did for a living. *Who would take the time?* He would. That was his job. The images that infiltrated her mind made her stomach twist. Lane being patient and gentle with some stranger. Lane putting his hands on the woman and coaxing a response from her body. Lane giving her something no other guy had been able to accomplish.

Elle wanted to maim the woman in the fantasy, and she was only imaginary—which further confirmed that Elle had made the right decision. Shutting things down with Lane was the smart thing to do. She was already feeling territorial. Way, way too dangerous a feeling for some guy she'd only slept with once.

She shook the images from her head and tried to focus on the movie. But then her mind tiptoed off in another direction. Lauren Hutton gazed at Richard Gere with that hungry look of a woman who knew she'd won some kind of sex lottery. In the movie, she was playing the older, married woman to his hot, young prostitute. In a way, she *had* won the lottery. Cake and eating it, too. And all she'd had to do was offer to pay for the privilege.

Elle took another long sip of wine, her thoughts now softening with the alcohol. She'd done the same. Offered money to Lane. She'd done it out of panic, knowing it would piss him off, knowing it would push him away and end things without her having to reveal how much he'd gotten to her. But what if he hadn't been offended? What if he'd pocketed it and asked when they could do it again? What would she have said? Would she have agreed to *pay* for sex?

The idea seemed gross and pathetic on the surface, but did it have to be? When her muscles hurt, she paid for a massage. When she needed something done around the house, she hired someone. Why was sex so different from that?

If there was a man out there who was open to it and healthy and not forced into that kind of lifestyle, what would be the problem? It was simply a business arrangement. An exchange. She'd get what she wanted without the strings, he'd get money and hopefully enjoy himself as well. Did it have to be seedy? In the movie, Richard wasn't hanging out on street corners and turning tricks. He was a high-end escort. He spoke three languages, could have intelligent conversation, and liked giving women pleasure. He lived a lifestyle that he enjoyed. Well—until he got framed for murder. Being in a movie was tough that way.

But hiring someone seemed like it could be the ideal set up. Neat. Clear. Lane would never go for it, but what if she could find someone like Lane? Someone who was capable of pushing edges? Someone who wouldn't be insulted by the prospect of a business exchange, who would happily take a woman's money and play by whatever rules she set?

She knew they existed. Gossip was a high-level sport in the circles her family had moved in. She'd heard her mother and her friends whisper about some of the men Mrs. Dawson would take to parties after her husband left her. They were always handsome, younger than she was, and amazingly attentive. Mrs. Dawson had claimed she'd met them in the sculpting classes she was taking at the local college, but no one believed that. Male escorts. That had been the rumor. Men who were trained in the art of being gentlemen in public and pleasing women behind closed doors.

Elle sat up a bit on the couch, the whisper of an idea becoming a bit louder in her head. At first blush, it made her feel like she'd officially hit *desperate*. Hell, maybe she had. Finding a man to sleep with wasn't difficult. She could go to one of the many bars closer to the city and meet someone. But even when she found a guy she was attracted to, the sex was usually vanilla and not all that exciting. How could it not be? She wasn't going to bring up kinky stuff with a stranger, especially if the guy showed no predisposition for that kind of thing. And the ones who did show that predisposition day one—well, she probably wouldn't feel safe going home with them.

How many times had she wished she could just write out a checklist and then make that guy appear? It was a fantasy, but what if it didn't have to be? What if she could hire a guy who would enjoy what she liked to do and who wouldn't require any commitment from her except a payment?

In a lot of ways, it sounded ideal. It also sounded crazy.

But what she'd been doing had been failing miserably for a long time. Maybe it was time for a little crazy.

chapter six

Carlotta clutched the edges of her robe, groaned, and tipped her face toward the ceiling, her long dark hair falling along her back. "I feel so stupid."

Lane sat in the metal fold-out chair he'd set up in the room. "Take a deep breath. There's no rush and you're not stupid. Anxiety is a badass villain to take down."

"But we *are* in a rush. I need to get over this shit. I know they're this close"—she pinched her fingers together—"to firing me. I mean, why deal with all of my drama when they have a hundred other actresses who'd kill for this role and have no problem dropping trou?"

Lane gave her a sympathetic smile. "I'd say the fact that they're giving you some extra time shows that they really want *you* in the role. That you're not so easily replaced."

She sighed and finally met his eyes. "Everyone's replaceable, Lane."

The softly spoken words dug at something inside him, but he didn't let it show on his face. Positivity. That was what Carlotta needed. "Maybe so, but you're not going to have to worry about that because you're going to get past this. I'm awesome at my job."

She laughed at that, some of the tension lines in her face softening and revealing just how stunning she was. Long, shining hair, olive skin, and bright hazel eyes that would catch anyone's attention. So many people would watch her on screen and envy her, thinking they want her life, but would never know how much Carlotta struggled with feeling good enough.

This was their fourth session in two weeks, and she hadn't made it through one yet without a panic attack. Wednesday night, it'd happened with her just stripping down to her bra and modest underwear. But today, she'd insisted on trying to go topless with a G-string like she'd wear in the movie. She was convinced the only way to get it done in the timeframe she had was to rip the bandage off, but Lane had his doubts. He appreciated the determination but deep wounds didn't get fixed overnight.

"Why don't you try to do some of the choreography with the robe on?" he suggested. "Close your eyes and imagine that you're topless when you're doing it. Get into the head of your character and don't open your eyes to break that. You'll still know I'm here and watching. Pretend I'm a customer in the strip club scene."

Carlotta chewed her thumbnail as she pondered and then nodded. "Yeah, okay. I can't take this off yet. My heart's about to jump out of my chest."

"Practice the deep breathing you learned with Dr. Rush. Get your heart rate back down before we start. I'll get the music set up."

He rose from the chair while Carlotta practiced her breathing, and he cued up her music. But while he was doing that, he got another idea. He'd set up the session in a private rehearsal room at a dance studio so they'd mimic a little of the real scene she'd have to act out, but every light in the place was on and the mirrored wall was a distraction.

"You can start it," Carlotta said, a tremor in her voice.

"Hold up for a sec. Let's try something." He walked over to the panel of light switches and messed around with them until there was only one shining spotlight in the center of the room. Carlotta was standing right at the edge of the lit circle.

She gripped the lapels of her robe again. "What are you doing?"

"Let's do this in stages. I want you to start with dancing in the dark. I won't be able to see you. In fact"—he grabbed a bandanna he used at the gym from his bag—"I'll blindfold myself so you know for sure I can't see you. I'll put my chair near the light. Try to work your way toward me, pretending I'm a customer in the scene. If you feel comfortable enough at any point, take off the robe. I won't be able to see you unless you want me to. You can pull off the blindfold whenever you want. Or not at all, if you're not ready."

Carlotta eyed him. "You promise you can't see through that thing?"

"You have my word."

She rolled her shoulders and shook out her hands. "Okay, I guess it's worth a shot."

Lane hit play on the music and dragged the chair over to the small circle of light. He tied the bandanna around his head and closed his eyes. He wasn't used to being the one blindfolded, but he hoped this would help. He was giving her privacy while still pushing against her fears. Carlotta was afraid of being evaluated, of the judgment. He couldn't do that if he couldn't see, but she would have someone else present, which would be a step in the right direction.

She inhaled a yoga-deep breath in time with the music and then the sound of her bare feet against the smooth wood floor filled his ears. He could get a sense of where she was in the room but didn't turn his head toward the sound in case she was worried he was looking.

The music increased in tempo, the beat heavy and grinding, music appropriate for a strip club, and a hand brushed over his knee. He forced himself not to smile as the heat of her body swept by him. She was close enough to touch. She was in character.

He cheered silently for her. He couldn't seem to get passing grades in his classes, but at least he could do this. He could help someone.

The sound of swishing fabric drifted over him. The robe being removed? He dared to hope.

"You look like a guy who'd do dirty things to me." The words whispered against his ear, husky and full of promise. It was a line from the script delivered with the perfect amount of come-hither sex appeal. Carlotta had slipped into character.

But the tone and her nearness had his brain cutting Carlotta out of the picture and inserting someone else into the scene. Not the dark-haired beauty working through her issues, but instead a sharp-tongued blonde with a voice that went raspy when she got turned on.

You look like a guy who'd do dirty things to me.

Lane tried to shake the image from his head. He did *not* need to be thinking about Elle right now. He was working. He needed to focus on Carlotta. She deserved his full attention.

Hands curled over his shoulders and lips brushed his ears. "What if I said I *want* you to do dirty things to me?"

Fuck. He had no idea if Carlotta really sounded that much like Elle or if his mind was screwing with him. But his dick certainly had an opinion. He could feel the beginnings of a hard-on pushing against his zipper.

Focus. He tried to talk himself down. He was a master at self-control with his clients. He'd worked with some of the most beautiful women of Hollywood and had managed to temper his reactions to only what the patient needed. He didn't get hard unless it was necessary. But right now, his body was rebelling.

In his mind, it was Elle dancing around him, Elle's voice in his ear. "Carlotta…"

"Shh…" A finger pressed over his lips. "My name's Ginger."

Lane swallowed hard, trying to bring himself back to what was actually happening. But before he could, Carlotta took his hand and placed it on her breast—her bare breast. Somewhere, his mind registered victory. She'd stripped down. But the other part of him was still fighting the fantasy of Dr. McCray. He forced the other woman from his thoughts and caressed Carlotta, searching for what he was supposed to be doing. "I thought customers couldn't touch, Ginger."

"For you, I'll make an exception."

Feeling Carlotta beneath his palm helped drag him back to reality. Her skin was soft and supple, but her breasts were small, nothing like the lush handful Elle had offered. Lane didn't usually have a preference either way. He'd been with enough women to appreciate the many different variations of the female form, but right now his libido seemed to be hung up on the doctor. And feeling the differences helped center him.

Carlotta shifted in front of him and he felt her fingers playing along the back of his head. Then she was tugging. The blindfold fell away and he opened his eyes.

Carlotta was in front of him, nearly straddling him, and wearing nothing except the tiny gold G-string. She braced her hands on his shoulders and he left his hand where it was. She was shaking beneath his touch.

He lifted his eyes to hers and found worry on her face, but also fierce determination in her gaze. Her throat worked as she swallowed. "Like what you see?"

That was still Ginger talking, but it wasn't a line from the script. Carlotta was facing the fear of being observed through her character.

Lane let his gaze travel along her body and trailed his hand down from her breast to her hip. "I like it so much I think we need a visit to the VIP room."

Carlotta let out a whooshing breath and stepped back. She put her hands on her knees, her back rising and falling with quick breaths. Lane recognized the panic attack but didn't rush to help. She was strong enough to work her way through it. They'd been practicing how she could handle it if one happened on set.

He calmly got up, retrieved her robe, and draped it over her. He placed a hand on her shoulder. "That's it. You're in control of it, not the other way around. Breathe it down. I'll get you some water."

When he returned, she was in the chair, the robe wrapped around her. And though her skin had a sheen of sweat, she was grinning. She took the bottle of water from him with a shaky hand and kept smiling. "I fucking did it."

He nodded with pride. "You totally did."

"Then I lost it." She let out a laugh. "But I'll take it. I'm not in a heap on the floor crying, so I'll call it a win."

He smiled and squatted down in front of her so he wasn't looming over her. "Absolutely a win. You did awesome."

"And...I made you cop a feel and now I feel kind of awkward. Was that okay? I mean, I know that you said touching can be part of the therapy but you probably meant with, like, discussion before or whatever and you taking the lead on that."

"It's not a problem at all. This is about your comfort level and what you feel you need. Bradley is going to touch you in the love scene, so I think it was a logical next step if you were comfortable with it." He stood and helped her to her feet. "Did anything in particular trigger the panic attack or did it just hit you?"

She tied the belt on the robe and color appeared on her cheeks as she shrugged.

His internal sensors went off. "What was it?"

She wet her lips and dipped her head. "I...uh. Well, when we were acting out the scene, I noticed you...getting into it, you know, physically, which helped actually. It put me fully in the head of my character. But then when you opened your eyes, my effect on you...went away."

Lane cringed inwardly and tried not to show his frustration at how his body had gone rogue. "Carlotta—"

She lifted a hand. "No, it's fine. It's just that reaction triggered those *what doesn't he like about my body?* thoughts, which is dumb, I know. Because how you feel about how I look is not supposed to matter. I don't want someone else's opinion of my body affecting me. That's the whole point of this. But it's still a knee-jerk reaction."

"Stop calling yourself dumb. You're not. Being able to pick all that apart is insightful and self-aware. My body is going to react how it's going to react. But my head stays in professional mode, so you can be assured of that." Even though, in truth, he'd wandered way off the professional reservation fantasizing about Elle mid-session. "And I'm not going to spend time reassuring you or telling you what I think about your body. My opinion of it, and anyone else's, needs to be completely irrelevant to you."

"I know. I'm working on not caring." She gave him a brief smirk. "So fuck you and whatever your opinion is, Lane Cannon."

He laughed. "There you go."

"And I'm going to take your initial reaction as a sign of my superior acting skills. I made *you* slip into the role, too." She tilted her chin up in faux haughtiness, making her look even younger than her twenty-four years.

He grinned. "You're going to nail the role."

"God, I hope so." She closed the distance between them and surprised him with a quick, tight hug. "Thanks so much for today."

He gave her a pat on the back and then stepped away, forever conscious of keeping boundaries clear in a very blurry job. "It was all you."

"No way. I think your idea about the blindfold was genius. It helped me get into character without having to think too hard. Next time, maybe I'll be able to do it without making you close your eyes. I'm going to rock your world, Seedy Strip Club Guy."

With that, she turned on her heel and headed toward the restrooms to change and leave. Lane shook his head. *Genius.* Yeah, that wasn't a word thrown at him often.

He walked over to the stereo to shut off the music system and checked his watch. He was supposed to meet with one of his professors tonight. Dr. Arquette was his favorite teacher, but when she'd pulled him aside yesterday and asked to meet up with him to discuss his struggles in her class, his stomach had flipped over. He'd told her he couldn't stop by during her office hours, but she'd said she'd be happy to meet him for coffee tonight.

So whatever it was, it couldn't be good if she was going out of her way to set up a meeting with him on a Friday night. He grabbed his backpack off the floor and waited for Carlotta to leave before locking up and heading to his fate.

chapter seven

The Pecan Street Café was busy with students and people in suits with loosened ties at this time of the evening. Dr. Arquette was already at a table sipping something steamy with foam. A half-eaten pastry filled the plate in front of her. She lifted her hand in greeting when Lane walked in, and he was jarred by how different she looked from when she was teaching class. Instead of slacks and a blouse, she was in jeans and a soft cream-colored sweater, her dark hair piled on top of her head in a messy bun. For the first time, it registered that she was probably around the same age as he was.

He put in a quick order as the waitress passed him and tried to keep a pleasant expression on his face as he walked over to the table. He nodded her way. "Professor Arquette."

"Lane." She smiled and motioned for him to sit. "And please, call me Allison. We're both grown-ups and not on campus."

He pulled out his chair and sat. "All right, Allison."

She glanced at him in that way that let him know he made her a little nervous. He'd gotten used to that look when he'd worked as an escort. Tentative attraction. A certain brand of awareness a woman could get when she was interested in a guy but not sure how to proceed.

The waitress dropped off his black coffee, and he fought back the wariness that kind of look stirred up. This wasn't a meet up before a "date" with a client. This was his professor. And he couldn't imagine Professor Arquette being anything but professional. So even if she was interested, he doubted she'd go there. "I appreciate you meeting me so late."

She waved a dismissive hand. "It's not a problem. I usually stop here on my way home a few times a week anyway. Their chocolate croissants are a weakness of mine."

"Yeah, I haven't tried anything here that I haven't liked." He took a scalding sip of his coffee. "So what did you want to talk to me about?"

Her affable expression flickered. She smoothed the napkin in front of her, little frown lines touching her lips. "I read over your latest paper the other night."

Lane nodded, already hearing the song "Taps" playing in his head at his failing academic career, the sad wail of the bugle. "Okay."

"And...well..."

She seemed to be struggling to find the words, so he filled in some for her. "It's so bad, you don't know how to break it to me?"

She glanced up at that, surprise on her face. "No, it's not that at all."

His eyebrows lifted in challenge.

"It's...smart and insightful and shows so much potential." She reached down and pulled papers out of the messenger bag by her feet and set them on the table between them. "But it's an absolute mess with spelling, format, and the structure of your sentences."

He blinked, his brain hung up on the first words. "How could you say it's smart if it's a mess?"

She frowned fully now and tapped the pages. "Because the ideas are smart. I can see the points you were trying to make. They're good points. Fresh perspective on the topics. But if I use the grading rubric to score this, you're going to end up with a D, Lane. There's no recovering from that with this being such a big percentage of the semester. And my class isn't optional for the degree program you're in."

Lane's fingers tightened around his coffee cup. "So you called me out here to tell me I'm going to fail your class?"

She sighed and folded her hands on the table, all professorial now. "Yes and no. I wanted to talk to you because there's still time to fix it." She met his gaze. "How do you think things would change if you tried to rewrite it? Took your time. Focused on following the directions and putting your thoughts into a more cogent form."

"You told us there are no redoes."

"I know, but I'm also not unreasonable. There can be exceptions for certain circumstances. I know you're working a full-time job. I realize you're having to squeeze classes in between the rest of your life. If this is simply a matter of you had to rush through this because you have all that going on, I don't want you to fail because of that."

Lane's jaw flexed and he looked out the window at the people walking by on the street so that she wouldn't see the truth on his face. What she didn't realize was that he *hadn't* rushed the assignment. He'd spent so much time on it, he'd lost sleep for a few days. He'd been painstaking with it. And that had earned him a D. If he tried to do it again, he had no idea how to even go about fixing it or doing better. He didn't look her way. "That's the best work I can do. I'll just take the grade."

"That's a bullshit answer."

His attention snapped to her. "Look, I don't know what to tell you—"

"Have you ever been tested for learning disabilities? I think—"

Everything inside Lane went cold. "I don't need to get tested. I'll take the grade."

Allison straightened at his harsh tone. "There's no shame in getting tested, Lane. If they find out you have something like dyslexia, which is what I suspect, accommodations could be made for assignments and I would have options not to fail you and—"

"I don't want special treatment. I don't need an exception to be made. If I get this degree, I want to get it legitimately on my own."

All he could see were the faces of his high school teachers from the fancy private school he should've never been in. Every time they handed him another failing grade, he got the same range of looks. Pity. Disgust. Looks that said he was hopeless, dumb, a charity case. Just the kid of the school janitor who was only there because his dad was an employee and he got free tuition. The teachers knew it. His wealthy classmates did, too. And things only got worse when they started making him go to remedial tutoring during his lunch period.

Allison gave him an exasperated look. "No one is going to give you a free pass to the degree. I'm certainly not. If you had impaired vision and I didn't accommodate that, it would be putting an unfair roadblock in front of you. Right now, I think there are roadblocks for you. We could help with that."

Lane didn't say anything. His muscles felt tight, his skin hot. He feared his face was flushed.

She pulled out a page from beneath his paper and pushed it toward him. "This is a referral letter from me to the Learning Services Center. If you at least get tested, I can hold off failing you on this paper. But you'd need to get there soon. If they find something, there are ways they can help and you can have another chance on this paper. You've got the brains and the insight, you just might need to come at learning and assignments from a different angle." She frowned, concern in her eyes. "Please don't make me fail you, Lane."

He blew out a breath and ran a hand through his hair, the earnestness in her voice getting to him. "Allison—"

"Is this degree important to you?"

"Of course." It was *everything* to him.

"Why?"

His hand curled against the table. He couldn't begin to explain how badly he wanted that piece of paper in his hand. It was more than a ticket to the job he wanted. It was a good-bye to everything that had come before it. A good-bye to that guy who couldn't do anything but fuck up. Maybe even a way to prove to his family that he was worth something. "I have my reasons. I—" He frowned mid-thought, a flash of blond hair near the back door of the shop catching his eye. "It's important to me."

His gaze followed the back of the blonde.

"Then prove it and stop being such a hardheaded man."

The tone in Allison's voice drew his attention back for a moment. Her eyebrow was lifted, making her look less professorial and more like a bossy friend.

"A hardheaded man."

"Yes." She took a sip of her coffee but kept her eyes on him. "Accepting that you—like everyone else in the world—may need to ask for help sometimes. And accepting that, hey, I may be right."

"That there's something wrong with me."

She groaned and set down her coffee. "No. That you're intelligent and talented, and it's going to get wasted if you don't get over your pride and figure out what you need to best work with your individual brain. I'll be really pissed if you fail out of my class because you can't get over your ego," she said, pinning him with a look. "This is my first year teaching this class and I will consider it a personal failing. And I'm really bad with failing. It makes me eat ice cream for dinner. And watch the home shopping channels and buy stuff I don't need." She leaned forward on her elbows. "I could end up ordering mom jeans and bedazzled sweaters. You don't want *that* guilt following you around, do you?"

He had to smile at that. "That would be tragic."

"So tragic." She put her hand over his. "The future of my dating life is in your hands. Save me, Lane."

He chuckled. "If you weren't my professor, I'd think you were flirting with me."

She shrugged and pulled her hand back. "If you weren't my student, maybe I would be. But you are and so I'm not. At least not until you've passed my class and moved on—emphasis on *passed* because you're going to get evaluated and not fail out."

The more he talked with Allison the person instead of Professor Arquette, the more he liked her. This was the kind of woman he should be pursuing. Someone who made him laugh and didn't take herself too seriously. She was pretty. Smart. A genuinely nice person.

"You're persistent."

"As a pit bull. Now tell me you're going to get tested, and I can put grading your paper on hold."

He opened his mouth to respond, but the glimpse that had caught his eye earlier flickered in his peripheral vision again. This time, instead of just getting a flash of a familiar shade of golden hair, he got the full side view. Elle McCray had taken a seat on the other side of the restaurant. She had a glass of iced tea in front of her, was bouncing her crossed legs, and eyeballing the main door as if she were waiting for someone.

Just the sight of her sent a bolt of electric awareness through his system. She looked so damn prim and proper—forever perturbed. Like the world was constantly letting her down with its idiocy and she didn't have time for its bullshit. The attitude should be a turn off. But he couldn't pull his gaze away and forgot what he'd been about to say.

"Lane?"

"What?" He looked back to Allison and her expectant face. "Oh, sorry. Uh, yeah, I'll go."

The words were out before he could consider them, but if nothing else, at least the answer bought him time. The thought of getting evaluated made him want to punch things and he wasn't sure he'd do it, but he wasn't going to make that decision now. He wasn't going to seal his fate quite yet with the failing grade.

Her face lit like a happy child's. "Really? Excellent. That's great news."

"Yeah. Great," he said without enthusiasm. His gaze drifted to the other side of the cafe, but he dragged his attention back to his professor. She'd gone out of her way to meet with him, to try to help. It would've been a hell of a lot easier for her to just slap a D on his paper and call it a day. "I appreciate you talking to me about everything and taking the time. I'll let you know how it goes."

"Thanks, Lane. I'm really glad you're going to give it a try. I'll hold off grading your paper until you get your results." Allison must've caught on that he didn't want to linger on this conversation any longer, and she was smart enough to get out when the getting was good. She pulled a few bills from her purse and pushed her chair back. "Well, I've got to get going. I've got more papers to grade and a *Walking Dead* marathon to watch."

He peered down at the money and picked it up to hand it back to her. "I've got it, Professor."

She looked down at the money. "I don't mind buying you coffee, Lane."

He shook his head. "I've got it."

She pressed her lips together at his determined tone but nodded. "Okay, well, thanks. I'll see you in class."

He let her go with a polite good-bye and then zeroed his attention back on Elle. He didn't want to think about what he'd just agreed to. And he didn't want to ponder why he hadn't turned on the charm to flirt with Allison when she was exactly the kind of woman he probably needed in his life. All he wanted to do right now was figure out what Elle was up to. She was checking the time on her phone and her posture was stiff, her movements unsure. She kept dipping her straw in and out of her glass as if she were fishing for her lemon, but she'd already taken that out and put it on the table.

Lane frowned. The obvious nerves looked strange on someone as poised as Elle. Was she waiting for a date? Was that why she was nervous? The thought didn't sit well with him—her waiting for some other guy. But he'd told her no drama and they'd walked away from each other. He had no claim.

The caveman part of him grunted in indignation at that.

He grabbed his coffee again and took a gulp of the now lukewarm brew. He should leave. No good would come of this. But he didn't get up. He sat there and drank the not-great coffee and tried not to feel like a stalker. Maybe seeing her on a date would be what he needed to get her out of his head. Make it clear to his rogue libido that she wasn't an option. Then he could move on and stop obsessing about the night they'd had together.

That was the rationale in his head. The plan.

But a few minutes later, when a tall black man with movie star good looks, a designer suit, and a smile that had melted off more than one woman's panties walked through the door and strolled up to Elle's table, Lane's best intentions disintegrated into a ball of flame.

The man was a friend.

An old one.

And Lane only had one kind of old friend.

Everything inside him rallied into one loud battle cry. *Oh, hell no.*

chapter eight

Elle gathered every bit of her internal reserves to remain calm and businesslike as Isaiah walked up to her table. She'd left two lemon wedges in the center of the table on a napkin. That was the subtle signal they'd agreed to, but she hadn't noticed him glance at what was on the table. He'd walked in the door, tall, confident, and gorgeous, had locked eyes with her almost immediately, and had headed her way as if he'd known without a doubt she was the one he'd come here for.

She didn't know whether to be comforted by his confidence or concerned that she somehow looked like the woman who would hire an escort. But she didn't have time to worry about it because he was at her table in the next breath. He smiled down at her, revealing friendly brown eyes that crinkled at the corners and a perfectly executed five o'clock shadow. "Elle?"

"Yes." She stood too quickly and her knee bumped the table, making her tea slosh. *Real smooth, Elle.* She put out her hand, her doctor's handshake ready to go. "And you must be Isaiah."

"I am." He took her hand, but instead of letting her get away with a formal, businesslike shake—which would have helped her get herself together—he squeezed her hand gently, put his other hand over their clasped ones, and kissed her cheek. All warmth and ease. "It's a pleasure to meet you."

The word *pleasure* rolled off his tongue and somehow managed not to sound seedy. She was thankful for that. If he got cheesy in any way, this wasn't going to work.

He released her hand and nodded at the table. "Shall we?"

His accent was one she couldn't quite place, easy on the ears, like a bit of Brit underneath something else. "Of course."

He pulled her chair out for her and then took his seat, motioning for the waitress at the same time. He put in an order for a sweet tea and then turned to look at Elle. "You want to order anything, love?"

The endearment startled her for a second, but he'd said it in a friendly way, as if he'd call a stranger that. She *was* a stranger. A stranger who was about to discuss paying him for dirty, kinky sex. She cleared her throat and said the first thing she saw on the appetizer menu. "How about the balls?" Everything inside her cringed. "The artichoke balls."

The word *balls* seemed to echo in the cafe like she'd said it with a bullhorn, and her cheeks went hot. God fucking dammit. She was blushing. She didn't blush.

This was ridiculous. She was a grown woman. She could do this. So what if this very attractive man was here as an escort? No one else knew that.

Isaiah grinned. "The balls sound fantastic."

When the waitress walked off, Elle pinched the bridge of her nose.

"What?" he asked, a smile in his voice. "Balls *are* fantastic.

I've always been quite fond of mine."

She snorted, unable to hold back the awkward laugh. "I promise I'm usually more put-together than this."

He tapped her hand. "Hey, truly, no worries." He leaned forward on his forearm, creating a quiet space between them. "This is out of pretty much everyone's comfort zone. Give yourself a break. As for the balls joke, it's going to happen. You'll find that no matter how hard we try, we'll hear double entendres in our conversation. It's inevitable."

She took a breath, trying to regain her composure. "Thanks. We should've met at a restaurant that served wine."

"No can do. I have a rule that first meets can't involve alcohol. This is a decision you have to make with a clear head." The waitress dropped off his tea, but his gaze remained on Elle. "And this part is going to feel awkward at first because we don't know each other yet. It'll be fine. Just relax. Awkwardness never killed anyone."

She rolled her shoulders, trying to release the tension there. "You're right. I know that. Part of my job is lots of awkward first meetings."

He lifted a brow, which reminded her that she'd been scant on the personal information when she'd gone to the kink club and asked if the owner could set her up with a reputable service.

She took a sip of her tea. "Sorry. I'd rather keep my work life stuff separate."

The waitress dropped off the appetizer and made sure they didn't need anything else before leaving them alone again. Elle stared at the food. The artichoke balls were their specialty and a New Orleans mainstay—little baked bites of mashed artichoke hearts mixed with parmesan, egg, and breadcrumbs.

They smelled delicious, but Elle doubted she'd be able to eat anything tonight.

Isaiah nodded, tossed his straw aside, and sipped his drink. "Not a problem. It's up to you to decide what you want me to know and what you don't. But for what it's worth, my job is built on discretion. I wouldn't have it anymore if I couldn't keep people's secrets."

She smoothed her napkin on her lap. "How long have you been doing this?"

His lips hitched up at the corner. "I'm getting that you don't want to play the game of we pretend we're just two people on a date."

The let's-put-the-cards-on-the-table response soothed her some. "No. This whole thing is only going to work if we go the straightforward route. I'm not fooling myself that this is something other than it is. And I'm not so delicate that I can't handle the idea that you do this for a living. This is a business exchange. I want it to be a mutually agreeable one. So we talk, lay it all out there. Then, if you're not into what I'm suggesting or if you find me unappealing in some way, we end it here and move on."

He leaned back in his chair, easy and comfortable. "You're a beautiful woman who knows what she wants. I have a feeling I'll be into that. And to answer your question, seven years."

The accent was gone now, the façade dropped. "Wow. That's a while."

He laughed. "That surprises you?"

"A little. I guess I imagined it's a job someone does in the interim to make money for the next thing."

He shrugged. "It started that way. I became a dancer—a

stripper, if we're going to be no bullshit about this—to earn money for grad school. But then I got the opportunity to go this route, and it stuck. I still have my degree. I could do something else. But I'd take a pay cut, and it'd be a hell of a lot less fun. I'm not here under duress, if that's what you're wondering. This is my choice. I'll stop doing it if it ever feels like it isn't."

The words settled something inside her. Part of her *had* been worried about that. That she was taking advantage of some guy who was forced into the role either by need for money or by someone else.

"Thank you. That's good to know." She took one of the artichoke balls and put it on her plate, splitting it in half and thinking.

"And *you're* not here because you can't find a man willing to sleep with you."

She looked up, surprised. "What?"

He had popped a bite of food into his mouth and he waited until he was done to explain. "I'm just letting you know that I'm aware of that. I'm not sitting here thinking you're desperate. You're an attractive, intelligent woman who I'm guessing has a pretty high-powered career. It wouldn't be hard for you to go out and pick up an equally successful guy. So you're talking to me for other reasons. Maybe we should discuss those, so I can know what you need from me."

She appreciated that he was so matter-of-fact about it, but him asking what she needed from him didn't settle right inside her. He was telling her he could be whatever she wanted, and she knew that was how it worked. She was paying, and as long as she didn't ask for something outside of the parameters of what he was willing to do, he could be what she asked. The doting boyfriend. The kinky lover. The sexy stranger. That was his job. To play the role she wanted. And God knows, he was hot enough to inspire fantasies. Everything she could want—good-looking, intelligent, straightforward, good sense of humor.

But she was having trouble imagining him sparring with her in the way she craved. He seemed so *nice*. And nice was great for a friendly chat, not so great for what she needed. Though, she hadn't really given him a chance. He could be a wild sadist behind closed doors. He'd been an escort for seven years. There probably wasn't much he wasn't capable of. She needed to keep an open mind and be honest about what she was seeking. She also needed to accept that it'd be a role for him. There was nothing authentic about this arrangement. That was the trade-off for the neat, clean boundaries.

She smirked and shook her head. "To be honest, what I probably need from you is for you not to like me."

His eyebrows lifted at that. "All right. Explain."

She rubbed her lips together and tried to figure out how to word it. "I don't like to be doted on. I don't like romantic. I… my ex-husband was really good at that. And it was a lie. I don't react well to…sweet. I know it probably sounds screwed up, but sweet can trigger panic in me and ruin the moment."

"Because you always think it's bullshit?"

"Because, in my experience, it usually *is* bullshit."

He considered her. "But what if it's not? What if a guy would genuinely enjoy taking care of you?"

She shook her head. "I'm not sure that guy exis—"

"Excuse me." The smooth, cool voice cut right through her words.

Elle's attention flicked upward, the familiar voice sending a dart of alarm through her. Lane was standing a step away from the table, his gaze fastened on her and his eyes full of challenge. Her thoughts scattered like a strong wind had hit them.

"Uh…"

"*Cannon?*" Isaiah's voice pulled Elle out of her two-worlds-colliding stupor. "Well, I'll be damned."

Lane's attention slid to the other man, a devil-may-care smile touching his lips. He stepped closer and put out his hand. "Hey, man. Good to see you."

They did the half-hug, half-thump on the back like old buddies and Elle just stared. Her escort and Lane knew each other?

Isaiah glanced her way and smiled. "Elle, this is Lane, an old friend from school. Lane, this is Elle."

Elle. Well, that was vague enough.

Lane smiled. "Yes, we already know each other."

Isaiah looked between the two of them again. "Oh?"

Elle tried to force the shock off her face and act like a normal human being. "Yes, we work together."

"Oh, great. Well, Elle was just indulging me by listening to my pitch about why I am a far superior financial planner to the one she has now. I'm hoping she'll move her accounts over with my company, but she's a tough customer." Isaiah handled it all with smooth social grace. He was clearly used to being on his toes and playing it by ear. In his job, he no doubt traveled in some high-powered circles and would have to know how to hold his own and have a cover story.

Lane's attention returned to her, something dangerous in his eyes. "Oh, she's a tough customer all right. She'll be your toughest one yet."

Isaiah glanced her way, a thoughtful look on his face, but he gave the appropriate laugh for Lane's joke-that-wasn't-a-joke. "Well, it was good seeing you. We should get together for a drink soon and catch up."

"Absolutely," Lane agreed. He gave Isaiah a pat on the back and then stepped closer to Elle. "Elle, it was good seeing you." She stiffened as he leaned down to kiss her cheek. His mouth brushed past her ear. "Bathroom hallway. Be there in two minutes."

The whispered words shot through her system like a flare of heat, but she sent him a narrow-eyed look. Who the hell was he to order her around? "See you at *work*, Lane."

The head shake he gave was nearly imperceptible but she got the message. Not that she was going to heed it. She turned back toward Isaiah and smiled. "So tell me more about your plan."

Lane walked off but not out the front door. He turned the corner and she knew he'd be in the bathroom hallway, expecting her to show up. Well, he could hold his breath and wait. If nothing else, seeing him had cemented her reasons for inviting Isaiah here. Isaiah was the right choice. No drama. A sexy, friendly guy who was willing to provide what she wanted without requiring anything else.

"Sorry about that," Isaiah said, settling back in his chair. "If it helps any, I don't know where Lane works. I haven't seen him in a long time, so he didn't reveal anything about you."

She shrugged, giving up on the hope of total anonymity. "It's fine. Things like that are going to happen. I need to be prepared to run into people who may know me. I'm a doctor."

He smiled. "I'm impressed."

"But now you understand why discretion is so important."

"Of course. Like I said, your secrets are safe with me. Now, back to—"

But he was cut off by the waitress stopping by to take their orders.

Elle ordered a random sandwich from the menu and her gaze strayed to the clock. How many minutes had passed since Lane had walked off? Was he still in the hallway? What did he want to talk about? Her heart was still beating too fast from seeing him here. She shouldn't care, but she couldn't shake the thought that he was there waiting for her. No way was she going to be able to concentrate on the conversation she needed to have if Lane was hovering in the back of her thoughts. Damn that man.

After Isaiah put in his order and turned his smile back to her, she slid her chair backward. "Excuse me for a second. I'll be right back."

"No problem. Everything okay?"

"Of course. Just too much tea."

He smiled an easy smile and she made her way to the restrooms. When she turned the corner, she didn't see Lane, and some weird combination of relief and disappointment filled her. She let out a breath. He'd left. Okay. Good. Now she'd be able to work this thing out with Isaiah and not think about the way just having Lane's words brush against her ear had sent a trail of goose bumps over her skin.

She pushed open the door to the ladies' room, deciding she might as well go if she was there, and then touched up her lipstick afterward. The woman staring back at her in the mirror looked determined, resolute. She could do this. Just because Isaiah hadn't yet sparked that rush of desire in her didn't mean he wouldn't. They just needed to get past the awkward planning and negotiating phase first.

Elle stepped back out into the hallway, feeling calmer, and was quickly blocked by a wall of muscle. She let out a startled gasp and almost ran right into Lane's chest. He smiled down at her. "I knew you couldn't resist."

chapter nine

I knew you couldn't resist. Elle's fists curled tight at Lane's pompous words. The words were one-hundred percent true, but no way in hell was she letting *him* know that. "I had to pee."

"Uh-huh. I need a minute." Lane reached down, grabbed her wrist, and tugged. Before she could protest, he pulled her through a half-open doorway behind him.

"What are you doing?"

"Finding privacy." He closed the door. The storage room was small, half-lit, and smelled like industrial cleaner and stale coffee. Various discarded decor items were propped against the wall. An old menu board. A mirror with a crack in it. A broken chair. He turned and faced her, leaving barely any space between them. "I figured this chat was best had without an audience."

"Chat? No. I don't have time for this. I need to get back to my date."

He smirked. "You mean your financial planner, right?"

She gave him a warning look. "Maybe he's both."

"Or maybe I know exactly what he is."

The words punched the air from her lungs but she forced her face not to react. "Whatever, Lane. Let me out of here before I scream."

He moved aside. "You know what they used to call Isaiah?"

She scooted by him. "I don't care about stupid college nicknames."

"The Golden Tongue."

She stiffened, the words halting her step.

"Because he could sweet talk his way into a rich housewife's bed like no other." Lane's voice was quiet in the small space. "He could get the ones you'd never think would go for that kind of thing. But the temptation he'd lay out for them was too much to say no to. Because he knew how to tell them exactly what they wanted to hear. How perfect they were, how smart, how talented, how he couldn't bear to see such beauty wasted on a husband who didn't take the time to take care of his wife."

Elle went cold all over and turned to face him.

He stepped close again, his eyes holding challenge. "Is that what you want, Elle? Some smooth-talking guy to whisper lies in your ear and then get you off on time so he can get paid and go to the next appointment?"

She closed her eyes, her breath stuttering. "I don't know what you're talking about."

He pressed a finger beneath her chin, tilting her face up and forcing her to open her eyes in the dim light. His gaze was intent now, edging on concerned. "Look, I *know* what's happening out there. Let's not stand here and play the who-can-lie-better game. He's not your financial planner and he's not your date. You're about to pay for sex. I'm telling you it's a bad idea."

Her jaw clenched and she had to breathe through the urge to

lie again. "Why? Because it's not the *therapeutic* kind you dish out, so you get to judge me?"

Lane's expression hardened. "No. Because I don't know Isaiah from college."

The words didn't register at first. She blinked a few times. "What?"

The smile that touched his lips was a bitter one. "I guess this is the part where you get to hear that you were right when you called me a whore. I'm not now, but I used to be. Isaiah and I were roommates and worked for the same company—if you could call it a company."

Her lips parted, words extinct.

He released her chin with a sound of disgust. "Yeah. So I know exactly what game is being played out at that table. And I'm telling you that you need to walk away. It's not for you."

The shock of finding out Lane used to be an escort was enough to have her ears ringing. She had questions. So many questions. But the last part of his declaration set off a knee-jerk response. "And who are you to tell me what's not for me? Is he a bad guy? Dangerous?"

"No."

"Then we're done here. I know what I'm doing. I don't need you to school me on it. I'm not some pampered debutante who's going to pretend this is something other than it is. All I care about is having a good time with a guy without having to worry that it's going to get complicated. This is a business exchange and you're interrupting the deal. Now let me get back to it."

He didn't move. "So that's your kink, then? You want to have a rent boy you can pay? Want to call all the shots and make him do your bidding?"

Her stomach dipped, but she didn't let him see her flinch. "So what if it is?"

"It's not," he said, stepping fully into her space, his voice softening. "And you know it. If it was your thing, I'd tell you to go for it. But that's not what gets you off. You could have that any day of the week without spending a dime. Willing men wanting to please the pretty doctor. You've tried that already, haven't you?"

She had to fight not to look away, not to reveal he was hitting targets.

"Did you have to imagine filthy things while they were fucking you to get off? Pretend that they were holding you down or being rough instead of gently coaxing an orgasm out of you?"

Her heart thumped hard against her ribs, but she refused to let any emotion show on her face. His observations were painfully accurate. How many times had she squeezed her eyes shut with a guy and pretended the things happening were so much darker, more dangerous?

The look on his face said he knew he'd hit the mark. "Isaiah can't give you what you want. He might be able to play the role, but that's not his natural way. He's not mean enough for you. He can't do what I did for you. I know that's what you're hoping."

The words pushed needles into her. "You're such an egotistical jerk."

"Doesn't change what's true." His hand slid onto her hip, the heat of his palm searing her through her dress. "You're too smart to trick yourself. You think you'll be able to pretend it's all real, but you'll always know in the back of your mind that he's in your bed because you're paying him to be. That he'd be following *your* orders, not his own desires. And I promise you, that's going to take the fire right out of it. You'll see the strings at the magician's show. The magic will be gone."

She shook her head, not wanting to hear it. That, of course, had been her fear all along. She'd fooled herself in her marriage, tricking herself into believing she was loved and cherished, that she meant something to someone. When, in reality, she'd meant nothing—not to her husband or her family. She'd sworn she'd never let herself fall into that kind of fantasyland again. Since then, she couldn't help seeing the hard truth of things. She couldn't read books with happy endings anymore. Fairy tales were bullshit. Even when she weaved fantasies in the privacy of her own head, reality had an ugly way of pushing in and marring them.

Some of the fight went out of her, a cold, empty feeling pinging through her. "Maybe so. But this is what I have to work with. You don't think I get that I'm fucked up about this? That this isn't normal? I get it. But it is what it is. I'm a solution-focused person. And no solution is perfect, but this is the one that's the closest for me. So please, let me go back to my fake date so I can go home and get fake laid."

"Elle." Lane frowned, his eyes scanning her expression. She thought that'd be the end of it, that he'd drop it and let her go. Instead, he kissed her.

The shock of his lips against hers stunned her into instant silence, and without thinking, she reached up and grabbed his shirt. At first, she did it with the intent to push him away, but then found herself dragging him closer and parting her lips.

His tongue slid against hers and he groaned, a whole-body sound that sent a flash of heat to all her best parts. The enticing scent of him had already been too much in the tight space, but adding the taste of him against her tongue put her brain into shutdown mode. Her fingers curled into his shirt and she made a noise that sounded way too close to desperation.

His hand grasped the back of her head and his other slid behind her thigh, lifting her leg so he could step even closer. The hard press of his zipper dragged against her belly and he pressed the heat of his body against her now spread legs.

Everything inside her went warm and needy and ready. She clung to him and kissed him back hard, unable to do anything else but follow where her body wanted to go. Fingers in his hair, breasts pressed against his chest, body melting into him.

"Doc, *fuck*." The words were mumbled between hungry kisses and grabbing hands. He left her leg hooked around his hip and dragged his hand up to squeeze her breast. Not a light, tender touch, but a rough, possessive grab that made her gasp and writhe. She wanted more, his hand against her bare skin, his teeth tugging her nipple.

But they shouldn't be doing this. They weren't supposed to be doing this. "Lane, please. Isaiah is—"

He didn't let her finish the sentence. He pulled back from the kiss and grabbed her hips to spin her around to face the wall. "You have a word that will make me stop."

His erection pressed hard against her backside and when she didn't say a damn thing, his hand slipped between her and the wall and cupped her through her dress. Just the burning heat of his palm was almost enough to bring her to her knees. But of course he didn't leave it at that. He pressed kisses to the side of her neck and rocked his fingers against her, putting pressure right where she needed it most. Her forehead tapped the wall.

"Tell me what you would've done if I'd taken the money that night?" he asked, the words rough against her ear.

She squeezed her eyes shut, the pleasure of what he was doing with his fingers in direct opposition to the anxiety the question caused. "I knew you wouldn't take it."

"You wanted to piss me off, chase me out?" His fingers made circles around her sensitive clit, the silk of her panties sliding over it in a maddening glide.

"Yes."

She gasped as he moved his hand and abruptly hiked up her skirt. His fingers pushed aside her panties, finding her wet and wanting.

"Why?"

Her nails curled against the wall, thoughts harder to put together now that his fingers were on her, inside her, touching her exactly where she needed.

"Because I can't handle complicated."

His fingers slowed down to a sensual rhythm, one that had her lifting up on her toes and breathing hard, and the scent of arousal filled the small room.

He kissed behind her ear and then nipped at her lobe. "You never answered my question. What would you have done if I'd accepted the money?"

She swallowed past the dryness in her throat, fighting not to beg for more of his touch or ride his fingers like some desperate, needy thing. She was so close. "I would've asked you to come over the next night. And the next."

"To use me."

She scoffed, though it came out sounding more like pleasure than disbelief. "To use each other. Don't act like you want me for anything but this. You and I have nothing in common besides this."

He plunged his fingers deep at that. "Why, because I'm a lowly former hooker and you're the fancy doctor?"

She shook her head, somehow wanting to laugh at that notion. "No."

"Why then?" he demanded.

"Because life hasn't killed off the good parts of you yet."

His pace stuttered at that and she regretted letting the words slip out, but he didn't give her time to take them back. "You give me too much credit, doc. Life's done a hell of a lot to me. And I promise you, none of it's good."

His fingers found her clit again, and he stroked her with expert precision and no reprieve. Her thoughts blurred around the edges and her breath soughed out of her in quick, loud bursts. Orgasm wouldn't be far behind.

"Make me the offer again, doc," he growled as his fingers worked her.

She couldn't think, couldn't focus. "What?"

"Tell me you want me to fuck you for money."

She was sweating, her hair and makeup would be ruined. She couldn't find it in her to care. "I want you to fuck me. For money."

"Good. Here's the catch, doc. I'm in control. I set the rules. You're paying me, but you're *my* plaything. And only mine."

Her need to come was so strong her entire body was pulsing with it, but she forced herself to focus on the words. "I'm not a submissive."

"Don't need you to be. Don't want you to be. You can fight me as much as you want. And you'll always have your safe word. We can even keep it quiet at work so that you don't taint your precious reputation. But I come over when I want. I'm in charge of how things go. That means I won't be treated like a dog who needs to be sent home after getting his scraps. If I want to stay over, I'll stay. I've had enough rich bitches send me home after they've used up the help. I'm not the help anymore. No fuck is worth going back to that. Not even one with you."

She winced.

"But I will give you the guarantee you want, the one to fix that thing that scares you so much."

"What's that?" she whispered.

"I won't expect more than you're capable of giving. I know who you are. You don't have to pretend you're something different with me. And when it's time, I'll walk away. I've spent my whole life walking away. I'm good at it."

"Lane..."

He pressed the length of his body against her back. "Now come for me, doc. Come all over my hand and then walk back to that table with your soaked panties and throbbing cunt and tell Isaiah that you're off the market."

She gasped, fighting hard not to make too much noise, and writhed on Lane's fingers, her entire attention focused on the pleasure coursing through her. She couldn't think about the fact that she was in some dark storeroom or that she'd made some crazy deal with Lane. She'd worry about that when her world wasn't exploding behind her eyelids.

"That's it," Lane said softly against her skin. "Show me how sexy you are when you come, how hungry you are for this."

Lane banded his other arm around her waist and turned her with him, putting his back to the wall and her front toward the cracked mirror leaning against the other side.

The broken reflection stared back at her. Her dress was hiked up and her panties pushed aside. Lane's fingers worked her, a knee-weakening orgasm making her shamelessly rock herself against him. She was the picture of a woman utterly undone. And his expression was pure male intent. Determined. Stern. Almost grim.

Going on expression alone, she'd guess he wasn't enjoying things. But his body said otherwise. His erection was like steel against her ass and his heart pounded against her back. What that did to her was visceral and potent. She knew Lane could fake interest if needed. His job required that. But that wasn't the case with her. He wasn't doing this for the money or an easy lay.

That both comforted her and scared the shit out of her. Because if not for one of those, why was he going through the trouble?

But the thought escaped her as her mind went blank with pleasure. Her eyes closed and she let herself fall into the bliss of all that sensation. She'd think later. Right now, she'd just feel.

"That's it," he said after a few moments, the words quiet against her ear and his hand slipping away. "It's a deal, then."

Her mind snapped back into focus at that. "Lane…"

"No more talking, cupcake." He shifted behind her and righted her clothes. When she turned to confront him, he pressed his slick fingers to her lips in a mock kiss. "Get rid of Isaiah. I'll send you my account number so you can deposit the money. And I'll be in touch."

"But—"

"We're done here." With that, he walked out, leaving her there with a pounding heart, boneless legs, and a spinning brain. Something had dropped out of Lane's pocket on the way out, but she didn't have the energy to call out to him or to go over and pick it up. She sagged against the wall and ran a hand over her forehead, trying to get her mind back together.

Somehow, she'd gone from having a formal, maybe-this-might-happen conversation with Isaiah to being manhandled in a storeroom and coming at the hands of a guy she'd sworn off for good. A man she'd now agreed to pay.

And frankly, that wasn't what was freaking her out.

No, what was making that tremble move through her body was something entirely different.

She'd just agreed to give Lane Cannon control.

What the fuck had she been thinking?

chapter ten

W hat *the fuck* had he been thinking? Lane took a long gulp of beer and flipped through Carlotta's case notes without seeing them. He was supposed to be concentrating on his clients and making a decision about the school testing his professor had suggested, but all he could think about was the stupid deal he'd made with Elle yesterday at the café. He'd been in a haze of possessive lust, wanting to do whatever it took to make sure it was him in her bed and not someone else.

He'd broken so many personal codes it wasn't funny. Keeping the drama factor low in his life. Gone. Not poaching another escort's client. Done. Never *ever* taking money for non-therapeutic sex again. Fail.

He groaned and ran a hand through his hair. That last one was such a stupid, stupid move. Not only because he'd made a personal vow to himself to never go backward, to never return to that life. But he was putting everything at risk. He'd worked hard for his current position and was busting his ass to get his degree so he could move to the next level. Make something of himself. This could ruin it all. If anyone got even a whiff that he was taking money for recreational sex, he could kiss his job and his license good-bye. It was the stereotype surrogates fought against—that they were just glorified whores—and now he was agreeing to an arrangement that was anything but therapeutic.

Fucking destructive was more like it.

But the alternative wasn't an option either, anymore. Elle had infected his entire system and he needed to cure that obsession. Hearing her words yesterday had put a knife through him. *Life hasn't killed the good parts of you yet.* In that moment, it hadn't been about how hot she was or the challenge of her. He'd gotten a glimpse of the real woman beneath it all. Heard an echo of something that he'd thought way too often when he'd lain in a woman's bed, cash stacked on the bedside table. He'd sold his body. He'd sold his compliments. He'd sold his affection and some I-love-you's. Those kinds of thoughts had stalked him. *What if there's nothing good left to give? What if I've sold it all to the highest bidder?*

Elle had never been a hooker, but somewhere along the way, she'd given things away, too—or maybe they'd been stolen. He didn't know, but that was what had kept him from taking back his reckless offer. He'd realized in that moment that she didn't know how to deal with things in a different way. She wanted him as much as he wanted her. But paying for it was the only way she could feel safe acting on it.

So be it. He'd do it.

But that didn't mean he was going to let her do things her way. If she wanted to give him some token cash to put a nice clear line in the sand for herself, fine. He'd funnel the cash into the domestic violence shelter The Grove helped fund. But he wasn't going to be her whore. He wasn't going to do her bidding. He wasn't going to act out some role. He wasn't that guy anymore.

He'd told her as much. But what she didn't know was that she was going to have to pay a much higher price for his services than she ever anticipated.

He didn't require submission. Or trips to the kink club. Or even blow jobs—though, those were always nice. No, what he was going to require would terrify her more than any of that.

She was going to have to let him in.

Seven days. Elle collapsed onto her couch with a bowlful of banana ice cream that she'd drowned in chocolate sauce. Seven goddamned days since Lane had dragged her into the storeroom. And five since she'd deposited money into his account. She hadn't heard a word from him. He'd told her he'd be in touch, but that had obviously been a lie. Or he'd been playing a game.

She'd seen him on campus yesterday and had planned to confront him, but then a woman had run up to him and started walking with him. The woman had been young, pretty, and smiling way too eagerly at Lane. The warm smile he gave her was one he'd never given Elle.

Elle had immediately typed out a text, telling him not to bother calling her, but she hadn't been able to send it. She didn't want to look as if she'd been hanging by a thread and waiting for him to call. She'd rather let him believe that she'd forgotten about the whole thing entirely. If he called, she wasn't going to answer. Let him think she'd moved on without a thought.

She shoved a spoonful of ice cream into her mouth, full of righteous indignation, and flipped on the news. She should've stuck with Isaiah. The guy had been nothing but gracious when she'd told him she'd changed her mind. He hadn't tried to persuade her but had instead given her his card and told her he was always open to hearing from her. She needed to dig out that card and go with her original plan.

But she didn't move from the couch. She just took another big bite of dessert and fumed.

Her phone rang next to her on the couch, and she hated the way she perked up like a Pekingese being offered a treat. But the screen showed it was her mother again. She knew she should answer. She'd avoided two of her mom's calls already, but she didn't have it in her. It wouldn't benefit either of them for her to answer in this mood. She sent it to voicemail, knowing her mother would never leave one, and tossed her phone to the other side of the couch.

Maybe she should've picked up the Friday night on-call duty and saved herself this ruminating. Fridays were always busy on-call nights. At least she could be useful up at the hospital. She'd sat for two hours with a new patient this afternoon, listening to a former child actress describe all the things she'd done in exchange for roles so that she could keep money coming for her family. The woman had turned to drugs to blot out all the memories, but they were roaring to the surface post-detox.

It'd made Elle want to personally maim every single adult who had taken advantage of this talented young woman, including the family that hadn't protected her. The woman had ended up bawling in Elle's arms. Elle didn't make it a habit to hug patients because of boundary issues, but sometimes people in pain just needed to be held and told that they were going to make it through whatever it was. When the patient had thanked

Elle and even managed a hopeful smile, Elle's chest had filled with warmth. She'd felt useful. Happy.

Work seemed to be the only place she felt that way.

The doorbell rang. She startled, nearly dropping her bowl of ice cream, and glanced at the clock. Almost ten. Her stomach clenched.

Was her mom at the door? Was that why she was calling?

Elle set her bowl aside and let out a breath, dismissing the thought. Her mom hated driving at night. She wouldn't go through that much trouble to see her. It was probably some issue at the hospital. Late-night knocks weren't all that uncommon since she lived on the grounds of The Grove's sprawling campus. Maybe they needed extra help. She pushed herself off the couch and headed to the door.

When she swung it open and found Lane lounging in the doorway with that smug look of his, it took her a second to process his presence and what it meant. But when she did, her anger shot straight to the surface. "What the hell are you doing here?"

His brow lifted. "I believe the agreement was I'd be doing *you*."

The words raised all her hackles—and she had a lot of those. "That's not how it works." She braced her hand on the door, ready to shut it. "You can't just show up. You're supposed to call first."

"Never agreed to that." He ducked under her arm and stepped past her without invitation, his fresh-laundry scent drifting in with the night air. "I had a late session, thought I'd stop by."

"A session," she said after quickly peering outside to make

sure no one was nearby to see Lane coming in. She shut the door behind her. "Meaning you slept with someone else and wanted round two?"

He tilted his head, his gaze traveling over her *so*-not-for-public-viewing outfit of plaid PJ pants and an old T-shirt from a pharmaceutical company. "You know I can't discuss clients."

She crossed her arms. "Right. Of course. Well, how about we don't discuss a thing at all? You can leave."

"You don't want me to leave," he said, as casual as you please. "You just hate getting caught off guard."

"No. I was going to cancel our agreement anyway. And even if I wasn't, I would now because if you think I'm going to take sloppy seconds when you haven't even showered off the last woman, you can go to hell."

He grabbed her melting ice cream off the sofa table, took a big bite, and smiled a lazy smile. "Take off your clothes, Elle."

She scoffed. "You're delusional."

He took another bite and watched her, those green eyes daring her as he licked chocolate syrup off the back of the spoon. "Well, we could watch a movie instead. You've paid for my time."

"You have even less of a chance of that. Keep the money. I don't care. Just leave."

He set the bowl aside and strolled closer, his movements calm, but his gaze not leaving hers. She took a step back, hitting the sliver of wall separating her entryway from her living room.

He braced a hand above her shoulder on the wall. "You got your feelings hurt because I didn't call on your timeline. No need to shut the whole thing down over that."

"There are no *feelings* about this. Don't give yourself that much credit."

"So self-centered. It's all about you, huh? Did the busy doctor ever consider that maybe I have a lot going on, too? I have clients. I'm in school." He leaned close to her ear. "That doesn't mean I forgot. That doesn't mean that this morning when I woke up hard and hot from a dream, that I didn't stroke my cock thinking about what I wanted to do to you when I got the chance."

The heat in her body spiked at that image, but she fought to hold onto the threads of her irritation. "You should go home and do that again. That's all you're going to get."

His lips brushed her ear, sending shivers down her neck. "Take off your clothes and show me that you're not wet, then."

Her jaw clenched. She was not going to give him the satisfaction. She was not going to let him win. Or see that she was more than a little turned on with him this close, with her mind painting pictures of his hand pumping his cock, of him spread out naked on his bed and coming with her name on his lips. "No."

"No isn't the magic word. Take off your clothes or safe word."

She closed her eyes, her heart pounding hard. So much of her wanted to comply, wanted to just give in and feel good and not think. She could let him touch her. They could have a hot night, scratch each other's itch, not sleep alone tonight. But the fantasy wasn't enough to eclipse the reality. She had rules. Standards. Promises she'd made to herself.

He didn't get to do this to her. He didn't get to come in and take what he wanted, when he wanted. He didn't get to do this after he'd had sex with someone else tonight.

Even so, the word didn't want to come out, the sound stuck

in her throat, but she forced it. "Birthday."

The word was whispered but powerful—a whoosh of air that snuffed the flame burning in the space between them, a chilly breeze replacing it.

Lane instantly pushed away from the wall, giving her all the space she could need. His expression was unreadable but all traces of smugness were gone. He gave a brief nod. "Okay then. I'll leave. Good night, Elle."

She blinked, the simple declaration catching her off guard. "That's it?"

"Yes. That's it. That's how it works. The safe word isn't a game. It's a promise and a parachute cord. If you're not ready for this, I'm not going to try to persuade you."

He said everything so matter-of-fact that it startled her out of her anger for a moment. "Oh."

He blew out a long breath, suddenly looking exhausted. "If this were a normal arrangement, like if we were at a club or something, I'd talk with you about what made you safe word. We could see if there were ways to adjust things to make it work for you. But you've made it perfectly clear that you don't want to talk about...anything at all with me. I thought maybe we could work around that, but this proves we can't. There's got to be some level of trust there and there's not. And if you're not willing to talk to me like a human being, there never will be."

Elle stared at him, absorbing the words and trying to process them. She didn't know how to deal with him when she wasn't fighting with him. So she said the only thing she could. "I don't know how to do that."

Something akin to relief loosened his expression. "Okay, honesty. Good. I can work with that." He stepped closer. "How about you start by telling me what made you safe word? There's no wrong answer. You can call the word for any reason at all, but I can't help or adjust things if I don't know. Was I scaring you? Are you just not into it tonight?"

She closed her eyes. Breathed. "No, it's the other thing."

"What other thing?"

"You having sex with a client and then coming here. I can't—" Her voice caught and she shook her head.

"Hey…" The word was soft against her senses.

But she didn't let him finish. If she was going to say it, she needed to do it now before she chickened out. "My ex-husband cheated on me, all right? He used to fuck someone else and then would crawl in bed with me." She dared a glance up. "I found out later that he'd sometimes…get me to go down on him, knowing he hadn't used a condom with *her*. Some private joke or fetish or whatever."

Mild horror crossed Lane's face and his breath whooshed out of him.

The confession hung heavy in the air, and she immediately wanted to snatch it back. It was so goddamned humiliating. She closed her eyes again, shame burning through her.

Hands cupped her shoulders. "Elle…"

The pity she heard in his voice was enough to snap her out of the moment. She opened her eyes and shrugged out of his hold. "Never mind. Just go please. You're right. I don't want to talk to you."

But Lane didn't move away. Instead he shifted closer, putting his hands on her face. "Hey, look at me."

"Don't therapy me, Cannon. I swear to God, I will knee you in the balls."

He met her eyes, his gaze steady. "I didn't have sex with someone else and then come here. I wouldn't do that to you. That's the trust part we have to find."

She let out a breath. "Oh."

His hands moved down to her shoulders. "I'm not going to pretend I have a different job, but I also respect you enough to be upfront. I spent most of my day trying to rewrite a paper, which has sucked up a lot of my week, and then tonight I sat in on a session with Marin and a client we're both working with. I planned to call you tomorrow, but when I drove by and saw the TV light flickering, I couldn't resist. That's it. No ulterior motives or plans to piss you off." He smiled. "Okay, maybe I enjoy pissing you off a little."

She smirked. "And getting me to confess my embarrassing secrets."

"That's not embarrassing. That's your ex being an abusive asshole. Don't discount what it was."

"Knee to the balls, Lane," she warned. "Knee. To. The. Balls."

He raised his palms. "No therapy, I promise. Plus, I don't want you to turn that shit around on me. I was an escort. My tales of things I've had to do would keep a therapist in business for *years*."

She smiled at that. "Well, now you've got me curious. I need the most embarrassing one ever. Then, we can be even."

He shook his head. "No way. I made no deals."

Now she was the one to stalk forward. "Come on, Cannon. Don't be a scaredy-cat. We're building trust here, right? Trust involves dirt. You've got some of mine, now I need some of yours."

"*Now* you want to talk about trust? When you can scent

blood in the water? You're ruthless, doc."

She stopped in front of him and put a finger to his chest. "Spill."

He gave a put-upon sigh. "Fine. I was once hired for a bachelorette party. They used me for party games."

Elle let the hand she'd pointed with flatten out on his chest, enjoying the feel of his heart beating against her palm. Based on the quick beat, he was more nervous saying this stuff than he was letting on. That comforted her somehow. "What kind of party games?"

He pressed his hand over hers and slid it lower until it was resting at his waist. "One was naked charades. Another involved tossing plastic rings at me. I'll let you figure out what they were trying to ring."

She winced. "Ouch."

"You're telling me. Try staying hard while drunk women with terrible aim throw things at your junk."

She snorted and let her fingers explore a little, sliding along the warm strip of skin between his shirt and jeans. "What'd you think about to stay…up for the job?"

"Boobs," he said with a solemn nod.

A laugh burst out of her. "That's it?"

"I was eighteen. Didn't take much back then."

She looked up, frowning. "Eighteen? When did you start—"

He lifted his hand and pressed it over her lips, cutting off her question. "I'll tell you, but if I agreed not to play therapist, I need the same assurance from you."

She nodded.

He lowered his hand. "I was sixteen the first time. I was failing out of school, my parents were about to kick me out of the house, and someone made me an offer I couldn't turn down. The rest is history. *Buried* history."

Her stomach twisted at that. Knowing Lane was an escort as a grown man was one thing. Thinking of someone preying on a vulnerable kid and dragging him into that kind of life was another. But she'd promised not to psychoanalyze, so she held her tongue.

"And now we're done talking," he said, giving her a look. "Do you want to un-safe word, Elle? Or should I go home?"

She wet her lips and tugged at the hem of his shirt. "Option one. Happy Un-Birthday, Lane Cannon."

"Great. So we're going to watch a movie, then?" He grinned wide.

She pushed him, almost tipping him over the edge of the couch, but he grabbed ahold of her and took her down with him. They landed in a heap, almost rolling right off onto the floor. "No movie. Unless it's reenacting one where the hot stranger does really bad things to the lady of the house."

He stared up at her. "I'm all for that. But tell me one thing first. Were you really planning to call things off?"

She settled on top of him, feeling the heat of his growing interest pressing against her, and braced her hands on his chest. "Yep."

"Because I wasn't calling you on your schedule or doing things the way you wanted me to."

She shrugged. "Basically."

"And now I am?"

"Pretty much."

His smile was slow. "You may not be submissive, doc. But you certainly have a masochistic streak." He took her by the wrists, rolled her off of him, and sat up.

She blinked at the sudden change in position. "What are you doing?"

He took her hands and kissed her knuckles. "Go to your bedroom, take off all of your clothes, and wait for me."

She stared at him for a moment, wary of his tone, but when he didn't say anything else, she nodded. "O...kay. Not a do-it-on-the-couch kind of guy?"

"No more questions. Go. Do what I asked and don't leave the room unless I call for you. If you leave your bedroom without my permission, I'm going to go home without touching you."

She frowned.

"My rules," he said, cocking his head in challenge. "That was the deal. I'd take your money. You'd deal with me calling the shots. Or are you backing out of that deal?"

"I'm—" She cut herself off before she could give her knee-jerk response and tell him no. He was right. They'd made a deal. He would be in control of this part. She took a deep breath. "Okay."

He released her hands and smiled. "See you soon."

But that turned out to be a lie. Because after stripping off her clothes and sliding into bed, she waited. And waited. The clock minutes seemed to drag. And with each one, she got more annoyed. And then angry. And then downright pissed. She knew he hadn't left because she could hear him downstairs, watching television, probably eating more of her ice cream. But she couldn't go and see what exactly was taking so long because if she left the room, he would keep his threat and leave.

So, she waited more.

Her vision began to blur after looking at the clock so often. And right past midnight, she couldn't focus any longer. It'd been a long day and her anger had burned the last remaining bits of her energy. This was some sort of test. She mentally told Lane to fuck off, but she wasn't going to fail it.

Sometime before one, she fell asleep.

chapter eleven

Lane stared down at the woman curled on her side in the bed. Her shoulder rose and fell with steady breaths, and the thin sheet draped over her revealed every gorgeous dip and curve of her naked body. In sleep, her face was blessedly relaxed, the usual frustrated wrinkle in her brow gone for a little while. He wanted to reach out and run his thumb over the smooth spot, but he kept his hands at his side.

He honestly hadn't expected her to make it as long as she did. It'd been a test, but a particularly hard one for her. She thought she wanted control. She thought she wanted to dictate every little thing, but that was what she did every day and it wasn't satisfying her. It was too easy. People were too easy to push away or cow into submission. And that response from everyone else told her exactly what she suspected—that she wasn't worth the trouble of pushing back. That'd they'd rather comply than deal with her.

She was trying to prove Lane fell into that category. She'd threatened to pull the plug on this because he hadn't done things her way. He needed to show her that her method wasn't going to work with him and that it wasn't what she really wanted anyway. So he was testing her. She probably didn't realize that she was testing him right back.

What are you going to do about it, Lane Cannon? That was what she asked in every move she made with him. But he saw through that haughty facade. She gravitated to him despite their personalities clashing because she wanted the challenge. In school, she would've never taken filler classes. She'd look for the teacher who would make her work, the subject matter that would push her capabilities. She needed that in bed, too.

She also needed to trust that he could give it to her, that he wouldn't be scared off by her attitude and defensive tactics. So he'd waited her out. Now, this was his prize. Seeing the all-powerful doctor as vulnerable as anyone could be. Naked. Asleep. No shield or barbed words to protect her.

Not that he blamed her for the shields. She hadn't told him all the reasons they were there, but he'd gotten a glimpse tonight. Her ex-husband hadn't just betrayed her, he'd humiliated her, abused a sacred trust. Used her for some sick-minded game or ego-stroking. Lane didn't know the guy, but he already wanted to nut-punch him.

Lane stepped closer to the bed, feeling a bit like a creeper for watching her sleep but unable to help himself. She was always beautiful, but in a sophisticated, untouchable way. That cool attitude was actually a turn on for him. She wasn't the only one who enjoyed a challenge. But like this, she seemed ten years younger. Sweet, even. He glanced at the bedside table. She had a notepad and pen next to her cell phone—ever the efficient doctor—but he smiled when his eyes skimmed over the note.

Go to hell and burn long, Lane.

He chuckled under his breath and ran his fingers over the deep scratch of the writing. Ah, a love note. Lucky for her, making them both burn was exactly what he had in mind.

The pressure on her wrists woke Elle. Her nose itched and when she went to scratch it, her arm didn't cooperate. Her eyelids flew open and she blinked in the filmy darkness.

She was on her stomach, cheek against her pillow, and her arms were above her head. Something soft but restrictive was around her wrists and she was blindfolded. She yanked but the bed frame just squeaked in response. Her heartbeat kicked up. "What the hell?"

"Stay still or you're going to hurt yourself."

Lane.

The quiet voice in the dark was enough to break through some of the fog of sleep and reassure her that she wasn't in some nightmare, but it wasn't enough to calm her down. She yanked again. "What are you doing?"

A light smack to her thigh had her words catching in her throat. Lane pressed his hand against the spot he'd popped. "I said, stay still. Play nice and I'll be nice. You always want me to do things your way. So, lady of the house, meet your stranger."

"My str—" Oh. *Oh.* Her words from earlier in the night came back to her. The movie she'd joked she'd want to reenact. "I didn't mean—"

He smacked her again, this time on her ass and with more oomph. The sting burned, but also sent tendrils of hot sensation over her skin. Her fingers curled into her palms as she fought not to squirm.

"Next time, be careful what you wish for, then. Because

now you're mine. Just try to escape or fight me and see what happens."

Mine. The words should've bothered her, but she could tell he was slipping into a role. A dangerous one, but one that was pushing hot buttons she'd rather not analyze. She found herself wanting to fall into her own part as well. She tried to pull her arms free. "You're sick. Tying me up while I'm sleeping."

"Mmm, is that your professional opinion, doctor?" The bed dipped and he clamped a big hand over her wrists, pinning them down. He straddled her thighs, his weight pressing her into the bed. "I told you not to fight."

"I told you I'm not one of your submissives."

A quiet laugh rumbled through him, vibrating through her as well. "Never have truer words been spoken. That doesn't mean I can't make you submit. I'm bigger than you. And meaner."

He ran a hot finger over her tailbone and down, lazily tracing the crease of her ass. The simple touch sent electricity racing over her. She wanted him to touch her everywhere. She wanted to feel good. To feel him. But as usual, that little voice inside her wouldn't let her give in. She tried to buck beneath him. "Get off."

The bed springs groaned, but there was no dislodging the beast of a man straddling her. His finger teased lower. "Get off? That's the idea. At least for me."

She grunted and twisted her body, or tried to, but he shifted along with her, anticipating her movements. His other hand released her wrists since they were effectively tied anyway and he pressed his entire body along hers. His naked body.

Every part of her became acutely aware of that fact in one quick instant. Not having her vision dialed up everything else to eleven. The crisp hair on his legs brushing against her smooth ones, the hard planes of his chest heating her back, and the thick length of his cock marking the path his finger had followed.

She wanted to part her legs, to pull herself up on her knees and just have him take her like that. Every female molecule in her body hummed with the knowledge that there was an aching, throbbing, empty place inside her that wanted to be filled with a big dose of Lane. But the words that came out didn't match the need that raced through her veins. "This gets you hard? Tying up some woman in her sleep and forcing yourself on her?"

"No," he said against her ear, his breath making goose bumps track over her skin. "Knowing that it's *you*, and that you want me to, makes me hard."

"I don't—"

He shifted his weight, lifting his hips, and his fingers pushed between her legs, finding her embarrassingly wet. He slid a long finger inside her. "You don't what, doc? Tell me what you don't. But speak up. I may not be able to hear it over the slippery sound of your needy cunt."

She bit her lip at the dirty words, fighting back the moan that wanted to escape. His finger felt like too much and not enough all at once. Involuntarily, her hips rocked back, deepening his movement.

Deftly, he slipped his finger out before she could get the angle just right, and he teased her outer lips instead, a gentle, blunt fingernail tracing an electric pattern over her flesh. "You want to come, cupcake?"

"Don't call me that," she said through gritted teeth. His teasing finger was going to drive her mad. She'd been so keyed up when she'd come to the bedroom earlier that her body remembered how unfulfilled she'd fallen asleep.

"You didn't answer my question, and I can call you whatever I want right now." He caressed her slick skin in a maddeningly slow stroke. "Because this pretty pink pussy makes me think of those cupcakes I brought you. All covered in icing and begging to be licked."

Only Lane could talk about a bright pink cupcake and make it sound filthy. And the thought of him licking every bit of her had her burning hotter. His finger grazed over her clit and the moan finally broke through. *Fuck.*

"Just ask me, doc. Ask me and you get to come."

She squeezed her eyes shut behind the blindfold. Part of her still wanted to fight, but her body had taken over and the need to come turned frantic. Like her nerve endings would just light on fire and burn her up if she didn't get relief. "I want to come. Please."

"Mmm, even a please. Very nice."

"Fuck you."

He laughed and rolled away from her.

"Where are you going?" She couldn't help the edge of panic in her voice.

"Shh"—his hand brushed over her hip—"don't worry. I keep promises. Pull your knees beneath you and show me how badly you want this."

She let out a breath, and before she could think too hard about it, she did as he said. It was only a game. She'd agreed to this. She could play by his rules for a little while. But before she could calm herself fully, cool liquid slid between her ass cheeks. She tensed. "Lane."

The flat of his thumb rubbed the lubricant over her sensitive back opening, sending oh-my-God awareness to every part of her. She'd been touched there a time or two before, but nothing beyond that. She didn't stay with guys long enough to move pass the basics. This was not just beyond the basics, this was you-should-know-the-name-of-my-childhood-stuffed-animal-and-why-I-don't-like-celery familiarity.

"Easy," Lane said, his tone soothing and commanding all at once. "I won't hurt you. Just give yourself a second to relax and see how it feels for you."

She pressed her face into the pillow and when the tip of his thumb breached her, she let out a gasp. But it wasn't of pain. It was a foreign sensation but also one that made every erogenous zone on her body stand at attention, fully aware, all cells reporting for duty. He slowly moved his thumb deeper, and rubbed the fingers of his other hand along her sex at the same time. She bit the pillow.

Lane inhaled deeply behind her. "You should see how wet you're getting, doc. Your scent has me hard as a rock." His thumb slid almost all the way out then back in. "I wanted you like this that day at your office. Wanted you in just your white coat and bent over your desk like this."

Her breath came in short bursts.

He stroked her with maddening patience. "I would've taken one of those cupcakes, smeared the icing right here, and licked it off you."

At that, he ran his tongue over her ass cheek and bit.

"Oh, fuck." That was all it took. The images, the feel of him stroking her, tasting her. She couldn't stop it. *"Lane...please..."*

The orgasm rolled over her like a dump truck, flattening her and making her cry out and buck against his hands for more.

Begging him with her body and her words.

"That's it," he said with utter male satisfaction. "Feel what I can give you."

Then his tongue was on her, licking her in the most lewd, shameless way as she worked herself on his fingers. Every tether inside her broke loose and she screamed, the orgasm too much and just right all at the same time. Her wrists pulled tight against the bindings and she lost her sense of where she was on the bed. But he kept her where he wanted her and stroked and licked until she was vibrating and squirming and she couldn't bear it anymore.

As if sensing everything had become too much for her, he shifted back, his hands leaving her for a few breaths, and then returning to her waist before she could settle. She heard the tear of the condom packet. His big palms gripped her hips. "My turn."

"I can't," she gasped. "Need a minute…"

"No, you don't." The tip of his cock pressed against her sex. "You want to find your control."

He was exactly right. Her thoughts were shattered, any shred of pride in a tattered heap on the floor. She'd *begged*, for God's sake. "I—"

His fingers dug into her, grounding her. "Am I hurting you, Elle? Tell me now if I am and I'll stop."

The words were strained to her ears. He was fighting to get them out.

Hurting her? "No."

The word was the truth but she hadn't meant for it to slip out so easily.

"Good." He pushed forward, burying his cock inside her

and making her body clench hard around him.

"Oh, God," she groaned, her face pressing into the pillow again. She had a word that would stop him, but suddenly she had no interest in using it. His weight on her, the feel of him sliding deep, were all she could think about.

He pumped into her with long, determined strokes—the ragged sound of his breath an erotic soundtrack. And then his thumb was back, pressing against her asshole. The lubricant eased his way and he stretched her as his cock glided against sensitive flesh and his thumb added more fullness. "One day, I'll take you here. Fill you up everywhere and show you how good I can make you feel, how much you'll crave the things we do. You won't be able to go to sleep without thinking about it. You'll touch yourself imagining me here with you. And you won't be able to stop it. I'll be in your head, Elle, and you won't be able to get rid of me."

The words were painting fears in her brain, but she couldn't process them the right way. Instead, all those threats only ratcheted up the sensation more. She got off on a little show of force, on roughness. That wasn't news to her. But never before had a guy threatened to force his way into her head, to leave a mark on her thoughts, on her fantasies. She didn't want any man invading that territory, but the threat added a layer of danger. And when Lane angled just right inside her and whispered a few words in her ear, she came so hard she saw colored light behind her eyelids.

He came along with her, gripping her hard enough to leave bruises. But those marks weren't going to be what she remembered tomorrow or the next day.

No, what would stay with her longer were the words he'd

whispered next.

"You can't escape me, Elle. Even if you make me leave, I've already got you."

chapter twelve

"You're a pompous asshole. You know that, right?" Lane, who'd been rubbing his hair dry after a shower, lowered the towel to look at Elle in the steam-filled bathroom. "What?"

"What you said to me. That's such a dude thing to say. Like you can own my fantasies or invade my head if I don't want you there. Don't flatter yourself." She stuck her chin out and wrapped a fluffy, white terry-cloth robe around herself, the bathroom version of her doctor's coat. Her armor. "If women said half the things guys do in bed, we'd be laughed right out of it."

He smirked. "Cupcake, if some woman told me she was going to invade my fantasies and make me think about her when I jerk off, I may get on my knee and propose right there. I don't know about other guys, but I like a woman with a filthy mind and dirty mouth. Bring it on."

She sniffed, back in Elle McCray mode already. "My fantasies are my own. You're not invited."

He tossed the towel aside, not bothering to cover up. He could tell Elle was trying to pull herself together, slide that mask back in place, but her poker face was on the fritz. His naked presence in her bathroom was affecting her. Her quick, stolen glances down his body gave him no small amount of satisfaction. He liked knowing that she was as attracted to him as he was to her. And he wasn't going to let her shut down. "Oh really, I'm not welcome? Who's invited to that party then? What celebrity is lucky enough to get a starring role in the great Dr. McCray's fantasy montage?"

She opened her mouth to respond then frowned.

"What?" he asked, leaning against the sink, amused. "Too embarrassing? Is it a guy who plays one of the superheroes? No, that's probably too generic for you. Maybe some actor from a brainy British miniseries or something."

The line was back between her brows. Always deep in thought, his Elle.

Wait—*his* Elle? Maybe she wasn't the only one who needed to get her armor on. He picked up the towel and wrapped it around his waist.

She shook her head. "No, no one like that. I guess I never really thought about it. Any fantasies I have, the guys are usually faceless."

Faceless. The idea struck him as sad. But who was he to judge? Men objectified women and reduced them to faceless sexual objects all the time. If that was what she did to guys in her fantasies, that was her business. "Guys? More than one in there at the same time?"

She tilted her head, almost coquettish if not for the wry expression. "So what if there are? Maybe there are whole orgies of men in my head granting my every wish."

He laughed, happy to see her playing along instead of locking him out. "An army of manservants servicing the illustrious Dr. McCray, huh?"

She shrugged. "Maybe. Too bad for you, you'll never know. Only I get to be in my head, which is my point in the first place."

"Right. I'm not allowed in. I get it." He stepped closer and wrapped an arm around her waist, pulling her against him, surprised and pleased that she didn't resist. "But my guess is those orgies of men aren't serving the good doctor. They're holding her down and doing hot, depraved things to her. Forcing her past where she thinks she wants to go. Making her feel used and helpless."

Elle wet her lips, the pupils of her eyes dilating a bit, letting him know that he'd hit the right nail.

He reached up and pushed her damp hair off her forehead. "See, maybe I can get in there just a little bit." Her lips parted, no doubt to protest, but he pressed his fingers against her mouth. "That's not me trying to screw with you, doc. I only know what's in there because it's in mine, too."

She moved his hand away. "Manservants?"

"No. Dark fantasies. Some anger mixed up in the sex. Desires that most people don't get. Things that could get you in trouble if done with someone who doesn't understand it." He let out a breath, dropping his own guard. "Feeling a little fucked up about it because you can't tell how much is you and how much is what other people have done to you."

Her eyes met his at that, some of her usual shields falling away for a moment. "You think I'm like this because of my husband."

A statement, not a question. He was careful not to break the eye contact, the moment feeling tenuous. "I don't know enough to say. But I'm guessing you didn't always need this level of impersonal sex. Just like I didn't start out wanting so much control. I didn't crave it until all of it was taken from me over and over again."

Her mouth curved downward, something akin to concern in her expression.

He pressed on. "We were both humiliated and maybe reacted in different ways. And who knows, maybe we each had a tendency to be kinky or whatever from the start. But we'll never know, right? So it always feels a little wrong, like what we're enjoying was created by the very people or experiences we hated so much."

Her shoulders sagged with a long, slowly released breath. "Ugh. How did we end up on the goddamned therapy couch? We both promised."

He gave her a grim smile. "Because you're a doctor at a mental health hospital and I'm a wannabe therapist?"

"A going-to-be, not wannabe."

He looked away at that, the words like a bucket of ice water over his head. One of the reasons he'd been drawn to come here tonight was to distract himself. He didn't want to think about the paper he wasn't going to be able to fix or the form he had in his car that would withdraw him from all his classes. He'd considered his professor's suggestion. But every time he'd tried to get himself to go to the learning center, he'd felt sick to his stomach, remembering all the times in high school that he'd ended up in the counselor's office, getting talked down to like he was stupid. He'd decided he wasn't meant for a degree. He was doing just fine with his current job. "Not quite."

"What do you mean?"

He cleared his throat, trying to force the words out. "I'm dropping out of my program. I'm too busy with everything at The Grove right now. So a wannabe, I'll remain."

"Wait. Hold up. You said you were working on a paper all week."

Lane lifted his gaze to find her wearing a deep frown. "I was trying to fit everything in and realized I couldn't. The paper's not going to get finished. It's not a big deal."

She stepped out of his hold and eyed him in that way that made him think she'd missed her calling as a high school principal. "It is a big deal, actually."

His defenses went up. "What? Don't sleep with men who don't have fancy letters behind their names?"

She scoffed. "Oh, don't give me that crap. You know that's not what I'm saying. Do you know what percentage of people who drop out of college actually go back?"

"I'm not a statistic. I dropped out of high school and got a GED years later when no one expected I could. I'll go back when the timing is better." The last part rolled off his tongue. A lie to her. A lie to himself.

She scrutinized him, eyes narrowed, lips pressed together. He turned his back to her to open the medicine cabinet in search of a spare toothbrush, avoiding her reflection in the mirror.

"Does this have anything to do with you getting referred to the Learning Services Center?"

Lane stilled and his hand gripped the edge of her sink. "What?"

She crossed her arms, her reflection misted in the glass. "When you accosted me at the café, you dropped something on your way out. It was a referral to test for learning disabilities."

Heat tracked up the back of his neck and flooded his face. He turned around. "I have no idea what you're talking about."

"Lane."

He stepped past her. "Look, it's late. I need to get going."

"Get going?" she asked, following him into her bedroom, a bloodhound on the hunt. "It's the middle of the night. What happened to you'll sleep here if you want to?

He searched for his jeans and boxers on the other side of the bed, digging amongst the pillows and blanket they'd knocked onto the floor. "If I want to. I can't tonight. I have to be somewhere in the morning."

She stalked over and stepped in front of him before he could grab his jeans off the floor. She gave him a pointed stare. "Bullshit. Don't try to lie to me. I work with addicts and actors for a living. Your professor referred you because she thinks you have dyslexia. Did you get tested?"

He reached between her feet and grabbed his jeans, some weird fight-or-flight response welling in him. He didn't want her to see this side of him. When he was with her, he felt confident and in control and like the version of himself he wanted to be. This conversation made him feel like that stupid kid all over again. "No. I don't need to. School's just not for me."

Elle huffed with disgust. "Oh my God, you are *not* doing that male pride thing."

He didn't respond.

"Come on, Cannon. You're better than that. If you're having trouble, get yourself evaluated and they'll give you help."

"I don't want help." He shoved his leg in his jeans, giving up on finding the boxers. "I wanted to do it on my own. If I can't get it that way, I don't want it."

At that, she stepped forward, put her palms onto his chest and, taking advantage of his off-balance state, shoved him onto the bed. "Stop getting dressed like you're leaving. And that's ridiculous logic. Get over yourself."

His jaw flexed, his fingers gripping the side of the mattress. "I'm sure that's easy for you to say. Let me guess—you graduated top of your class, went to some fancy university on scholarship, everyone's always told you how brilliant you are? I bet you didn't even have to study because it just came naturally to you."

Defiance flared in her eyes. "I worked my ass off, for the record. But what does that have to do with anything?"

"Because you don't get it," he said, voice rising. "You don't get what it feels like for someone to look at you with pity because you want something, but you're not smart enough or because you came from the wrong place and the wrong family and had the wrong life. That you're just faking it. That you're smoke and mirrors."

The words spilled out of him, and he wanted to gather them back the minute they were out there. But if he expected a free pass from Elle, she wasn't going to give it. "Don't do that, Lane. You got dealt a shit hand. Okay, fine. That sucks. But it doesn't mean you get to use that as an excuse."

"It's not an excuse."

"Right. Sure, it's not. You know what I'd write in your chart if you were a patient? Self-defeating behaviors and pride too big for his own damn good."

"You sure you're not reading your own chart?" he tossed back.

She narrowed her eyes as if he'd hit the mark but then shook her head. "Oh, don't turn it around on me. We can worry about my fucked-up-ness later."

He smirked. "Your fucked-up-ness?"

"That file is too thick to get into right now. We're talking about you."

"No, we're not. I'm leaving."

She put her hands on his shoulders and straddled him before he could get up. Her thighs squeezed around him with more strength than he would've expected, and his feet tangled in his jeans. "No, you're not. And, yes, we are."

His body responded to her climbing on top of him of its own volition, but he couldn't have this conversation with her. "Leave it alone, Elle."

She met his eyes and held the gaze, something determined but uncharacteristically gentle there. "Give me one therapy moment. Humor me and you can have your own with me at the time of your choosing. Then I will take off this robe and we will get back to what we're good at."

Lane let his hands rest on her waist, enjoying the feel of her despite his frustration with the conversation "You're baiting me with sex? Dr. McCray, I thought you were above that."

"Don't think so highly of me."

He let out a breath. "Fine. One doctor moment. *One*."

"Good," she said, her tone all business. "I get that it's hard to accept that you need help with something. That you can't do something one-hundred percent your way. Believe me. But you're not going to drop out of school."

"Elle—"

She put her fingers over his mouth. "Because if you do, you're proving all those people who told you that you weren't good enough right. Dyslexia or any other learning disability is just something that is. If you couldn't walk, you wouldn't reject a wheelchair. This is just like that—a thing that can be addressed and accommodated. It's not something you caused and it literally, scientifically, has zero to do with your level of intelligence. You're not dumb. But if you drop out of school over it instead of getting help, then you *are* an idiot and they win."

His body was tense all over, but he tried to keep his tone even when she moved her hand away from his mouth. "This is how you talk to your patients? Call them idiots?"

"You're not my patient. But I know what it feels like to think you're a fake. After my marriage fell apart, I almost didn't come back to this line of work. How was I supposed to guide people through life and their relationships when I couldn't even manage my own? When I was depressed and could barely get out of bed because of some guy?"

She said the words matter-of-factly, like she was reporting the weather, but Lane's chest tightened. "Elle…"

She shook her head. "I don't want to talk about it, but I can tell you that it took someone talking to *me* like this to make me get help and get back on track. Who knows where I'd be if I hadn't listened? I don't pretend I'm the best doctor out there, but I know I've helped a lot of people. I know I'm good at what I do and care about my patients. And that's how I say 'fuck you' to my ex and the people who let me down." She held his gaze, something earnest in hers. "I know you're good at what you do, too. People who aren't the best at their jobs don't get positions at The Grove. But you obviously want a bigger role. To get that, you're going to have to get over your pride and fear and fight for it. Don't be a fucking coward."

The words were digging into him, one by one, sharp little needles, stabs of truth. She'd pinned him to a board like a butterfly and laid out the guts of it. Fear. Shame. Insecurity. "You're one to talk about not being a coward. You can't even sleep with me without paying me like I'm your whore."

She shifted on his lap, leaning back to eye him, and braced her hands on her on thighs. "That's not about pride. That's about learning from my mistakes. I know you don't need the money. I know you're here only because you want to be and the minute you don't or you get bored with this, you're gone. The money keeps my head in the right place. It gives us both boundaries."

"That we're not dating," he said flatly.

"Yes. I can't date. I won't. My emotional tolerance for that sort of thing is nonexistent. I was...broken after my divorce." She ran a hand over her still damp hair. "I'm better alone, Lane. That's the only time my life goes in the right direction, when I'm on my own. But you're the type of guy who will be a great husband one day and maybe a dad. You're still young, and throwing away a potential career because you're embarrassed to ask for help is ridiculous. Don't sabotage yourself like that."

He sighed, some of his anger draining out of him. He wasn't going to blame Elle for being honest. He knew what he was signing up for when he made the offer in the first place and expecting her to be something different wasn't fair. "Maybe it's dumb, but I don't want to have to sit with some college-age kid to tutor me on how to read and write better. It just feels like a repeat of high school, and I never want to go through that kind of humiliation again."

She considered him for a long moment, her brows pinching together again. "What if I could help?"

He blinked, his original trail of thought cutting off abruptly. "What?"

She shrugged. "If you get tested and it's dyslexia, I can help. I worked for a while at the learning center at my college in undergrad. If auditory stuff works better for you than print, there are resources for that. Apps that will read documents aloud, dictation software, even simple things like bookmarks that isolate lines of text can help. It can take a while to get used to all of that stuff, but in the meantime, I could help you finish your paper and whatever else you have to do to get to the end of this semester. I could read aloud references to you. You could dictate your paper to me, and I can help you organize how you want to say things."

"You want to *tutor* me?" He grimaced. "That sounds like the least sexy thing ever."

She lifted a brow. "You're saying I wouldn't be a hot teacher?"

The haughty expression broke the tension strumming through him for a moment and he smiled. "Your humility is overwhelming."

"Said the pot to the kettle."

He ran his hands over her arms, sliding beneath the sleeves of her robe. "I don't get it. Why would you want to do this? You don't want to be friends. You've made sure to hammer that point home. This would require spending actual time with me that doesn't involve you begging to come."

"I did not beg."

Now it was his turn to give her the don't-be-coy look. "There was begging, McCray. Pleading, even." He pushed aside one lapel of her robe and drew his knuckles over her breast, watching the nipple tighten in awareness. "I bet I could get you to do it again right now."

She put her hand over his, pressing his palm against her but stilling his movement. "Don't try to distract me with your wicked hands."

"You didn't answer my question. Why?"

Her lips pursed, her frustration obvious. "Maybe because I feel like this whole setup we have is uneven. I know I'm paying you, but you're humoring me."

He met her gaze but didn't deny the accusation.

She sighed. "So maybe this makes it feel better for me. I provide you with a service…"

"…and I pay you back with one," he finished, his tone flat.

She nodded. "Yes. Exactly."

He let out a breath, wishing they could just go back to tussling in bed instead of discussing all of his shortcomings and their screwed-up arrangement, but he had a feeling she wasn't going to let this go. And really, he didn't *want* to drop out of school. He'd worked hard to get to the point he had and still wanted to be a degreed therapist, to be able to help people with more than his body.

Getting tutored by Elle would probably be maddening but more fun than dealing with some eighteen-year-old kid who was trying to teach him for class credit. Plus, the more he and Elle annoyed each other, the hotter the sex would be. But if they were going to be spending more time together and working on things that affected his career, he had to put a lid on this back-and-forth act she was pulling. She'd almost ended the whole thing when he'd come over tonight. This dance was wearing him out. He didn't want that same thing playing out with the tutoring. But he didn't know how to fix that unless…

An idea popped into his head. A dangerous, barbed one, but a good one. He smiled. "I'll agree to this on one condition."

"A condition," she said, obviously skeptical.

"Yep," he announced. "No more clandestine stuff."

Her frown was instant. "What?"

"I have a few months left of this semester. You agree to help me get through that. I agree to make it worth your while in bed. But in public, we're friends."

She bit her lip, a deer-in-the-headlights look in her eye. "Lane…"

"It won't be real and we can go our separate ways when the agreement comes to an end. But I've spent years being women's secret. It's too exhausting to be yours, too, especially if we're going to be seeing each other a lot."

Elle shifted off his lap and sat next to him on the bed, her eyes wary. "I can't do that."

"Sure you can. People know you're human. They won't be that shocked that you made a friend."

She shook her head, her entire posture closing. "You don't get it. It's just—people will talk—and my reputation at the hospital and—"

Elle never stumbled with words, so the way she stopped and started put a chill in his chest that spread out wider the longer she babbled. There were reasons mixed up in her speech and explanations and lots of you-wouldn't-understands.

But Lane understood. He understood exactly.

He felt his own shields going up, his gates locking in place. He lifted a hand to cut her off. "I get it, Elle."

She let out a relieved breath. "Oh, good."

"The surrogate is good enough for your bed in private, but we couldn't have people of importance thinking you're slumming it with someone below your pay grade. Got it." He reached for his jeans.

She stiffened at that. "That's not—"

"I've got to go."

She grabbed his arm. "Please, don't. Come on. What I'm saying isn't coming out right. I didn't spend time with Donovan publicly either. It has nothing to do with you. I just—you're part of that social world at work. I'm not. I don't want to be. This saves us both the awkwardness."

His fingers paused while buttoning his fly. "You think I give a fuck about awkwardness?"

He turned to find her eyes pleading—a sight he never thought he'd see outside of sex. "Please. Don't go. We're both exhausted. I'm not explaining myself well. Can we just go to bed and talk about in the morning? It's almost four."

He stared down at her, his anger still roiling but exhaustion waging a battle as well. He didn't get where she was coming from but for some reason, he sensed that it really wasn't about him. This was much more about her.

He didn't know if it would be a deal breaker for him, but suddenly he felt too tired to decide. Getting a few hours' sleep and talking about it in the morning wouldn't hurt anything. With a groan, he tugged off his jeans, walked to the other side of the bed, and slid beneath the covers.

Elle shrugged out of her robe and settled into the spot next to him, turning on her side to face him. "Thank you."

The words were quiet in the dark. Sincere.

He closed his eyes, wondering what in the hell he'd gotten himself into.

chapter thirteen

The knock on the back door came way too early and way too loudly. Elle startled at the sound and almost spilled coffee on herself. She muttered a curse and glanced at the clock on the microwave. Just past seven. Who the hell would show up at this hour on a Saturday morning?

She set the steaming carafe down on the kitchen counter and wiped her hands on a dishtowel before heading to the door. But when she peeked past the curtain and saw who it was, every part of her went icy. *Oh, hell no.*

The knock came again. "Ellie, I know you're in there. I saw the curtains move."

Ellie. No one dared call her that these days. No one but her mother and…*Nina.*

Her stomach twisted and her hands balled. How did Nina even find her house on campus? They usually didn't let anyone past the gates this early except employees.

The brisk knock came again, louder this time. "Seriously? I'm not going away."

Elle cringed. Lane was still sleeping upstairs and the last

thing she wanted to do was rouse him, especially with this guest at the door. Elle cursed under her breath and unlocked the latch. She cracked the door open a sliver. "What are you doing here?"

Despite the early hour, Nina looked perfectly stylish and put together. Her honey-brown hair in a loose twist, makeup that accentuated her blue eyes and hid her freckles, and a navy-blue sundress that was probably off this spring's runway. "Let me in. We need to talk."

"We don't talk."

Nina winced ever so slightly but then pursed her lips. "Yes. I get that. But we need to today, and I didn't drive to the boondocks from the city to stand out here and talk through the door."

"That's your own fault for showing up uninvited."

"I tried to call from Mom's number because I knew you wouldn't answer mine, but apparently, you don't give a shit about her anymore either."

That did it. Elle moved to shut the door, but Nina put her hand out and stopped it. "Don't. Sorry. Please. Do you think I'd be here if it wasn't important? I don't exactly love the idea of talking to you either. And if you shut the door, I'm just going to sit here and wait."

Elle sighed. Her little sister always had been a stubborn thing. If she said she'd wait it out, she would. Elle pulled open the door. "You've got ten minutes."

Nina slipped inside, her heels clicking along the floor. Her sister glanced around at Elle's place with appraising eyes. It wasn't anything like the lavish home in the Garden District of New Orleans where they'd spent their teen years, but Elle loved the little renovated cottage.

"This place has nice bones. It'd sell for a ton in the city."

Elle poured herself a cup of coffee and begrudgingly poured another for Nina. She pushed the mug across the bar. "I doubt you're here to give me a house appraisal."

Nina took the coffee and added milk and sugar, a pensive look on her pretty face. She still took way too much milk in her coffee. She'd been doing that since she was a kid. Elle would make her a cup of warm milk and mix in a few tablespoons of chicory coffee because Nina wanted to feel like a grown-up. They'd pretend they were having high tea and scones. Back in the days when they didn't hate each other, when all Elle wanted to do was see her little sister smile, when they were just two lonely kids whose parents worked too much.

Elle cleared her throat. "I'm waiting."

Nina looked up, the expression revealing faint dark circles under her eyes, the makeup not quite enough to hide it. "I'm getting married."

Elle's grip on her mug tightened but she took a sip, trying to look wholly uninterested. "I heard. I got the announcement in the mail."

And tore it into shreds. Then spit on it. Not one of her finer moments.

"Congratulations," she said with no sincerity at all.

Nina set down her mug and rubbed the spot between her eyes. "Look, I don't expect you to be happy for me. Believe me. I get it, all right. All I can say is what I told you from the beginning—I didn't mean to fall in love. I didn't do it to hurt you."

Elle lifted her brows. "You didn't mean to sleep with my

husband. Is that what you didn't *mean* to do? Somehow you just tripped and fell on his penis in *my* bed after I generously let you move in with us?"

Her jaw flexed but she didn't back down. "I was lonely and did a dumb thing. We both did. He didn't mean for it to happen, either."

Elle scoffed at that, almost choking on her coffee. "Wow, you said that with a straight face." She gave her a mean smile. "You really believe that, don't you? That he was so overcome that he just couldn't help himself? That the beautiful hand of fate pushed you two together? That he accidentally married the wrong sister and the world needed to right it?"

She crossed her arms, looking more like the stubborn child she used to be than the thirty-three-year-old woman she was now. "You didn't love him. You never really did. He was just the easy choice for you because on paper it made sense."

So that was the story Nina was telling herself to justify things. Nice. If only that were the case. In the end, Nina had done her a favor because her ex was a scumbag. But Nina was wrong. Elle had loved him. He had put on a good show of loving *her*, especially in public and in front of her family. Elle had been committed to making their marriage work even after she'd noticed Henry getting resentful about how many hours she had to work. She'd tried to adjust her schedule, tried to go out of her way to be attentive. She'd thought they were making progress. Then, she'd come home from a business trip early and walked in on Henry and her sister naked in her bed.

Henry had declared that he'd fallen in love with Nina and was leaving Elle.

Then, when Elle had expected her family to be outraged

on her behalf, to support her when she was falling apart with anger and grief, they'd informed her that it would be best if she would let it go and move on. Henry worked with her father, so he wasn't going anywhere. These things happened. *It's better to find out now that the marriage wasn't meant to be before you had kids. You two were never really well-suited. Don't make a scandal out of it.* As if the neighbors talking about it was a fate worse than death.

But Elle had been trained for that tactic all her life. Always put on a happy face. When Dad drank too much night at night— *he just needs that to relax after work.* When her mother would miss yet another important event in their lives—*you should be proud your mother's so successful.* When she caught her dad kissing his assistant and told her mom—*that's not what you saw. She's like family. They were just being friendly.*

Don't trust your gut. That had been the message. Appearances are more important than the truth. Which was why Elle avoided family get-togethers and only had minimal contact with her mom. Her dad had died a few years ago without ever telling her he was sorry for standing behind Henry. She didn't have the energy to play the game anymore, especially not with her sister because that one hurt the most. They'd been soldiers together in the same bizarre war, always on the same side. Until Henry.

Henry, whom she was marrying. "You still haven't told me why you're here."

Nina clasped her hands in front of her. "We've moved up the wedding. It's in two weeks. I need you to come."

Elle laughed, actually laughed loud enough that she had to cover her mouth so she wouldn't wake Lane. "You've got to be kidding me. Are you high? I'd rather get a root canal without anesthesia. Why would you even—"

"Mom's got breast cancer."

Elle's coffee cup hit the counter with a thunk. "What?"

Nina's throat worked as she swallowed. "She tried to call you and tell you but, obviously, you're not answering her calls. They want her to have surgery, but she doesn't want to do anything until after the wedding. I think she's worried she's not going to make it out of surgery."

"Jesus." Elle's heart was thumping too hard, her hands clammy. "What do the doctors think?"

"They have a more positive outlook than she does, but you know doctors."

"We can't make promises."

"Right." Nina was looking at her hands, absently turning her sparkling engagement ring. "And I know it's a shit thing to ask. I know I betrayed you in the most epic way possible." She looked up, her eyes shiny. "And I'm sorry. I truly am. Not that I found Henry, but that he was yours and I didn't have the right to him back then. I never wanted to hurt you. It was never about that."

The apologies were long-coming but Elle couldn't quite absorb them. Some things were beyond forgiveness.

"But Mom wants nothing more than for all of us to be at the wedding next weekend. She…" Nina looked up to the ceiling. "She thinks that all this family drama, the tension between you and I, contributed to the cancer."

"*What?*"

"She said she doesn't talk about it, but you and I being estranged and you being depressed and living this lonely workaholic life weighs on her."

Elle put a finger to her chest. "Me? I'm not depressed. I'm

fine."

Nina met her eyes, a get-real look on her face. "You live alone on the grounds of a mental hospital. You realize that's messed up, right? Like, normal people wouldn't want to do that. This basically screams I want to be a hermit, never get married, and never have kids."

"Like that's some requirement in life? And I *was* married, Nina."

She waved a dismissive hand. "Go ahead and throw it in my face again. You were married. I messed it up. That doesn't mean it's my fault that you're almost forty and bitter and *alone*."

The words were like knives hitting all the tender parts, tearing strips off her. She wanted to throw something, to scream. But before she could get any words out, footsteps sounded behind her.

"Doc, how could you let me sleep this long? I have a full schedule, you—" Lane's words cut off as soon as he rounded the corner and stepped into the kitchen, standing there in nothing but a pair of unbuttoned jeans, his discarded T-shirt casually tossed over this shoulder. "Oh. Sorry. Didn't realize you had company."

Lane quickly fastened the button on his jeans and offered a chagrined smile as he tugged on his shirt, looking as sexy as Elle had ever seen him in his sleep-mussed and half-naked state. But that view wasn't as satisfying as her sister's stunned face.

"Uh," Nina said, looking at Lane with wide eyes. "Hello."

Lane jabbed a thumb toward the back of the house. "I didn't mean to interrupt. I can…"

"Oh, you're not interrupting, honey," Elle said, coming back to herself.

Honey?

Lane looked her way, question marks in his eyes. But she hoped she gave him a sign that said, *Please, for the love of God, just roll with it.* "This is my sister, Nina."

Lane's brows went up, his smile widening. He stepped closer to Nina and put out his hand. "Nice to meet you."

Nina still looked shell-shocked. "And you are?"

Elle jumped into action before she realized what she was doing. She walked over to Lane and slid an arm around his waist. "This is Lane. My..." *Lover. Hooker. Co-Worker.* "Fiancé."

The word leapt out before she could stop it. Lane's muscles stiffened beneath her fingers. *Oh, shit. Oh, shit. Oh, shit.* That was absolutely one-hundred percent not what she was supposed to say.

Nina's eyes went round. "Wait, your what? *You're engaged?*"

The wonder in Nina's voice was too much to ignore. Elle liked that she'd shocked her, proved her wrong, even though she hadn't really at all. She couldn't find it in her to take it back. Not yet. "Yes, it's all pretty new, so we haven't announced it yet. And, of course, I didn't want to take attention away from your wedding plans."

Lane looked at her, his face revealing nothing, but she could feel him vibrating with tension. She smiled at Lane. "Hon, Nina's getting married in two weeks. To my ex-husband."

Awareness dawned on Lane's face, his lips parting. "Oh, that's...wow."

That was one word for it. "Yep. She was here to invite me to the wedding. It seems the date's been moved up."

Nina had a pasted-on smile, the McCray way. Pretend in front of others. Everything was great. Everything was fine. We're the bestest sisters ever! That whole adultery thing is *so* water under the bridge. "So you'll be there, then? And obviously, Lane, you should come, too. I'm sure our mother would be thrilled to hear Elle's engaged. She's always worried Elle is wasting away her best years out here in the boonies."

"Yes," Elle said, deadpan. "The pre-Botox years."

Lane's gaze flicked to her and then he turned to her sister, his grin as genuine as Elle had ever seen it, clearly a way better actor than she was. "I'll have to check my schedule, but that sounds great."

"What is it that you do?" Nina asked.

"He's a therapist here," Elle filled in. "And a student."

"A student? I thought you looked young," Nina said sweetly. Elle gritted her teeth.

"Not that young," Lane said, his tone buttery smooth, but Elle didn't miss the sardonic undertone. He was losing his patience with this charade.

"Well, Nina," Elle said, breaking in. "I told you I had ten minutes and that was true. Email me the details and we'll figure everything out." She put her hand on her sister's elbow and lowered her voice as she guided her to the door. "Does Mom need anything before then? Is she happy with her doctors? I know a good surg—"

"We've got it covered," Nina said peevishly. "Henry has taken care of everything. We don't need your help. I just want you to put on a happy face and make her believe all is well with us at the wedding. I can't believe you didn't even bother to tell her you were engaged. You know that would've thrilled her."

"It only happened a week ago. The ring isn't even sized yet. Plus, I haven't had time to call."

Nina stepped outside with Elle and turned to her, pinning her with her gaze. "Don't back out on this. I'm going home and telling her that you'll be there. Don't you dare let her down. She needs this."

A pang of guilt hit Elle. She'd never been very close with her mom. Her mother had been married to her career and not all that interested in the day-to-day drudgery of motherhood, but her mom was also the one who'd shown her a woman could be the strong one in the family, the breadwinner. They'd at least connected there. So though it was a tenuous relationship, there was love there. She wanted her mom to be well. "I'll be there."

"And no drama. Henry isn't going to bother you, so you don't bother him."

Elle's nails bit into her palms. "I wouldn't waste the breath."

"Right." Nina sniffed. "I'll email you the details. Plan to come down for the whole weekend. Rehearsal supper is Friday night. Mom would like us all to stay at the house."

A whole weekend at her family's house? *Shoot me. Just take me out to pasture and put me out of my misery.* "Whatever."

Nina smiled but it held no warmth. "'Til then."

Her sister turned, hiked her purse onto her shoulder, and walked toward her Mercedes with her shoulders back like an evil queen. Elle shook her head. She remembered when they used to raid her mom's closet to make costumes and do that walk, pretending they were ruler of the land. Now they were the heads of warring kingdoms.

Elle let out a tired sound and turned back to the house. She didn't want to go in. How the hell was she supposed to explain this mess to Lane? He was going to be beyond pissed. He had every reason to be. But what else could she do? She straightened her spine and headed back into the kitchen to face him.

She found him sitting on her island, drinking her coffee. His attention swung to her the second she stepped inside.

"Lane—"

"Don't you mean *honey*?"

She pressed her thumb and forefinger to her temples. "Shit. I'm sorry. I don't know what got into me."

"So last night we can't be friends in public and now we're engaged."

She cringed and looked up. "Maybe? Sort of. I'm not sure how that happened."

"I think you've watched too many romantic comedies. You realize you can't actually do that in real life, right? Get engaged to someone without their permission."

She groaned and went to the cabinet to get another coffee cup. "Yeah, I got that. Look, I'll figure this out. We'll make up an excuse as to why you can't come. I know that was ten kinds of messed up. But she said all these horrible things to me, and once you walked in and she saw you, the lie just came out. I couldn't take it back." She blew out a breath. "She's so goddamned convinced that she's got me figured out, and I wanted to—"

"Prove her wrong."

"Yes."

"You didn't tell me your ex cheated on you with your sister. That's taking fucked up to a new level. Who does that?"

"Henry does that. And apparently was doing it for a while before I figured it out. I had suspicions toward the end that he was cheating, but I never would've considered Nina was the one he was cheating with. I had let her move in when she was in between jobs. I was working long shifts back then. They were both home a lot without me. She thinks he stopped sleeping with me when he started things with her, painted some picture of the frigid wife, but he didn't. He was sick enough to get off knowing he was bedding us both."

Lane made a sound of disgust. "This guy sounds like a real winner."

"Yeah, and my family loves him still. He works in the law firm my dad started. Now he'll be my brother-in-law."

"Your parents don't care that he cheated on you?"

"My dad passed away a few years ago, but when it happened, neither he nor my mom stood up for me. Henry gave them some bullshit story about how we'd fallen out of love and had been like roommates for a long time and then he met his soul mate in Nina." She held out her cup and Lane poured coffee into it. "They also didn't want a scandal or, God forbid, any uncomfortable moments at family dinners. They expected me to get over it and move on. That's the McCray way. And really, I think what it comes down to is they believe it was my fault. That I'm too cold or career-focused or whatever." She gave him a tight smile. "You know, hard to love. Things you already know about me."

Lane frowned at her as she took a sip of coffee. "I don't know that at all."

"Right." She cradled her cup, warming her chilled hands. "Let's not pretend you haven't called me a bitch in your head. I *am* a bitch."

The consternation on his face deepened. "I haven't, for the record, but what's wrong with being opinionated and tough? You do realize that no matter if you were cold or busy or whatever, you didn't deserve to be betrayed like that, right?

What he did wasn't just cheating. What you told me he made you do after he'd slept with your sister or God knows who else—that's fucking abusive, Elle. It's sick and cruel. Not to mention a risk to your health."

She looked down, the words like acid in her stomach. Those weeks after everything had come out, she'd gone to her doctor, had gotten tested for all the diseases, had been racked with anxiety, left wondering how many people's sexual histories she'd been exposed to via her husband's penchant for unsafe sex. She'd gotten a clear bill of health eventually, but the waiting had been like having her head in a steel trap with a hair trigger.

Abuse. She hadn't labeled it as such, but if she'd heard the story from a client instead of it being her own, how would she have seen it? She swallowed hard. "It doesn't matter now. He and Nina deserve each other. I'm sure he'll be cheating before the first wedding anniversary, if he's not already."

"Then why would you even consider going to this wedding?" he asked, genuine confusion on his face. "Tell them to go get fucked and save yourself the trouble."

She sighed and peered up at him, an ache moving through her. "That was my plan, but Nina told me my mom has cancer."

Lane's face fell. "Damn. I'm sorry."

"Yeah, me too. But apparently, me being there and mending fences is Mom's wish before she has surgery." She ran a hand through her hair, bone-deep tired all of a sudden. "We don't have the best relationship, but I can't turn my back on my mother when she needs me. If she wants me there, I'll be there and be civil with Nina. I can manage not to murder Henry for three days. Probably. Maybe. I might just sprinkle some laxatives on his Cheerios. Nothing permanently damaging."

"Right. Sounds fun."

She gave him a what-can-you-do shrug. "I've dealt with worse. I'll manage."

Lane levered himself off the island and turned to her. "You just have to ask, you know."

She sipped her coffee, though it now tasted burnt in her mouth. "Ask what?"

"If you want me to go with you, I will."

She set down her cup and blinked. "What?"

He glanced at the door Nina had left through and then looked back to her. "You told your sister you had a fiancé. So bring him. If nothing else, it will irritate your ex."

She stared at him like he'd spoken a different language. "Are you nuts? That would be a disaster. I have to go for three days and stay at the house. No escape. They'd see right through us."

He crossed his arms and smirked. "You think this is my first rodeo, doc? You know how many times I've had to play the new boyfriend for a divorcée? I've never done full-fledged fiancé, but believe me, they wouldn't see through us. We're sleeping together. I work at the same hospital as you do, so that part makes sense. We have chemistry. The only thing we'd have to get the hang of is acting like we're in love."

"That's a big goddamned jump, Lane."

He put a hand over his heart as if deeply wounded. "Are you kidding? I am super lovable."

She snorted, his mock puppy dog look breaking through some of her angst over this whole screwed-up situation. "You're insane."

"Probably," he agreed. "But teasing aside, I don't think it's good for you to go into that kind of situation alone."

"I go into every situation alone. I'll be fine." Maybe if she said the words out loud, it would make them true.

He frowned, concern plain on his face. "Family shit is different. They can tear you up with just a few words. Do real damage. Believe me, I've been there."

She tilted her head, wanting to ask what he meant, but he didn't give her the chance.

"This sounds like it's going to be a soul-crushing gauntlet. You need at least one person on your side, and it doesn't sound like you're going to have any in your family. If you want to go and be able to focus on your mom, I can give you the space to do that." He reached out and placed his hands on her shoulders, expression serious. "Because I can guarantee you, I'm not going to let your ex mess with you. I can be a nice guy. I like to think I *am* a nice guy. But I also can be an intimidating motherfucker when the situation calls for it. I'm still a street kid at heart and don't let anyone mess with my friends."

The fierce look in his eye and his words had unexpected emotion gathering in her. "Last night I told you we couldn't be friends. I insulted you. Why would you even give a damn if he hurts me?"

Lane's stern expression softened and his mouth curved. "The same reason why you give a damn if I fail out of school. I know it may shock you, but this thing right here—where we talk to each other about what's going on in our lives and the issues we're dealing with—is what people call *forming a friendship*." He said the last few words as if he were speaking to a toddler. "Whether you want to be seen in public with me or not doesn't change the fact that this is happening. You're beginning to like me, McCray."

She straightened, resistance rising in her like a scrappy army.

He lifted his hands from her shoulders and held his palms up. "Don't freak out and don't blame yourself. It was inevitable. I am inherently likable. You really had no shot."

She groaned and tipped her face toward the ceiling. "I seriously hate you."

He chuckled. Gleefully. Then he leaned in and kissed the tip of her nose. "You say the sweetest things, dearest. So when's our wedding date?"

Her attention snapped back to him. "What?"

He shrugged. "You jumped my case last night because I wanted to do everything on my own for school. You told me to get over myself and accept help. I'm turning your advice back on you. Bring me to the wedding weekend and let me play interference. Accept. Help."

She crossed her arms and considered him. This had disaster written all over it. She'd seen movies with the fake boyfriend. They never went well. But this wouldn't be funny hijinks fit for romantic comedy. Her family could be a nightmare, and her ex wasn't the type to stay in the background. He'd dig into Lane, ask a thousand questions, try to make him look inferior in some way. And all of them would cut into Elle. They could wield passive-aggressive comments like ninjas with throwing stars. She didn't want anyone to see her in that situation. Her family and ex were the only people who made her feel weak, who reminded her of that desperate, insecure person she used to be when she was with Henry.

But she couldn't help but be tempted by the lifeline Lane was dangling in front of her. He'd already seen her in weak moments—at the party, last night when she'd lashed out at him, today with her sister. Her secrets were already exposed. He already knew she was screwed up. What did she have to lose? If he went, Lane could be a distraction and run interference. Her family was always better behaved in front of strangers. Maybe his presence could tamp down some of the drama that was sure to ensue if she went alone. They would be the smiling, everything's-all-right McCrays for him.

The urge to handle everything on her own was a deeply ingrained instinct, but she forced herself to loosen her hold on those reins. She let out a slow breath. "Okay. If you're willing to sign up for this domestic nightmare, I will let you come with me and help—on one condition."

Lane's smile dropped into a grim line. "I go to the Learning Services Center."

She nodded. "Yes. If I have to swallow a spoonful of pride, you do, too. You get tested—today. If it's something I can help with, you let me. If it's not, you find someone who can. You get this paper written and no dropping classes. Doctor's orders."

He sighed. "You know they might just tell me I'm dumb and they can't help me. I've had more than one teacher tell me I should just find a workable blue-collar skill."

She rolled her eyes. "You're not dumb."

"How can you be so sure?"

She stepped into his space and put her hands to his chest. "Because despite what you think you know about me, I have only one absolutely undeniable fetish when it comes to guys."

He lifted his brows.

"I only get turned on by smart ones. My vagina is very discerning and can spot a hot IQ from a mile away. And you, Lane Cannon, have revved my engine from the very first time I met you—which, of course, has always pissed me off."

He grinned at that and slipped his hands inside her robe to grip her waist. "So if your vagina is so discerning, how about I skip this testing and she can just whisper to my dick what my issue with this paper is?"

"Have we just personified our private parts?"

"We totally have."

She lowered her forehead to his shoulder and laughed. "What is my life? I need more coffee."

He laughed and peeled back the lapels of her robe. "No, we need our parts to have this very serious discussion. Mine just woke up early for the meeting." He gathered her fully against him, the state of his growing erection hard to miss even through his jeans. "He's very interested in today's agenda."

Her skin warmed at the feel of him and she looked up, letting her hands loop around his neck. "Is that right?"

Lane smiled. "Yes. Agenda item number one: Make Elle come before breakfast." He pushed her robe off, leaving her in just a T-shirt and panties. "Agenda item number two: Come on Elle after breakfast." He traced a finger down her sternum. "Agenda item number three: Lick her clean for dessert."

She shivered at the promise and the filthy-sexy images. "I'm liking this agenda."

He dragged her T-shirt up and off, his gaze eating her up, and then cradled her breast in his hot palm, his thumb teasing her. "Good. Because I have a feeling this meeting's going to get messy."

"Yeah?" His words moved through her, echoing in another place, far from her sex-addled thoughts.

Get messy.

The words sent a shimmer of anxiety through her.

Because the truth was, they were already there. This was getting messy. But she shoved the thought away, not wanting to evaluate it too closely.

Lane lowered his head and took her nipple into his mouth while his hand tracked downward, finding her wet and wanting. Always wanting when it came to him. A sharp pulse of desire fanned outward from his touch, and all those dangerous thoughts blissfully slid away into the background.

This was just sex.

Her brain needed to shut up and enjoy it.

She'd figure out the rest later.

Because in this moment, all was right in her world.

chapter fourteen

"It qualifies as a disability." Lane shifted in the hard plastic chair of the Learning Services Center, his skin going clammy as he listened to the bespectacled counselor go over his test results. "A disability."

The counselor, Mitchell, gave him a brief, emotionless smile. "Yes, Mr. Cannon. That's good news."

Lane couldn't contain his derisive snort. "Oh, having dyslexia is good news. That's great to hear. I didn't realize I'd won some contest."

Mitchell adjusted his glasses and gave Lane a patient look. "I'm sorry. I didn't mean it that way. Of course, it's a challenge. But it's one you've faced your entire life, I'm sure. Now that it's been identified and qualifies as a disability, you can get some accommodations—technology aids, tutoring if needed, extra time on assignments and tests. It opens up options that can help you be successful here at the university."

The words made Lane feel like he'd ingested bad cafeteria food, leaving his stomach turning and a bad taste lingering in his mouth. Despite agreeing to do this, the idea of getting special treatment to get through school still pushed all his *fuck no* buttons. The whole point of getting his degree was to prove to himself that he could. He wanted to walk across that stage, get his diploma, and know that he'd done it the same way everyone else had. On his own. That the janitor's son, the kid who got kicked out of his house at sixteen, the former escort, could be a college graduate.

"I don't want special treatment."

Mitchell folded his hands atop Lane's test results. "I understand, Mr. Cannon. I do. But this isn't special treatment. It's accommodation for the way your brain is wired. There's a difference. You have what it takes to be successful here if you learn to work *with* your dyslexia." He pushed the file folder toward Lane. "When you get a chance, you should go through your results in more detail. The evaluation found far more strengths than deficits."

Lane took the folder but barely heard the words. He had no interest in a bunch of test results, just the bottom line. "So I get more time to turn in my paper?"

"Yes," he said, reaching over to wake his computer screen. "And I'm going to give you a computer program that takes dictation. That way you can speak your paper instead of typing. But there's a bit of a learning curve with it. I have a student worker who can train you on it. Then, once we get this paper out of the way, we can set up some sessions with one of our specialists. She can show you some methods and tricks that will help with your writing and reading comprehension. Your auditory comprehension is very strong, and you don't seem to have trouble organizing ideas if you speak them aloud, so that gives us a lot to work with."

A student worker. A specialist. Lane's mouth filled with a whole bunch of *nope, nope, nope,* but he bit his tongue and took a breath before speaking. "I don't need a student worker. I'll just take the program and figure it out. Until I get the hang of it, I have a friend who is going to help me with the paper. She said she could take dictation for me."

The guy glanced at him with a lifted brow. "You sure? This won't cost you anything."

Except his pride. "I'm sure."

"Okie dokie." Mitchell typed something into the computer. "Well, our specialist is booked up until the end of the month, but I'll get you on her schedule after that. I'll email you the time and date."

Lane wasn't up for that either but it would buy him some time with his paper, and he could always decline the appointment later. "Thanks."

Mitchell wrapped things up and gave Lane the computer program with a few more instructions, but Lane just nodded and did what he had to do to end the appointment as quickly as possible. He was so ready to get out of there, he was surprised his shoes didn't leave scorch marks on the carpet as he escaped.

He climbed into his car, thankful for the solitude and quiet, but it didn't last long. His mind got loud fast, the words *disability* and *accommodations* rolling around in his head and rattling old ghosts as he drove back to The Grove.

Ghosts from his fancy prep school: *Did you hear Lane try to read in class? What is he? Retarded?*

Ghosts from his family: *Son, don't get ideas in your head from those rich kids. You get your diploma and then find a trade. You'll do just fine.*

Ghosts from his escort days: *Oh, sweetheart, we don't need to talk. I'm not paying you for stimulating conversation.*

Lane pulled into the parking lot of The Grove, not missing the irony that he was heading into a mental health hospital while hearing voices in his head. Maybe he should be checking in instead of offering help. *Get it together, Cannon.*

The unseasonably warm afternoon enveloped him and sunlight hit Lane's face on his way into the building. He rubbed his fingers over his brow, trying to chase away the dark memories. Logically, he knew that a learning disability wasn't something to be embarrassed about. It wasn't something he'd caused. If he had a client share that information about herself, he would tell her as much. But shame still burned hot in his chest, the demons from his past vicious and relentless. He took a deep breath through his nose, shoving down his own internal drama as best he could, and pasted on a pleasant look as he stepped inside the building. Here, his problems couldn't exist. When he was working, he needed to be fully focused on the clients.

A few of the staff waved or nodded at him as he made his way through the hallways. Psychiatrists, social workers, doctors, nurses. People were friendly here. But now more than ever, he felt like he was cast in some movie role instead of actually belonging there. *I'm not a real therapist, I just play one on TV.* Because when it came down to it, he was only allowed at an elite facility like The Grove because he wasn't scared to sleep with strangers—a job that was undesirable to most— and because he was appealing enough not to be a turn off to a wealthy clientele that placed a high value on looks. He was here because he could make women feel comfortable, get them talking, and get them off if they were having trouble with that. A hired dick with a fancier title. Maybe Elle had been right about him from the start.

Elle.

She was somewhere in this building. They'd agreed not to interact at work unless it involved a patient, but she'd told him to let him know how his test results came back and suddenly, he had the urge to see her. He checked his watch. He had an appointment in twenty minutes. He probably had time to swing by her office to see if she was busy. He could always make up an excuse that he needed to discuss a client case if anyone was nearby.

He took a left, hopped into an elevator, and once he'd reached the right floor, headed toward the addiction wing, or the R and R wing, as most of the staff called it. Because it contained the rehab facility, that section of the hospital was a secured unit, so he had to use his keycard to get in. Oriana was walking out right as he was walking in.

She gave him a bright smile when she saw him, her brown skin glowing with her trademark friendliness. "Hey, it's my cupcake savior."

"Reporting for duty." He gave her a mock salute. "Any other baked goods need rescuing? I skipped lunch so I'm willing to take one for the team."

"Sadly, not today. There are some bran muffins in the break room but I don't recommend them unless you need a colon cleanse."

He chuckled. "Yeah, I think I'll pass on that."

"Good move." She leaned in conspiratorially. "But thanks again for helping me out. You saved my butt. McCray has been in a better mood and she never figured out that I screwed up. Whatever you said to her worked."

"A better mood, huh?" he said, trying to sound only mildly interested and not one-hundred percent smugly satisfied that his hookups with Elle had helped her mood.

She peered back over her shoulder to verify they were alone. "Yeah, to be honest, it's freaking me out a little. I love working with her because she's hella brilliant and a great teacher, but I'm not sure how to handle her being...somewhat pleasant. It's like the earth's off its axis or something. I keep expecting an explosion. Or to find out she's been taken over by a body snatcher or something."

He had to bite back his grin on that. Well, *he* had been snatching her body on a regular basis, but he couldn't tell Oriana that. "I'm glad things have improved. Is she around? I had a case I needed a consult on."

Oriana pulled her phone out of her jacket's inner pocket and checked the time. "Yeah. She's wrapping up a training in the education room, but should be done in a little while. You can probably catch her before she goes on rounds. And the session's open to employees if you want to slip in the back."

"What's the training on?"

She dropped her phone back into her pocket. "Working with patients who have a dual diagnosis of bipolar disorder and substance use disorder. That's her specialty."

"Is it?" he asked. He should probably know that about her, but she never brought up work and he never asked.

"Yep. She did a groundbreaking study on it a few years ago, researching the incidence of that particular dual diagnosis among people in the arts. That's what got her the job here. She's one of the country's leading experts in that area." She jabbed a thumb behind her. "You should go pop in and hear her speak. Any time people talk shit about McCray, I tell them to withhold judgment until they see her with a patient or hear her give a training. The woman's a genius."

Genius. He didn't doubt it. She was a genius, and he was getting assigned student tutors to help him read. Fantastic. He rolled his shoulders, shaking off the disturbing thought. "Which room is it?"

"E-one."

"Got it. Thanks."

"No problem. Enjoy." She smiled and gave him a little wave before heading past him and out the door.

Lane wound his way through the main part of the rehab unit, which was decorated in muted grays and dark navy and looked more like a lobby at a posh hotel than a hospital. A couple of the patients were chatting in a squared-off section of plush couches. A few others were solo—reading, listening to headphones, writing in notebooks. He recognized a couple of faces from magazine covers and movies. That wasn't uncommon. The Grove, particularly the rehab unit, often had its fair share of who's who in Hollywood or the music industry—at least in recent years.

Initially, The Grove had mainly served wealthy southerners and the occasional actor or actress who happened to be filming in New Orleans, which had become known as Hollywood South after some favorable tax laws were put in place a few years back. But once word spread in the right circles about the level of care and privacy, The Grove had quickly become the facility of choice for those who didn't want to be stalked by the relentless paparazzi in L.A. and New York. Even now, it was still a pretty well-kept secret, tucked away in the Louisiana bayous behind big gates. And the level of confidentiality employees had to agree to in order to work there was no joke.

When he'd gotten hired on, they'd required a full background check and he'd had to disclose his past, including a few minor criminal charges. He'd thought that would be the end of it, but Dr. Suri, the director, had been surprisingly accepting. *You've come a long way to get to this point. I imagine in your previous profession, your job depended on keeping people's secrets. You will find it is the same here, only with confidentiality clauses that will cost you a lot of money and legal problems if you break them.* Straightforward and no bullshit. He'd liked her instantly. She'd also, as far as he knew, never shared his background with anyone else.

He skirted the edge of another seating area, trying not to disturb anyone. The door to the education room was only a few steps away, but he could already see the handwritten sign on the door. *Session full. Come back later.*

He let out a sigh.

"You lost?"

He turned at the voice, finding a woman watching him from one of the couches, a notebook and pen clutched in her hand. He hadn't paid close attention when he'd first passed, but now he wondered how he'd missed her. She had the kind of rocker-girl beauty that would get her cast as the cool chick in a movie. Dark eyes lined darker, straight black hair with a pink streak in it, eyebrow ring. But she didn't need a movie role, she was already the real deal. Jun Alexis, lead singer and bassist for Fractured Sun. He had all their songs on his playlist and had seen them play an arena show last fall. He loved their stuff and

Jun was a badass.

He had a brief rush of starstruck-ness, but he'd learned to play it cool around here so kept his expression even. No one wanted to be fan-boyed while they were in rehab.

"Who am I kidding?" she said before he could answer. "We're in rehab. Everybody's lost." A wrinkle appeared between her brows. She glanced down at her paper and scribbled something, humming a few notes to herself. "Hmm, that could be a good."

He waited until she looked up again before he responded. "I'm not lost. Just looking for Dr. McCray."

Jun glanced at the closed door. "Ooh, are you fresh blood? I've been in here two weeks as the new girl, and I officially hate everyone. Please tell me you're checking in and that you're not a self-involved douche canoe."

He huffed a laugh. "Sorry to disappoint."

She sighed dramatically and collapsed back against the arm of the couch. "So you *are* a self-involved douche canoe?"

"Probably at times. But it's not that. I work here."

She blanched. "Great. A white coat. So you're someone I'll be begging for a sleeping pill later?"

"No, I'm not a doctor, and I'm in a different department. I have no pills to give. The doctors around here aren't so keen on giving them out either."

"I've noticed." She tilted her head. "That is really cramping that whole addiction thing I have going."

He smirked. "This place is a total buzzkill."

"Literally. They should just call rehab Buzzkill U." Her lips pursed again and she pointed at him. "And that, my new friend, could be a great song title." She scribbled another note and then gave him a rapacious grin. "Ooh, you're muse-y. Sit down and keep talking, cute doctor man. I'm Jun and I've got half an album to fill and a whole bunch of group therapy to avoid."

He couldn't help but be charmed. Jun was spellbinding on stage, but in person, she was pure charisma. He peered toward the still closed door and then stepped around the couch to take a seat opposite Jun. If he was going to wait for Elle, he might as well sit and chat while he did. "I'm still not a doctor."

She tilted her head. "So what's your name and what do you do?"

"Lane. And I work on the sex therapy wing."

Her pierced brow twitched up. "Like fixing people's sex problems?"

He nodded. "Something like that, though I'm not a fan of the word fixing. It implies something's broken. I assist."

Something flickered in her dark eyes. "Right. So if I were to get a referral to that wing, you could end up assisting me?"

Her tone had his *uh-oh* sensors flickering to life. "In theory."

She stared at him, her eyes narrowing. "Huh."

"What?"

She lifted a shoulder. "Nothing. It's just not in theory. Oriana, my social worker, wants me to talk to"—she flipped back two pages in her notebook—"a Dr. Rush while I'm here."

Lane straightened. "Oh."

Her lip curled. "Yeah. So I guess I can't let you be my muse if there's a chance that in the near future, I'm going to be telling you how I hate sex and haven't had an orgasm in five years. That kind of kills the vibe."

He frowned at her admission, his want-to-help instincts surfacing. Five years? The woman who wrote some of the sexiest fucking rock songs out there hated sex? And had she not had an orgasm in that long because she didn't want to or because she couldn't? Questions filled him, but he couldn't delve further. She wasn't his client at this point. "If you end up as a client of Dr. Rush's, you could end up working with me at some point, yes."

She sighed. "Damn. Way to kill the dream, man. I prefer to keep my muses separate from my fucked-up therapy sessions. I need my muse to think I'm wonderful and funny and brilliant." She closed her eyes and rubbed the bridge of her nose. "I need someone here to look at me like I'm something other than a Dumpster fire."

Lane sat forward, bracing his forearms on his thighs, empathy swelling in him. He'd never been to rehab, but he knew what it felt like to have people look at you like you were screwed up or hopeless. "That's not what they're thinking about you."

She looked up, skepticism all over her face. "Yes they are. And they should be. I *am* a Dumpster fire. I'm surprised you can't smell the smoke."

"Even if you are right now, even if you've made a complete mess of things, that doesn't mean the other things aren't true." He reached out and tapped her notebook. "You *are* wonderful and funny and brilliant. You write songs that make people feel things and create music that chases away bad days."

Her eyes met his, a little of the tough girl facade slipping. "You don't know that. I don't write happy songs."

"I do know that, and no happy songs required," he said resolutely. "When I've had a crap day, I can put the *Bright Fall* album on full blast in my car and no demons are left standing afterward. It's like an exorcism."

She stared at him. Then her smile appeared like a sunrise,

slow but brilliant. "An exorcism."

"Yeah. Everything but the pea soup and head-turning-backward thing."

"Man, if I could do that to people, that'd be hardcore." She playfully made the devil horns sign with her hand. "But messy. And I hate peas."

"Peas suck," he said with a smile. "And I don't know your story or what you're going through, but I can say that if everything feels like it's on fire right now, you're in the right place. You've called the best fire department. Now all you need to do is let them help."

"Fuck," she said with a sardonic grin.

"What?"

"You realize how doctor-y you sound? You are such a white coat."

The words threw him a little, and he didn't register why she was climbing off the couch.

She stepped over to him and gave him a hug before he could intercept. "A white coat with incomparable taste in music. Thanks, Lane from the Sex Therapy Wing."

He froze for a moment. He hugged clients he was working with if the person initiated and it seemed appropriate, but Jun wasn't his client and she was a patient here. He gave her an awkward pat on the back and was about to extricate himself from the embrace when he heard a loud throat clear.

Jun straightened, releasing Lane, and he turned to see where the noise had come from.

Elle was standing a few feet away, her lips in a thin line. "Ms. Alexis, aren't you supposed to be in group right now?"

Jun blanched. "I was just about to head over. Lane was

waiting for you and giving me some advice on a song I'm writing."

Elle's expression remained implacable. "We can discuss it later in session. Right now, please head to group."

"Yes, Dr. McCray." Jun looked appropriately chagrined but when she put her back to Elle, she gave Lane a quick eye roll, like they were co-conspirators who were trying to get away with something in front of the principle.

Lane gave her a tight smile.

After Jun had gathered her things and left, Elle turned to face him. "Why are you here, Mr. Cannon? I don't recall having an appointment with you."

Her voice was one part professional, nine parts frosty. He stood and frowned. "I wanted to run something by you before you went on rounds."

Her gaze narrowed but she cocked her head to the left. "I have to drop off my laptop in my office. You can walk with me."

She didn't say a word as they made their way across the main floor. Not until they were safely ensconced in her office did she turn on him and drop the Dr. Ice routine.

She set her laptop on her desk with a thunk. "What the hell was that?"

For a moment, he wondered if her ire was jealousy. She'd walked out to him hugging another woman—a famous, beautiful one at that. But that wasn't Elle's style. Elle was patients first, everything else after. He lifted his palms. "It was absolutely nothing. I was waiting for you and Jun struck up a conversation. We talked for a few minutes. When she shared some of her current struggle with being here, I gave her some encouragement and told her she was in good hands. She surprised me with a hug. That's all it was."

"That was not your place," she said, words sharp. "This is my unit. My patients. I am responsible for their care. She was supposed to be in group, not talking to some—"

"Some what?" he challenged. "Some untrained lackey?"

She tipped her head forward and pinched the bridge of her nose. "You know that's not what I was going to say. You wouldn't want me interfering with your clients either. Jun's looking for any excuse to not do the work here. She's isolated herself from the rest of the patients, won't open up in sessions, and has generally been acting like a brat. She needed to be in group, not flirting with you."

He sighed. "She wasn't flirting."

Elle put her hands on her hips, an elegant snort escaping her. "You think I didn't catch the look she gave you before she left? Please." She batted her eyelashes and tucked her hands beneath her chin, her voice etching up an octave. "Oh, Lane, you've been so helpful. I could write sappy love songs about you."

Lane's mouth curved. "You couldn't possibly be feeling a little possessive, could you, Dr. McCray?"

"Yes," she said flatly. "Of my patient."

"Uh-huh. I think the doctor doth protest too much." He stepped closer, letting his hands slide onto her waist. "Did you know you're kind of adorable when you're jealous?"

Her lips thinned, defiance in her eyes. "I. Am. Not. Jealous. And never adorable. I'm not a goddamned puppy."

"I was thinking in more of an angry wildcat kind of way," he amended. "Did I mention Jun's the lead singer of one of my favorite bands? Or how much I love her music? That shouldn't bother you, though. That I'm a fan."

She groaned and tried to wiggle away from him. "You are such a sadistic asshole."

"I am." He touched his forehead to hers. "That little twitch in your eye, the one that says you're working so hard to not break, is definitely giving me half-wood. The more you protest, the more it does it for me. Keep telling me how it didn't bother you one little bit."

"Ugh. Fine," she said, giving him her most ferocious look of disdain. "Maybe I was a *little* annoyed to see the guy I'm currently sleeping with embracing a beautiful young thing who's sold a metric ton of records."

"Downloads, babe. Downloads," he said, amping up his old California accent.

Her jaw unhinged, a haughty expression crossing her face. "Did you just call me old? Oh, now that's your ass, Lane Cannon."

She reached between him and grabbed his balls with a not-yet-painful-but-definitely concerning grip. All the air puffed out of him as his body went into protect-the-man-parts-at-all-cost mode. "Doc."

"Say you're sorry, Cannon. And say it nicely." She smiled sweetly.

"Now who's the sadist?"

She arched a brow.

The arrogant look only made him want her more. He licked his lips. "I was not calling you *old*. I was *teasing* you because it's becoming a favorite pastime of mine and I love how riled up you get. You have nothing to worry about from some twenty-something singer." He took a breath when her grip eased ever so slightly. "And here's what you need to remember, doc. I don't have trouble getting laid. *You* don't have trouble getting laid. Neither of us are here because we're out of options. We're choosing this option because we're good together."

A cornered-animal look flashed through her eyes and she released her grip entirely.

"In bed," he added, hoping that would soothe her flight response. "We're good together in bed. Your kink and my kink line up just right."

She sighed and some of the tension leached out of her body. "I know that. And this isn't even—well, I don't really know what this is, but I guess when I saw you two hugging it just set off old stupid shit."

He rubbed his hands along her upper arms, a kick of guilt in his gut. "I'm sorry. I didn't think when I was teasing you—"

She shook her head. "Stop. It's fine. Please don't coddle me."

He frowned. "I won't, but know that while we're together, I won't sleep with anyone outside of what I need to do for my job. That's a promise. I'm not him. And I know you haven't known me long enough to necessarily believe it, but when I give my word, I keep it."

She met his eyes and gave a little nod. "Okay."

"Okay?"

She graced him with a reluctant smile. "Yeah. Now why are you on my unit, besides to torment me and make me late for my rounds?"

He dipped his hand in his pocket and pulled out what he'd tucked in there before his meeting at school. "First, I came by to give you this." He held out a vintage gold wedding ring. "What do you think?"

Her eyes widened and she took the ring. She held it up and

the light sparked off the cluster of diamonds at the center that formed a flower shape. "Lane, this is gorgeous. You didn't have to do this. I could've…"

He shrugged. "I got a good deal at the local pawn shop near the college. It's vintage and one of a kind, which I thought suited you and would impress your family. I can sell it back to the shop when we're done."

She glanced up at him, something tender flickering there. "It's perfect. Honestly. It's something I would've picked out for myself. Thank you."

He beamed and put a hand over his heart. "A compliment. I might fall over."

She rolled her eyes but her smile stayed in place. She slid the ring on her right ring finger for now. It was a little loose but not enough to be a problem. "So you said, first. What's the second reason you're here?"

His shoulders slouched. "Test results."

"And?"

"Hi, my name is Lane Cannon, and I'm dyslexic."

She crossed her arms, her all-business face replacing the smile. "So it's what your professor suspected. That qualifies as a disability and should get you some help and some more time on your paper."

"Yes. Plus, a dictation program to learn," he said, failing to keep the derision out of his voice. "And a student tutor to teach me how to use it. I told them to keep the tutor. I have a mean-as-hell doctor to take my dick."

She reached out and pinched his hip, hard.

"*Dictation,*" he said quickly, taking her wrists in his hands to thwart further torture. "To take my dictation. And then my dick. Because let's face it, after all that work, we're going to need some fucking."

She groaned and let her head fall against his chest. "I hate you."

He set his chin atop her head and closed his eyes, feeling strangely contented for the first time all afternoon. "I hate you, too, doc."

She tapped her head against his chest. "Why does that make me want to kiss you?"

"Because you loathe me so hard?"

She lifted her face to him, humor in her eyes. "So hard."

He released her hands and cupped her face. "Feeling's mutual. You're a nightmare."

She smiled and looped her arms around his waist. He didn't need any further invitation than that. He lowered his mouth to hers, taking what he'd wanted since walking in the office, taking what she'd refused him that first night together.

When his tongue touched hers, her softly expelled moan was enough to get his blood rushing straight south. Elle in her doctor's coat, all buttoned up and late for rounds, melting like butter in a hot skillet under his touch. He wished she had more than a minute. He wished he could lift her onto her desk and put the *In Session* sign on the door, give her the afternoon work break they really needed.

He let his hand slide to her ass, cupping her and angling her against him as he deepened the kiss.

A knock sounded to his left and before he could register what that sound meant, the door swung open. "Dr. McCray, I—"

chapter fifteen

Elle jolted back from Lane at the sound of the intruding voice, and Lane lifted his hands as if he were being held up by the police.

Both of them turned to the door to find an emoji version of Oriana—all wide eyes and O-shaped lips—staring back at them.

Elle's mind raced, trying to come up with some conceivable reason why she was on duty and in a lip-lock with The Grove's sex surrogate. But her ability for speech had apparently bolted out the door hand in hand with her dignity.

Ori spoke first. "Uh, I am *so* sorry. You didn't have your sign up and—I just…" She jabbed her thumb behind her. "I'm leaving."

"Ori, wait." The words jumped out of Elle's mouth unbidden.

"Wait?" She looked like a bird trapped in a cage, begging to be freed from the situation. "I really should go."

Lane gave Elle a what-the-hell look, but some of the blood had rushed back into her brain, kicking it into gear. "Yes. Shut the door for a minute. Please."

Oriana sent Lane an S.O.S. look, but when he didn't jump in

to help, she reluctantly shut the door. She gripped her elbows. "Dr. McCray, I—"

Elle held up a palm. "Ori, please. You don't have to apologize. It's my fault I forgot to put the sign up on my door. But I need you to understand what you saw."

She winced and glanced away. "I can figure it out. I really don't need—"

"I'm considering seeing Mr. Cannon for…therapy."

Lane's attention snapped to her, shock in his eyes. Shock and…hurt.

Elle cleared her throat, pushing through the pang of guilt that sent through her. She could not have her co-workers think she was dating Lane. She wasn't *dating* Lane. And that rumor would spread like wildfire. She couldn't handle that kind of attention. The whispers. The jokes. The raised eyebrows when she referred patients to Lane.

Making it a therapy thing insured the rumor would stop here. Confidentiality was law at this place. "It's a very private matter and we were just seeing if there was enough…compatibility to proceed with sessions." She fought not to cringe at the words. "I'm sure you understand that this is very confidential."

Ori's lips rolled inward and she nodded. "Of course, Dr. McCray. I would never say anything to anyone. Therapy or otherwise."

Ori was giving her the opportunity to come clean, but she couldn't bring herself to do it. Elle nodded, her gut telling her she could trust Ori when she said she wouldn't say anything. She had always been a consummate professional. But Elle couldn't let go of the lie. "Thank you. I appreciate your professionalism. Now, was there something you needed?"

Ori straightened and glanced between the two of them. "Nothing that can't wait. I'll go over it with you after rounds."

"Fine."

Ori took that as her cue, gave them both one more darting look, and then she hurried out the door, shutting it behind her. Elle heard her *In Session* sign being slipped into place.

Elle let out a defeated breath and turned to Lane, feeling the weight of his stare on her. "I'm sorry."

His jaw flexed and the warmth he'd had in his eyes earlier was gone, flint replacing it. "What? You're sorry that you're so embarrassed by me that you'd rather tell someone you had sexual *problems* than admit we're seeing each other? Is that what you're sorry about?"

Her stomach hollowed out. "Lane. It's not that, it's—"

"Whatever," he grated out. "I can't deal with this right now. I have a client arriving any minute. Your time renting me for the afternoon is done. Someone else requires my services."

The way he said *services* and *renting* sent terrible images through her mind. Was he off to kiss someone else? To put his hands on her? Make her feel good?

She'd known that all along but had managed to compartmentalize it since they'd made their agreement. But now he was throwing it in her face because, why shouldn't he? She'd just denied him like he was some disease. She'd hurt him.

And that hurt her. More than she expected.

"Please don't walk out like this. We should—"

"Later, Elle. You don't want to talk to me right now. It won't end well for you." He strode past her, his gait calm but his quiet fury palpable. The door shut with barely a click.

She almost wished he'd slammed it.

It'd be easier to be mad, but the feeling wouldn't come.

Instead, she sank into her chair, her chest burning and hot tears jumping to her eyes. Tears of frustration. Of shame. Confusion.

Why couldn't she have just told Ori the truth? Elle and Lane hadn't been breaking any rules. They'd been in a private office. Oriana wouldn't have betrayed their confidence.

But no, Elle had to screw it up. Do the most hurtful thing possible and deny Lane. Embarrass him. Push him away like she did everyone else.

She stared down at the sparkling ring on her finger, a ring so perfect she couldn't have picked out a better one herself, and tears slipped down her cheeks.

Seeing the ring made her ache for a life that could've been, a woman who could've been, if she'd met someone like Lane before she'd become...this. Before she'd learned that no one in her life could be trusted to have her back, that if you let your guard down, the people closest to you could rip out your heart without warning and leave you. She didn't want to always be waiting for that knife in the back, but if she couldn't trust her heart to her husband, her parents, or her own sister, how was she supposed to trust a man she'd just met? Especially one who had the job Lane did.

If she let her feelings get involved, she wouldn't survive another betrayal like that. It would break her.

She'd worked so hard to get to this point. She was proud of how far she'd come after her marriage had fallen apart and she'd fought her way out of depression. She loved her job. Loved being able to help her patients. Loved the research she did. This way of life worked for her.

No, that little voice inside her taunted. It *had* been working for her

Because right then, staring at the closed door, face damp with tears and shame burning in her belly over how she'd treated Lane, she'd never felt so epically alone.

And lost.

And she had no idea how to fix it.

L ane showed up at her door at seven that night with a bag of takeout and his backpack. The sight of him standing on her doorstep was almost too much to take in. Relief stole her breath. After what had happened in the office that afternoon, he hadn't returned her calls and she'd been convinced that she'd wrecked everything, that he'd never speak to her again. But Lane didn't look mad. He just looked…normal. And handsome. And like everything she needed tonight.

She wanted to talk to him. To explain.

"Lane," she said, her voice coming out more earnest than she wanted. "I'm so glad you're here. I didn't expect…about this afternoon—"

He shook his head and handed her the bag of food. "Later. I'm here to eat and to work on my paper. Are you still willing to help with that?"

She frowned. "Of course. It was my suggestion."

"Fine. Let's get to it, then. It's been a long day." He stepped inside and headed toward the kitchen.

She shut the door and followed him to the back of the house, a chill left in his wake. When she got to the kitchen, he was already grabbing plates from her cabinet like he knew the place. She cleared her throat, searching for a topic other than their argument. "How'd your appointment go this afternoon?"

He cut a look her way. "You know I can't discuss clients that aren't yours."

"Of course." She tried to busy herself with taking the boxes of fragrant Thai food out of the bag, but her brain wouldn't shut up, which meant her mouth wouldn't shut up. She dumped some noodles onto one of the plates. "I tried to call you, but I guess you were busy. Was it an...extensive session?"

"You mean did I have sex with her?" The words were clipped, the tone pointed.

She winced. "I—"

"It doesn't matter. You and I aren't sleeping together tonight."

She swallowed hard. "Right. That's not what I—"

"Or ever again."

The flat statement had her head snapping upward. "What?"

"That part is done." He stabbed his chopsticks into the other container and served himself some food. "I was being delusional this whole time. I thought we could have some fun with each other, maybe even be friends, but this afternoon confirmed what I already suspected. This arrangement can't work. You never wanted it to. I should've just let you go with Isaiah and saved us both the trouble."

The stinging words were delivered without emotion or humor, none of Lane's trademark good nature seeping into them. "But...you're here."

"I'm here because we made an agreement, and I told you I keep my word. You'll help me with my paper. I'll still pretend to be your fiancé to help you get through the wedding weekend. But sex can't be a part of that." He looked up, green eyes clear and resolute. "I made a rule for myself when I walked away from hooking. I would never fuck someone who didn't respect me—as a lover, as a friend, as a human. Maybe that's what sent me down the path of becoming a dominant, but the rule still stands outside of that world, too."

The words cut into her like ice shards. "Lane, I didn't—"

"Imagine if I had done what you did today. If we had run into some of my friends and I said, *Oh her? Are you kidding? No, I wouldn't date that bitch. She's just good at getting me off when I'm too lazy to masturbate.*"

Her spine went straight. "That's not what I said."

He shoved a bite in his mouth and shrugged. "Same sentiment. Only replace *bitch* with *trash*."

Angry words burned in her mouth, her old defenses rising. She wanted to swing, to fight, because this was hurting more than it should. But she fought the instincts that told her to lash out. Lane was right. She'd realized her mistake as soon as he'd walked out of the door today. She'd screwed up, so she swallowed back the ugly retort and took a breath.

"I'm sorry. You're right. What I did was wrong. I reacted—badly. I don't think you're trash. You can't really think that."

He leaned back against the counter, his gaze cool. "Those are just words, Elle. Actions speak the truth. And today, you acted like you'd rather someone think you had sexual problems than let them think you're seeing someone like me."

"I panicked."

His brow arched. "Right. So if we were to go up to the main building right now, you'd hold my hand and tell your night staff we're seeing each other? Because if that's the case, let's go, Elle." He put out a hand. "Bring me up there and let's tell them."

She glanced at his hand and pressed her lips together, trying to find the words that could explain why that sent so much fear coursing through her, but none would come out.

He smirked and lowered his hand. "Exactly. Words are just words."

"Lane—"

"But no hard feelings," he said, peering back down at his food as if it were more interesting than she was. "At least not on my end. We'll take sex out of it and make it easier for us both. We each need help with something outside the bedroom. I'm still willing to hold up my end. Are you?"

She stared at him, hating the emotionless facade, hating that there was a wall and now he was on the other side of it. The teasing, playful, infuriating man was gone. In his place was this cool, polite professional. She wanted to scream.

But she tucked all that emotion down and didn't make a sound. He was giving her an out. Plus, he'd managed to tell her what his ultimate goal had been anyway—to have some fun and maybe make a friend. Not to fall in love or have something lasting, which proved she'd already gotten too attached and made this into more in her head than it was in reality.

This was for the best. This arrangement had been doomed from the start.

She should've known better.

She gave him a prim nod, gathering up her composure like armor. "I can still help you, but you're released from your word with me. I'll go to the wedding alone."

"Nope," he said, reaching for his drink and sending her a look he probably used on submissives. "That's not the deal. We both help or both walk away. I don't want to owe anyone any favors."

She crossed her arms. "But you don't even like me. And you're angry with me. What good are you going to do me at the wedding?"

His lips lifted into the briefest humorless smile. "You're forgetting who I am. Playing the part of liking someone used to be my job. I promise you an Academy Award-winning performance. I didn't get to be number one boy at the agency because I couldn't fake it."

Her stomach dropped.

With that, he picked up his plate and headed to the living room, calling out over his shoulder. "Time to get to work. I have a paper to rewrite."

Lane watched Elle at her keyboard, typing his words at a rapid pace, her back ramrod straight, and a hollow feeling pinged through his chest. He'd come here and said what he'd needed to say. The words had tasted like sand in his mouth, but she hadn't left him any choice. He couldn't keep this going with her when every few days, she would say or do something to cut him down.

"You should probably put this paragraph at the beginning of this section," she said, not looking his way. "It will provide a good intro. It draws the reader in and asks a compelling question that will make them keep reading to find out the answer."

"Good idea," he said, closing his eyes and rattling off more sentences for his paper.

Her fingers went to work again, the clicking of the keyboard the only noise in the room, but his thoughts got louder, drowning it out.

In the beginning, this thing with Elle had been a game for him. He could field her insults and prickly attitude. He'd gotten used to people belittling him throughout his life, so he could let it roll off his back these days, dismissing their opinions. But then he'd made a mistake and had started to care about Elle, had seen hidden sides of her, had shared things about himself. Her opinion had started to matter to him. And when people he cared about threw knives his way, it hit those old unarmored parts of him, tearing into tender flesh.

Today in her office, he'd felt so…diminished. With a few words, she'd knocked him from lover, maybe friend, to hired fuck. To something she needed to sweep under the rug. No way was he going to volunteer for that kind of bullshit. So, he'd shut it down. He'd still help her because the thought of her going into that wedding weekend alone would keep him up at night, but he couldn't get in any deeper with her.

One thing he'd learned early on in life and then again with therapy—you can't help those who don't want help. Elle didn't want his friendship. She didn't want to change. Didn't want to let anyone in and would sabotage anyone who tried. He'd been pompous to think he could change her mind.

So now, he'd treat her like a client who'd hired him to be her date. He'd be convincing, he'd play the part, and then when they got back, he'd shake her hand and wish her luck.

He'd already told her good-bye, she just didn't know it yet.

chapter sixteen

Elle hadn't seen Lane since the night they'd finished his paper. She'd gotten a text from him on Monday letting her know that he'd turned it in and would meet her at ten on Friday morning to head to New Orleans. She'd also seen the money she'd originally deposited into his account reappear in hers. But other than that, there'd been no communication. She hadn't even seen him at work except from a distance in the cafeteria, where he'd been sitting with Dr. Rush and laughing at something she'd said. That full, hearty sound had traveled across the cavernous room and hit Elle in the gut like a flaming spear. He wasn't going to grace her with that laugh anymore. Access had been revoked.

Elle sighed, and as she sat on her porch swing with her roller bag by her feet, she considered taking off on her own to the city. She could save herself the awkwardness of spending a weekend with Lane, relieve him of that obligation, but the thought had a fist tightening around her windpipe. Facing her ex-husband and sister alone was too daunting of a specter to ignore. Lane had been right. She could handle herself but having an ally would make it more bearable—even if it was a fake ally.

Gravel crunched in the distance and Lane turned into her driveway, his sleek black Corvette feeling like an omen instead of a welcome wagon. No more delays. She was really going to this wedding. She would have to face the people who'd ripped her life down the middle and try to show them how fabulously fantastic she was doing. Put on a show.

She hated that her first instinct at seeing Lane's sports car was to wonder what Henry would think of it. He'd probably dismiss it as immature and impractical. He was a luxury car guy. The manufacturer had to be foreign and the price tag unfathomable or it didn't warrant his respect.

Ugh. She shook the thought away. She wasn't trying to prove anything to him. She didn't need to impress anyone. She didn't need Lane to fit into some kind of mold.

Lane climbed out of the car, his blond hair styled in that messy-on-purpose way he used on the weekends and his clothes casual but sharp—pale blue polo shirt and dark jeans that made him look downright edible. The man didn't just know how to dress, he knew how to wear his clothes like they'd been made for him, like he was one-hundred percent comfortable in his own skin. She wanted to drag him into the house and take him out of those clothes, touch that skin.

She curled her nails into her palms, trying to use the sting to shut down her rogue libido. *Not yours.*

Anymore.

Or ever, really.

Lane sauntered up the drive, a surprisingly pleasant expression on his face. "All ready to go?"

She stood, smoothing her dove-gray slacks on the way up,

and grabbed the handle of her roller bag. "I'm packed, but I'll probably never be ready. You sure you want to do this?"

"Yep. I told you I keep my word. Plus, I owe you." He reached behind his back and pulled something from his pocket—a paper. He turned it around and showed her the front. It was the title page of his research paper. A bright red *A* was scrawled on the front.

A gust of pride swept over her. "You got an A?"

"*A-minus.* Not too bad." He shrugged but the curl of his lips betrayed him.

She had the sudden urge to hug him, which was weird in and of itself. She wasn't a hugger. But she didn't know where the boundaries were with him right now. They weren't at her mom's house yet. They didn't need to perform for an audience. She lifted her hand in a high-five motion instead, feeling like a complete dork. "Lane, that's great. You did it."

He tapped her hand with his but then curled his fingers around her palm to give it a squeeze. "*We* did it. I owe you a big thank you. Not just for typing but for forcing me to get tested so I could get an extension. This grade feels good."

The heat of his palm against hers and the appreciation in his eyes made her stomach hurt. She wished she could rewind time and never invite him into her office, never have Ori catch them. Right now, they'd be in full celebration mode. He'd kiss her. She'd tease him. She wouldn't feel as if there were an ocean of complications between them. She slipped her hand from his. "You're welcome. But you deserve the credit. It's your words in that paper."

"They are, but you got them on that paper for me and made sure I put them in the right order. So"—he tucked the paper under his arm and took her bag from her—"you deserve a thank you."

"Your thank you is you being here. I can't believe you're still going through with this." She grabbed her purse from the porch swing and looped the strap over her shoulder. "You have a masochistic streak hidden in there?"

"No. I'm keeping my promise and paying you back. But believe me, this is going to feed the sadist in me far more than anything else."

The statement and his accompanying smirk made her spine go stiff. She cleared her throat and walked down the steps past him, keeping her shoulders back even though she wanted to fold in on herself. "Yeah, I guess there's no better way to get back at me for insulting you than to spend a weekend watching me get humiliated by my family and ex. Good plan."

"What?"

She kept walking down the driveway to the car, hating the way her eyes burned. She would not let him see how he was affecting her. She'd been fielding barbs from him since the beginning. This should be no different.

Lane grasped her elbow, halting her brisk march to the car.

"Hey." He stepped in front of her, his eyes searching hers. "You honestly think that's what I meant? That I'd enjoy seeing you get hurt?"

Her teeth clenched and she inhaled a deep breath through her nose, trying to maintain her I-don't-give-a-shit face. "What else could you mean?"

His mouth sank into a frown. "Jesus, Elle. I meant I was going to enjoy irritating your ex-husband because the guy deserves it. I can't believe you'd think—" He exhaled loudly and ran a hand over the back of his head. "Look, I'm not happy with how things went down with us, but I don't wish bad things on you. I'm not cruel. I wouldn't be here unless I was here to help."

She blinked, his words making her stomach fizz and her anxiety about this whole weekend bubble over. She looked down, trying to hide her face from him. "I'm sorry. I just—I guess I was thinking what I'd do in your place. If someone hurts me, I want to hurt them worse."

"Well, that's you. I'm a way nicer person than you are."

She snorted, the laugh surprising her and getting caught in her nose. She peered up to find him grinning. "Asshole."

"There she is." He put a hand on her shoulder and gave it a squeeze. "And I'm serious. I've got your back this weekend. Nothing will give me greater pleasure than pissing in your ex-husband's and bitchy sister's Fruit Loops—or their healthy, organic, non-GMO, gluten-free, sugarless tree bark. Whatever their pretentious asses eat for breakfast."

She couldn't help but smile at that. "It will definitely be something pretentious."

"Good. I'd be disappointed otherwise."

She sighed and put her hand over his, some of the tightness in her muscles easing. "Thanks, Lane."

He lowered his hand to the handle of her bag again and gave a quick nod. "No worries. We've got this."

He turned to the car and rolled her suitcase behind him, her heart giving a completely unhelpful kick. This man could've been her friend, her lover. She liked him. He was a *good* guy.

But that was the problem.

Lane wanted more than she was capable of giving. Deserved more.

She couldn't be that woman for him. She would always hurt him.

This weekend he'd see why.

Lane picked up speed, the engine purring like a big cat, as they turned off the two-way roads that cut through the bayous and the towering cypress trees and made it to the interstate that would bring them into the city. Elle kept her eyes on the scenery, trying to focus on anything but where she was going. She needed to remember her mother was ill. This was about her mom. Her sister and ex were just a sideshow. Hopefully, they'd be too wrapped up with wedding shit to bother with Elle anyway.

"Hold up," Lane said, his voice startling her out of her thoughts. "You got them a *wedding present*?"

She turned to him. "Huh?"

He nodded toward her purse, which had come open at her feet. A present with silver and white wrapping stuck out. She reached down and tucked it back in before snapping her purse shut. "Yes. It's the proper thing to do."

"The proper thing?" He gave her a you-must-be-out-of-your-mind look. "What the hell did you get them?"

She adjusted her seatbelt and smoothed her expression. "A nutcracker."

Lane's eyes lit with amusement. "Nice. A metaphor to your ex?"

She smirked his way. "No, I'm not that subtle. It's a straightforward fuck you. Henry's allergic to nuts."

A laugh burst out of him, one of those like she'd heard in the cafeteria. The hearty sound filled her like helium, making her feel lighter inside. He shook his head. "You're something else, Elle McCray. Remind me to stay on your good side."

She sniffed. "Who said I have a good side? Or that you're on it?"

His smile turned smug. "I've seen you naked. I assure you, there are lots of good sides. Mainly the front and back. And I've been on both."

She rolled her eyes but warmth crept through her, making her skin tingle. She knew it was harmless flirtation, Lane's way. But to her it felt like much more. It felt like an olive branch. He was showing her that at least for this weekend, they could leave the heavy stuff back at The Grove and be relaxed around each other.

They both got quiet for a few minutes, the interstate taking them over the Bonnet Carré spillway, a wide expanse of water that took the overflow when the Mississippi River and Lake Pontchartrain got too high. When she'd first moved here with her parents from Napa Valley, a local had laughed when she'd pronounced it in proper French. *No, dawlin', not that fancy. We say it Bonnie Carrie.*

She'd felt like a stranger in a strange land. California had been home. But her parents had fallen in love with New Orleans on a vacation and the cost of living had tempted them here when she was fifteen. In Napa, they could live well. In NOLA, they could live like royalty. What did it matter that it completely uprooted their oldest child right in the middle of high school?

"So what's my story?"

Lane's question broke her from her thoughts. "What do you mean?"

"What's the story we're giving your family about me? I

assume you don't want to say I'm a professional surrogate."

He said it casually but she knew that was still a raw wound. He should be able to say what he was. But she cringed inwardly at the thought of announcing that to her family and ex. They wouldn't understand what that meant. They'd dismiss him out of hand.

Like she had.

She frowned, hating that she was anything like them, and absently turned the fake engagement ring round and round on her finger. "I told my sister we work together. We can say you work in the couples therapy department and are in school to... wait, what are you in school for? What's your end goal?"

"What?"

"What's your goal for school? Do you just want to add the degree to get a raise or something?" She'd never thought to ask him. He didn't need a degree for what he did, just training and a certification.

He looked back to the road, his jaw flexing. "Right now my goal is not to fail out, but when I started, my hope was to get a master's degree in counseling or clinical social work. It's probably a pipe dream, but I'd like to do what Donovan and Marin do."

She stared at him, the revelation surprising her. "You don't want to stay a surrogate? I thought you liked your job."

He sent her a wary look. "I do. But I also would like a job one day that doesn't involve sleeping with strangers. I believe in the work I do, but I don't want to be doing it when I'm fifty. The therapists get to dig into so much more with the clients. I only get to help with one aspect."

She considered him, the new information giving her a fuller

picture of the man she kept trying to box up neatly in one category. "Why does it have to be a pipe dream? You get the hang of those accommodations at school and you can go for whatever you want."

He grunted in an utterly male, we're-not-talking-about-this way.

She sighed. "Well, either way, that's what we'll say. You're going to school for your master's degree. Henry will probably ask why you waited so long and what you did before school."

He shrugged. "I'll tell him I lost my parents when I was sixteen and needed to get a job to make ends meet and save up for school."

Her breath caught. "Is that true?"

His knuckles whitened against the steering wheel. "For all intents and purposes. That's when I failed my junior year of high school. I refused to repeat the year, and my dad didn't bother to ask me why I was having such a hard time in school. He just kicked me out of the house because I was a 'lazy and ungrateful punk' who needed to see what the real world was like. My mom would've never done anything to stand up to my dad, so she didn't intervene. I think they expected me to come crawling back when I ran out of money. I didn't."

Her lungs compressed, the matter-of-fact way he'd said it hitting her more than anything. "I'm sorry."

He shrugged. "Old news. A teenager doesn't start taking money for sex because his home life is awesome. My story isn't as bad as most of the guys I worked with. Once I got enough money to be comfortable, I got my GED and started looking into ways I could get a legitimate career. One of my former clients was actually the one who made the suggestion that I look into surrogacy. I'd helped her after her husband had passed, and she said I had an empathetic ear and a calming nature. I figured it was worth a shot. Turned out to be the best decision I've ever made. God knows where I'd be otherwise."

Elle watched him for a long minute, this polished, intelligent, kind-hearted man. How he'd gotten himself to this point all on his own was a testament to an iron core of strength. Hell, she often felt sorry for herself because of her screwed-up family, but she'd had every advantage given to her. Private schools. Tutors for outside lessons. A college fund. A car as soon as she could drive. She hadn't had to work until she was out of school.

And what had she done to Lane to convey how impressed she was by the epically difficult mountain he'd climbed? She'd denigrated him for what he did. Made him feel less than. Bile burned the back of her throat.

People often called her a bitch, but in that moment, she felt like one.

"Is this the exit I should take?" Lane asked.

She'd typed in the address on the GPS for him, but it was giving them two route options.

"Yeah. This way's the quickest."

Lane followed the GPS directions, taking them off the interstate and into the city. The streets went narrow and bumpy and the buildings grew older, history rising up around them in a city that cherished its age and didn't feel any driving ambition to modernize. She appreciated that about New Orleans. It didn't change for anyone or try to be something besides itself. You either loved it for all its quirks and grit and personality, or you could get the hell out. Despite missing Napa when she'd moved here, she'd always felt a connection to NOLA in that way.

They took a few more turns until they were on her mom's street in the Garden District. The sunlight became dappled along the windows and enormous oak tree shadows painted the road, the ancient branches looking both welcoming and threatening all at once—depending on if your ex and betraying sister were waiting for you, or if you were just on a stroll after having brunch and a cocktail at Commander's Palace. Unfortunately, Elle hadn't had a cocktail.

"Wow," Lane said, leaning forward to peer at the houses on the right side of the road. "This isn't bad living."

"Yeah." Even Elle had to admit that this part of the city was nothing short of gorgeous. Beautiful, historic homes in white and sometimes frothy pastels displaying the best of New Orleans architecture. Lush gardens and short iron fences that were art pieces in their own right, with all the intricate designs and scrollwork. If she'd been a child when she moved here, she may have thought she'd entered some kind of fairytale land. But as a teenager, it'd looked like a gilded cage.

"I've never really driven through this part of the city. I didn't realize it'd be so beautiful." When she didn't respond, Lane glanced over, brow dipping. "You okay?"

She rolled her lips inward and nodded. "I'm good."

He reached out and gave her knee a squeeze. "I'm sorry. I shouldn't be fawning over this like a tourist. This place isn't a happy one for you."

She shrugged, trying to shake off the feelings with it. "I can't blame the neighborhood."

He nodded and gave her an empathetic look. "Believe me, I know that pretty houses can hide ugly situations. I used to visit a lot of pretty houses. I'm sure it was hard living here, everyone thinking you were leading a charmed life, but feeling lonely and out of place inside."

She swallowed back the emotion that his statement sent rushing through her and forced herself to take a breath. "It's the second one on the right, with the two-story porch and white columns. You can park on the street."

Lane gave her one last concerned glance and then eased into the spot in front of the house. The lantern-style light above the front door was on even though it was daytime. Other than that, the house looked postcard pristine—every bush pruned, the crepe myrtles winter-naked but still pretty with their smooth, pale bark, and the steps leading up to the porch free of debris. Perfect as always. Her stomach knotted.

Lane looked over. "You ready?"

"No."

"Want to go to the French Quarter and get hammered on hurricanes instead?"

"Yes."

His mouth kicked up at the corner. "Don't say that. I'll do it."

She sighed and reached for her door handle. "How about we go in and do this, and if I say my safe word, you immediately haul me out of there and we'll go do exactly that."

He smiled fully. "That's a deal, doc."

"You can safe word, too," she said gravely.

He laughed. "That bad?"

"Worse."

They climbed out of the car and headed for the front door. The silver garden sign stabbed beneath a large English boxwood said *Bienvenue*. Welcome.

Elle filled in the rest: *to your personal nightmare.*

chapter seventeen

Lane kept Elle in the corner of his vision as she prepared to ring the doorbell. She took a deep breath and seemed to grow two inches as she made her spine poker straight and tilted her chin up—Elle's armored stance. He'd seen it from time to time, had witnessed how intimidating and unflappable she could look. But he knew her too well now, could almost hear the pounding of her heart. This was taking everything she had.

He reached out and grabbed her hand, linking his fingers with hers, feeling the ring he'd given her press into his skin. She glanced over as if surprised to see him still standing there, like she'd forgotten she didn't have to face this alone. He squeezed her hand and her steely expression softened a bit.

"Want me to knock?" he asked.

She shook her head and peered back at the door, burning a hole through it. Her grip tightened on his hand and she raised her other to push the bell. Some elaborate chiming song started up that reminded Lane of church bells, and a yipping dog joined in with the tune. Elle frowned. "They got a dog?"

"Sounds like it," he said. "And sounds like it's on fire."

She smirked. "My dad always said dogs make too much mess. I guess Mom didn't feel the same way."

Clicking footsteps sounded on wood floors and Elle's lips flattened into a line. The door swung open and a small ball of black fur and purple ribbons launched through the gap and barreled into the yard. A squirrel who'd been gathering pecans that'd fallen off one of the trees raced through the gaps in the iron fence with a slew of get-the-fuck-away-from-me noises.

"Dammit, Roux, get your butt back inside," Nina yelled.

The dog barked at her and then spun in circles, trying to catch the ribbon that had come loose at her ear.

Lane smiled. That seemed like the dog's version of *Screw you, lady. I'm busy.*

Nina sighed and gave Elle and Lane a cutting smile. "Sorry. Mom got a dog a few months ago because she'd heard they can be stress relieving, but Roux is a menace and doesn't listen to anything anyone says. She already peed on the ring pillow for the wedding."

Elle glanced back at the dog and smiled. "I like her already."

Lane coughed, choking back the laugh that tried to come out.

Nina's pretend smile dropped. "Really, Elle?"

Elle shrugged, coolly unapologetic.

"Fine," Nina said through tight teeth. "Look, let's just get this out of the way now. I know how you feel about me. You've made that crystal clear. But I'm asking you to please keep it away from Mom. As far as she knows, we've mended fences. Don't let her think otherwise. She doesn't need any drama."

Elle's jaw flexed and her hand gripped Lane's painfully tight. "The only reason I'm here is for Mom. I can pretend as well as the rest of you. That's what we do, right? It's the McCray way."

Nina glanced at Lane, her gaze wary.

"He already knows what the situation is," Elle said, following Nina's look. "Neither of us are here to cause drama."

Lane nodded. "Elle's here for your mom. I'm here for Elle."

Nina's shoulders lowered and she returned the nod. "All right, come on in."

They stepped inside the foyer, the narrow entrance typical of a historic home, but all the finishes fine. Medium-tone, polished wood floors, pale cream walls, a beautiful oak staircase, and expensive artwork. A show home.

"Honey, was that the door?" The male voice echoed down the hallway as Lane shut the door behind him. Elle's breath hitched.

A dark-haired man in khakis and a forest-green button down stepped into the hallway. The self-satisfied look on his face told Lane exactly who he was. Henry. The cheater. The asshole. Lane had to bite back his frown.

Nina cleared her throat. "Yep, it's Elle and her...guest."

"Elle." Henry smiled and headed their way. Like he was happy to see her. Like they were old friends. Like this wasn't ten kinds of fucked up.

"Henry." Elle shifted closer to Lane and he released her hand so he could place his palm on her back instead. Her muscles rippled beneath his fingertips, but he had a feeling that was more anger than nerves.

Henry reached them and immediately leaned in to kiss Elle on the cheek. "So glad you could make it. I knew Nina would be able to smooth things over between you. It's no good for sisters to fight."

Lane was surprised Elle didn't knee the guy right in the balls for daring to touch her. He had to stop himself from taking the dude by the collar and teaching him manners. But Elle smiled a smile dripping with acid. "Yes, sisters should be there for each other."

Henry kept his smile as if Elle's words hadn't been laced with arsenic. He looked to Lane. "And who's your friend? One of your interns?"

Lane's teeth ground together. Yes, he was younger than Elle but not by that much. Henry was taking a dig at Elle's age.

Elle leaned into Lane. "No. This is Lane, my fiancé."

Henry's eyes flashed at that, a brief break in the genial facade, but then his eyebrows went up with exaggerated surprise. "Your fiancé? Well, I guess it *is* possible to meet people when you live at a mental hospital." He reached out to shake Lane's hand. "Nice to meet you. Henry Blanchard. Hope you weren't one of the patients."

Henry gave a hearty chuckle, like that was a funny joke, and Lane gripped his hand firmly, barely resisting the urge to squeeze until the guy cried *uncle.* He didn't want to give the dude the satisfaction of thinking he'd gotten to him on any level. "Lane Cannon. And no, I'm one of the therapists."

"That's convenient," he said. "Free therapy. Good thinking, Elle."

Henry moved to release the handshake, but Lane held on, making Henry's gaze jerk back his way. Lane smiled with pointed pleasantness. "Henry, I know we don't know each other, but I know enough. And I would recommend that while Elle and I are here this weekend that you speak to her respectfully, or you and I will have a problem. She is here for her mother because she is the bigger person. She is not here for whatever show you're trying to put on right now. Worry about your wedding and your woman. Leave *mine* out of it."

Lane released Henry's hand.

Red splotches appeared on Henry's cheeks and his attention flicked to Elle. "You're going to let your meathead boyfriend threaten me in your family's home? I didn't say anything insulting to you."

"Hmm," Elle said, as if she were utterly bored and unimpressed with Henry's tantrum. "You should probably go take a walk, Henry. It's no good to get your blood pressure so high—you know, with your age and all."

Henry's face went redder.

She linked her fingers with Lane's. "Sweetheart, why don't I show you the back garden? It's really lovely and peaceful, and I bet we'll find my mom out there."

"Sounds fantastic," Lane said, sending her a warm smile as a bloom of pride went through him. Elle's hard shell could be frustrating sometimes. But right now, seeing her so calm and collected in the face of this disgusting human being, he just wanted to forget that they were playing pretend and kiss her. The woman was tough as hell and elegant as fuck. He brought their linked hands to his mouth and kissed her knuckles before they stepped around Henry and Nina and headed toward the back of the house.

Elle's heart pounded a little faster than she would've liked, but she felt triumphant as she walked away from her sister and Henry. Henry had tried to play his normal games, the sugar-coated jabs, the said-with-a-laugh insults. It was the same stuff he'd done toward the end of their marriage. Back then, those kinds of jokes had cut her, made her bleed, made her insecurities rush to the surface. She'd since learned to be a pro in letting that kind of thing ping off of her, but she hadn't realized how satisfying it would be to have someone else on her side. Just when she'd been ready to tell Henry off, Lane had stepped in with a brutally calm, don't-fuck-with-her tone that had set Henry back on his well-heeled shoes.

And Lane had called her his woman. Not in so many words but the sentiment was there. *Leave mine out of it.* His.

This was a farce, but those few words had sent a ripple through her. In that moment, she'd wished them to be true. She didn't need a man to take care of her. Or a family. She'd proven that. She could do whatever she needed to do on her own. But feeling that layer of protectiveness, that glimmer of belonging to a couple instead of fighting the battle on her own had felt good, like a relief.

"You okay?" Lane asked under his breath.

She glanced up at him as they walked and nodded. "Yeah. Thanks. You make him nervous. That was fun to watch."

Lane grunted. "He needs to be nervous. I won't stand by and let him insult you again. He needs to watch his manners or he'll be introduced to the meathead side of me."

She laughed and bit down on her lip so the sound wouldn't travel. "You're not a meathead."

"I can be if a situation calls for it."

She didn't doubt it. Lane could be a gentle soul. It was what made him good with patients. But a guy didn't survive on the streets like he had without knowing how to intimidate others and protect himself. If Henry had any sense, he'd take heed.

They reached the back of the house and Elle peered out the

glass door. As she'd guessed, her mother was on the brick-paved back porch, drinking something from a frosty glass and reading a book. The dog had made it to the backyard and looked to be unsuccessfully stalking a butterfly. Despite her anxiety at seeing her mother, a smile touched Elle's lips.

Her mom hadn't been around much when Elle was growing up, but when she did take days off work, this was where she'd always retreat to, no matter what city they were in. The outdoors in the shade with a book. As a child, Elle had often taken the seat beside her and sipped on something colorful so she could feel grown up. Her mom would read to her from whatever book she was reading, quizzing Elle on what some of the bigger words meant.

Her mother had given Elle her work ethic. She'd also given her the love of reading and learning. Unfortunately, she'd skipped a lot of the other stuff in between. And when she'd needed her on her side the most, her mom had let her down.

She opened the back door and stepped out with Lane following behind. Her mother glanced up from her book, as elegant as ever with her white-blond hair in a side-swept bob, and her eyes lit with surprise. "Ellie."

Elle stepped forward. "Hi, Mom."

"Nina told me you were coming, but I wasn't sure I believed her." Her mom set her book down and swung her legs to the side of the lounge chair to get up. She was moving a little slower than the last time Elle had seen her, but she still looked strong. "I'm so glad you could make it."

Elle went over to her mother and they shared a quick hug. A knot of emotion clogged Elle's throat. She didn't want to accept that her mom was sick. Cassandra McCray was the toughest woman she knew. She was supposed to be invincible. "I'm sorry I never called you back. I was busy and I didn't realize anything was going on."

Her mom leaned back, gripping Elle's hands, and shook her head. "I understand. You're just like me. Work always comes first. I didn't want to leave a message and worry you."

"Mom—"

"And you brought a friend," she said, peeking over Elle's shoulder at Lane. "Hello there."

"Hi, Mrs. McCray." Lane stepped over and put his hand out. "I'm Lane Cannon."

Her mom shook Lane's hand. "Cassandra McCray." She eyed him up and down. "And you are what to my daughter? Friend? Boyfriend? Bodyguard?"

Elle shifted closer to Lane. "Fiancé."

Her mom arched a brow, her skeptical face on full throttle. "Right. *Your fiancé.*" She gave a little laugh, like she was entertained by the idea. "Well, you always were an overachiever, Ellie. The apple didn't fall far from the tree."

Lane's lips parted and his gaze skated to Elle. "Uh…"

But before Elle could process what her mother meant, her mom turned to her and smirked. "I knew you'd bring someone to drive Henry up the wall, but you didn't need to go all the way to fiancé." She patted Lane's arm. "My daughter doesn't think I pay attention, but I know her well enough to know she'll never get married again. Henry and Nina will buy it, though, so it'll be effective nonetheless."

Elle stiffened. "I never said I wouldn't get married again."

Her mom shrugged. "You didn't have to. You're too smart to put yourself in that position twice. Plus, you're the type of person who does better on her own. I thought that even before you married Henry. I was proven right."

Elle crossed her arms, suddenly feeling like a petulant child. "So it's my fault my marriage didn't make it?"

"That's not what I said." She swept a hand out, dismissing the words. "I'm saying you are better on your own and you know that." She turned to Lane. "So who are you really? Friend? Co-worker?"

"Fiancé," Lane said smoothly. "And co-worker. And friend. But I understand where you're coming from, Mrs. McCray." He turned to Elle with a fond look. "Elle is brilliant, talented, and tough as nails. She definitely doesn't need a man in her life." He brushed her hair away from her face with a sweep of his hand, his green eyes holding her gaze without wavering. "But somehow, she's let me into hers, and I feel like the luckiest guy around because of it. Our engagement is new but if she lets me, I will spend my life making sure she's as happy as I feel every time I'm in the same room with her."

The words were a lie delivered by a talented actor. Her brain knew that. But somehow the rest of her body didn't get the message. Her chest compressed and her throat narrowed with that horrible feeling that preceded crying. No one had ever said something like that to her. Not even her ex when things were good. Tears stung her eyes. She needed to pretend back. That was what she told herself she was doing when she let the tears fall. Oscar-worthy acting. Sure.

"Oh, honey." She pushed up on her toes and pressed her lips to Lane's.

His hand slid to the back of her neck and he kept the kiss brief and chaste, but she felt the tenderness of it deep in her gut. He smiled down at her when he pulled away and wiped her tears with his thumbs. She couldn't seem to look away from him.

Her mother cleared her throat, reminding Elle that they weren't alone. She turned to look at her mom and found her with an unreadable expression. Her lips finally tipped up at the corners in a tentative smile. "Well, if that's the case, then I'm sorry for making assumptions."

That wasn't her mother saying she believed them, but Elle sensed they had her questioning herself a bit. Mission accomplished. Too bad that mission had also left Elle's heart pounding, her knees a little weak, and her mind scrambled.

Lane released Elle and shifted on his feet. "I should probably go and get our things out of the car."

Elle had the knee-jerk instinct to grab his shirt sleeve and ask him to stay, but he was trying to give her alone time with her mother. Plus, she probably needed a few minutes away from him to get her head back together after his romantic faux speech and kiss. "That's a good idea."

"Do you need any help?" her mother asked.

"No, we didn't bring much."

"Okay, well, you two will be staying in Elle's old bedroom. Second room on the left once you go up the stairs. Make yourself at home."

"Thanks, Mrs. McCray."

"Cassandra," she corrected. "After all, we'll soon be family, right?"

Lane smiled that disarming smile of his. "Of course, Cassandra."

He gave Elle a quick kiss on the cheek, as if he just couldn't bear to leave without another little peck, and then he headed out the side gate. Elle shook her head. The guy had said he was good at this, but she hadn't expected he'd be quite this good. He was making *her* question the situation, even when he'd made it perfectly clear where they stood. How many times had he pulled off this kind of farce? The thought made her stomach hurt.

"He's very good-looking," her mother said as she grabbed her drink and sat back on the chaise.

"He is."

She gave Elle a pointed look. "Is he smart enough to keep up with you?"

Elle stared down the path Lane had just tracked over, turning the question over in her head but already knowing the answer. "He is. He's pretty brilliant, actually. And he's great with the patients."

"Money?" she asked, as if that were a completely acceptable question.

Elle fought not to roll her eyes. "He doesn't need mine, if that's what you're worried about."

"So you're really engaged?"

Elle sat on the other chaise with a tired sigh and poured herself a glass of lemonade. "Mom, how long are you going to grill me to avoid telling me what's going on with you?"

Her mom's lips pursed like her lemonade was too tart, and she turned to look at the bubbling bird fountain at the edge of the patio. "What's there to know? It's cancer."

The word sent dark tendrils of anxiety over Elle's nerve endings, but she didn't let it show on her face. Her mother wouldn't want sympathy. She'd kick her right off the porch.

So Elle channeled her physician mode. "What are they recommending?"

"Double mastectomy." She said the words with no emotion but her knuckles were white against the frosty glass. "They think they can get it all with that, but they won't know for sure until they get in there. Now you can act like everyone else and tell me about all the advances and how my percentages for survival are good and that I shouldn't be so terrified at the thought of the surgery."

Elle frowned. "I'm sorry, Mom. I'm not going to tell you any of that. This sucks. Your chances *are* good, but that doesn't make any of this easier or less stressful. Do you like your doctors?"

"They're a little too nice," she said, sending her a wry smile. "Even when I bite their heads off, I can't get a rise out of them."

Elle smiled and sipped her drink. "I'll put in a request for more ruthless doctors."

"Please do. I'd feel so much better if they'd yell back at me instead of treating me like a dying woman."

Elle's heart sank. "You're not dying, Mom."

"Damn straight I'm not," she said, some of the steel coming back into her voice. "I have a business to run. And now I need to be around for your wedding. Every wedding needs a bossy mother."

Elle smirked. "Didn't you already do that the first time?"

She flicked a dismissive hand in the air. "No. I was only learning that first time. If I'd been more on my game then, I would've never let you marry Henry in the first place."

Elle leaned back in the chaise and stretched out her legs, the condensation from her glass dripping onto her slacks. "Yet, you're letting Nina marry him."

Her mom peered over with a knowing look. "I love Nina. She is my youngest and my dreamer, a romantic at heart—which is hard for practical people like you and me to understand. But the downside is that she has always been insecure. She needs someone like Henry to fill in those gaps for her. She wants someone to take care of her. And despite his past bad behavior, I think he actually loves her."

Elle snorted. "Henry loves himself."

"Yes, that's true, too. But he's sweet with her. And I at least know he's not cheating."

Her attention flicked back to her mother. "How would you know that?"

Cassandra gave an unapologetic shrug. "I had a private detective follow him for the last year. He's been faithful. And he'll support her. So I'm not going to stop them, despite the unpleasantness he brought into our family."

"Is that what we're calling it?" Elle asked, unable to hide the vinegar in her tone. The complete destruction of her marriage, the life she thought she would have, and her relationship with her sister was simply *unpleasantness*? Good to know.

Her mom reached out and patted her hand. "Don't begrudge your sister her version of happiness. I know how it happened has hurt you and it was wrong, but in the end, she saved you from a miserable life."

Elle frowned.

"Henry made you weak. He made you question yourself. He wanted someone to need him and you didn't, so he tried to break you down and create that neediness. You would never have gotten to where you are now if you had stayed with him. You'd be some broken version or yourself or you'd become me—working all the hours you have to avoid dealing with your gallivanting husband and then stressing yourself so much about it, you give yourself cancer after he's gone."

The words echoed around her head, almost too much to take in, but the last sentence registered just fine. "You didn't give yourself cancer, Mom. And Nina told me you blamed our riff for that."

Her mom lifted her gaze to the heavens and shook her head. "Oh, Nina. That girl should've been a lawyer. She bends the truth just enough to make it believable." She looked back to Elle. "I told her to mend things with you or I wasn't paying for the wedding."

Elle's lips parted. "You what?"

"This has gone on too long. Back when it happened, I didn't want our family to be the center of gossip. After what you'd been through, I wanted to save you that kind of humiliation. I'd been there before. It's why we left Napa."

Elle blinked. "What?"

"You girls were too young to know, but one of your father's indiscretions landed me in the center of nasty gossip. I wouldn't wish that on anyone. Somehow the wife always gets blamed. So when things happened with your marriage, I tried to make it seem to everyone like your marriage was already done before things started up with Nina and Henry. But by protecting you, I also protected her. No more." She sipped her drink, clearly annoyed at the memory. "She made the mistake. She needed to fix it. I've got bigger things to worry about right now than you two sniping at each other. I don't have much family left. I need my daughters around me for what I'm about to face. *Both* of you."

Elle nodded, a pang of guilt moving through her. "I'm sorry, Mom. You know I'll be here for whatever you need. Nina and I will make it work."

"I have faith that you can do more than that. Your sister betrayed you. That will never be undone, but I think you can both move forward. You won, after all. Who do you think is going to end up on the better end of things? She's got to spend her whole life with Henry." She gave Elle a conspiratorial smile. "You get to spend yours with that good-looking man who almost made you swoon like a schoolgirl with just a kiss."

Elle straightened in the chair. "I—"

"Honestly, Ellie, I never thought I'd see the day when you looked at a guy like he hung the moon and stars just for you. I almost didn't recognize you. It was like some other woman had appeared in my garden." She reached out and squeezed Elle's arm. "I'm happy for you, sweetheart. Women like us often end up with marriages that are practical instead of magical. But I think you and that new man of yours may have found some fairy dust."

The words landed on Elle like winter rain, sending a chill into her bones that sank deep. She forced a smile to her lips. "I don't believe in magic, Mom, but I am lucky to have found him."

chapter eighteen

Lane pulled a tie from his suitcase, looped it around his neck, and listened to the shower water run as Elle got ready for the rehearsal dinner. The scent of her shampoo—fresh mangoes—drifted from beneath the door and invaded his brain like a sensual fog, making him picture things he shouldn't and forget how to tie his tie. He cursed under his breath, pushing away thoughts of fruit-scented bubbles sliding over naked skin, and started his knot again.

This was his own damn fault. He should've never said those things to Elle in the garden and kissed her earlier this afternoon. He'd done it to convince her mother, to play the part he'd promised to play, but the whole thing had come too easily. He'd looked down at Elle's face, had seen the strength and beauty there, the determination to survive this gauntlet of a weekend, and the words had just tumbled out.

He'd feigned relationships and affection more times than he cared to count. He'd sold those words and smiles and kisses. Had sold more than that. But this afternoon, he hadn't had to pull from some script. He'd spoken the truth. No, they weren't engaged. But Elle *was* brilliant, talented, and tough. Elle *didn't* need a man. But in that moment, he'd wished like hell that she needed him.

His words had brought tears to her eyes and that had punched him right in the sternum. Elle could put on a front like a champ, but in that moment, that show of emotion was real. Elle wouldn't fake cry. She would find that silly and weak. He'd hit some nerve, had gotten a glimpse of something tender and vulnerable beneath all those honed steel layers.

When he'd wiped away her tears, he'd felt this surge of protectiveness that he'd never experienced before. Not the brutish, I-want-to-beat-up-your ex urge that he'd felt when they'd met Henry—though that was there, too—but more this aching desire to be the one she came to without armor, the one she could trust not to wound her. The one she'd trust with those tears.

From what he could tell, Elle had never had that soft place to fall. She had to have her guard up with everyone. Even her mother, who seemed to genuinely care for Elle, believed Elle was meant to be alone. The untouchable queen in her castle of ice, meant to share her brain and talent with the world but nothing else. Elle seemed to buy into that fate, too. And who could blame her? The one guy she'd given her trust to had treated that gift like it was some throwaway trinket at the bottom of a cereal box. And her family hadn't rallied behind her when he'd crushed that trust.

Elle was smart enough to recognize when something was a bad bet. She'd learned what a relationship could do to her. She would avoid becoming that layman's definition of insanity: doing the same thing over and over again and expecting different results. She hadn't done the same thing ever again. She'd changed course and protected herself. Was still doing it. Pushing people away.

She'd hurt him. Maybe on purpose. Maybe because that was all she knew how to do. And he'd set a boundary, one to protect his own pride...and heart.

But his plan wasn't working.

The more time he spent with her, the more he wanted her, the more he felt for her. But he couldn't tell what was driving that. Lust? The challenge? Something more than that? The last possibility was what had him worried.

Because knowing why Elle was the way she was helped him understand her better, but it didn't mean he could accept that treatment from her. She'd let him know how she felt time and again. She was embarrassed about his job. She wouldn't date him publicly. Even now, her family believed he was someone he wasn't. This could never work. He had to get that through his head.

But when she walked out half an hour later in a sexy royal-blue dress that would guarantee she'd outshine the bride tonight, his body forgot to listen to that advice.

She put her hand on her hip and tilted her head. "You all right? Did I smear my makeup or something?"

Lane got up from the side of the bed and cleared his throat, trying to keep his eyes off the plunging neckline of her dress. "Uh, no, sorry, just lost in thought. You look great."

Her gaze glided down his matching blue tie and his gray suit. She walked over and adjusted the knot on his tie and then gave it a playful flick. "You clean up nice, too, Cannon. You'll be the beau of the ball."

"No one's going to notice me if you're on my arm."

A half-smile touched her lips. "You don't have to pretend right now. We're behind closed doors."

He reached out and centered the pendant on her necklace, indulging in the feel of her skin against his knuckles. "Elle, we're pretending we're a couple. I never have to pretend that you're beautiful. That's just a verifiable fact."

Her gaze met his, her mascara-darkened eyelashes making her eyes look electric blue in the lamplight. She wet her lips and her throat worked. "Thank you."

"You're welcome."

"Not for the compliment," she said, pressing her fingers against her necklace, the place he'd just touched. "But for all of this. No one..." Her throat worked. "No one's ever done something this nice for me. You're...an amazing guy, Lane."

He shook his head and tucked his hands in his pockets so he wouldn't be tempted to touch her again. "I'm just a guy, doc. This is how you should be treated. Don't let the people outside these doors make you think you deserve any less than that. They've given you a warped view of what you should expect from people."

She smirked, though it seemed more sad than sardonic. "They have. But I also know that I've done enough not to deserve this from you." She gripped his tie again and then pushed up on her toes. She brushed her lips over his cheek in an all-too-brief kiss before pulling back. "So, thank you."

There was so much he wanted to do in that moment. He wanted to haul her against him, part her lips and taste her, feel her body fitted to his and hear his name on her lips. He wanted to convince her that it didn't have to be this way. He wanted her to show up to the rehearsal dinner with flushed cheeks and a wrinkled dress and a satisfied smile on her face. He wanted it all.

He inhaled a deep breath and let it out slowly. "Anytime, doc."

She rolled her lips inward and nodded. "Okay, guess it's time to go play bridesmaid and not lose my shit in front of everyone. Fingers crossed."

"Worried you're going to throw a punch?" he asked. "Because frankly, I don't blame you. Your ex could use a good knock to the head. Or the soft parts."

"I wish it were that. Anger actually helps me keep it together. This isn't that." She lifted her hand and showed him how it trembled. "I don't think I've been this close to a panic attack in years. I should probably have a stiff drink before I get there. The thought of all those people looking at me and thinking—*oh, she's the one he left for her sister.* It shouldn't bother me, but..."

He took her hand and sandwiched it between his palms, pressing heat into her cold fingers. "Of course it bothers you. You're human."

She groaned. "My worst nightmare is having Henry or Nina see me fall apart. I don't want to give either of them the satisfaction of knowing I'm bothered at all. But I feel like I have a live wire inside me. Everything's setting me on edge. Maybe I should've brought a Valium."

He smiled. "Let's not recreate the *Sixteen Candles* wedding scene, all right? I don't want to have to carry you out over my shoulder."

"At least I wouldn't be panicking. People would just assume I have a drinking problem. That's way more acceptable in this social circle."

"Tell me what I can do to help," he said, taking both her hands in his. "Do you want me to tell everyone you're feeling sick?"

She shook her head. "They'd see right through that. I don't want to be a coward. I need to be there." She rolled her shoulders. "I just wish I could shake it off. It's dumb. What the hell do I care what these people I never see think of me? I'm a grown woman. This shouldn't affect me."

"Worrying about those people's opinions was ingrained into you growing up. It's embedded deep. Just like my issues with school. We know it's not a life or death situation, but our body still reacts like it's a real threat. So, don't be so hard on yourself. We all have some fucked-up wiring. Life is an inefficient electrician."

She lowered her head and pressed her forehead to his shoulder with a groan. "You are such a therapist sometimes."

"I'm not a therapist yet. I just play one this weekend."

She lifted her head and gave him a look. "Don't do that. You help people. You just have a different title."

He lifted a brow and released her hands. "Says the lady who once told me I was just a hired dick with a certification."

Her mouth dipped into a frown. "I'm sorry I ever said those things to you. I was wrong. If you haven't noticed, I have an uncanny habit of saying the most damaging things possible when I see someone as a threat."

The words weren't what he expected. No pretense, no excuses, just the bald truth. "Why was I threat?"

She shrugged but her gaze slid away. "Because you're everything I'm not. Fun. Social. Well-liked. You're everything

I try to avoid. Someone who's easy to get attached to, someone who, by definition of his job, can't be faithful. But…I wanted you anyway. Even when I knew it wasn't good for either of us. Even now, when I know I can't fix the situation or offer you what you deserve. You still make me…wish things were different, wish *I* was different."

His breath gusted out of him.

"We're going to be late." She stepped past him and went to the bed to get her purse and slip on her shoes, putting her back to him.

He closed the distance between them and put a hand on her shoulder. She stiffened beneath his touch and he dropped his arm to his side. But she turned around to face him, her expression closed off.

He sighed. "Doc, you realize that I never wanted you different, right? Who you are was always what drew me back to you. I like how determined and tough you are. I like that you don't take any bullshit and push back. I like that your kink is my kink. I like you *because* you're different."

A muscle in her cheek twitched, her eyes flashing with an emotion that had escaped her fortress.

"We're not rolling around in that bed right now because *I* don't fit into *your* mold of who you wish I'd be, not the other way around."

She winced. "I've never asked you to change."

"You didn't have to," he said softly. "Hiding our relationship told me all I needed to know."

She blinked, a stark sadness coming over her face. "Lane…"

"We better go," he said stiffly. "If we walk in late, you'll have even more eyes on you."

He didn't wait for her response. He grabbed the keys off the nightstand and headed out the door. He couldn't have this conversation right now. It hurt too much. It tempted him to go against his personal code, to accept her terms, to be with her in secret so he didn't have to walk away from her after this weekend.

But he'd spent the first part of his life accepting scraps. Scraps of attention. Scraps of affection. Used only when needed.

He couldn't do it again.

Even for her.

chapter nineteen

Elle stood in the back of the courtyard, holding a thick book of Shakespeare her mother had asked her to carry in and trying to look unperturbed but feeling like a swarm of bees had set up shop in her chest.

The cobblestone courtyard outside Hotel Bienville had been draped with vintage string lights, the burning bulbs artfully arranged to illuminate all the gorgeous flowers and statuary. It looked elegant and old-fashioned and magical—like the event could be taking place in a different era or on the cover of a book. She'd thought the same thing when she'd chosen it for *her* wedding ceremony, but Henry had nixed the idea immediately. His mother had insisted they marry in the family's preferred church. He'd told her he believed in saying his vows in front of God, so she'd relented, respecting his beliefs.

But apparently he'd changed his stance on that, because his new wedding was going to be in this courtyard garden. Or maybe his church frowned upon lying, cheating bastards and he couldn't get a spot. If so, maybe Elle needed to take up religion because she'd sing a hallelujah for that. But of course Henry and

Nina would pick this place to get married. It was breathtaking. Who cared if it was the same place Elle had wanted? Nina may not even know that detail, but Henry sure did.

He'd take pleasure in taking that away from her, in needling her. How she'd ever let herself love a man like that, she didn't know. Her past self had been skilled in making horrible decisions. She wasn't sure her present self had gotten much better.

She took a deep, steadying breath and let her eyes travel to the back of a blond head in the third row of chairs—Lane, sitting casually and talking to another guest. Her stomach tightened into a fist.

He'd been cordial on the drive over, their conversation from the bedroom closed, but the feelings lingered in her like the aftereffects of a camera flash, setting her off balance and altering how she saw things. *I like you because you're different.*

She'd known she'd hurt him by hiding their relationship. He'd made that clear before. But she'd convinced herself that she was doing him a favor. He didn't need someone in his life who had her temper or her hardheadedness. She could be a complete pain in the ass and didn't want to change that. But he'd yanked her reasons right out from under her.

The things he liked about her were the very things that made others turn away. He didn't put up with those things. He was drawn to them.

She'd found someone who saw *her*, who she really was, and he'd stepped closer instead of running in the other direction.

And she'd fucked it completely up. Was still doing that.

"It's really big of you to attend the wedding, but you probably shouldn't be the one to do the poetry reading."

The familiar voice startled Elle out of her thoughts and sent disgust slithering down her spine. She didn't turn to look at the man who'd sidled up next to her. "Go away, Henry. I'm holding this for my mother."

"I was making a joke."

"Did you not hear me?"

He gave a put-upon sigh, as if she were being so very unreasonable. "You know, it doesn't have to be this way. I have no ill feelings toward you, Elle."

She couldn't help the snort that escaped. She looked at him. "Oh, you don't harbor ill feelings toward me, the wife you cheated on. Duly noted. That's very *big* of you, as you'd say."

"Right, I'm always the bad guy." He gave her a disgusted look and tucked his hands in his pockets. "Let's not pretend like I destroyed our marriage on my own. You abandoned me way before Nina became a factor. You were married to your job and in love with your own status. When we slept together, you acted like you were doing me a favor. When we were out with friends, you always had to one up me, make me look like I wasn't as smart or as successful as the precocious doctor."

She stared at him, not believing the words coming out of his mouth. "So you get a free pass to cheat because I wasn't the doting wife who worshipped her husband and made him feel like the big man? Insecure, much?"

"Whatever, Elle. I was just trying to offer a truce for Nina's sake. I hate seeing her unhappy, and the gulf between you two eats at her."

"It should. That's what happens when you stab someone who loved you in the back. She deserves whatever she got."

Henry's eyes narrowed. "Goddamn, you always had a

mean streak but when did you become such a bitter bitch?" He glanced out at the audience. "No wonder you had to hire some hooker to drag here with you this weekend."

Her body went cold, her muscles stiff, but she fought to keep her expression unchanged. "If you're talking about my fiancé, you need to—"

"Come on, Elle," he said, cutting her off and looking her way. "Be a better liar. He's years younger than you and you're not going to jump into marriage. I called a cop friend and checked Lane out because something didn't feel right. He has a prior arrest on his record for solicitation."

Elle's heartbeat thumped like a bass drum in her ears.

"So either you hired a prostitute or you're marrying one. I'm sure your mother would love to know she has a gutter rat staying under her roof."

Elle's rage meter climbed, making her vision blur at the edges. "Do not...call him that."

"So, I'm curious," Henry said, on a roll now. "Are you just paying him to be on your arm or are you actually letting his filthy dick touch you? Because God knows the places he's stuck—"

Elle wasn't sure how it happened. But one second her fingers were digging into the heavy book of The Bard's greatest hits and the next, she was swinging it at high velocity. The move was so quick, she surprised herself, but more importantly, she surprised Henry. The massive tome connected with the side of Henry's face with a satisfying thwack, and Henry let out a high-pitched howl.

His hands flew up to his face and blood poured from his nose. Elle could hear the shocked voices of the people who'd been preparing for the rehearsal, could see them in her periphery, but she didn't turn away from Henry.

"Doc!" Lane's voice sounded urgent but distant.

Someone shrieked, maybe her sister.

Henry's eyes filled with rage, the man behind the polished mask. He launched himself at her, grabbing her roughly by the arm and shaking her, his fingers digging into her flesh. "You fucking bitch! What is the matter—"

That was all he got out before a hand was darting out, grabbing Henry's other arm and wrenching it behind his back.

"Let her go or you're going to have a broken arm to add to the nose. And I might not stop there." Lane's voice was a growl, vicious in its calmness

Henry winced when Lane jerked a little harder, and he released Elle. But a sneer filled his face. "So your whore fucks you *and* acts as bodyguard? Hope you're paying him well."

Lane's eyes met hers over Henry's head and he roughly released Henry's arm.

Nina ran up, eyes wild. "What are you doing?" She glanced at Henry's bleeding face. "What did you *do?*"

"I hit him in the face with Shakespeare," Elle said simply. "Tell your fiancé not to insult mine and to stay the hell away from me."

Henry pulled a handkerchief from his pocket and held it to his nose. "Her *fiancé* is a hooker. She had the nerve to bring that kind of filth into our wedding."

Everyone was gathered around now. Hearing it all, looking Elle's way, shock on their faces. Her mother was among them, eyebrows lifting high on her forehead, silent questions stacking up.

Lane's expression was a stoic mask.

"Henry, what are you talking about?" Nina said, her voice bordering on hysterical as she tried to help him clean up. "She didn't hire him. Lane was at her house when I went to visit her. Why are you fighting with her? This is our wedding rehearsal."

"I'm not lying." Henry said, anger still rippling through his words. "I checked his record."

"Illegally checked," Lane finally said. "You saw a charge that was false and dropped."

"They're lying," Henry said, looking to the crowd gathered. "She knows who he is."

All heads turned toward her, the faces of family, her mother's friends, some curious, some appalled, some eager for gossip.

Elle set the book down on a nearby table and pulled her shoulders back, keeping her expression placid even though her arm was stinging from where Henry had gripped her and her anxiety wanted to take over. She stepped around Henry and his mess and went to Lane to take his hand. "Yes, I do. He's a brilliant surrogate and counselor in the sex therapy department at the hospital I work at. He's a man with a kind heart and the patience of a saint." She looked up at Lane, finding his gaze heavy on her. "And he's the best man I know. So yes, I know exactly who he is."

Lane's eyes softened, a ghost of a smile touching his lips. He rubbed the tender spot on her arm where Henry had gripped and he kissed the top of her head. "Ready to celebrate your birthday, doc?"

Birthday. The safe word. She'd never been so happy to hear it. She smiled and leaned into him. "So very ready."

Without worrying about who was looking or what they were

saying about her, she slipped her arm around Lane's waist and let him lead her out of the courtyard.

She'd miss the Shakespeare reading.

A shame, really.

She'd heard it was very impactful.

Especially when swung at full speed.

Lane and Elle's footsteps went silent as they escaped into the carpeted hallways of the hotel. The blast of air-conditioning hit her heated face and made her suck in a breath. She was still trembling, but now it had nothing to do with nerves and everything to do with adrenaline.

Lane grabbed her hand and turned to her as they made tracks toward the lobby. "You okay, doc?"

"I'm not sure. I think so?" She couldn't think straight. Part of her was soaring because she'd just stood in front of everyone and told the truth, but the other part was reeling from what Henry had said to her about her role in the breakdown of their marriage. The words were eating at her like hungry caterpillars.

They passed a large potted fern and Lane tugged on her hand, dragging her into an arched alcove.

"What are you doing?"

Lane pulled her to him and captured both her hands between their bodies. His eyes scanned her face, searching. "Did you mean those things you said?"

She blinked, temporarily dazzled by the intensity in his gaze. "Which part?"

"The things you said about me. Tell me they were an act. Tell me they were to piss your ex off, that you were putting on a show."

"Why?" she asked, her voice breathless to her own ears.

"Because then I won't have to break the promise I made to myself."

Her heart picked up speed and she wet her lips. "The book was for him. The words were the truth."

Something broke in his expression, the scaffolding giving way. Lane released her hands and cupped her face. "You just told everyone you know that I sleep with people for a living."

"I know," she whispered.

"They're going to be talking about you for months."

She swallowed past the dryness in her throat. "Let them. Their opinions don't matter to me anymore. I'm tired of trying to…prove that I was unaffected by what happened, that I just brushed myself off and moved on. I didn't. I shouldn't have been expected to. It changed me. Something like that is *supposed* to. The woman I used to be would've never gotten involved with a man like you."

He flinched slightly.

She let her hands flatten along his chest. "But I'm not her anymore. I don't want to be. I don't ever want to feel like I did after Henry cheated on me, but I'm tired of being scared to feel something for someone. Hearing him tonight, I realized he's still controlling me. What he did to me is puppeteering my life. And that"—she met his gaze—"pisses me the hell off."

Lane nodded, his expression not revealing anything.

She took a deep breath. "You might hurt me. This might blow up in my face. But I'm tired of playing his game. These last few weeks with you, even the hard ones, have made me feel things I thought were long dead. You matter to me, Lane. I'm sorry I keep pretending that you don't."

"Elle." He closed his eyes and said the word like a prayer,

like he was letting out a long-held breath.

She didn't know how he was going to respond. Vulnerability blanketed her and her heart tried to jailbreak through her ribs. Every instinct was telling her to run, but she forced herself to stay in his arms.

When the silence stretched on, she began to sweat. "Say something, Lane. I don't know what to...do with this."

He looked down at her, a rueful smile touching his mouth. "I don't either. But how about we start here?"

He tilted her face toward him and kissed her. The connection started off slow, a simmer, a let's-figure-this-out-together kiss, but soon her fingers were curling into his shirt and she was making a needy sound in the back of her throat. The whimper seemed to flip a switch in him. His tongue dipped into her mouth and her hands mapped his back. This was not the chaste nonsense they'd done in front of her family. This kiss held the fire of those early kisses back when they were hating each other and sparring. Urgent. Needful. Wild.

Her back hit the wall and his body aligned against hers, hard fitting to soft. Her skin burned through the thin material of her dress and her lungs protested for air, but she didn't want to stop. This. She needed this. They'd been pouring water on this forest fire since the day she'd ruined things in the office, had tried to ignore how they were flint and steel to each other, but all of that thwarted need poured into the kiss now, singeing her from the inside out.

Lane's mouth trailed down to her neck and she gasped for breath, her head tilting back and her shoulders rising with panted air. He caressed her breast through her dress, a gentle thumb grazing her nipple, his voice a growl against her throat.

"It took everything I had earlier not to go back on everything I said and peel you out of this dress. You look like fucking sin, Elle. One I'd commit over and over again and happily go to hell for."

She groaned, her hands gripping him as if she'd float away if she didn't have something to hold on to. Over and over again sounded like an excellent plan. She cosigned that plan. She shifted her hips, a shiver racing through her as the hard length of him brushed against the place that ached most.

They had too many clothes on. She needed him against her naked. Her eyes flitted open and she caught sight of the tiny security camera in the corner, reminding her where they were and where they were not. "We might not go to hell, but we might get arrested if we keep this up."

Lane lifted his head and followed her gaze. His grin was pure wicked schoolboy when he turned back to her. "Someone is getting a show during their night shift."

He waggled his fingers at the camera in greeting.

She laughed. "We should charge."

He leaned in and kissed her again. "No. No more money exchanging hands."

"Good idea."

"But let's skip jail tonight." He stepped back, adjusting his jacket, and then held his hand out to her. "I've got a better idea. Come on."

She took his hand, her blood still pumping with desire and her flaming cheeks probably telling the tale for anyone who passed. He guided her toward the lobby, but instead of heading out front to the valet, Lane parked her on one of the pretty Victorian couches and went to the front desk.

A few moments later, he returned and held up a keycard. "How about a little more privacy and a few less family members?"

Her lips curved. "We don't have any of our things."

He offered his hand. "I only need one thing tonight—you out of that dress in a room with thick walls and a plush bed. We'll worry about the walk of shame tomorrow."

She took his hand and let him drag her against him again. She pressed her lips to his for a quick kiss. "No more shame. I'll proudly walk into my family's home tomorrow with you on my arm, looking like I've been manhandled."

He touched his forehead to hers and cupped the back of her neck. "Oh, you're so going to be manhandled, doc. I need to pay you back for all this torture you've put me through."

She gave him an I-dare-ya smile. "I'd like to see you try."

chapter twenty

The door to the hotel room had barely clicked shut when Lane hauled her up against it and fitted his body to hers, his mouth capturing her lips with fevered urgency. She melted into the door and shoved his jacket off his shoulders, trying to keep herself steady while he kissed her senseless. She needed him naked. Now. His jacket hit the ground.

Big hands roamed her body, seeking, owning. He pushed her wrists above her head, pinning her with ease. She could feel that dominant side of him in every movement, every fevered touch. It was barely leashed, that need to take over. Their lovemaking had always been combative. He pushed, she pushed back. She didn't submit. She loved that game. But being trapped against the door and feeling the intensity of it all had erotic curiosity pinging through her. Curiosity and...trust.

The feeling was unfamiliar. Powerful. Freeing.

Lane worked his way down her plunging neckline, his lips making heat streak straight downward, and she moaned, every muscle in her body straining toward him. She tried to hold on to her thoughts. "Lane..."

"Hmm," he murmured as he pushed her dress aside and then dragged his tongue over the curve of her breast, sending smoky desire curling through her. "Do you need me to fight with you?"

She loved that he asked but hated that he had to.

"No." Her senses homed in on his touch, the pressure on her wrists, her damp panties, her pounding heart. "You said I owe you for the torture. I want to pay you back."

He stilled and looked up, shadows crossing his face. "No more paying."

"Not money. I need my hands." He released her and she flattened her palms on his chest and eased him back, giving herself room. He watched her with careful eyes as she kicked off her heels. Without giving her old demons time to catch up with her, she lowered herself to her knees. "I mean, this." She wet her lips. "I'll give you the control. I'll…be whatever you want tonight. Show me who you are when you go to those clubs."

Lane's brows lowered, his expression dark. "Elle…"

She reached for his belt buckle, her hands shaking a little. She hadn't gone down on a guy since her ex, had never want to put herself in that subservient position again or risk those memories ruining things mid-moment. But right now, the desire to touch Lane, to taste him, to give him the kind of pleasure he gave her, was stronger than her past.

She unbuttoned his fly. His cock was a hard outline beneath his slacks, the sight alone making her sex clench. But when she reached for his zipper, he put a hand on her wrist, stilling her.

Her gaze jumped up to his.

His jaw flexed, like it was taking everything he had not to let her get on with things. "Don't do this because you think you owe me something. I don't want you to be my submissive."

Her hand trembled in his grip, her nerves fully surfacing. Was he saying she couldn't be what he needed? That she couldn't fulfill that part of him? "Why not?"

He ran his thumb over the top of her hand, his attention heavy on her. "Because that's not who you are."

She grimaced. "You don't know that. Maybe I have a side you don't know about."

His eyes narrowed and he released her wrist to cup her chin. "Okay. Beg me to suck my cock, Elle. Tell me how desperate you are to taste it, how you'll do anything for the privilege."

The words sent her gulping, the images making her skin heat—her lips wrapping around him, his taste on her tongue. But she couldn't make the words come out of her mouth. She wanted him. She was ready to push past this mental block she'd had for so long. But *beg* him for the privilege of getting him off? "You've got to be kidding me."

He grinned, mischief in his eyes. "And that, is exactly what I mean. Not a submissive."

Her fingers curled into fists. "But you're a dominant. That's what you're into."

He traced her bottom lip with his thumb. "I like being dominant in bed. That doesn't mean we have to fit in some neatly labeled box. I'm into *you*. You feed that part of me more than you realize. You like to fight back and be overpowered and give me hell over it. You don't submit until you have no other choice. You know what that does to me?" He guided her hand to his rock-hard erection, wrapping her fingers around him. "It pushes all of my buttons, doc. All my dirtiest, darkest buttons."

Her muscles clenched, low and tight, her body aching for

him.

"You do that even when we're not sparring. So we don't have to follow someone else's rules. If you want to play, we do it our way. No one doing anyone favors. Both of us getting what we crave."

Our way. The words reverberated through her. There could be an *our* now. The notion filtered through her system, making her feel confident. In her skin. Sexy.

She heard the words loud and clear. What they did in the bedroom didn't mean they were broken in some way. Or that they were doing kink wrong. All that mattered was that they both were on board and enjoying the hell out of it.

"Maybe the first man on earth to turn down a blow job," she teased.

"I never said I turned you down." Lane lowered his hand and finished dragging down his zipper. The faint sound of the zipper releasing had her teeth digging into her lip. He took his cock in his palm, looming over her, teasing her with the sight of his thick erection. He gave himself a leisurely stroke, spreading fluid over the head. "You should see your face right now."

"Annoyance? Disdain?"

He chuckled. "More like I just offered you a big, fat slice of chocolate cake and you're starved." He brushed the tip of his finger over her bottom lip, spreading some of his fluid there. "Suck my cock, gorgeous. I know how much you want to. I know how wet it's going to make you."

She sent him a wry smile even as a ripple of anticipation went up her spine and his taste hit her tongue. "Someone's confident."

The green of his eyes was almost black in the lamplight.

"Don't think it's going to do it for you?"

She shrugged, feigning indifference. In all honestly, she really didn't know how she'd react. She wanted this, but she wasn't ruling out bad memories taking over the minute she got into it.

"Stand up."

The command confused her, but she got to her feet. Lane reached out and dragged her dress up her hips. Hunger flared in his gaze when he discovered she was wearing garters and stockings along with her satin panties. But if he approved, he kept any thoughts to himself. "Looks like you've made a mess of yourself already. Unsnap the garters and take your panties off."

She did as she was told, enjoying the way his eyes followed her every move, how he casually stroked himself at the sight of her.

When she stood upright again, he put out his hand. "Give them to me."

She handed them over and he stepped closer, the tip of his erection brushing against her hip. He kept his eyes on her face as he tucked his hand between her legs and swiped at her with her panties, drying her damp skin but also dragging satin over her clit and making her knees want to buckle. Every nerve ending was on high alert.

"There," he said against her ear. "I'll see what state you're in after. If having my cock in your mouth doesn't make you wet, you win."

Her nipples were hard against his chest, her whole body tingling now, every inch sensitive. "What do I win?"

"What you like the best. Being right. And you'll be in charge the rest of the night."

"And if I lose?"

He slid his hand down to her ass and squeezed. "You're mine to use however I want."

Anticipation rolled through her like a tidal wave and she nodded. "You're on."

"On your knees, doc. Let's see if that mouth is useful for more than smartass comments." He gripped her shoulder and guided her down, using just enough pressure to make her feel like she was resisting and he was forcing.

She didn't know why that did it for her, but it did. She wasn't going to question it any longer.

Her knees landed softly on the hotel carpet and she reached out, placing her hand over his where he gripped his erection. They stroked together for a moment and then he braced a hand above her on the door and guided himself to her mouth, but he didn't push his way in. He brushed the tip over her lips, painting her mouth with the salty fluid that had escaped, but making it clear she was going to have to make the next move. He wasn't going to force this.

Part of her wished he would. Anxiety was trying to invade her brain. The last time she'd done this to a man, she'd tasted another woman on him. She closed her eyes and inhaled deeply, the scent of Lane filling her senses. She would not let Henry ruin another thing for her. This was Lane, a man who meant something to her. A man she wanted to enjoy, to give pleasure to.

She parted her lips and enveloped his cock with the wet heat of her mouth. Salt. Warmth. Velvet skin. *Lane.* A wash of hot desire went through her.

"Doc...fuck." Lane groaned and his free hand went to her

hair, lacing his fingers in it and gripping.

The unedited reaction, the clear appreciation in the way he'd whispered the words was all the encouragement she needed. There was no room for any of the ugly stuff to steal the moment from her. All that was left were the two of them, connected in one of the most intimate ways possible, making each other feel good.

She eased back and then took him deeper, swirling her tongue around him and sliding her hands up his thighs to hold on, to feel the muscles tighten and flex beneath her fingers, to feel how she was affecting him. She didn't have to think about if she was doing it right. Lane's reactions were visceral and generous, sexy. The sounds he made, his flavor on her tongue, the almost harsh grip on her hair.

"No half effort from you, doc. You trying to get me to come so that I can't do all the bad things I was promising?" he asked, his voice gritty but tone still teasing.

She pulled off and then dragged her tongue over his sac and up the length of him in one long swipe, taking her time and enjoying the torture she was meting out. When he cursed, she peered up at him and smiled, sending a silent challenge. But instead of his normally cocky expression, a tender look crossed his face, one that said he saw *her*, that he knew what amount of trust this was taking for her to do this.

It nearly undid her. She closed her eyes again, the feelings welling in her more than she wanted to deal with right now, and took him back into her mouth. She doubled her efforts, wanting to focus on the sensations, on the act, on worshipping his cock with her tongue. Not on the heavy stuff. On the what happens next. She couldn't think that far or she was going to panic.

"Elle." His grip in her hair tightened, his hips rocking into her now, his own control waning. "Baby, pull away if you don't want me to come in your mouth."

She appreciated the warning but she didn't back off. She could feel how close he was, the tension, feel the victory of knowing she'd brought him to his edge. He was at her mercy now. She would finish what she'd started.

Seconds later, he ground out her name and held her head against him, his release spilling against her tongue and flooding her with his taste. Even though she'd prepared herself, the force of it still caught her off guard, throwing her off her rhythm. She sucked and swallowed down what she could, not managing all of it. It was messy and primal and hot.

So. Very. Hot.

Her body flushed warm everywhere. Aching. Needy. Throbbing.

The potent reaction knocked her off balance. Was this what it was supposed to be like? Never in her life had giving head been so erotic. Every erogenous zone in her body pulsed as if she'd been the one being stimulated. She wanted to yank off all of his clothes, tumble him to the floor, and demand he get hard again so she could have him inside her.

Lane pulled her to her feet before either of them had caught their breath.

"Christ," he whispered. He pressed a kiss to her hair and breathed her in like he was still getting himself together, but then he backed away, his attention going to her mouth. Her hand flew up to fix things, but he blocked her. He brushed his thumb over the corner of her mouth where some of his release had escaped and he held it to her lips. "Finish."

She sucked the pad of his thumb, holding his gaze and watching the way his pupils dilated.

"You are the sexiest woman I've ever met, Elle McCray," he said, his tone dead serious.

"I bet you say that to all the girls who give you a blow job," she teased, her voice light and breathless, her heart beating too fast.

"No. I don't." He leaned in and kissed her long and deep, his taste still lingering on her tongue and his appreciation clear in every move.

She groaned into it, her breasts rubbing against his chest, her need to be skin-to-skin making her dizzy. He'd teased her about begging earlier, but now she might be ready to do it for real. He slid his hand down her body and found the throbbing heat between her thighs. His fingers slid over swollen, embarrassingly slick flesh.

He smiled against her mouth. "And in a crushing defeat..."

She couldn't help but laugh. "You don't play fair."

He tucked two long fingers inside her, making electricity spark over her skin and her words lodge in her throat. "Who said anything about playing fair? I like to win. I especially like to win when it means getting my cock sucked and having a beautiful doctor so wet her thighs are slick."

Her head tilted back against the door. "Somehow I don't feel like I'm losing right now."

"That's the best part. Even the loser gets a prize. Me."

She snorted but the sound cut off halfway through because Lane lowered himself to his knees, his fingers still buried deep inside her, and put his mouth to her. Her body bucked instantly, the feel of his hot mouth almost too much at once. Her hands went to his shoulders, grappling for balance in case her knees gave out.

But soon he was guiding her thigh over his shoulder and pressing her into the door, holding her in place. Her body opened for him like a book, one his velvet tongue would read every page of. She gasped for air and all the blood in her body rushed downward.

His fingers pumped deep, and his lips and tongue worshipped every sensitive, needy part of her, making everything hum with awareness. Her back bowed and her head tapped against the door in some erotic Morse code. *Need to come. Need to come.* Lane shifted and kissed her deep between her legs, his tongue working with his fingers to bring her to the edge of her control.

"Lane." The word was a plea, but she wasn't sure for what. She felt like she was going to break apart. "Please."

He made a sound, his lips vibrating against her, and she shattered. It'd been too long and he was far too good at what he was doing for her to hold out any longer. She cried out, probably giving anyone in the hall a shock, and came in a whole-body rush of sensation that had her wanting to collapse to the floor in a puddle of useless limbs.

Lane didn't let her fall, though. He held her in place and continued to pleasure her until her body began to quake, and then he softened his approach, kissing her thighs with feather-light brushes of his lips.

He slipped her leg from over his shoulder and helped her to the floor. There was no fight left in her body. She settled into his lap and he cradled her against him, soothing words drifting from his lips.

"You're so beautiful," he murmured against her hair, stroking his fingers gently through the strands. "I don't know how we got here, but I'm glad it's now."

The words filtered through the filmy afterglow in her mind but instead of warming her, the compliment hit some old open cut. Anxiety shimmered through her.

She must've stiffened because Lane stopped stroking her hair. "What's wrong?"

She shook her head, trying to fight the reaction.

But he didn't let her get away with the rebuff. He tipped her face toward him, his eyes searching hers. "Tell me."

She wet her lips, her throat tight. "The sweet words. They're making me...it triggers..."

His eyes flickered with understanding, but there was an edge of sadness there, too. "This makes me want to go kill that man downstairs in that ballroom. Make him pay for the things he did to you."

She closed her eyes as her body trembled.

He pushed her hair away from her face. "Look at me, Elle."

She forced her eyes open, panic trying to claw at her, and met his steady gaze.

"I will not lie to you," he said firmly. "I'm not trying to manipulate you. I can't tell you where this is going or that I'll always do or say the right thing, but I can swear to you that I am not him. I will never betray you like he did. If I tell you you're beautiful, it's because I think you are, not because I'm trying to feed you a line. If I tell you I'm happy that it's now, I am. Okay?"

The words hit her hard, made her want to cry, but she nodded. "Okay."

"Good." He gave her a brief kiss and smoothed his hand over

her hair. "Now, the bad news for you is that you lost the bet."

She blinked.

He traced his finger down her sternum, sending goose bumps in its wake. "Take off everything but the stockings and garters and meet me in the bedroom. I get the control now. And I know a real effective way to chase the memory of any other man from your mind."

The words zipped through her, dragging her anxious mind back to the matters at hand. A sexy dominant Lane and a lost bet.

She scooted off his lap and held her dress to her chest. "What do you have in mind?"

He didn't look at her as he got up and headed toward the bedroom. With his back to her, he called out, "Don't make me wait, cupcake."

She took a breath, trying to shove away the remnants of the chill that the panic had brought on, and quickly undressed. She crossed the posh hotel room in just her stockings, feeling equal parts excited and vulnerable. But the feeling amplified when she walked into the bedroom and saw that Lane had put his clothes back to rights. His slacks were zipped, his tie perfect, his hands casually tucked in his pockets as though he were there for a business meeting.

But the look in his eyes was what had her breath leaving her. Lane in full dominant mode.

Holy hell. The guy really should come with a warning label.

He held up a hand when she stepped inside and she stopped, her mouth going dry. His eyes tracked over her slowly, head to toe and back up again. A man in control. A man on a mission. She had a feeling her sexual fantasies would be faceless no more. Lane made a shirt and tie look like the male version of lingerie, but the attitude was what had hot shivers moving over her skin. The cool, evaluating look Lane was giving her set off all her erotic switches.

"Now about paying me for the bet you just lost." He cocked his head toward the bed. "Sit."

She lifted her eyebrows even as she made her way across the room and sat on the end of the crisp white duvet, trying to channel her haughty side even as her body ached for him to touch her. "Paying you? I just gave you a blow job."

His lips curved into a barely there smile. "That was for you."

"Oh, really?" she said, not hiding the sarcasm from her voice. "My mistake."

He turned and stood in front of her a few paces away. "You're going to fulfill your end of the bet with something else."

She tipped her chin up in challenge. "And what's that?"

He stepped closer and tugged at the knot on his tie. He pulled it off and held it in front of her. "Close your eyes."

She eyed the strip of silk. "Blindfolding me with a tie is a little cliché, don't you think?"

He smirked. "This is for you, too. It will make it easier."

She had no idea what he was talking about, but she closed her eyes and he tied the warm silk around her head, blocking out the light. She'd played this game with Donovan before, so the loss of sight didn't unnerve her, but his talk of something being hard for her had her belly tightening.

He brushed the tips of his fingers down the back of her neck. "Very good."

She noticed he didn't say *good girl*. She'd told him once and he'd never forgotten. Every limit she'd ever laid out, he'd respected. That calmed her some.

The sound of a chair dragging across the carpet filled her ears and she sensed him parking himself in front of her. His knees brushed hers, sending goose bumps along her thighs. "If we're going to do this and move forward, my request is simple. All I want is honesty."

She frowned. "When have I not been honest?"

"I haven't asked the question yet."

She clamped her lips shut.

"Are you willing to give this a real chance?"

She frowned. "Sex?"

His hands closed over her knees. "No. Us. I want you, Elle. Not just in my bed but in my life. Do you want that, too?"

She took a long, steadying breath, old feelings waging war with new ones. "I do. I'm...trying. But even this kind of conversation is freaking me out."

"I know," he said softly. "But you're still here. You just faced a panic attack out there and didn't run. You didn't lash out at me. You let us have a sweet moment and you're still here."

The words made her throat tight, but she managed a quivery smile. "You better not be therapy-ing me, Lane Cannon. I will punch you."

He took her hands in his. "Indulge me. Can you give me your trust tonight?"

"With what?"

He touched his forehead to hers. "I want to make love to you, Elle. No mean words, no fighting. Just let me make you feel good my way."

Any erotic drive she'd had walking into the room went dormant. Her stomach was a pit. Honest words fell from her lips. "I don't know how to do that. I can't promise I won't panic"

His palm cupped the back of her head. "That's okay. Trust that I've got you, that I'll take care of you. And there's always your safe word."

Fear tried to grip her. She didn't make love. That wasn't part any relationship she'd had since her marriage, but she didn't want to shut this down, not after all that had happened tonight. She needed to trust that Lane would keep her safe. She needed to give them both a chance. She took a breath and nodded. "Okay."

chapter twenty one

"**O**kay."

The word was a simple one but the trust it required from Elle sent relief sweeping through Lane. She was freaked out, but she trusted him enough to give him a chance. Now he had to make sure he didn't screw it up.

Elle had been totally in for everything tonight—her guards down, the fun, sensual woman he'd suspected hid underneath all that armor on full display. Hell, she'd announced in front of her whole family that he was a surrogate. But the minute he'd said something sweet to her, he'd triggered her demons and the panic had tried to take her down.

If she were a patient of his, he'd want to talk it out. But Lane knew that'd only make it worse with Elle. They'd talked enough. So, he was turning to the only thing he had left—his instincts.

If they really wanted to make a go of this, of trying to date, he wasn't going to walk on eggshells. He wanted to be able to tell the woman he cared about how he felt.

"Lie back on the bed," he said, keeping his voice calm.

"Spread your legs."

The command seemed to snap her from whatever thoughts were making her body tense up. She took a breath and scooted back on the bed. She lay on her back and parted her legs. He ate up the view as he shucked his shirt. Even though he'd only come a few minutes ago, his cock stirred with interest at the sight. Elle's breasts smooth and full in the warm glow of the lamps, her body bare and open to him, those lacy garters making her look like a confection. Goddamn, the woman was sexy.

He reined in his galloping libido and went to the closet, searching for what he wanted. He'd checked for possible supplies when he'd come in and had been pleased to find that the swanky hotel had rubber-tipped clothespins on their hangers. God forbid any guest wrinkle their clothes with metal teeth. Their attention to detail was his boon.

He grabbed a few and tucked them in his pocket before walking over to the bed. He ran the back of his hand over Elle's breast, brushing the nipple with a barely there touch and bringing it to a hard point. Her belly dipped with a breath.

"Have I ever told you that you have the most beautiful breasts?" he asked, tracing a circle around her areola and watching goose bumps rise.

Her fingers curled into her palms. As he'd expected, the simple compliment unnerved her. Her lovers weren't supposed to be kind or complimentary. That was what had been burned into her brain by that asshole lacing his lies with sugar. Well, Henry wasn't going to steal that from her anymore if Lane had anything to do with it.

He brought her nipple between his fingers and clamped the clothespin on it.

She gasped. "What the hell?"

She tried to sit up but he put a palm in the center of her chest and guided her back down. "The more you move, the more it will sting. Just let the feel of it move through you. And try not to think about how it will feel when I pull them off later. The pain of that is going to make you call me bad names."

"I want to call you bad names right now."

He smiled, pinched her other nipple, and clamped it without ceremony. "Be nice."

She made a sound in the back of her throat, some combination of pain and frustration. He flicked the clamp and watched as a flush moved up her body. The familiar scent of her arousal drifted on the air, and satisfaction filled him. He had her attention and she wasn't bailing on him. He'd take every shred of good news he could get.

He walked toward the end of the bed and undressed. "We know what your kinks are, but we haven't gotten to the extent of mine. Dominance is one thing. Sadism is another. I haven't had the pleasure of sharing that part of me with you yet." He traced his fingers down her knee, watching the muscles twitch in his wake. "And I know you're not a submissive, but I have a strong suspicion that you don't mind some sharp edges with your pleasure." He smacked the inside of her thigh. "I told you to keep your legs open, cupcake."

She grunted and huffed a breath but parted her legs. The sight of plump, slick flesh was enough to get his dick rock hard again. He took the cold metal end of another clamp and traced it over her clit.

The shock of the cold made her back arch. "Lane."

"Look how wet you are again. I love how hot you get." He

traced the lips of her sex with the clamp. "I'd like to wake up each morning to your pretty face and then lick this sexy cunt for breakfast."

Her knees pulled up and her toes curled into the duvet.

"I can see that, you know?" he said, keeping his voice steady. "Where this could go. Our future. Sharing a bed. Maybe a house one day. Kissing you good-bye each morning and looking forward to seeing you each night. I'd be a damn lucky guy. I never considered how much I wanted that kind of life until I met you. You make me want things I thought I could never have."

The truth was hard for him to say, his own vulnerability on display, flapping in the wind like a flag in a storm. But if he expected her to take this risk, he needed to be willing to take some, too.

Her body stilled, the panic obviously gripping her, but he'd expected that. He clamped one side of her labia with the rubber-tipped clip. Her breath hissed out through her teeth and her head tilted back, the panic no competition for that shock. But her legs opened wider and her teeth bit into her lip. No safe word came. She was in the good kind of pain.

He let out his own breath, sending a silent thank you to the universe that his instincts hadn't been off base. He'd suspected this might be an option, since she enjoyed rough sex and she'd had a thing with Donovan, who wasn't vanilla himself, but he didn't want to assume. Now he could see it in front of his eyes. She could get off on a little erotic pain.

More importantly, though, it could jam the other signals her brain and body were trying to give her. Calm that fight-or-flight response.

This was what he could give her. A way to sink into the sensation during sex, to clearly separate it from the type of sex she'd had in her marriage, but without arguing or insults always having to play a role. A way to simply be with each other. To be dirty and rough and sweet all at the same time.

"Still with me, gorgeous?"

Her throat worked and she licked her lips. "Yes."

He leaned down and kissed her inner thigh, moving higher and higher until he reached the center of her. He licked over her swollen clit.

She bowed up on the bed and made the most delicious, decadent sound he'd ever heard. "What are you doing to me?"

"Bad things."

"They don't feel bad," she said softly.

He smiled. "Because I'm good at this." He slid a finger inside her and gently tugged at the clothespin with his other hand. Her inner muscles clenched hard around him. "And because you're good at this, too. You're super filthy, doc. I love it."

A quiet laugh escaped her.

He swallowed hard. "I could love *you* if you let me."

His words cut off her laughter like a knife had gone through it. She sat up on her elbows, her mouth in a deep frown. "Lane—"

"I didn't tell you to get up. And I don't need you to freak out."

She yanked off her blindfold, her eyes finding his, accusation there. "What are you doing?"

"Tonight's about honesty. That's me giving you mine." He channeled the inner calm he'd learned from being a counselor, showed no emotion on his face, and pulled off the clamp from between her legs.

She fell back to the bed. "Fuck."

He didn't wait for her to recover. She had a safe word if she needed it. He dropped down between her thighs and sucked her clit between his lips. She moaned, the sound obviously out of her control, and he vowed to make her do it again and again.

Elle couldn't think. Half her brain was running around like it was on fire, Lane's words setting off every alarm in her head, but the other half had lost all functioning because all she could think about was the oh-my-God sensation of Lane's mouth on her again and the tight burning of her nipples beneath the clamps. Her body felt as if every erogenous zone were connected by wires, a touch or tug in one place setting off a cascade of sensations through the others.

Lane could love her?

He slipped his hands to the backs of her thighs and opened her wide, lashing her with his skilled tongue and digging his fingernails into her flesh. Somehow the pain kept her from flying apart. Kept her glued to the bed and rocking against Lane's mouth, begging for another orgasm, even when every other logical part of her screamed she should shut this down.

But why?

The dangerous thought whispered through her mind as she let herself open her eyes and watch this man who was pleasuring her. Just seeing his blond head made a warm feeling move through her. When he'd said he wanted to wake up to her face every morning, she'd wanted to shove the comment back, un-hear it, but the images had entered her head anyway. Tempting, sunrise-dappled scenes of Lane lying next to her in bed, all messy-haired and shirtless. Sharing coffee and their plans for the day. Touching. Cuddling.

And what *the fuck* was that about? She didn't cuddle.

That wasn't what her life was meant to be. She'd accepted that she would always live alone. She wanted to continue seeing Lane, but she'd meant in a dating capacity, not in a let's-fall-in-love-and-move-in-together capacity.

Lane pinched her thigh and she yelped, the sting bringing her back into the moment. He lifted his head. "Don't think so much, doc. Just feel what you feel."

"You can't expect me to—"

But before she could get the words out, he crawled up the bed and kissed her. He tasted like her and smelled like sin and sent her thoughts whizzing out of her head. She groaned into his mouth, his chest bumping against the clamps on her nipples and his cock brushing against her thigh.

Her sex throbbed and her legs opened wider. She didn't know what to do about the thoughts, about the words, but her body had one mission in mind and it pulled rank. She needed this man inside her. Right now.

She reached between them, taking him in her hand and guiding him to her entrance. *Need you, need you, need you.* His cock breached her, the feel of him like the answer to a prayer.

But Lane broke away from the kiss with a gasping breath. "Hold up. Condom. Not on yet."

The words didn't make sense at first, the erotic fog in her brain thick, but then they snapped into place. The bedside table where the condom was seemed so far away. And he felt so good. She didn't want the barrier. "I'm on the pill. And tested regularly. You?"

"I was tested a month ago, but I've never not…"

"Your call."

His eyes met hers, something breaking open in his gaze, something vulnerable and real. He grabbed her thigh and sank deep.

The velvet heat of him nearly sent her over the edge again. The orgasm from earlier seemed years in the past. But she breathed through the surge, trying to keep from ending this too quickly.

He tipped his head down, his cheek to hers, his eyes closed. "Thank fuck I already came once tonight because I would've just lit you up on the first thrust."

She laughed, the sound bubbling out of her and unfurling something inside her, lifting some of the weight of the night, making her forget why she was supposed to be worried. "Hold it together, Cannon. If you come before I do, I'm going to kick your ass."

He lifted his head with a wicked grin. "Oh, don't worry. I'm going to take good care of you, gorgeous."

He buried himself fully and ground his pelvis right against her clit, making tension coil low and deep. "Oh, God."

"Hold that thought," he said, and quickly pulled the clips from her breasts.

Sharp, fiery pain radiated outward as blood rushed back into her nipples and set them aflame. Her eyes watered and she gasped, but almost as fast as it started, the sensation changed course, linking up with the rocking, grinding pressure against her clit. Pleasure exploded low and fanned outward like a sonic boom, sending her crying out and grappling for Lane.

He held on and pumped hard into her, angling just right,

hitting the place she needed most and launching her into an orgasm. She called his name and scraped her nails down his back. He lowered his head and latched onto her tender nipple, pressing his teeth into it and setting off more fireworks. Release arced through her and pushed her higher. She peaked with a loud, desperate cry and felt his muscles ripple beneath her fingers. He plunged deep, his release bathing her with hot, wicked pleasure.

He buried his face in her neck and breathed through his orgasm, whispering sweet things and praise and finally one simple sentence. "I might not even wait for your permission."

He could love her. Even if she didn't let him.

The words should terrify her.

Make her run.

But in that moment, she couldn't find it in herself to be scared. She just wanted to curl into him…and cuddle.

chapter twenty two

Lane was quiet on the way back to her mom's house early the next morning, occasionally mentioning something inconsequential or pointing out interesting things they passed in the city, but nothing beyond that. Elle sensed that he was giving her space.

She appreciated that gift and clung to it.

She'd lain next to him all night, barely sleeping, her brain on blender mode and her heart trying to elbow its way into the mix. This was territory she hadn't traversed before, and she felt as if she were wearing flip-flops and a cocktail dress to climb Everest. She had no clue how to even…process this. She brought her coffee to her lips and sipped, wishing it held answers instead of just a jolt of caffeine.

"You sure you want to go back to your family's place?" he asked. "I could just go in and get our stuff."

She shook her head. "No, I'm not going to run away from it. I caused a scene, which I'll apologize for because that wasn't my intention."

"You were provoked."

She sighed. "Even so, I should've walked away. I doubt they still want me at the wedding, but I don't want to look like I'm turning tail and running. Plus, I came here to visit with my mother. I can still do that at least."

His big hands flexed around the steering wheel. "Do you still want me to go in with you? I could leave you with the car and rent one to get back to The Grove."

She frowned. "Why would you do that?"

He peered her way. "They know what I do now. If that's going to be awkward for—"

"No," she said. She wasn't sure of a lot of things but she was sure of that. "No shame, remember?"

"Right." He nodded. "Doc, about last night—"

"I can't."

His expression turned guarded. "Can't what?"

She took a breath. "Talk about last night right now. I need to handle the drama with my family first. When we get back to The Grove, we can deal with last night."

His jaw twitched and he looked back to the road. "Right. Deal with it."

She caught the edge in his tone but didn't know what to say. She didn't have answers for him. She didn't regret last night, hearing the things Lane had said, sharing the things they'd shared. But the light of day brought things hidden by the fog of sex into sharp relief. The problems they'd left behind at The Grove didn't go away just because they weren't there right now.

Maybe she could learn to take a compliment, to be sweet with Lane, to trust him. God knows they had enough chemistry to set the world on fire. But one thing kept sticking pins in her balloons of hope no matter how she tried to find her way around it.

How was she going to accept being in a serious relationship with someone who slept with other women for a living? The thought had gnawed at her last night until she'd wanted to scream. She wished she could be so self-assured that his patients wouldn't feel like a threat, but she saw who walked into The Grove. Beautiful, young actresses, sexy musicians, wealthy businesswomen. She would have to share him with those people, and she couldn't imagine swallowing that particular pill down without choking.

And that's what had her gut churning this morning.

She was falling for someone who wasn't hers to have alone.

They pulled in front of her mother's house, the sky still dark at this early hour but the porch light burning.

"Looks like we're not the only ones up," Lane said.

Elle's gaze drifted to the far side of the porch, where a woman bundled in a blue shawl sat on one of the rocking chairs. Elle frowned. "That's weird. Nina's always been a late sleeper."

Lane sniffed. "She's getting married. That'll keep anyone awake. Lifetime commitment and all. Scary stuff."

She peered over at him and attempted to smirk. "Says Mr. Relationship."

"Mr. Relationship?" He lifted a skeptical brow. "Is that how you see me?"

She shrugged, though the move felt tight. "You said some pretty heavy things last night. Most guys would've been terrified to go there."

He stared at her and shook his head, wry amusement on his face. "You assume I wasn't terrified. That I'm not *still* terrified. That I haven't spent my whole life avoiding anything long term."

She blinked, the words taking a moment to register. "But the things you said…"

He glanced up at the porch and then back to her, his green eyes clear but a little sad. "You were worth the risk to me." He pulled the keys from the ignition. "I guess now it's your turn to decide if I'm worth the same."

With that, he unhooked his seatbelt and opened the door, leaving her staring after him, her heart sinking into her toes. He opened her car door to let her out, but he didn't wait for her.

He strode up the walk, greeted Nina briefly, and then disappeared into the house. Nina glanced out toward the car, obviously looking for her, and Elle's muscles froze in place. She didn't want to deal with any of this right now, especially not her sister.

But Elle was supposed to be the mature one. The logical one. The tough one.

With a heavy sigh, she grabbed her purse and coffee, slipped her heels back on and got out of the car. She tried to walk up the path like she didn't have a care in the world, but it was hard to look dignified when her feet were throbbing from the new shoes and her dress was so wrinkled it might as well have been made from tinfoil.

Elle felt her sister watching her. She gave Nina a prim nod. "Morning."

"Hey." Nina's eyes were bloodshot, her nose red around the edges.

Elle told herself to keep walking, but some old big sister habit decided to show up at the wrong time and had her halting her step. She let out a tired breath. "Are you okay?"

Nina sniffled. "Would you care if I wasn't?"

Elle frowned and set her coffee on the porch rail. "I don't know. It depends, I guess."

"At least you're honest." Nina took the shawl that was wrapped around her and swiped at her eyes. "I guess I wouldn't give a shit about me either if you'd done to me what I did to you."

Elle didn't answer that. What was there to say? *You're right?*

"I canceled the wedding."

The words dropped like a heavy stone between them. Elle stared. "What? Why? Because he has a busted nose?"

Nina looked down at the fringed edges of the shawl, separating the strings with her fingers. "Well, that would've made for some interesting wedding photos."

"Nina, you can't cancel the whole—"

"I didn't do it because of that." She shook her head, still staring down at her fingers working the shawl, her expression distant. "I did it because last night I realized what this has been about all along." She smirked, no humor in it. "This wasn't about love or fate. I was part of a revenge mission. Henry wanted to marry me to get the final word with you."

Elle sank into the other rocking chair, her mind whirling.

"I mean, I'm not dumb. Or at least not *that* dumb. I suspected that was part of it early on, when our relationship first started. He was so *angry* with you. The things he would say about you."

Elle swallowed past the squeezing tightness in her throat. Henry had never shown that to her back then. He'd played the part of doting husband, the resentments manifesting in more quiet, insidious ways instead. If anyone had been dumb, it'd been Elle.

"But I thought that eventually…we fell in love for real. That it was meant to be. That's why I gave up so much to have him, pushed down the guilt. I thought *I'd* be the one shunned from the family. I was willing to give it all up for him. I never thought they'd expect you to…accept it." Nina rubbed the spot between her eyes. "But then you were so hateful afterward and it just confirmed all the things he'd told me about you, the side I didn't see."

Elle stared. "You slept with *my husband*. How did you expect me to react? Did you want me to throw you a party?"

"I know," she said, her voice breaking, her tone desperate. "I know how horrible I was, okay? How wrong. I'm the worst sister in the world. But…" Tears pooled. "I loved him."

"More than you loved me," Elle said flatly, wholly unmoved by the tears.

Nina stared at her lap, tears falling onto her wringing hands. "I was blinded by it. Haven't you ever been blinded by love? It's like a goddamned drug. You make dangerous and stupid decisions. You're willing to sacrifice everything."

Elle's stomach tightened and she glanced warily toward the house, picturing Lane tucked away in her old room.

"We've been happy," Nina said, her voice catching on the last word like it'd gotten sticky in her throat. "I thought it was all meant to be. But when you showed up this weekend, he was so…unhinged by you and Lane. Why would he care who you brought to the wedding? Why would he go through the trouble of digging up your fiancé's record?" She swiped at her nose. "And then after everything went down last night, all he could do was rant about you. You bringing a guy here has driven him crazy. The jealousy was so transparent it was laughable. It was like I wasn't even there."

Elle frowned and pulled a tissue out of her purse, handing it to Nina and not knowing what to say.

She took it and crumpled it in her fist. "I'm such an idiot. All this time, it's just been about you. I'm a tool to get back at you. You must've thought I was such a joke."

Elle released a breath, a bone-deep weariness settling in and dampening some of her anger. Betrayed or not, she had a hard time watching her little sister in pain. "I don't think that's really the case. Henry wouldn't have stayed with you this long if there wasn't something there between you. I haven't been in the picture. Seeing me probably just triggered old resentments. He may genuinely love you, but he's also a selfish, self-centered asshole who couldn't stand seeing me happy with someone else. The two things can exist concurrently."

Nina looked up, eyes puffy with tears, reminding Elle of the baby sister she used to be instead of the grown woman who'd stabbed her in the back.

"*Are* you happy?" Nina asked softly.

Happy. Elle's chest compressed with some unfamiliar emotion and she rolled her lips inward, trying to keep her composure as she thought about the last two months with Lane. Was she happy? Could she even recognize what that felt like anymore?

But warmth moved through her as pictures filled her head, of last night, of the evenings she'd shared with Lane, of the way she felt when she was curled up in his arms or even just bantering with him.

She didn't know what exactly that feeling was, if it could be called happiness, but she knew it made her stomach dip and her lips want to curve. "I could be. Maybe. I'm working on it."

"With Lane?"

Elle clasped her now damp palms in her lap and nodded. "Yes. With Lane."

She tilted her head. "Is he really your fiancé?"

"No," she admitted. "We're...dating."

"And he's a sex surrogate? Like, sleeps with strangers? I googled it last night."

Elle adjusted the hem of her dress. "Yes. It's an important position at The Grove. He helps people who have sexual problems. It's not seedy like people think. It's a legitimate form of therapy."

"Wow." Nina leaned back in her chair and shook her head, an awed look on her face. "You must have confidence of steel, Ellie. I'm not sure I could deal with knowing that the man I was with had that kind of job. He must be a really great guy to make that worth it."

Elle smiled, though a hollow feeling pinged in her chest. "He's an amazing guy."

"And super hot," Nina said with a smirk. "Like, had to pick my tongue up off the ground when he walked into your kitchen shirtless that day. Christ."

"That doesn't hurt." Elle laughed, the sound drifting between them and into a foreign space. She didn't laugh with her sister anymore.

Nina pulled her knees to her chest and wrapped her arms around them. "I'm glad he makes you happy. You deserve that more than any of us."

Elle looked down.

"What we did, what *I* did, was unforgivable." Her voice wavered. "I know I've said it before, but I mean every word of it. I'm sorry. I am so sorry, Ellie."

Elle's teeth pressed against each other, emotion bubbling up past her guards. Nina had said she was sorry before but this one hit home. The regret seemed genuine. But Elle didn't know how to close the chasm between them. So much had been lost. "I just don't understand why you did it. Or why you didn't come to me when he first made a pass at you or you started having feelings for him. At least give me a way out with dignity instead of making me the fool. You could've given me that."

"I know," she said, quiet tears surfacing again. "I was a coward and selfish. I let Henry tell me that fate intervened and that we couldn't help ourselves and that you pushed him away, that it was just bad timing. I wanted to have that romantic story, the we-were-meant-to-be thing. But I chose to believe those things to make myself feel better." She let out a rattling breath. "Truth is, I was lonely and depressed. I'd been fired and didn't know what to do with my life. I resented you having it all together. You had the good-looking husband, the big-time job, the brains. It always looked like everything came so easy to you. So when Henry came to me, telling me I could give him something you couldn't, I wanted to believe it. It made me feel special."

Elle closed her eyes, the memories from back then assaulting her. Her sister sleeping in the guest room, the lost look on her face, their parents calling daily to see if Nina had gotten a job yet. She'd let Nina stay with them because she wanted to help, to give her encouragement, but she hadn't. She'd been too wrapped up in building her own career to pay attention.

"I'm sorry," Nina said again. "I don't know how I could ever fix it, but if it makes you feel any better, karma has paid me back.

I'm left with less than I had before. In my thirties, canceling a wedding, and working a job that I hate. I've wasted all these years on a man who used me to hurt someone else and I lost my only sister. I'm alone, and I deserve every bit of the pain that goes along with that."

Elle lifted her head, finding Nina's face tear-streaked but her eyes sincere. Her heart squeezed in her chest. "It doesn't make me feel better to see you hurting. You're my sister. You've broken my heart but I never wanted bad things for you."

Nina lowered her head to her knees, her shoulders jerking with a sob. "I'm so sorry."

Something broke inside Elle as she stared at her sister, a long-fossilized relic crumbling. Memories filtered through the haze. Nina falling off her bike when she was seven and running to Elle to fix it like a doctor. Nina curling up in Elle's bed on nights when the spring thunderstorms got too loud. Nina painting portraits of all the animals in the neighborhood and putting on an art show so they could earn money to buy a puppy—an idea her father had squashed even when they'd made enough.

They'd been each other's best friend for so long, their childhoods inextricably intertwined because their parents had rarely been home. They'd sworn to always be there for each other. They'd both broken that promise. Nina in a more dramatic way and Elle in a subtle abandonment, once she'd started her own career. She'd followed her mother's example, and Nina had been left behind. It didn't excuse what her sister had done, but it at least explained where her head had been. She hadn't done it out of vindictiveness. She'd done it out of loneliness, and Henry had smoothly offered her an enticing solution.

Elle stood and walked over to her sister. She put her hand on her shoulder, the contact feeling foreign. "I believe that you're sorry."

Nina lifted her head, a glimmer of hope on her face. "Really?"

Elle sighed and stepped back, putting her hand out. "Come here."

Nina's brow scrunched in confusion at first, but then it registered. She rose from the rocking chair, the shawl falling to the porch, and Nina stepped close to her, unsure and awkward. Elle put her arms around her sister and hugged her.

"You're going to survive life without Henry. You deserve better than someone like him, anyway. We both do."

Nina crumpled in her arms at that and pressed her face into Elle's shoulder. "I've missed you so much."

Tears slipped down Elle's face, her muscles unknotting. "I've missed you, too."

And that was the truth. Elle had felt the loss of her failed marriage. But she'd mourned Nina more. She didn't know if they'd ever be able to recapture the relationship they'd had before Henry, but maybe they could find a new path where they could be in each other's lives.

Nina sobbed softly and they stood holding each other for long minutes. The sun peeked over the horizon, slanting warmth along Elle's back, and hope bloomed fresh inside her. The start of a new day...and maybe the start of a lot of other things in her life.

Only when their mother stuck her head out the door did they pull apart.

"Come on, girls," her mom said softly, her eyes brighter than Elle had seen them in a long time. "It's time for breakfast."

chapter twenty three

Lane climbed out of the car after pulling up in front of Elle's house and set her bag on the porch. Elle busied herself digging her keys out of her purse. The entire road trip home, they'd managed to stick to safe topics like Elle's new truce with her sister and if her mother needed anything before her surgery. They'd dutifully avoided talking about the state of their relationship—or if there even was going to be one.

He wasn't going to take back what he'd said on Friday night. He'd been honest. But he also wasn't going to force the issue. She'd had life-changing shit thrown at her this weekend. He didn't plan to add to the pile. He could push her boundaries in the bedroom. He wouldn't on this.

"I want to try," she said from somewhere behind him.

He turned, distracted. "Try what? Visiting home more?"

That had been the last topic they'd covered, and he figured she was ruminating over it.

She frowned and hitched her purse higher on her shoulder. "No. Try with you."

"Try what with me?" he asked cautiously.

She straightened her spine, looking somehow fierce and adorable at the same time. "Dating...with intention. And an open mind."

An open mind. Which meant an open road. None of the rules and restrictions they'd been messing with. Freedom. His lips curved on their own. "Yeah?"

She exhaled and squinted toward the pond in the distance, as if looking at him was too much. "Yeah. I think..."

When the sentence drifted off and she still wasn't looking his way, he reached out and touched her elbow. "You think what, doc?"

She tipped her head back and looked at the sky like she wished she could beam herself up to some other place. "I think you make me happy, okay?"

The words hit him right in the sternum, unexpected and breath-stealing. *He made her happy.* But the perturbed look on her face had a laugh rumbling out of him. "You sound kind of pissed about that."

She groaned and finally looked at him, those bright blue eyes drilling right into him. "I am, a little. This wasn't the plan. You were supposed to be..."

"Just a hot piece of ass on a lonely Friday night?" he supplied with a smirk. "Let's face it, I'm still that on every night of the week. All is not lost."

She snorted. "You're not going to make this easy on me, are you?"

He crossed his arms, all too pleased. "Nope."

"Fine." She rolled her shoulders, looking ever the put-together doctor, though anxiety flickered in her eyes. "Yes, you were supposed to be a hookup. You weren't supposed to matter.

You weren't supposed to make me want things I'd given up on. And you definitely weren't supposed to make me feel…lost at the thought of you walking out of my life."

His heart gave a hard thump in his chest, all desire to joke draining out of him. He took her hands in his. "Doc…"

"I don't know if I'll be any good at this because Lord knows I've made a disaster of it so far, but I want to try. I want to be happy…with you." She shrugged a shoulder. "You know, if you want that, too."

He laced his fingers with hers and pulled her to him, guiding her hands around his waist. He gazed down at her, a surge of affection welling and nearly choking off his words. "I want that. So much. You make me happy, too, doc."

She closed her eyes, released a breath.

"Well, when you're not driving me absolutely batshit crazy," he added, hoping to take some of the pressure off. He could see how hard this was for her, how frightening. It scared the hell out of him, too. Things between them had been fast and intense. They were both driving headlong into unknown territory, but neither of them were ready to jump out of the car.

A quiet, derisive laugh escaped her. "But fair warning, I have no idea what I'm doing."

"If it makes you feel better, I don't know how to do this either." He cupped her face and tilted it toward him, catching her gaze. "But I know how I feel when I'm with you. That's what matters. We can figure out the rest as we go along."

A softness crossed her face, one he'd never seen on her. It nearly broke his heart in two. This was the woman behind the layers of armor. This was the woman who'd been hurt and betrayed, who'd been let down by the people who loved her.

This was her trusting him not to crush her.

He hoped to God he was worthy of the gift.

He slid his hands into her hair, bent his head, and kissed her. Because one more second without her lips on his would've been too much.

She melted into the kiss like she'd been needing it just as badly as he had. Her lips parted, granting him entry, and she aligned her body to his. Soft and pliant. But when he slid his hand along her nape and gripped, she groaned, and the sweet turned steamy almost instantly.

He put his other hand to her hip and fitted her against him, his cock stiffening at the feel of her heat. His tongue stroked hers, and he guided her against the column of her porch, pressing her into it. He wanted to slide her skirt up her hips, stroke her, push aside her panties and see if she was as ready he felt, but he reined in the impulse.

She was willing to go public with their relationship, not get naked on campus. He had to remember that they both had professional reputations to maintain. He broke away from the kiss. "How about we take this inside, gorgeous?"

"Good idea," she said, her chest rising and falling with panted breaths.

She hurried to unlock the door and he grabbed her bag. The door hadn't even clicked shut behind them before he was dropping the suitcase and lifting her over his shoulder. He kicked the door shut behind him.

"What are you doing?"

He wrapped his arm around the back of her thighs and flipped her skirt up with his other hand, revealing lacy, cream-colored panties. He gave her a quick smack to her ass. "Claiming you."

She grunted against his back. "Caveman."

"Sometimes," he admitted, carrying her down the hallway. "But that gets you wet, so what does that make you?"

She sighed heavily, feigning boredom. "Don't be so proud of yourself. I'm not turned on by this, you know."

He smiled and halted his step in the hallway in front of a mirror. With his free hand, he tugged aside her panties, the view of all that pretty pink flesh making his cock go painfully hard against his zipper.

"What are you doing?"

He dragged his fingertips over her, his fingers coming away slick and a tremor working through her body. "You're such a liar, doc. A filthy liar with a needy, wet pussy."

The words were crude, but the mirror gave him all the confirmation he needed. Her muscles clenched, her body reacting to the dirty talk like he'd stroked her again. Heat suffused through him and all his blood rushed south.

"You're disgusting," she said, but the breathlessness in her voice gave her away.

"You fucking love it." He swung away from the mirror, carrying her to the bedroom with singular purpose.

When they got inside, he lowered her to the bed onto her back, and she sat up on her elbows, fire in her eyes. He could stroke himself off to that image alone, Elle's hair mussed, her knees spread, and challenge all over her face. *I dare you to fuck me.* That was the overt message. But another, more dangerous one whispered at the back of his mind.

I dare you to love me.

Everything in that look said she wouldn't make it easy on him. She wouldn't hide that fact. She'd challenge him, keep him on his toes, not let him get away with any shortcuts. He fucking loved that about her. Elle was a lot of things—smart, beautiful, tough. But what drew him to her over and over again was that intense confidence that made him bring his A-game.

She demanded more of him. He wanted to be more for her.

"Take off your panties and show me how *not* turned on you are," he challenged.

She cocked an eyebrow at him, reached down to tug off her underwear, and then bold as you please, dragged the material over herself, removing any evidence of how wet she'd become. She parted her knees, giving him an X-rated view that had his tongue pressing against the roof of his mouth.

He smirked, trying to look unimpressed even though his dick was about to break through his zipper. "That's cheating, sweetheart."

"I don't know what you're talking about," she said breezily. "This is doing nothing for me."

He unbuckled his belt and slid it through the loops, making sure it snapped when he pulled it fully out. "Well, if you're not going to play by the rules, then I don't need to either."

Her gaze jumped to the leather in his hand, a flicker of unease crossing her face. "What are you doing?"

He stalked over to the bed, taking his time, enjoying how warily she watched him. Two predators sizing each other up. Without giving her warning, he lifted her up and flipped her over. She let out a little sound of protest, but he had her hands behind her before she could offer much of a fight. He gripped her wrists in one hand and held her in place as he used the looped belt to flip her skirt up. Her wrists twitched in his grip, but she didn't try to pull free. He smiled at the silent permission.

He dragged the warm leather over her ass, relishing the way she shivered. "Your scent's filling the room, doc. One would think you might be begging for me to stripe you with this belt."

"Fuck off."

"That's not the magic word."

He lifted the belt and let it fall along the lower part of her ass, not too hard since they hadn't played this way before but enough to make her feel the sting and make her skin go pink.

She gasped and her hips rocked back automatically...toward the belt, not away.

He licked his lips at the sight. He could give up pain play if Elle wasn't into it, but her eager response had his engine revving. To be able to play these kinds of games with her, walk these lines, and know that they were both getting off on it...that was magic.

No, not magic, a miracle. A miracle to find it in someone like Elle, someone who he was just as drawn to outside the bedroom as he was in it. He'd never found both sides of his desires met in the same person.

He brought the belt down again, this time right above the first spot. She groaned into the mattress. That was all he needed to hear. He held her in place, wielded the leather in short bursts, and turned her ass pink all over. When she was writhing and cursing into the mattress, he leaned over and dragged his tongue along her heated skin, then bit.

"Son of a bitch." The words were sharp but the tone was much more *God, yes* than insult.

He drew his fingers along the slippery flesh between her legs. "Beg me to fuck you, Elle. I can make that ache you're feeling go away, can make that burn turn into something much more satisfying."

"Who says I need you to take care of it?" she shot back.

He smiled and wrapped the belt around her wrists, binding her so he could release his grip on her. "Oh, you'd rather your narrow little fingers? Or maybe the good doctor has a toy supply. I bet you do." He checked the tightness on the binding, making sure it was holding her but not cutting into her skin. "Now that I have you tied up, maybe I should check."

"Stay out of my stuff, Cannon."

He smiled. Still not a safe word. "Where would the good doctor keep her stash?" he wondered aloud, teasing her. "She's too rude to let anyone sleep over, so she probably wouldn't go through too much trouble to hide it."

He went over to one bedside drawer, naming the contents as he went through. "A novel, batteries, a remote control…aww, a journal. I wonder if you've drawn hearts around my name."

Elle turned her head his way, worry flashing across her face. "Not the journal."

He could hear the change in tone, the lack of playfulness in it. He reached over and tapped her chin, getting her to look at him. "I was kidding. I wouldn't do that to you. Got it?"

She swallowed hard. "Okay."

"But these"—he pulled out a flesh-toned dildo/vibrator combo and a small bottle of lubricant—"these are exactly what I was looking for."

Her gaze followed him as he walked around the bed and stopped behind her again. He ran his palm over her reddened skin, loving the shiver she gave him in return. Everything would be sensitive now, the tingling nerves making her aware of every part below her waist. He grabbed a pillow from the top of the bed and positioned it under her hips.

"What are you doing?"

"You said you didn't need me. I'm proving your point. You should be thankful. I'm agreeing with you." He reached around her hips and angled the dildo inside her, pushing slowly and getting the small silicon attachment to press against her clit.

She hissed out a breath. He smiled, pleased with the response, and positioned the pillow so it'd hold the toy in place. Then, he turned it on.

"Fuck." Her body gave a start as if she'd been shocked and her fingers curled into the sheets.

"Someone went for high voltage last time she got herself off." He dialed the speed down. "Don't want to rush you, doc. That'd make it too easy."

He dragged a wingback chair from the corner of the room and positioned it in her line of sight. Her cheek was pressed into the bed and her gaze burned into him, focused even though the vibrator was obviously working some magic on her. He sat down for the show.

"You're just going to sit there?" she demanded.

He smiled and casually unbuttoned his jeans. "You said you didn't need me, so I thought I'd just enjoy the view."

He slipped his hand inside his pants and freed his aching erection. He gave himself a slow stroke, and Elle's hips rocked, probably of their own volition based on the frustrated wrinkle in her brow.

"Better be careful how much you move, don't want to dislodge the vibrator." He ran his thumb over the head of his cock, spreading the fluid there and enjoying the feel of it as he kept his eyes solidly on Elle. "That wouldn't be any fun for you, watching me come with no help for yourself at all."

"You're a selfish bastard. I doubt you'd care."

He shrugged. "You're probably right. But remember, if you need me to fuck you, I can. You just have to ask...nicely."

"Screw you."

He tilted some of the lubricant in his palm and then fisted his cock, sending a ripple of pleasure through him but enjoying the hungry look on Elle's face more. Her hands twisted in the binding of the belt and she rolled her hips against the pillow, trying to get more stimulation. He'd set it low enough that it was probably a losing fight. It'd be just enough to get her riding the edge but not enough to put her over. He wasn't above stacking the deck when it came to these games. He liked to play dirty, too.

"How's the silicone feel, doc?"

"Bigger than you."

He smirked, knowing that wasn't true. "How many times have you fucked the vibrating wonder? Do you imagine it's attached to someone or do you get off knowing you're doing it to yourself?"

"I don't need to imagine anyone. I'm a pretty good lay."

He chuckled. "Confident."

Her gaze dipped back down to his hand and he spread his knees wide, cupping his balls and glossing himself up in the lewdest way possible. Elle was riveted, and that only drove his need for her higher. He was playing the game like he didn't care, but his whole body ached to plunge deep into hers.

Patience. That was going to be the name of the game.

Who would break first?

Elle thought her body might implode. Lane's big hand stroked lube over every inch of his cock until it was thick, hard, and shiny, and all she could think about was how good it would feel to have him inside her. Her trusty vibrator was betraying her with its gentle, maddening hum against her clit— just enough to make her toes curl but not enough to give her any relief. She ground her hips shamelessly, trying to get more stimulation, but it only teased her more.

Meanwhile, Lane looked as if he had all the time in the world. He was sprawled in that chair like a decadent king, legs wide, eyes half-mast, pleasing himself but teasing the hell out of her. She wasn't sure she'd ever seen a man look more enticing. Lane wore his eroticism like a second skin, like he was one-hundred percent comfortable with himself.

He had to be with his job, she imagined, but she couldn't think about that now. Right now, all she could think about was getting him back to the bed with her. She needed him, and both of them knew there was only one way she was going to get him.

She cleared her throat, a needy tremble working through her body as the vibrator pushed against her clit again. "You win," she said hoarsely. "I want you. I need you to fuck me."

Lane's brows lifted. "I didn't hear a please."

She swallowed past the instinct to argue back. In this game, they would both win. "Please fuck me. I would be ever so grateful."

He smiled despite her mocking tone. "Wow, look how nicely the doctor can beg. I even believe she half means it."

"Yeah, the bottom half means it wholeheartedly. The top half is giving you the finger."

A low chuckle rumbled from him. "Good thing I only need

the bottom half right now."

He stood and walked over to her, hand still absently holding himself. He bent close to her ear. "You trust me, doc?"

The words sent prickly awareness through her. With any other man she'd been with since her divorce, she would've instantly answered, *No, back the hell off.* But the answer came easily this time. "Yes."

He kissed behind her ear. "Good. Because I plan to make us both feel very, very good."

She wasn't sure exactly what he had in mind, but a calmness filled the space inside her head that would normally start analyzing everything. This was Lane. He'd take care of her. And if anything went amiss, he'd respect her safe word. She was safe with him.

Lane released her hands from the belt's binding. "Get your elbows beneath you, pretty girl."

The little endearment would've freaked her out in the past, but now it warmed her. She settled on her arms and took a deep breath as Lane trailed a palm over her backside. He grabbed the base of the vibrator and gave it a few pumps, angling it inside her and hitting all the right places.

She sighed into the mattress.

"I'm thinking our silicone friend here might help us out. Maybe I'll keep him right where he is."

She didn't know what he meant but when he dragged a lubricated finger over her asshole, she automatically clenched.

"Easy," he said, as if he were soothing a horse. He kissed her tailbone. "I can make you feel really good, but you'll have to do your part. You'll need to trust me and relax."

She inhaled a deep breath, trying to recapture that calm

place inside her, but her heart was hammering against her ribs. She remembered him threatening this that first night together. The thought had both intrigued and terrified her. The fantasy of it pushed all those sexy, forbidden buttons, but reality didn't always match fantasy. There were a lot of things she could fantasize about that she didn't believe would be all that fantastic in real life. But the calm confidence in Lane's voice soothed her. He wouldn't try anything with her that he didn't think she'd enjoy. He was dominant in bed, but generous, and had always focused on her pleasure. If he wanted to do this, it was because he believed it'd feel good for them both.

"Still with me, doc?" he asked, voice soft.

She swallowed past the initial kick of anxiety. "For now."

"Good." His finger pressed against her opening, and the touch alone sent nerve endings waking up and standing at attention, but instead of the expected discomfort, a wash of pleasure went through her. The vibrator had keyed her up so much already that it was converting everything into sweet, liquid oh-hell-yes sensations. He eased his finger inside, giving her body time to catch up and soften. She groaned into the mattress.

Lane whispered words of filthy encouragement, his own voice dipping into an octave that meant this was driving him wild, too. One finger, then another, Lane worked her sensitive opening while keeping the vibrator moving just right with his other hand. He was the musician and she his instrument. She'd never heard this song before but she was ready to buy the album and a ticket to the concert.

He scissored his fingers with slow, steady attention and a tremor went through her muscles. A curse slipped past her lips.

"I want to take you here, Elle," he said, his voice deep and gravel-filled. "I want to feel you squeezing my cock as I fill you up and that vibrator works on us both."

She writhed against the touch and at the words, her body slick with sweat and demanding more. Right now, he was making her walk the edge but not letting her fall over. She wanted to fall over. "Get on with it then, just let me come."

She could almost hear him smile behind her. "Such a bossy woman."

"You love it," she bit out, another kick of pleasure making her body clench around his fingers.

"I do." He angled the vibrator right against her G-spot, making her gasp. "That makes it more satisfying when I bring the great doctor to a whimpering, begging mess."

"I. Do. Not. Whimper." But her panted breaths lied.

"Don't speak too soon, sweet thing." His fingers slipped out of her, making her feel oddly empty, and the rustle of clothing sounded behind her.

She closed her eyes, concentrating on the slow, steady pleasure the vibrator was offering and trying not to overthink about what the next step might feel like. But when the head of Lane's cock pressed against her ass, instead of fear rising, a bone-deep need shuddered through her. She wanted him. In all ways.

He stroked her hip. "Just breathe easy, baby, and relax your muscles. Push out when I push in. I'm nice and slick. I'm going to make us both feel good."

She did as she was told, not wanting to question at this point, and felt the head of his cock stretch her. A brief dart of panic chased up her spine. Everything felt like too much, too big, but then he eased in and her tension gave way, accepting him into that most private space. Lane groaned as he seated deep, his fingers digging into her hips, and she let out a gritty moan as her nerve endings lit up.

Everything felt alive and sensitive and oh-so-fucking good.

"Hold the vibrator in place," he said, his voice strained.

She slipped her hand between her legs, doing as she was told, and Lane slowly pumped into her again.

Her brain blinked off and everything became sensation. The heat of them skin to skin, the full feeling of his cock and the vibrator inside her, the slow, steady hum of the toy teasing her clit and converting everything into pure epic pleasure.

"You okay, doc?" Lane asked between breaths.

"Yes."

"Ready to beg yet?" he teased, though the words sounded labored, like he was waging his own battle to keep it together.

"No."

He rocked back and slid deep again, groaning. "Fuck."

Her body trembled, the need for release nearly breaking her. "I lied. Please. *I need you.*"

His grip tightened and he reached down to click the vibrator to a higher speed. "Come with me, gorgeous. Let me feel you fall apart."

He picked up the pace of his thrusts, but didn't get too rough—just smooth, long, and deep—as if he sensed exactly how precarious the pleasure/pain balance was. But everything inside her hummed with the anticipation of oblivion. So close. So close. Then Lane whispered her name like it was the most sacred word in the English language, and the blackness behind her eyelids broke into a thousand fragments of light. Her orgasm swept over her, blurring all the sensations together and making her cry out in a pitch she didn't even know she was capable of.

Lane's thrusts became quicker and more fervent as he pushed her pleasure higher, not relenting with just the quick burst of an orgasm but dragging it out and transforming it into a whole-body event. She cried out his name, panted through the blinding sensations, and forgot where she was for a second. Lane's shouts joined hers and he gripped her hips tight before pulling out and painting her backside with his hot release.

Every muscle in her body quaked with aftershocks, and her lungs fought for a deep breath. But never had she felt so damn sated.

She eased the vibrator out, tossing it out of the way, and collapsed bonelessly onto the bed. Lane lay atop her, breathing hard, their bodies sticky and sweaty, but she didn't care about the mess. She didn't care about anything else right now but the man on top of her and the way he made her feel.

She turned her head to the side, her vision unfocused and her muscles still twitching with post-orgasm. "Well, that was a passable attempt at sex. I mean, if you're into that kind of thing."

Lane laughed softly and kissed the back of her shoulder. "I adore you, Elle McCray."

She closed her eyes, a sated happiness filling her veins and stirring feelings she hadn't thought she was capable of anymore. "I adore you back, Lane Cannon."

chapter twenty four

"You want to do dinner?" Elle asked Wednesday morning as she put down her mascara wand and enjoyed the view of Lane standing in her bedroom with just a towel around his waist.

Lane dug through his bag, which he'd been working out of since they'd gotten back from her mom's on Sunday, and pulled out some fresh clothes. He dropped the towel, offering her a view that had her wanting to tumble back into bed—broad body, hard muscles, ass that was begging to be bitten—but he tugged on his boxer briefs before she could make herself late for work.

Lane ran the towel through his wet hair and turned her way. "Sure, but it might not be until late. I have class most of the day, am supposed to meet with Marin and a new referral this afternoon, and then have a late session with a client. That should wrap up by eight."

Elle's stomach dipped. She wasn't in denial. She was all too aware of what Lane did for a living, but this was the first time since they'd decided to try a relationship that he'd be seeing a client. She wanted to be mature about it. She wanted to act nonchalant. "Involved session?"

She cringed inwardly. Could she be more transparent? *Ugh.*

He frowned. "You know I can't share details. But not... intercourse."

Something loosened in her chest—though didn't unravel completely. "What percentage of your clients require that... level of intervention?"

He draped the towel around his neck, holding both ends taut. "A smaller percentage than most people would guess. It's usually a lot of talking, building rapport, developing a comfort level. Often there's trauma in the past so things progress very slowly and deliberately. Most common issues I see are anxiety around sex, orgasmic disorders, problems with arousal, phobias about sex or their bodies. The majority of my job is giving clients a safe place and patience to tackle those things. Lovers have a tendency to rush their partners even if they're trying to be understanding about an issue. I'm not there to get off, so I can be as patient and focused as necessary. It's all about the client, always."

The clinical breakdown gave her some comfort. She didn't doubt Lane was a professional, but she also didn't want to picture him in those sessions with strangers. "A late dinner is fine. I can get takeout from Vincent's if that works for you."

He tossed the towel aside and pulled on his pants, his expression a little warier than it had been a minute before. "You know, one day we could try eating in public. I've heard it's all the rage."

She didn't miss the dig. He was still worried that she would try to hide their relationship. She wasn't avoiding a public place per se. They'd just both been busy the last two days. "We can go out. Do you want to meet me here after your late session?"

"I'll actually be at that dance studio on Collins, so I won't be on campus. If you want to meet me there around eight, we could find something nearby."

"Dance studio?"

"Yeah. This case required some out-of-the-office work."

"Right." She couldn't imagine what a dance studio would have to do with anything but he wouldn't be able to answer any questions without breaking confidentiality. "That works."

He buttoned his shirt then walked over to her. He cupped her chin and bent to kiss her, the simple connection sending pleasant warmth tracking through her. He leaned back, his gaze holding hers. "You sure you're okay? Honestly?"

She sighed. "I'm a work in progress on the possessive, jealousy thing."

He nodded, no censure in his expression, and lowered himself to his haunches so he could be eye to eye. "I know this is asking a lot, doc. I know it's a weird job, but it *is* my job. It's important to me, and I've worked hard to get it. I don't plan on it being a forever thing but it's a right-now thing. And I like knowing I'm helping people." He took her hand and sandwiched it between his. "But what I can promise you is that I am absolutely one-hundred percent professional with my clients. I am always safe. I have never had or wanted to have a relationship with a client. I don't derive sexual pleasure from them. It's about their issues and how I can help. I imagine it's similar to if some hot A-list actor has to strip down in your office for an exam. You know how to be a professional. And so do I."

She took a deep breath and tried to blow out some of the

tension. He was right in that she knew how to separate professional and personal modes. Good-looking men got naked for her on the regular at work, but it was clinical. Not sexy at all. However, she was only seeing them naked and examining them, not actually having sex with them like Lane sometimes had to. "I know there's a difference between work and pleasure for you. But you realize this takes confidence of steel, right?"

He smiled. "I do. I honestly never thought I'd meet any woman who'd be able to accept the job I had, but if any woman can, it'd be you. I don't think you realize how much every other woman pales in comparison." He pressed his lips to her knuckles. "You've got me on lockdown, doc."

The words soothed some of the jagged edges inside of her, but her stomach was still knotted. "I'm going to work on getting used to it."

He leaned over and kissed her cheek. "And I'm always willing to talk it through. Just promise me you won't let stuff build up and not tell me. We're figuring this out as we go along…together. All right?"

She nodded and sighed. "Yes. Together."

"Good." He rose to his feet and grabbed his bag. "I'll see you tonight, doc. Go convince people drugs are bad."

She sniffed. "Go convince people sex is good."

He came over and gave her another quick peck. "Thank you."

Lane headed out and Elle finished getting ready. She wasn't going to let herself dwell on the conversation or obsess about what he might be doing with his client tonight. Like Lane said, they were figuring this out as they went along. She would see · how this felt, how she'd deal with knowing he'd spent time with someone else tonight. Hopefully, she'd be okay with it. If not…well, if not, she had no idea where they would go from here.

She didn't want to think about it.

Elle walked onto her unit ten minutes late, which raised a number of eyebrows as she passed some of the staff on her way in. She was a notorious stickler for being on time and had been known to give quite a lecture to anyone who was late. But her staff was smart enough to not tease her about her own lack of punctuality this morning. She was definitely not in the mood.

Oriana fell into step beside her as Elle made her way to the office. "Good morning, Dr. McCray."

"Morning," she said, keeping her gaze forward as she scanned the unit, taking quick inventory of who was awake already this morning and who wasn't. The early birds tended to be the ones doing better with treatment. "How are things?"

"A little unsettled," Ori said, handing her a stack of manila folders. "According to the night staff, Belinda threatened Jeremy at late-night group and he spit in her face. Some other residents got involved in the altercation, so everyone had to be sent to their rooms for the rest of the evening."

"Anyone injured?"

"Nothing but a few scratches," she reported. "I've talked to a few from the group this morning. Jeremy seems to have been the main instigator. He's blaming his meds for his outburst. Says we're 'fucking with his head.' His words."

Elle opened the file and scanned down Jeremy's list of medications, noting that none of them were known to cause violent outbursts. "So he's blaming that and not the withdrawals from the amphetamines he's been subsisting on for two years or the fact that his wife just left him?"

"Basically."

She took a pen from her pocket and scribbled a note in the file. "I'll put him on my schedule for this afternoon. I doubt it's the meds but I'll talk to him, check for any other side effects. If he wants to try a different combo, there are some options."

"Thanks." Oriana paused outside of Elle's office and faced her. "Also, Dr. Rush stopped by to talk with you about Jun. I had referred her to the X-wing."

"Right. I saw that in the notes."

"Dr. Rush had two sessions with her and wants to run some potential treatment options by you, make sure they don't interfere with Jun's plan over here."

Elle tried not to blanch. She and Dr. Rush had learned to work together, but their shared history with Donovan always carried a layer of awkwardness neither of them could escape. "She's waiting now?"

Ori jerked her thumb toward the door. "She's inside. She said it wouldn't take long."

Elle sighed. "Okay. I'll speak with her. Any other fires right now?"

Ori smiled. "None that I can't handle."

"Good." She had full confidence in Oriana. The woman was a brilliant social worker and didn't let any of the patients manipulate her, which was saying something. Addicts were often skilled at the con to begin with, but add award-winning performance skills to the mix with their clientele and even the most seasoned professional could fall into a trap. "Let me know if anything else comes up."

"Will do. And Dr. McCray?" she asked, concern flickering across her features.

"Yeah?"

Ori lifted a shoulder in an awkward shrug, which was odd because the woman was usually as comfortable and casually elegant as one could be. "I know it's none of my business, but is everything all right? You've seemed...different lately. Distracted."

Elle stiffened.

"I know working here can feel like a boarding school sometimes. Clique-y, you know?" She shrugged again. "So I just wanted to put it out there that even though you're my boss, if you ever wanted to grab a drink after work or chat about something other than work, I'm game. I've found it helps to have friends here. We get how hard this job can be. And how isolating living out here in the bayou can get. So I...just wanted to put that out there."

Elle stared at her for a moment. Her initial instinct was to brush off the offer. That was her standard go-to when she'd first started working here and people had offered to socialize. *I like to keep my work and home life separate.* She didn't want to build bonds, get attached, make things more complicated. But she couldn't bring herself to say it.

She liked Oriana, respected her. And Elle knew what kind of reputation she had developed around here. Approaching her prickly boss with this brand of kindness was a big risk for Oriana. She was reaching out. And not to kiss the boss's ass or to get gossip on her. She could see it in her face, the open expression, the offered hand. This was genuine.

I'd like to get to know you. I'd like to be a friend.

The offer touched something inside Elle that made her throat go tight and words burst out. "I'm dating Lane Cannon."

Ori's eyebrows jumped up. "Oh."

Elle put her fingers to her lips, surprised that the statement had escaped. "Shit. That wasn't what I meant to say."

Oriana grinned. "That wasn't what I expected you to say, but I guess that explains why you're acting differently. And explains a whole lot about what I saw that day in your office."

Elle shook her head and rubbed her brow. "I guess I just needed to say it aloud to someone."

Ori tipped her head to the side, her dark halo of hair making her look like an angel with a secret. "I'm honored I get to be your confessor today. Lane seems great."

"He is."

"And your secret's safe with me."

Elle nodded. "Thanks." She should've told her it didn't have to be a secret anymore. There was nothing forbidden. Lane wasn't in her department or a direct report, so she didn't need any kind of special approval. But she couldn't quite say the words. "And I'll definitely take you up on an after-work drink sometime."

Ori's face brightened. "Excellent."

She cocked her head toward her closed door. "I better stop making Dr. Rush wait."

Ori lifted her hand in a good-bye and headed toward the group room. Elle turned around, took a breath, and stepped inside her office. Marin Rush was in the chair across from Elle's desk, texting on her phone, a secret smile on her face and a little flush on her cheeks.

She was probably texting with Donovan. Elle waited for the

jolt of jealousy to go through her, but nothing came. She felt…
nothing about the two of them being together. Huh.

"Good morning, Dr. Rush."

Marin glanced up, turning her phone over in her lap, and
her expression smoothed into a polite, professional one. "Dr.
McCray."

"Oriana said you needed to speak with me," Elle said in a
measured tone as she took her seat behind her desk.

"Yes. I apologize for barging in on you first thing, but both
of our schedules are crazy today. I thought we could squeeze in
ten minutes before the chaos began."

Elle straightened a row of pens on her desk. "What can I help
you with?"

Marin tucked her phone in her jacket pocket and linked her
fingers around her crossed knees. "Jun Alexis."

"Okay."

"I had two sessions with Jun over the past week. I usually try
to delay any treatment on my wing until the clients over here
have fully completed your program, but Oriana told me that
Jun's sexual issues are deeply intertwined with her substance
abuse issues, and she doesn't expect Jun to come back for
separate treatment once her time in rehab is up. I wanted to see
how open she'd be to talking with me."

Elle flipped open a legal pad and wrote down the date and
Jun's name. "How'd the sessions go?"

"Promising, actually. She opened up about an assault a few
years ago, one that happened before she became well-known.
After a show at a club one night, she got attacked by two
guys who'd attended. Apparently, her stage performance was
provocative and they felt like she'd offered them the invitation

by paying attention to them during the song."

Elle frowned. "I knew there'd been a rape, but she hasn't shared the details with any of us yet. She insisted it wasn't relevant to her current situation and wouldn't go there."

"Yeah, I get the impression that she doesn't want to give the rapists that much credit—that they affected her enough to drive her to drugs. But after the assault, she pretty much locked the incident away. Didn't press charges. Didn't tell anyone. And apparently, she amped up the sexual tone in her stage show, like she was...I don't know."

"Giving the assholes a big fuck you."

Marin's smile was grim. "Something like that. Almost like a dare to prove that they hadn't changed her. But shortly after that is when she started experimenting with drugs. She's only slept with people while under the influence since then and can't orgasm, even on her own."

"So they stole even more from her," Elle said, anger sparking on Jun's behalf.

Marin nodded, frustration on her face. "It's horrible, and I hate that the disgusting human beings who did this to her just went on with their lives unscathed. But like you said, when Jun was first admitted, she didn't want to acknowledge the sexual issues from the trauma as a problem. She only wanted to focus on the substance abuse."

"But she was willing to talk to you," Elle said, impressed that Marin had gotten Jun to open up. "Any idea what changed her mind?"

"Ori's encouragement for one," she replied. "But that's not the only thing. She ran into Lane over here one day. Jun said he put her at ease and made the whole prospect of sex therapy seem less scary. So if she could work with him on the issue, she said she'd be open to trying."

Elle's fingers gripped her pen so hard she heard the plastic casing creak, but she fought to keep her expression stoic. "Is someone with Lane's specialization usually needed in this type of case?"

Marin shifted in the chair, expression thoughtful. "Lane's strength is working with anxious clients, so that's a good fit. He's also experienced with arousal disorder. He could teach her some techniques, provide a safe environment."

"Have sex with her, you mean," Elle said flatly.

A small frown touched Marin's mouth. "That would depend on the treatment plan he created. Intercourse could be part of it. But Jun would have to be on board with that, which may take a while with her anxiety from the trauma."

Elle couldn't stop the sick feeling from rising in the back of her throat. "Right."

Marin's brow wrinkled, her frown deepening at Elle's clipped tone. "Look, I know that kind of therapy can be controversial and not everyone buys into it. But if you're worried about that, I can assure you that Lane has helped a lot of people and he's very good—"

"I know he's good in bed, Marin. I'm dating him," she snapped.

Marin's lips parted and she blinked rapidly. "I, uh, was going to say he's very good at his job." She paused for a beat. "Wait. You're dating *Lane*?"

"That is not public information. Yet."

Marin bit her lip, but did a terrible job hiding the spark of amusement in her eyes.

"What?" Elle bit out.

Marin lifted her palms and shook her head. "Nothing. I didn't say anything."

"You look like you're about to laugh."

"Not in a mocking way, I swear," she said, her smile revealing itself now. "It's just, I sent him over to talk to you that night at the party, and you both looked like you were on death row, having to speak to each other. I would've never guessed. I think that's...great. Lane's a wonderful guy and a good friend."

"Then I doubt you'd want him with me. You're not exactly president of my fan club."

She shrugged. "He wouldn't be with you if you were a bad person. He doesn't put up with much bullshit in his life from what I can tell. And you and I...well, we started off in a bad situation. You were a threat to my relationship with Donovan. I don't put up with bullshit either."

"I understand," Elle said, shame bubbling up over the ridiculous way she'd acted when Donovan had dropped their tryst for Marin. Even when she'd seen how different Donovan was around Marin, how clearly in love he was, Elle had still tried to interfere out of pure spite. Not one of her finer moments. "The situation was...unfortunate."

"It was. And I wasn't exactly kind to you either. But I really don't know much else about you except that you're an accomplished doctor and that Oriana and your patients seem to have deep respect for you. That says a lot." She gave her a brief smile. "So if you and Lane have found something together then...I wish you both the best. Truly."

"Thank you," she said, sensing that Marin meant the words. "But I see now that this may be a difficult case to consult on," she said, releasing a breath. "Dating Lane or not, he still has the same job. One of your patients is in need of his type of therapy. But if it's too difficult to separate out personal from professional—and believe me, no judgment there because I know I'd have a tough time with that—I can make Oriana my primary contact on the case. We can handle this part of Jun's treatment so that you don't have to know the details."

Elle bristled at the suggestion that she couldn't keep personal and professional separate. She'd spent her life being nothing but professional, but her hands were trembling and her brain was trying to paint pictures she didn't want to see. The patient had to come first. Elle didn't trust herself not to let her personal feelings interfere. She forced out the words. "That might be for the best."

"Of course," Marin said. "Absolutely. Does Oriana know you and Lane are seeing each other or should I give her some other reason why you're not going to be consulted on this part of the case?"

Elle swallowed past the knot in her throat. "She knows."

Marin nodded. "Great. Well, we'll handle it from here. She'll be in good hands."

Hands. Lane's hands.

Elle's stomach sank to her toes and nausea shimmered through her. "Sounds good."

Marin got to her feet and headed to the door, but before she stepped out, she glanced back. "Nice chatting with you, Elle."

Elle let out a breath. They hardly ever called each other by their first names, and she recognized the peace offering for what it was. "Have a good day, Marin."

Marin smiled and slipped out of the office, clicking the door shut quietly behind her.

Elle put her head on her desk, her body feeling too heavy to hold up. Lane was going to have sessions with Jun Alexis. Beautiful, young, talented Jun. A rock star in her own right. Someone whose songs Lane listened to. Someone who wasn't Elle.

She was supposed to be handling this maturely.

She wanted to vomit.

chapter twenty five

L ane stepped out of the dance studio and into the night air with a smile on his face, laughing at something Carlotta had said. They'd had a victorious session tonight. Carlotta had been able to strip down fully to the costume she'd wear in the movie, no darkness, no blindfolds needed. She'd played the role of seductress with convincing confidence and had nailed her lines without a tremor in her voice. There'd been a few tears afterward but only of relief. She'd done it.

"I can't believe that was our last session," she said as they headed into the parking lot, the cicadas singing so loudly they almost drowned her out.

A breeze had picked up outside, chasing off some of the humidity from earlier in the day, and the parking lot's sodium lights were just coming on, casting an orange glow over everything. "I never doubted you'd make your deadline. You were determined from the very start. You should be proud of yourself."

She grinned, her face half in darkness. "I am. I kicked ass. But I couldn't have done this without you." She stopped in front of him and reached out, taking both his hands in hers. "Thank you, Lane. Seriously. You're a great guy. I thought there was no way this was going to work and then I met you, and...I'm not sure I've ever felt so safe with someone. You never made me feel uncomfortable or screwed up. I felt like a friend was holding my hand the whole time."

The comment warmed him from the inside out. That was the highest praise he could receive from a client, especially one who fought the types of demons Carlotta had to face. This was why he did this job, for moments like this when he could see the difference it made for someone. He gave her hands a squeeze. "You're welcome. Thanks for trusting me with your treatment. I don't take that lightly."

Her eyes shimmered in the soft glow of the lights and she stepped forward to hug him. He held her loosely and then she kissed him on the cheek. "I'll send you tickets for the premiere. You can come and see your hard work on screen. Plus, my boobs in high definition—which I will choose not to think about or I'll be back in your office in the fetal position."

He stepped back and smiled. "I wouldn't miss it. And you and your boobs are going to do great."

She laughed, the sound echoing through the mostly empty parking lot. "Well, I guess this is good-bye for now."

"I'll walk you to your car." He led her toward the red Mustang she'd rented and opened her door for her. When she'd driven away, he took a breath, relishing that feeling of knowing he'd helped someone.

He reached to pull his phone out his pocket to see if Elle was on her way to meet him, but the glint of orange lights off blond hair caught his attention in his periphery. He spun that way, finding a familiar face. Elle was sitting on a bench under one of the big oak trees next to the building. Her car was parked nearby, but he hadn't seen it in the dark.

She stood when she saw him coming her way. She was hugging her elbows, looking chilled despite the warm evening.

He smiled when he got close and gave her a quick kiss and hug. "Hey, you got here early."

She glanced toward the road then back to him, a far off look on her face. "Yeah, I had an errand to run in town and I finished up earlier than I thought. Figured I'd come by in case you were done."

"Sorry. We ended up needing the whole time. Were you waiting long?"

She shrugged and looked his way. "Not too long. I got to see the sunset. It was nice."

The words were casual enough, but something was off. Her whole demeanor was edged with something jagged. "What's wrong?"

"I didn't say anything was wrong."

Grim awareness hit him. "You saw me with my client."

Elle's mouth twitched at the corner, at attempt at nonchalance but one that she didn't quite pull off. "She's beautiful."

"That's her job."

"She likes you."

He sighed. "That's *my* job."

"Right."

"Elle..." He reached out for her, wanting to break through whatever wall she was standing behind. "Talk to me."

Her throat flexed as she swallowed. "We should get going before the restaurant gets too crowded."

A pit settled in his stomach. She was slamming the door on the conversation, a dangerous path in this situation. But he could see he wasn't going to get anywhere with her right now. Maybe she needed a little time to process what she'd seen. They could talk at dinner. "Fine. I'll follow you there."

The festive atmosphere of the restaurant with its mariachi music and beer bottle chandeliers didn't help lighten the stilted conversation over dinner. Elle talked about work and asked him about school. He told her about an interesting lecture he'd gone to today. But all through the meal, he could sense the crackle of tension underlying every word. He wanted to ask what was going on in her head, wanted to reassure her about what she'd seen tonight, but she shut down that lane of conversation every time he put a word in that direction. He decided it'd be best to wait until they got to his place or hers, where they could discuss it privately.

After he paid the bill, they made their way back out into the night and he walked her to her car. "Do you want to stay at my place tonight? It's closer and the traffic heading to The Grove isn't bad in the morning."

Elle turned to face him, keys clutched in her hand. "I don't know."

"You don't know if you want to stay at my place?" he asked carefully. "Or you don't know if you want to stay together tonight at all?"

She pressed her lips together and held her elbows, her entire posture closing to him. "You smell like perfume. Not my perfume."

So there it was. He frowned. "I can go home and shower. My client hugged me because it was our last session. That's all."

"This time. But what about tomorrow or the next night?"

He released a breath and ran a hand over the back of his head. "Elle, I don't know what you want me to say. We talked about this. This is my job. That's all it is, I swear. The only woman I want is you."

She shook her head and he could tell she was trying not to cry. "Jun Alexis is being referred to you."

"What?" Marin had told him earlier today that a new client was being added to his schedule, but he hadn't even had a chance to look at the file to know who it was or what the treatment was going to be.

Elle glanced away. "I stepped away from the case for obvious reasons, but I caught myself watching her today in group. I couldn't stop imagining you two together. Jun, whose album you love. Jun, who's fifteen years younger than I am. Jun, who made you laugh and who was completely enamored with you."

"Jun, who I have zero percent romantic or sexual interest in."

She blinked, her eyes shining, and wagged her head again. "I hear what you're saying and I believe you. I do. But I don't know if I'm tough enough for this, Lane. I want to be but..." She pressed her hand to her stomach. "I feel sick inside. I smelled that other woman's scent on you tonight and I just wanted to scream."

"Elle." He stepped closer, tried to reach for her, but she waved him back. He took a breath, reeling in the panic that shimmered through him. "Look, I know this is hard, believe me. I'm not pretending it's not. I'm asking a lot of you—the ultimate trust. But this is what my job is." He touched her cheek, encouraging her to meet his gaze. "All I can do is swear to you that none of them are a threat to us. I will treat Jun like a client. That's it.

There's only one woman I want to be with." His heart picked up speed as heavier words hovered on his tongue, in his heart. "The one I'm falling in love with. You."

Saying the words aloud sent a bolt of fear through him and a wash of vulnerability, but they were the truth. He wanted her to hear them.

"Lane." Elle closed her eyes, tears brimming at the edges and her anguish apparent. "I want to be with you…but I don't think I can do this."

The words were like razors to the gut. He reached out and cupped her shoulders, his heart squeezing tight in his chest. "Tell me what you need from me, doc. Tell me what I can do to help."

A few long moments passed, but then she lifted her head, her eyes red-rimmed. "You could quit."

The suggestion was like a bucket of ice water over him. "What?"

She wet her lips, her whole body trembling beneath his touch but her gaze earnest. "You don't need to do this. You said it yourself. This isn't your ultimate goal. You want to be a therapist. It's going to take twice as long with you working so much while you're in school. If you need it, I could…help."

His mouth turned dry and he lowered his arms to his side. "Help."

She nodded. "Whatever your job is paying for, I could help you with so that you can focus one-hundred percent on getting your degree. You could even move in with me if you wanted. My housing is covered by The Grove, and I have the space. I'd…like having you there."

His skin went icy from the inside out. "Are you kidding me

right now?"

"You could get to grad school faster," she said, her words rushed. "I would've never gotten my undergrad so quickly if I'd had to work full time during school. It's a win-win."

"Right. Win-win. You help me with housing. Pay for stuff I need. Sleep with me," he said, voice flat. "A kept man, then."

She reared back like she'd been slapped and frowned. "You know that's not what I mean."

"Isn't it, though? You know how many times I've had a rich woman who wants me in her bed make me the same offer?" His voice was careful, measured, but anger bubbled close to the surface, old demons rising from their graves. "What happens if this dyslexia turns out to be a major problem and I flunk out of school? Or decide not to go? Do you just pay my way until you get tired of me and then kick me out?"

"Lane."

"No," he snapped. "I get that this situation is hard. But don't you see how messed up what you're suggesting is? I just told you that I'm falling in love with you and you respond with an offer of money?"

"It's not about the money," she said, her voice rising. "I don't fucking care about money. Couples support each other's ambitions. One goes to school while the other works. It's not a bizarre scenario. If I quit my job to go back and get another degree, I wouldn't think I was prostituting myself if my boyfriend helped out with household costs."

His jaw clenched. "I never lied to you about what I do. You said you wanted to try."

"I *am* trying, Lane. I want to be with you so badly it hurts. This is fucking tearing me up inside. But I can't help how I feel when I think about you with a client. I'm trying to find a way to be together where I don't have to go to bed at night and smell another woman's perfume on your skin. I don't think that's out of bounds to want." Her voice caught, tears still flowing. "I need, for once, to have someone who's just for me. No one has ever been only mine, Lane. Not ever. I want to be the only girl you smell like."

The heartfelt words were launched at him and landed solid, despair filtering through him. He couldn't deny her logic, and he couldn't call her feelings unreasonable. Most women would agree with her.

He should've never let himself hope. He thought he'd found someone who could deal with his strange occupation, who could be with him as is. But his job was too much to ask of anyone, more trouble than he was worth to someone. To her. He understood, but it didn't mean it didn't rip him down the middle.

And even though he believed Elle was making her offer from a genuine place, he couldn't go there. He'd worked his whole life to support himself, to not depend on anyone else, had chosen the streets over taking money with strings from his parents. He couldn't let Elle pay his way. He knew how that would feel down the line after his savings ran out, knowing that the roof over his head, his food, his clothes were paid for by the woman he was sleeping with. It would taint what they had. Color it in shades that would make it feel ugly, would channel his past too closely.

He finally had a career he was proud of, that meant something to him. He'd worked too hard to get to this place in his life. This job had been the thing that had pulled him out of the gutter, the thing that made him feel like he was worth more than what people had told him all his life. He didn't know who he was without it.

And with his dyslexia, he couldn't guarantee that he could even make it through school. This job may be the only one in therapy he could ever get. He couldn't quit and just be the former hooker again, a guy mooching off a woman's money.

The reality of that settled over him like a hard, cold rain.

"I can't walk away from my career, Elle," he said quietly, meeting her eyes. "Please don't put that ultimatum on me. Don't make me choose."

She stared back at him, her eyes shiny and sad, and a look of defeat crossing her face. "You just did."

The simple words were like a punch to the heart, the finality of them stunning him for a moment. "So that's it?"

She looked down at the ground, her lips rolling inward. "I'm not strong enough for this, Lane. Love isn't strong enough for this."

Something spiked and painful burrowed into his gut. "Elle…"

She shook her head, heartbreak on her face, and turned away from him. "I've got to go."

She left him standing there in the dark parking lot, holding his keys and staring after her.

Love.

Elle McCray had finally said the word, and it was only to tell him good-bye.

chapter twenty six

Elle took a big gulp of her coffee as she made her way back from Saturday rounds. She'd pulled a couple of double shifts this week and her body was staging a protest over working the weekend, too, but the caffeine would have to push her past it. She didn't want to go home to her empty house. For years that little cottage had been her sanctuary, her peaceful escape from her high-stress job. Now it was just a reminder of who wasn't there.

Even in the short span of her relationship with Lane, every space was tainted with memories of him, of what could've been. She'd spent the first few days crying and not wanting to get out of bed, but she'd recognized the warning signs quickly, the old depression trying to grab hold of her. She'd forced herself to get out of the house and back to work. She couldn't mope when she had patients to take care of. They would be her focus. Her job would be her anchor.

But once she'd wrangled in some of the weepiness, the anger had swept in behind it. She'd wanted to be pissed. To rage. But she didn't even know whom or what to be angry at. Lane for being so determined to keep his job? Herself for being unable to turn off the possessive switch? Fate for bringing her someone so wonderful but whom she ultimately couldn't have?

He'd told her he *loved* her, dammit. They should be together right now, starting a life. Instead, here she was, miserable as hell, alone, and drowning her sorrow in non-stop work.

The coffee turned bitter in her mouth. All the ruminating wasn't going to change the situation. There was no fix. No prescription she could write to heal this. His job was non-negotiable for them both, and they were on opposite sides. Love didn't fix everything. That was a lie the world sold in movie theaters and in books with pretty covers.

She would figure out a way to move past this. She would have to.

Even if it felt impossible right now.

She turned the corner to head toward her office, her pager buzzing against her hip, and almost ran into Oriana. Her coffee sloshed onto the floor and she held it away from her body, narrowly missing spilling it down the front of her white coat.

"So sorry," Ori said quickly. "Isa from X-wing just called. She needs you over there immediately."

Elle frowned and checked her pager, seeing the extension for the sex therapy wing and the code that indicated it was urgent but not life-threatening. She tossed her coffee in a nearby trashcan and nodded at Ori. "You're in charge of the unit until I get back."

"Got it."

Elle swung by her office to grab a basic medical kit and hoofed it over to the other building. She rarely had emergencies that called her off her unit, but it was a weekend and there were fewer M.D.s working, probably none in the outpatient buildings. Last time she was called out of the blue like this, two kids in the teen program had gotten in a fight and a nose had been broken.

She pushed through the doors to the X-wing and stopped in front of the receptionist desk where Isa, the main assistant for the unit, looked up with relief in her brown eyes. "Oh, thank God. They got ahold of you."

"What's going on?"

"It's one of yours. Come on." Isa hurried from behind the desk and motioned for Elle to follow her, her shoes clicking on the shiny floors. Once they turned the corner, there was a forlorn sound coming from down the hall, a weeping voice. Raymond, one of the psychiatric aides from a different unit, was hovering near the doorway, his dark bald head gleaming in the light from the window but concern on his usually jovial face. Isa pointed toward the door. "One of your patients...she had some sort of episode in session and attacked. I called Ray but he...wasn't allowed to help."

"Wasn't allowed..." But Elle's words trailed off as she peeked into the open doorway and saw the scene.

Jun Alexis was in the corner of one of the therapy rooms in a robe, her face mascara-streaked and her arms around her knees. Lane was on the floor next to her, not touching her, his lips murmuring soothing words. Jun looked like she couldn't accept them. She was shaking her head, everything about her dialed up into some anxiety state.

"I tried to help, Dr. McCray," Raymond said, his voice library quiet. "She went after Lane and was hurting him. But he called me off. Said it would make her worse. I wasn't sure what to do, but he's got her calmer now. She was...out of her head."

Shit. She gave a quick nod. "Okay. Thanks for coming down here, Ray. Let me go and see what's going on. You mind sticking around in case we need help with a transport?"

"Not at all." Raymond slipped out of the way so that Elle could step inside, and she shut the door behind her, affording Jun privacy.

Elle cleared her throat, working to keep her voice low and calming so she didn't startle the woman. "Hi, Jun."

Lane looked up, flinching slightly when he saw that it was Elle but quickly recovering a professional mask. Deep scratches marred the side of his face, blood trickling down his cheek.

Elle took a breath. Jun hadn't lifted her head, so she directed her request to Lane. "Tell me what's going on."

Lane glanced at Jun, concern all over his face, and turned back to Elle. "We were having a session. She was practicing progressive relaxation while we did some touch exercises. She was doing fine until I touched her thigh. It triggered some sort of flashback and she reacted violently."

Jun sobbed softly and rocked, whispering to herself, something that sounded like *sorry* over and over again.

"I stopped the exercise immediately, but it was too late. She was lost to whatever memory it was and attacked me. Ray came to help, but she screamed at the sight of him. I didn't want to make it worse with"—his gaze held heartbreak on Jun's behalf—"two men restraining her."

Jun whimpered and scooted against Lane, seeking comfort from the man she'd apparently just attacked. He ran a gentle hand over her head, protective, almost brotherly. "It's okay, Jun. The doc's here to help. We're both here to keep you safe."

Elle's heart clenched.

"She's calmed some now," he continued. "But I didn't know what to do from here. Dr. Rush and Dr. West are off today. She's still trembling all over and she may have hurt her hands when she was hitting me."

Hitting him. Scratching him. Tearing his shirt from what Elle could see. The only way such a tiny thing like Jun could make a big guy like Lane look so ravaged was if he hadn't attempted to hold her back or restrain her at all.

But Elle couldn't worry about that now. Her first concern was Jun.

Elle squatted down to get eye level with her. The edgy musician who was usually so full of brash, bold attitude looked like a child trying to curl in on herself. Black eye makeup had made sooty streaks down her cheeks and her shoulders curved inward. "Okay, Jun. It's just me, Dr. McCray. I'm here to help and make sure you're all right. Let's see what we have going on, okay? I want to make sure you're not hurt."

Elle kept her voice gentle and didn't reach out to touch her. Jun shivered.

"Is it okay if I check your pulse?"

Jun nodded.

"Thank you." She gently took Jun's wrist and pressed her fingers against it, feeling the racing heartbeat and her clammy skin. She had her stethoscope but didn't want to spook Jun by touching her anywhere near her chest. "I need you to take some slow breaths for me, all right? Concentrate on filling your lungs all the way up and then releasing it slowly. You're safe now."

Jun attempted the deep breathing, and though the breaths were by no means long ones, they were sufficient to keep her from hyperventilating or worsening the panic response.

"Good."

"I feel like I'm going to pass out," she said between breaths. "My chest hurts."

"You're having a panic attack from the flashback, which may make you feel like you're dying. But it's just your mind trying to protect you, okay? Your body's acting like there's present danger, but it's sending a false signal," Elle soothed. "Whatever memory got to you is just that, a memory. You're here at The Grove on Saturday afternoon. You're safe. You're not hurt. No one here is going to hurt you."

"I hurt Lane," she whispered.

Elle glanced at Lane. The gashes in his cheek had to burn like hell, but his attention was solidly on Jun.

"Lane's a big boy. He can survive a few scratches."

Lane gave Jun's shoulder a gentle squeeze. "Don't worry about me. Just listen to the doc and breathe."

Jun pressed the heels of her hands against her eye sockets, her body still racked with a deep trembling. "Please give me a sleeping pill. I've never needed one so bad in my life. I can't... think about that night. I could see them, could smell their sweat, could feel—please. Just give me something to knock me the fuck out."

Elle frowned. Sleeping pills had been one of the things Jun had detoxed from when she'd come into the rehab program. Affording her that kind of oblivion would only make things worse, but she wasn't going to break that news to her right now. "Let's get you back to the unit and we can help you feel better. Okay?"

After a long moment, Jun nodded and whispered, "Okay."

Jun didn't fight when Raymond rolled in a wheelchair and they transported her back to Elle's unit. Lane followed them, wanting to make sure Jun was okay. Other patients gazed curiously at the group when they headed toward Jun's room, but the mind-your-own-business look Elle gave them quelled the stares.

Oriana was waiting for Jun when they arrived. Elle briefed her on what had happened and ordered the nurse to bring a dose of a non-addictive anxiety pill that would give Jun some relief without knocking her out. Ori would handle the talk therapy since she was the primary counselor on the case, and Elle would check in with Jun later. Jun's current diagnosis didn't include PTSD but if she was having flashbacks, Elle and Ori would need to dig deeper.

Once Elle had everything squared away, she turned to find Lane waiting outside in one of the cushy armchairs. He had cleaned off some of the blood but his scratches still looked angry and red. He stood, frown lines bracketing his mouth. "Is she okay?"

Elle blew out a breath and looped the stethoscope she'd been holding around her neck. "She's calmer and Oriana will help her talk some of it through. I also gave her meds to help."

He nodded, worry etched around his eyes. "Good. She was so terrified. She wasn't there with me anymore and to think I triggered—"

Elle held up a hand. "Why don't you come to an exam room and I'll get you cleaned up? We shouldn't discuss details out here. The rehab unit is all about the gossip."

He touched his cheek and flinched. "It's just a few scratches."

"And a torn shirt and a bite mark on your shoulder."

He glanced down at his shoulder like he hadn't even noticed.

She cocked her head. "Come on. You don't want to let bite marks or fingernail scratches fester. Lots of germs, high risk of infection."

He looked too tired to argue. He pushed himself up from the chair and followed her to a room near her office that doubled as a secondary exam room and a place where unruly patients were taken to cool down. She directed him to the paper-covered exam table and went to the cabinet for supplies.

As long as she kept moving, stayed focus on the task at hand, she didn't have to think about the fact that she was alone with Lane in a room. She snapped on latex gloves and stood in front of him, eyeing the gashes in his cheek and studiously avoiding his gaze. The cuts were deeper than she'd expected and ragged. "She got you good. That woman is probably a hundred pounds soaking wet. How'd she inflict this much damage?"

He ran a hand over the back of his head. "The power of mortal fear. I could see it in her eyes. She was no longer there with me. I was one of her attackers, and she lost it. I could've stopped her, but if I had tried to hold her arms or restrain her in some way, how bad would those memories have gotten? How much deeper into that hell would they have taken her? I'm trained in some things, but not how to bring someone out of a flashback. I didn't want to make it worse."

Elle's gaze flicked up, meeting his. "So you just let her attack you?"

"It was so hard to see her in so much pain." His eyes held sadness. "I thought maybe if she felt like she was winning, like she was taking back control, she would snap out of it or get some control over the memory. That maybe if she could lash out, it would help. Change the outcome of that memory. If that meant a few scratches or bruises for me, so be it."

Elle released a breath, all the starch leaving her. He'd wanted to absorb Jun's pain, take it from her however he could, even if that meant he'd bleed over it.

Goddammit, why did this man have to be so...so impossible not to want?

She'd met so few genuinely kind people in her life that she didn't trust it when people appeared that way. Her ex had looked like a nice guy at first, too. It was a lie. Everyone had an agenda. In the beginning, she'd assumed Lane did, too. But he'd proven her wrong time and time again. This man was a *good* man. He would rather get scratched and bruised if he knew it could help make his client's life less painful. That was who he was.

His *job* was who he was. Which was why he'd had to walk away from her when she'd made him choose. She'd thought it was pride and not wanting to accept money from her, but now she realized that was only a small part of it.

Lane had spent the first part of his life feeling less than—the "dumb" student who couldn't read, the poor kid among the rich, the child who was only loved conditionally, and then the hired body that was simply there for rich women's amusement. Becoming a surrogate had freed him from all that, had given him an identity and purpose. He'd learned that he was gifted at helping people overcome things, at guiding them to a happier life. He loved his job for many of the same reasons she loved hers. And needed it. Just like she did.

If he'd asked her to stop being a doctor, to let him cover her bills, what would she have told him?

The realization made her stomach hurt. She hadn't simply asked him to give up a job. She'd asked him to give up who he was. She'd asked for too much.

"That was a good instinct not to hold her down," she said quietly. "That could've made the flashback more vivid and traumatic for her. This will sting." She dabbed at his cheek with disinfectant, earning a soft hiss from him. "But it's also your right to protect yourself."

"I know. Maybe I'm a closet masochist," he said with a smirk.

She briefly met his gaze and moved to cleaning the teeth marks on his shoulder. "Well, you did date me, so I wouldn't rule that out."

He was quiet for a long moment and she kept her focus on treating his wounds, afraid to look him.

"Maybe we both are," he said finally. "I've certainly felt tortured since that night in the parking lot. We seem to be good at doing that to each other." He blew out a breath. "Maybe I should've left you alone at that party after all."

The admission sent a prickly pain spreading through her chest and tightening her insides. Would she take that back if she could? Go back to where she'd been? Save herself this pain?

Without that party, she would've never kissed him, touched him. She would've never stood up to her ex. She wouldn't be speaking to her sister again. She'd be home. Safe in her predictable world. Alone. She wouldn't know what it felt like to be loved and to lose it. Her heart wouldn't be broken.

She wouldn't know anything about Lane Cannon at all.

She could feel his attention on her as she spread antibiotic gel on the bite and bandaged it. Her heart was beating too quickly. Being near him was making the ten days they'd been apart hurt worse, the ache in her chest unbearable.

Say something.

The words wouldn't come. Why was she doing this to herself? Why did she always make everything so hard? The riot of feelings was like broken shards of glass in her throat, trying to get out but drawing blood.

She closed her eyes, her hand pressing over the bandage, and forced the words past her lips. "Please don't take that back."

His body stilled beneath her, no movement except the steady beat of his heart beneath her hand. "The party?"

"Any of it." She pressed on, needing to get it out. "The time I've spent with you has been…everything."

"Elle." Her name whispered out of him on an exhale.

"I know I asked too much of you. I'm sorry," she said, the apology freeing her from some of the tightness in her chest. "I'm sorry that I made your job sound like something disposable and that I insulted you with my offer. I'm sorry that I was so selfish."

"Selfish?"

She opened her eyes, finding his attention fixed on her, questions there. She licked her lips, her blood thumping in her ears. "I wanted you all to myself. I didn't think about what that meant for you or exactly what I was asking you to sacrifice. I was only thinking of what I wanted. I'd finally found someone I loved and I didn't want to share him, even with patients. So yeah. Selfish. And self-centered. And unreasonable. And—"

"Wait." His face went blank. "You *love* me?"

She groaned and pulled off her gloves. "Yes. Keep up, Cannon. I'm fucking miserably in love with you."

He blinked.

"And I thought I could get over it. I thought I had to. Because other women and perfume and...all the things!" She knew she probably wasn't making sense but she couldn't stop. "Then today...today you show up and let a patient go after you just to give her the chance to feel better. Just to help and be there for her." She tossed her gloves in the trash like they'd offended her. "How am I supposed to fight against that? You're...impossible not to love."

His eyebrows lifted at that. "I'm...sorry?"

"You should be, goddammit."

"Doc," he said, voice gentle.

She crossed her arms, frustrated tears threatening. "Don't *doc* me."

He reached out, caught the pocket of her white coat with his finger, and pulled her closer. "Doc."

The repeated endearment undid her. Tears slipped down her cheeks. "What?"

He cradled her face in his palms, holding her gaze. "I've got news for you. You're just as much to blame. You're impossible not to love back."

She sniffed. "That is empirically, verifiably untrue. Ask most people who know me."

"They don't know you like I know you. Not yet. When they do, you'll have them all on your side. You're an amazing woman."

She let her forehead touch his, the wave of emotion almost too much to weather upright. "I don't need you to quit you job, Lane. I'm sorry I asked you to do that. The patients deserve someone who is there for the right reasons. You are that person."

He sighed, his fingers lacing in her hair, his eyes closing. "We are completely ridiculous."

"What?"

"I've been a wreck since you walked away from me. I was going to come by tonight and talk to you."

She lifted her head, blinking hard. "About what?"

"I applied for a counseling internship on the X-wing."

She stilled.

"I've wanted that gig for a while but was too scared to take the written tests required to get the position. I knew I'd fail. But I told Donovan about my dyslexia, and he's set up accommodations. The pay isn't as good, but the experience will be everything I could want and it will count for my experiential hours for my degree. I'll get to work directly with patients on all kinds of issues, shadowing the psychologists."

Her heart pounded against her ribs. "But what about your surrogate job? I don't want you to do this for me, Lane. I want to be with you. No conditional clauses."

He pushed her hair away from her face. "I can't tell you what it means for me to hear you say that, but I'm not doing this for you. I believe in what I do, and I think it's an important role. But I realized after we broke up that I was clinging to it for the wrong reasons. It's my comfort zone. I know I'm good at it. It was my sure thing. The unknowns are scary. I don't know if I'm going to make it through school. I don't know if I'm skilled enough to be a full-fledged therapist with my own caseload. I don't want to fail. But if I keep dragging out my schooling, using this job to distract me from my ultimate goal, then I'm just being a coward."

Her ribs were cinched so tight she could barely breathe. "Lane."

"I love you, doc. I don't need your money, but I sure as hell need you."

She swallowed hard.

"So"—his green eyes held her gaze, a flicker of mischief there—"if the fancy doctor doesn't mind being with a lowly intern, maybe we could try this again?"

Try again. Her heart seemed to lift higher in her chest and a smile crept up her face. "Does this mean you're going to make inappropriate intern jokes that make me seem like a dirty old lady who's taking advantage of you?"

He gave her a come-on-now look. "As if I'd pass up that opportunity. Who do you think I—"

She didn't let him finish. She couldn't bear it any longer. It'd been one of the longest weeks of her life and a lifetime since she'd felt this brand of happiness. Her and Lane together. No contract clauses. No sharing. No hiding. She launched herself at him, wrapping her arms around his neck, and kissed him.

He groaned, his mouth opening to hers as his hands slid inside her coat and gripped her waist. He kissed her like he needed her air, like he'd been just as miserable being apart as she had. She deepened the kiss, stealing as much closeness as she could. Starved for him. But none of it seemed like enough for either of them. His hands grappled blindly and then lifted her up to straddle his lap. She put her fingers in his hair and eased him back along the exam table. Her hands roamed, careful not to touch his shoulder but not careful about anything else. Her hand fumbled with his buttons, dipped inside his shirt, mapped his abdomen.

"I feel like I'm getting a very thorough exam," he said between kisses.

"I'm good at my job," she said, yanking his shirttails from his pants. "Got to make sure you're okay."

"I'm so very okay." He cupped her breast with a warm hand and her stethoscope fell to the floor. They sank into another deep kiss. The protective paper covering the table bunched beneath them and made crinkly noises. She sent up a silent thank you that there were no surveillance cameras in exam rooms and that the hospital had thick walls.

Still they kissed. Heat shimmered through her, defrosting all the parts of her that had been cold since he'd left her in that parking lot, including the most important spot deep in her chest that had been iced over for far too long.

"I love you, Lane," she murmured against his lips.

"I love you back."

She slid her hands along his chest and kissed a line up his jaw, avoiding the side with the scratches. His cock was hard against the spot where their bodies met, and her own libido thundered through her, making demands, making her reckless. Nothing in the world seemed more important right now than being with this man, skin to skin, exorcising all the demons that had chased them, sharing their love for each other. She didn't want to stop. But her logical side tried to whisper through the erotic haze. She needed to get up and lock the door, mark the room as occupied. Let no one disturb them.

She would do that.

But just one more kiss and maybe a hand tracing the outline of his cock.

Hinges squeaked loudly, the door swinging open, air shifting.

Lane stiffened but Elle didn't even bother looking up. "Shut it and turn the sign to occupied. I'm on break."

The intruder laughed quietly. "No problem, boss. I didn't see a thing."

Oriana.

The door clicked shut and Elle smiled down at Lane. "Now, where were we?"

Lane cocked an eyebrow at her. "I think you were about to fuck me on an exam table in your doctor's coat. Please tell me that's the case. Please tell me I haven't passed out from blood loss and this is actually happening."

She grinned wider. "This is, indeed, happening."

He grabbed her by the collar of her shirt and dragged her down close. "Ah, pornographic dreams really do come true."

She brushed her lips against his, her chest filling with a frothy warmth, one that made her feel light and free and so fully in her skin that it made her breath catch. "I'm starting to believe the fairytale kind do, too."

His eyes softened and he tucked a lock of her hair behind her ear. "Ready to be my princess, doc?"

"No." Her lips curved. "I'm the queen. I'm *always* the queen."

He chuckled beneath her. "Of course. You know that's what I used to call you in my head. The Ice Queen."

She sniffed. "Asshole."

"I was." He slipped his hand under her shirt and dragged a thumb over her breast. "I was wrong about the ice part. Dead-on about the queen." He pressed a kiss to her mouth. "Now take off all your clothes, Your Highness, and keep the coat. Let's see if I'm worthy of being your king."

"Your wish is my command."

His face lit. "Finally, she follows a command!"

She poked his side. "Don't get used to it."

"I wouldn't dare," he teased. "You wouldn't be you

otherwise. And you...are perfect."

The words filtered through her, cutting through the tangles of bad memories and the failed marriage and the insecurities. He loved her. Not some polite, edited version. The woman she was, sharp edges and all. And she loved him back. Every last sweet, sexy bit of him.

They slipped off their clothes. She donned her coat, feeling wrong in the best way possible wearing only that, and Lane laid her out on the table.

He watched her with hungry eyes as he gripped her thighs and sank himself deep inside her. She let out a soft moan and held on to his biceps, her nails digging into the thick muscle. He canted his hips, angling just right, and the heat of him washed through her and made every agitated nerve sigh with relief. She couldn't remember ever feeling so filled up, not just physically but in every part of her psyche.

She didn't believe in one person completing another but now she knew what people meant when they said they'd found their match. Lane fit into her jagged spaces and smoothed them out, made her feel part of something instead of always on the outside looking in.

Made her feel...happy to be exactly who she was.

Lane shifted above her, one hand gripping the side of the table and the other tucked between their bodies, stroking her with confident skill and toe-curling accuracy.

Her brain buzzed with pleasure, making her back arch and a breathy sound come out of her. She wanted to savor this, to feel every sweet second, but her body felt ready to override the plan and go for the finale immediately.

A menacing grin appeared and Lane's gaze shifted to the

left. "What do we have here?"

He was asking her questions right now? She couldn't be expected to answer questions. She grunted but turned her head and tried to focus on whatever it was.

Lane braced himself above her, stealing away the blissful stroke of his fingers, and he lifted what he'd discovered. One of the arm cuffs of the four-point restraints they had for this table.

"What exactly goes on in this room, doc?" he asked wickedly, his hips still moving in a slow, tortuous rhythm that was making her pant.

"Patients. Danger. To. Themselves. Or. Others."

He dragged the soft, flexible material of the cuff over her breast, making her nipple tighten and a curl of pleasure go through her. "Well, you look very dangerous, doc. Definitely a threat."

"I will be if I don't get to come soon," she managed.

He laughed. "Defiant too. Definitely needs an intervention."

Lane slipped his fingers around her wrist and drew her arm down by her hip. He looped the restraint around one wrist and then gave the other the same treatment, pinning her arms at her sides.

She expected a bit of unease at being restrained, but a tremor of need went through her instead. Trust that Lane would make this good for her. But when he slid his cock from inside her, she groaned in protest.

He climbed off the table and found the ankle restraints and put her completely at his mercy. He traced fingertips up her thigh, admiring his handy work. "That's better."

"You're evil," she said, arching and testing the restraints with a tug. They didn't give. These weren't some novelty item from the lingerie store. These were medical grade. Meant to protect people.

But Lane looked poised for torture.

He trailed a path up her thigh and tucked two fingers inside her, finding her slick and desperate. "You want to come, doc?"

"You fucking know I do." She lifted her hips, seeking more. "And you've just blocked yourself. You're not going to be able to fuck me like this."

His lips kicked up at the corner. "Believe me. I don't plan to suffer."

He climbed back over her, bracing himself above her, and with all the patience in the world, he dragged his cock over her labia and along her clit. Her knees tried to bow up, the ripple of pleasure zipping over her, but the ankle restraints held.

She shuddered with need.

"Very nice," Lane said, voice dark with promise. "You can't go anywhere. You just have to take what I'm willing to give you."

He dragged himself over her in a hypnotic, sensation-laden rhythm, making every part of her aware of every inch of him. She needed to spread her legs, to feel him fill her up, to come and come and come. But she couldn't move, could only accept the sparking sensations, feel the erotic ache inside her.

She closed her eyes and swallowed hard. "Please, Lane. I need you."

"She begs," he said softly.

For once that didn't trigger her defiant genes. It no longer felt like losing a game. She could ask for what she needed from Lane without consequences. They were in this together. Both enjoying themselves. No shame. No apologies for what felt good to them. They could have their combative sex. They could play roles. But sometimes, she could just give in and let go.

She was free. "Please. I love you."

He leaned down to kiss her softly and then uncuffed her ankles. She hooked her legs around his hips, and he sank deep inside her. Her hands were still cuffed but she didn't need her hands to feel. Her breasts rubbed against the coarse hair on his chest, making her nipples tingle, his fingers stroked over her clit, making her blood pump, and his cock stretched her. In minutes, they both came with a chorus of quiet moans, hot words, and sweat-slicked skin.

She rode the wave of it. Every part of her was alight with feeling, with sensation. But when they finally settled against each other, coasting down from the high, something much more potent than the aftershocks of orgasm washed through her. In those private, quiet minutes, every hollow space, every dark corner inside her filled to the brim with contentment.

This was what she never knew she'd been searching for. This sense of knowing she was exactly where she was supposed to be.

Elle had always thought that villains had more fun in fairy tales, that happy endings were for childhood fantasies. Unrealistic. Boring.

But looking at Lane, feeling his heart beat against hers, seeing the future stretch out before them, she no longer wanted to be the Ice Queen in her tale.

She wanted to be the wide-eyed child who believed in the possibility.

Who believed that happily ever after wasn't so unrealistic after all.

That, in fact, it was hers for the taking.

She just had to close her eyes, take Lane's hand, and leap.

epilogue
Nine months later

Elle was starved after the drive back from New Orleans. She'd wanted to stop and grab a burger or something along the way, but Lane had asked her to hold out for dinner at a restaurant since he hadn't seen her in five days.

She'd been bummed he hadn't been able to come with her to visit her mother and sister, but he'd been in the home stretch of finishing a big research paper and needed some quiet time to dictate his latest pages. She also suspected that he was trying to give her bonding time with her family. Things had gotten much better with her sister, since they'd been together so often during their mom's recovery, but there was still work to be done, trust to be built. However, things with her mom had grown in a direction Elle had never dared hope for. They were getting along and actually enjoying each other's company.

Elle had taken time off and spent a few weeks with her mom after her surgery, rotating duties with her sister. And though it'd been tough to see her mother in pain, it'd been a gift to spend some one-on-one time with her mom. She got to see sides of her that she'd never been privy to as a child. They were also more alike than she realized—in good ways and bad—and that had opened up doors to conversations Elle had needed to have with her, healed wounds that had been left open.

She now spoke with her every few days because they enjoyed each other. That urge to simply chat with her mom was something she still marveled over.

Elle let out a sigh of relief when she saw the sign for Parrain's PoBoys gleaming neon against the worn wood of the building. Nothing sounded better right now than a sloppy roast beef po-boy, a pile of fries, and a sexy man to share them with.

She parked next to Lane's car and headed toward the building, surprised to see the parking lot full at this late of an hour on a weeknight. Usually, this was a weekend hotspot and more of a takeout place for the middle of the week.

The crushed oyster shell gravel crunched beneath her shoes as she passed a man leaving with an armful of sandwiches wrapped in white butcher paper, the grease already peeking through. The tempting smell of fried shrimp wafted after him and her stomach growled.

She picked up the pace and jogged up the stairs of the wide front porch. The empty rocking chairs creaked in the breeze, greeting her. But when she pulled the door open, the lights blinked off and she was hit with darkness. Only the neon Abita Beer sign behind the bar glowed. "What the hell?"

But before she could process why the neon would be on and not the overheads, a loud chorus of "Surprise!" nearly knocked her back out the door.

The lights flicked on and she yelped, putting her hand to her chest. A crowd of faces smiled back at her. The faces coming into sharp focus as her eyes adjusted. Oriana. Donovan. Marin. Ray. Members of her staff. Other colleagues. And then right at the center, Lane, smiling his wicked grin and holding out his arms in a *ta-da* motion.

She blinked, trying to take it all in, well and truly shocked. "What in the world is going on?"

Oriana held up a glittery sign. "Happy Birthday!"

The group clapped and whooped.

"Birthday?" Elle shook her head. "Mine's not until next month."

Lane grinned. "Hence the surprise."

She laughed and held her hands out to her sides. "Wow, well, I'm officially surprised!"

"Yes!" Oriana pumped a fist in the air. "Nailed it."

"Thanks, everyone. I've never had a surprise party." Or any birthday party as an adult at all.

She glanced around at all the colorful balloons mixing in with holiday decorations. Everything was festive and lovely, but her gaze caught on a table where a small pile of presents was stacked. Her breath caught. It was the table where she'd sat and first watched Lane cross the room toward her. She could almost see her former self still sitting there, separated from the group, back straight, expression annoyed. Last year, she'd been in that very spot on her birthday, more alone than she'd ever been in her life. Tears pricked her eyes.

Music from the jukebox started up and Lane stepped forward to gather her into his arms. He tilted his face close to hers, his voice low. "You okay? Because if this isn't your thing, I'll steal you away right now. I know you're not much of a party person, but your friends really wanted to do something."

Friends.

She rolled her lips together, overwhelmed at knowing that her co-workers put this together for her, but more overwhelmed that she was part of this group now. "They did this?"

He smiled. "Yes, my birthday surprise would involve a lot less clothes and probably ball gags. The night is young, though."

She laughed and half-heartedly shoved him. "I hate you."

He kissed her hand. "I hate you back."

She poked a finger to his chest. "I don't want to leave. But if I don't get my po-boy in the next two minutes, there may be blood."

He lifted his palms to her and backed away. "Someone get the doc some roast beef, stat."

She laughed as three different waiters stepped forward with trays of food. Lane got her a plate and piled it high, and then her co-workers descended on her, chatting, wishing her happy early birthday, and asking her about her mom.

The attention was overwhelming at first, but soon she fell into a rhythm that had become more and more familiar over the last few months, being part of a group, of a team...of a couple. She even caught herself laughing. Relaxing.

After she'd finished her food, Lane slid his hands onto her shoulders and leaned next to her ear. "I have fed you. Now we have reached the most vital part of the evening. It is time...to line dance."

She turned her head and gave him a you-must-be-on-hallucinogenics look.

"We reserved the place on country-western line dance night," he explained. "So we're obligated to do this. There has been line dancing on this night of the week here for ten years. It's bad luck to break tradition."

She smirked. "Bad luck? I am a dignified doctor of medicine. I *do not* line dance."

"You do now. Thems the rules, doc." He plunked a shot of something amber-colored in front of her. "Drink up, birthday girl, and let's fulfill our duty."

Elle groaned. "You're serious."

"I do not kid about serious matters such as these."

She gave him a look but tipped the shot back, hoping the liquid courage kicked in quick because this kind of dancing was going to require an altered state of consciousness. Her co-workers cheered her on, and Lane tugged her up from her spot.

A few of the others joined them on the dance floor and Marin pulled Donovan out there, her shiny new wedding ring glinting in the lights. Donovan sent Elle an S.O.S. look and mouthed *help.*

She laughed. "You're own your own, buddy. I've got my own problems."

Marin grinned her way, and it hit Elle how much had changed. She could joke with Donovan and Marin now. Their relationship had no pull on her anymore, no bitterness. And Marin had graciously given her a second chance after her bad behavior last year. The three of them had managed to forge good working relationships. But slowly, unexpectedly, they were also becoming her friends.

Lane spun her into position, looking way too pleased with himself. He waggled his eyebrows. "Know how to do this, doc?"

"Not even a little bit. You're doomed."

The music started before she was ready. She'd never be ready. But the beat wasn't going to wait. "Louisiana Saturday

Night" thumped from the jukebox. Or Loo-zee-anna, as the song declared. Everyone kicked off their shoes.

Elle groaned and slipped off her flats.

Lane took her hand and stood at her side. "Let's do this, doc."

The group started a long, weaving grapevine step. Elle tried to follow their lead but was looking at her feet and knocked into Oriana, who looked about as skilled at line dancing as she was. Ori laughed and put her hand on Elle's shoulder to keep from falling.

"I'd like to blame this on drinking," Ori said. "But I'm sober as hell. Can't we do 'Strokin' instead? I know that one."

The whole group spun and she and Ori ended up facing the wrong way. Lane didn't miss a step and looked as if he were just a pair of boots and a Stetson shy of being able to rope cattle. Elle found that oddly hot. She sidled up next to him again, trying to follow the steps through the end of the song, but she stomped on his feet three times. She was near tears with laughing by the end.

"I'm literally the worst line dancer ever."

"You are," Lane agreed with a grin. "You had to be bad at something."

When the song was over, she bumped him in the shoulder. "So where'd you learn your moves, cowboy?"

He laughed and tugged her to him, pulling her into some kind of two-step as a slower song came on. That was a little easier to follow. He bent his head close to her ear. "The agency I worked for in a previous life made us take lessons. Southern ladies like men who can dance."

"I'm scared to ask what other kind of lessons they gave you," she teased.

He got a wicked gleam in his eye and led her into a spin. "I didn't need those kinds of lessons. That just comes naturally."

He pulled her tight to him and a wash of heat went through her, mixing with the lingering warmth from the alcohol. Suddenly, she wished there weren't so many people around. "So how long do you think this party will go?"

"Already scheming how to get me alone, doc?" he asked, his hand sliding to her lower back.

"You have no idea," she said, looping her arms around his neck. "In my head, you're already naked. With cowboy boots."

His eyes twinkled in the lights and he dipped his head low to kiss her. "That can be arranged. And don't worry. Dessert's not too far away, I promise."

Lane sat, watching Elle give Raymond a quick hug good-bye and then thanking everyone for coming. He smiled at the sight. She was sparkling like the champagne they'd toasted with. Eyes alight, blond hair tousled, and her cheeks flushed from alcohol and a good party.

He hadn't been sure how Elle would react to the surprise get-together and had developed a back-up plan, but he'd wanted to give her the opportunity to see what her friends and co-workers had wanted to do for her. He was glad he hadn't shut it down before it happened. Elle had handled everything with grace. Not just grace but she looked…happy. Happy in a way that sent sunshine sneaking into the final worried corners inside him.

He waited until she'd said good-bye to the last guest and then grabbed the large white box from behind the bar. The manager gave him a nod and then slipped into the office, affording them some privacy.

Elle walked back into the main dining room, her eyes finding him in the low lighting at the corner of the dance floor. Her soft smile at seeing him sent Lane's heartbeat speeding up. He never got over how goddamned lucky he was to have Elle in his life. She saw *him*. Loved him. Every part of his life, of his past, his struggles and triumphs, and she embraced it all. He could joke with her on the dance floor about lessons he'd had to take when he'd been an escort and not have to worry about feeling judgment or pity from her. He could take her home and tie her to the bed and teasingly insult her and she only got hotter for it. They were oddly shaped puzzle pieces that, by some miracle, had found their match. He would never take that for granted.

"Hey, you," she said, crossing the dark dance floor. "Ready to get out of here? I think we've shut the place down."

He reached out and took her hand, pulling her down to the chair next to him. "We haven't had dessert yet."

She glanced at the empty bar. "Well, I don't think the manager would appreciate us doing dessert here in the restaurant."

He smirked and tapped the box on the table. "Actual dessert, horny lady."

She turned her head, noticing the box for the first time. She pressed her hands together with delight. "Ooh. You saved the cake all for us? Good plan."

"Open it."

She reached over and lifted the lid. He watched her face instead of the box. Her eyes widened and then a laugh tumbled out of her. "Pepto pink!"

"Of course." Lane nodded. "For your pretty, pretty princess birthday party. I even got little tiaras added to them."

She smiled wide. "I love them. They're perfect." She leaned

closer and poked at one of plastic tiaras. "But there are only eleven." She sent him a playful glare. "Did you already eat one again, Cannon? Show me those teeth."

He wet his lips and reached beneath his chair, grabbing the small white box beneath. He held it out to her. "No, there's a special one for the birthday girl. One that won't turn her teeth pink."

A wrinkle appeared between her brows. He took a breath and opened the box.

She blinked a few times, her gaze zeroing in on the cupcake inside, one made of blown glass he'd commissioned from a local artist.

Elle sucked in a breath and lifted the sculpture out of the box. "Lane, this is gorgeous."

"You're gorgeous," he said softly.

"Ooh, it opens." She glanced up at him and then slowly lifted off the top. He could see the moment she realized what was inside. Her eyes widened and her lips parted.

He couldn't see what she was seeing but he knew exactly what was there. A delicate vintage gold ring with diamonds in the shape of a flower, and all of his promises for the future weaved into it.

"Oh, shit," she whispered. "You said you sold this back months ago."

Lane didn't answer. He could've never sold that ring back. He'd seen how much she loved it. She'd told him it was what she would've picked out for herself. In his mind, it'd always belonged to her. He scooted his chair back and lowered himself to his knee.

Her stunned gaze darted to his.

He couldn't read if her expression was surprise, fear, or horror, but he had to get the words out. "Elle McCray, I know you swore you'd never get married again, so I'm not going to ask you. But I love you, and I can't imagine spending the rest of my life with anyone but you. So if you ever decide you're willing to walk down the aisle again, know that I'd love nothing more than to be the one doing it with you. But if marriage isn't for you, let this ring symbolize what I want to give you."

Her blue eyes went shiny and she gave him a tremulous smile. "And what's that?"

"Everything. Forever."

Elle set the sculpture aside and held the ring between her fingers, a tear slipping down her cheek as she stared down at it.

"Forever is a long time," she said softly.

He swallowed hard, feeling more vulnerable than he'd expected. "Yeah."

She lifted her gaze, her smile steadying, beaming, and slid down to the floor with him. "I have a feeling it's not going to be long enough with you."

All the breath whooshed out of him.

She took his hand and pressed the ring into his palm. "Ask me."

Every tense muscle in his body loosened, happiness suffusing through him and spreading wide. He took the ring and held it between them. "Doc, will you marry me?"

She reached out and cupped his cheek. "I would do it tomorrow."

He'd never heard sweeter words in his life. His hand trembled as he slid the ring onto her finger and then he brought her knuckles to his mouth, pressing a kiss there. "Me too."

"You mean that?" she asked, her brows lifting.

"Of course I do."

She peered down at the ring, a thoughtful look crossing her face. "Then, why don't we?"

He leaned back to get a better look at her, to see if she was kidding. "Like blow this joint and go to Vegas?"

"No one says we can't." She looped her arms around his neck, a wicked grin lifting her lips. "I've done the fancy wedding. It's overrated. Too many people. Too much drama. All I want is you. And I can think of no better way to celebrate my birthday than by making it official."

Something unlocked inside his chest, something he didn't even know had rusted shut. He knew Elle loved him. He knew they were right together whether there was a court document or not. But he didn't realize until that moment how badly he wanted her as his wife. How much he wanted her to take that risk on him. He leaned forward and kissed her long and thoroughly, letting the happiness sink into his bones and linger. He pulled back and smiled. "Let's do it."

"Yeah?" She laughed when he nodded. "This is insane."

He got up and pulled her to her feet. "Well, we haven't gone about this the normal way the whole time. Why start now?"

"Good point," she said, bouncing on the balls of her feet with giddy excitement. "Come on. Let's go home and pack. Or maybe make out first. And eat a cupcake. And then pack."

"Excellent plan." He grabbed the box of cupcakes and the sculpture.

Elle picked up a steak knife from a set of silverware on the table.

He glanced at the weapon in her hand. "What are you doing?

Is this the part where you confess you're a murderer?"

She rolled her eyes. "No, but there's something I need to do." She cocked her head toward the door. "Go donate a few of those cupcakes to the manager and stall him for a few minutes. I'll meet you outside in fifteen?"

He eyed her. "What are you up to?"

She shrugged. "Just need to take care of a little something."

He decided not to question her further and headed toward the bar to offer the dessert. The manager was more than happy to chat things up, but when Lane stuck his head out the door a few minutes later to check on Elle, she was crouched over one of the tables, the knife to the wood and a look of concentration on her face.

Lane stalled for a few more minutes and then headed out when he saw Elle was no longer out there. He walked to the table where Elle had been and looked at the fresh wood shavings scattered across the top.

A worn inscription was there, the edges smooth with time. $D + R = 4Ever$

But right beneath were freshly carved initials in the center of a crude heart. $L + E$

Not forever. Not always. Just their two initials linked without a time attached.

And that was exactly how it felt when they got on a plane that night to begin their future.

Together.

In love.

Limitless.

Thank You!

Thanks so much for reading *By the Hour!* I hope you enjoyed reading Lane and Elle's story as much as I enjoyed writing it.

If you did, I'd love it if you would **consider leaving a review online.** Reviews help readers find books, and readers finding my books means I get to write more, which means you get to read more. Win-win-win, yes?

If you'd like to stay in touch, get sneak peeks, find out when the next book will be out, and get helpful articles in your inbox on books, productivity, life, etc., sign up for the Fearless Romantics newsletter. I promise this newsletter is about 3% promotional and 97% interesting stuff. No one likes promotional newsletters, including me, so I work hard to keep mine helpful, entertaining, and fun. You also get a **free downloadable romance reading journal** when you sign up to track your reading.

Hope to see you around online! Now read on for a sneak peek of the first book in a brand new series, *The Ones Who Got Away,* and an excerpt of *Off the Clock* if you missed where the *Pleasure Principle* series started!

the ones who got away

Coming January 2018

chapter one

*N*othing *can save you.* Liv Arias rubbed goose bumps from her arms as she read the words scrawled on the sign taped under a maniacal-looking wasp painted on the wall of the gym. *Nothing can save you from the sting!* More hand-drawn posters hung crookedly around the ridiculous mascot, bubbly cheerleader handwriting declaring that the Millbourne Yellow Jackets were going to take down the Creekside Tigers. Some smartass had drawn a tiger with a swollen face and an Epi-pen with an X through it.

Nothing can save you. The level of artistic skill on the cartoon should've made Liv smile. Back when she was in high school, she would've never been the one making school spirit signs, but she would've appreciated the art and the sarcasm. Today, she couldn't find enthusiasm for either. Because it all felt off. The new name for the school. The weird, too smiley mascot. Her, being there.

This wasn't the gym where it had happened. That building had been knocked down within months of the tragedy. Spilled blood covered with dirt. A memorial courtyard was in its place now on the other side of the school. She'd taken the long way around and had avoided walking past it on her way in, afraid it would trigger all the stuff she'd fought so hard to lock down. Even after twelve years, she couldn't bear to look at a list of names that should've been in a graduation program instead of etched onto a memorial. People she'd sat next to in class. People she'd been friends with. People she'd thought she hated until they were gone and she'd realized how silly and superficial high-school hate was. Now they were just names on stone, memories painted on the walls of her brain, holes in people's hearts.

"You said you weren't in the gym when the first gunman came in."

The interviewer's calm voice jarred Liv out of her thoughts, and she blinked in the bright camera-ready lights. They'd been talking about the tragedy as a whole, but hadn't gotten into the details of the night yet. "What?"

Daniel Morrow, the filmmaker putting the documentary together, gave her an encouraging nod, making his too-stylish hair flop across his forehead. "You weren't in the gym..."

Liv swallowed past the rubber-band tightness in her throat. Maybe she'd overestimated her ability to handle this. She'd agreed to it because the proceeds were going both to the families of the victims and to research that could help prevent things like this from happening. How could she say no to that and not look heartless? But in that moment, she wished she'd declined. Old fear was creeping up the back of her neck, invading like a thousand spiders, the sounds and memories from that night threatening to overtake her. She closed her eyes for a second, focused on her breathing.

She wasn't that scared girl anymore. She *would not* be.

"Do you need to take a break, Ms. Arias?" Daniel asked, his voice echoing in the dark, empty gym.

She shook her head, the lights feeling too hot on her skin. No breaks. She needed to get this over with. If she took a break, she wouldn't come back. She opened her eyes and straightened her spine, rallying up her reserve of calm, that place where she went and pretended she was talking about things that happened to someone else, to people she didn't know, at a school she'd never heard of. "No, I wasn't in the gym. I'd gone into the hallway to get some air."

Not entirely true. She'd left the prom to sneak into a janitor's closet with Finn Dorsey. But she and Finn had never told that part of the story because he'd been there with a "proper" date, and he would've never wanted his parents or anyone else to know he was sneaking off with someone like Olivia Arias. She'd first dragged him into the closet to fight with him, to let him know how she felt about being passed over for his student council president date. But fighting had only stoked the fire that had burned between them back then. Young, misguided, completely inconvenient lust. They'd been rounding second base when they'd heard the first shots fired.

"What happened when you were in the hallway?"

Liv didn't want to picture it again. She'd wrestled with flashbacks for so long that it felt like inviting the devil in for another stay. Her only reprieve in the last few years had been one-hundred percent avoidance, cutting herself off from everything and everyone from back then. Letting the scene run through her mind could be too much. But there was no helping it. The images came anyway.

"When I heard the shots and screaming, I hid in the janitor's closet." She and Finn had thought it was some kind of prom prank until they'd heard Finn's date, Rebecca, shout the word *gun*.

Gun.

A tiny, three-letter word that had knocked their world off its axis and punted it into a different dimension forever.

"So you never saw the shooters?"

She wrapped her hands around her elbows, trying to keep the inner chill from becoming visible shivering, and she ignored the pine scent of the janitor's disinfectant that burned her nose as if she were right there again. She still couldn't buy a real Christmas tree because of that smell. "I didn't see anyone until Joseph opened the door."

Because Finn had left her. The second he'd heard Rebecca scream, he'd bailed on Liv. He'd said something to her, but she could never recall what. All she remembered was him leaving. And in his rush to save his real date, he'd inadvertently alerted Joseph to Liv's presence.

"He pointed the gun at me and yelled at me to stand up." Her voice caught on the last bit, snagging on the sharp memory, bringing back that all-encompassing fear that she was in her last minutes. She'd learn to mostly manage the panic attacks that had plagued her after that night, but that moment was always the image that haunted her most, where she saw the barrel of that gun pointing at her, the scared but determined eyes of her former lab partner drilling into her like cold steel.

"But Joseph didn't pull the trigger?"

Liv looked down at her hands, turning her mother's wedding band round and round. "No. He knew who I was. I...wasn't on his list."

"Meaning?"

There was no way Daniel didn't know what it meant. The media had latched on to killers' manifesto like ants on honey. Joseph and Trevor had chosen prom night for a very particular reason. Not to take out the popular people or people who'd wronged them. They wanted to take out the *happy* ones. *If you can be happy in a fucked up world like this, then you're blind and too stupid to live.* That'd been the motto of their mission.

Liv hadn't been deemed a *happy one* and had been spared. But she wasn't going to say it and open herself up to the question of *why* she hadn't been happy. There'd been enough speculation in the press back when it'd happened. What was *broken* with all those lucky survivors? Were they the mean kids? The depressed kids? The damaged kids? *Friends* of the killers? "Joseph and I had worked together on a project in chemistry. We weren't friends, but I'd been nice to him."

And he'd been nice to her. But she'd also seen part of him that would haunt her later. When she'd worried that their project wouldn't be up to par, he'd assured her that the rest of the class was filled with idiots, jocks, and assholes, so they'd look like geniuses in comparison. He'd smirked at her and said, *I mean, seriously, someone should just put them out of their misery. Save us the trouble of having to deal with them.*

Back then, she'd already been a subscriber to the church of sarcasm and had no love lost for many of her classmates, so she'd taken it as such and agreed with him. Now the memory of that conversation made her sick. She'd reassured a killer that he was right. Gave him more fuel for his bonfire.

"He cursed at me, told me to stay put, and wedged a chair

against the outside of the door." She rubbed her lips together. "After that, I heard more shots."

"Presumably when he shot at"—Daniel checked his notes— "Finn Dorsey and Rebecca Lindt."

Liv reached for her water and took a slow sip, trying not to hear the sounds of that night in her head. The gun going off in that steady, unrelenting way. The cries for help. A Mariah Carey song still playing in the gym. Her own rapid breath as she huddled in that closet and did—nothing. Frozen. For five hours. Only the chair against the door had alerted the SWAT team someone was in there after everything was over. "Yes. I didn't see any of it, but I know Finn was shot protecting Rebecca. You'd have to ask Rebecca about that part."

"I did ask her. I plan to ask Finn, too."

Her head snapped upward at that, the words yanking her out of the memories like a stage hook. "What?"

"Mr. Dorsey is my next interview."

She stared at him, not sure if she'd heard the words right. "Finn's *here*?"

She barely resisted saying, *He exists?* The guy had become a ghost after the awful months following the shooting. He'd gotten a ton of press for being a hero, and the media had played up the story to the *n*th degree. The star athlete and son of a local business owner taking a bullet for his date. But within a year, his family had moved out of town, running from the spotlight like everyone else. No one wanted to be that brand of famous.

She hadn't heard anything about him since, and he never gave interviews. She'd decided that he and his wealthy parents had probably moved to some remote tropical island and changed his name. She would've skipped town back then too if she'd had the funds to do it.

"Yes," Daniel said, tipping his head toward the spot over her left shoulder. "He got here a few minutes ago. He's declined to be on camera, but he's agreed to an interview."

With that, she couldn't help but turn and follow the interviewer's gaze. Leaning against the wall in the shadows of the darkened gym was a man with dark hair, black T-shirt, and jeans. He looked up from the phone in his hand, as if hearing his name, and peered in their direction. He was too far away for her to read his expression or see the details of his face, but a jolt of bone-deep recognition went through her. "Oh."

"Hey, we should invite him to join you for this part since you were both close to the same place at the same time. We'll get a more accurate timeline that way."

"What? I mean, no, that's not—"

"Jim, can you turn off the camera? I think this will be important. Mr. Dorsey," Daniel called out, "would you mind if I asked you a few questions now? The camera's off."

The cameraman went about shutting things down, and Finn pushed away from the wall.

Liv's heart leapt into her throat and tried to escape. She'd avoided Finn after everything had happened, not just from hurt, but because seeing his face, even on television would trigger the flashbacks. But she wasn't that girl anymore. Seeing Finn after all these years shouldn't concern her. Still, she had the distinct urge to make tracks to the back door. She slid out of the director's chair she'd been sitting in. "I think I've probably given you everything I have to add. I wasn't in the gym, and my story is really just me cowering in the closet. Not that interesting—"

Liv's words cut off, her voice dying a quick death, as Finn got closer and some of the studio lights caught him in their glare. The man approaching was nothing like the boy she'd known. The bulky football muscles had streamlined into a harder, leaner package. The smooth face was now dusted with scruff, and the look in his deep green eyes held no trace of boyish innocence. A thousand things were in those eyes. A thousand things welled up in Liv.

Finn Dorsey had become a man. And a stranger. The only familiar thing was the sharp, undeniable kick of awareness she'd always had anytime the guy was around. Time had only made the effect more potent. Without thinking, her gaze drifted to his hands. Big, capable hands that had once held her. When she'd known him, he'd always worn his football championship ring from junior year, the cool metal used to press against the back of her neck when he kissed her. Now he wore no rings at all. She took a breath, trying to reel in that old, automatic response to him, and smoothed her hands down the sides of her now-wrinkled pencil skirt.

Daniel held out his hand. "Mr. Dorsey, so glad you could make it."

Finn returned the offered handshake and gave a brief nod. "Not a problem."

Then, his gaze slid to Liv. His brow wrinkled for a second, but she could tell the moment he realized who she was. Something flickered over his face. A very distinct look. Like she caused him pain. Like she was a bad memory.

Because she was. That was all they were to each other at this point.

"Liv."

She cleared her throat. "Hi, Finn."

He stepped closer, his gaze tracing over her face as if searching for something. Or maybe just cataloguing all the differences time had given her. Gone were the heavy kohl eyeliner, the nose piercing, and the purple-streaked hair. She'd gone back to her natural black hair color after college, and though she still liked to think she had a quirky style, she'd chosen a simple gray suit for today's interview. Something teen Liv would've made snoring sounds over.

"It's good to see you," Finn said, his voice deeper and more rumbly than she remembered. "You look…"

"Like I've been through a two hour interview, I'm sure." She forced a tight smile. "I'll get out of your way so that you and Daniel can chat. I'm sure you'll be able to offer a lot more detailed information than I can. I was just the girl in the closet."

Finn frowned. "Liv—"

"I was hoping I could talk to you both," Daniel interrupted. "May provide extra insight."

Liv's heart was beating too fast now. Part of her wanted to yell at Finn, to demand why, to spew out all those questions she'd never asked, all those feelings she'd packed away in that dark vault labeled *senior year.* But the other part of her knew there was no good answer. In the end, all three of them had survived. Maybe if he hadn't left the closet, Rebecca wouldn't have made it. Then Liv would have that on her conscience.

She turned to Daniel and plastered on an apologetic look. "I'm sorry. This has wiped me out. I'd rather wrap things up here. I really don't have more to add."

"What if we took a break and then—"

"She said she's tired," Finn said, cool authority in his voice.

"It would only be a few more questions. The viewers would—"

Finn lifted a hand. "Look. I know you're doing this for a good cause, but you have to remember what this does to all of us. To the outside world, this was a tragedy. Something they discuss over dinner, shake their heads at, or get political about. To us, this was our life, our school, our friends. Asking us to come back here, to talk about all these things again...it requires more than anyone realizes. It rips open things that we try to keep stitched up. So let her go. She doesn't owe anyone more of her story than she wants to give." Finn peered at her. "She doesn't owe anyone anything."

Liv's chest squeezed tight, and Daniel turned her way, apologies in his eyes. "I'm sorry. You're right. Ms. Arias, if you need to go, please do. I appreciate all the time you've given me."

He held out his hand for her to shake and she took it. "It's fine. Knowing that the proceeds are going to the families helps. I know you'll do a good job with it. I just don't have any more to add."

She released Daniel's hand and turned to Finn, giving him a little nod of thanks. "I'll get out of here so y'all can get started. It was good to see you, Finn."

Finn's gaze held hers, for a moment kicking up old memories that had nothing to do with gunmen or violence or the way it all ended. But instead of stolen minutes and frantic kisses in the library stacks and his big, full laugher when she'd tell him her weird jokes. Before Finn had abandoned her that night, he'd saved her each day of that semester, had given her something to look forward to, something to smile about when things were so awful at home. He'd made her hope.

But even before the shooting, she should've known there was no future for the two of them. The signs had been there the whole time. She'd just been too dazzled to see them.

"It's been too long," he said quietly. "We should have a drink and catch up. Are you staying in town?"

She was. But she didn't feel prepared for that conversation. She didn't feel prepared for *him*. All those years after he'd disappeared, she'd had a thousand questions for him, but now she couldn't bring herself to ask one. This interview, the twelve-year anniversary, and seeing him had left her feeling too raw, exposed. And what difference would his answers make, anyway? The past couldn't be changed.

She wanted to lie and tell him she was heading out tonight. But she was staying at the Bear Creek Inn, the only decent hotel in their little Texas town, which meant that was probably where he was staying, too. If she lied, she'd run into him because that was how the universe worked. "I'm meeting up with some friends for dinner. I'm not sure I'll have time."

He watched her for a moment, his gaze searching, but then nodded. "I'm in Room 348 at the Bear. Call my room if you change your mind, and I can meet you at the bar."

She forced a polite smile. "Will do."

"Great." But she could tell by the look on his face that he didn't believe her.

This was all just a formality, and maybe his offer for a drink was the same. No matter what had happened between them before the night of the dance, all they were to each other now was bad memories and even worse decisions.

She told both men good-bye and turned to head to the door,

forcing herself not to look back. This place, this story, were her past. *Finn Dorsey* was her past. She didn't need anything or anyone reminding her of that time in her life, of how fragile she'd been. She'd worked too hard to lock up all that stuff in a fail-safe box so that she could finally move forward. She couldn't linger here.

She picked up her pace. Her high heels clicked on the gym floor at a rapid clip.

But instead of hearing her footfalls, all she heard were gunshots. *Click, click, click. Bang, bang, bang.*

Anxiety rippled over her nerve endings, and she tried to breathe through the astringent pine scent that haunted her. *No.* Screams sounded in her ears.

She walked so quickly, she may have been running. Finn may have called out her name.

But she couldn't be sure and she didn't turn back.

The faster she could get away from this place and the memories, the better.

She was not that girl anymore.

She would never go back.

Missed *Off the Clock,* book one in the
Pleasure Principle series?
Turn the page to get a peek at how it all started!

OFF *the* CLOCK

1

Then

"*I'm going to wrap my fingers in your hair and slide my other hand up your thigh. You have to be quiet for me. We can't let anyone know.*"

Marin Rush paused in the dark hallway of Harker Hall, her tennis shoes going silent on the shiny linoleum and the green *Exit* signs humming softly in the background. She didn't dare move. She'd been on the way to grab a soda and a snack out of the vending machine. Her caffeine supply had run low and watching participants snore in the sleep lab wasn't exactly stimulating stuff. But that silk-smooth male voice had hit her like a thunderclap, waking up every sense that had gone dull with exhaustion.

She'd assumed she was the only one left in the psychology building at this hour besides the two study subjects in the sleep lab. It was spring break and the classrooms and labs were supposed to be locked up—all except the one she was working in. That's what the girl she was filling in for this week had told her. But there was no mistaking the male voice as it drifted into the hallway.

"I bet you'd like being fucked up against the wall. My cock pumping in you hard and fast."

Holy. Shit. Marin pressed her lips together. Obviously two other people thought they were alone, too. Had students snuck into the building to get it on? Or maybe it was one of the professors. *Oh, God, please don't let it be a professor.* She should turn around right now and go back to Professor Roberts's office. Last thing she needed was to see one of her teachers in some compromising position. She would die of mortification.

But instead of backing up, she found herself tilting her head to isolate where the voice was coming from, and her feet moved forward a few steps.

"Yeah, you like that. I know. I bet you're wet for me right now just thinking about how it would feel. Maybe I should check. Keep your hands against the wall."

A hot shiver zipped through Marin, making every part of her hyperaware. .

"I'm so hard for you. Can you feel how much I want you?" That voice was like velvet against Marin's skin. She closed her eyes, imagining the picture the stranger was painting—some hot guy behind her, pinning her to the wall, his erection rubbing against her. She'd never been in that situation, but her body sure knew how to react to the idea. Her hand drifted up to her neck and pressed against her throat, her pulse beating like hummingbird wings beneath her fingertips.

She waited with held breath to hear the woman's response, but no voice answered the man's question. *Can you feel how much I want you?* he'd asked. And hell if Marin wasn't dying to know. She strained to hear.

"I tug your panties off and trail my hand up your thighs until I can feel your hot, slick..."

Marin braced her other hand against the wall and leaned so far forward that one more inch would've sent her toppling over. *Your hot...*

"Goddammit. Motherfucker."

The curse snapped Marin out of the spell she'd fallen into, and she straightened instantly, her face hot and her heartbeat pounding in places it shouldn't be. There was a groaning squeak of an office chair and another slew of colorful swearing.

Whoever had been saying the dirty things had changed his tone of voice and now sounded ten kinds of annoyed. A wadded-up ball of paper came flying out of an open doorway a few yards down. She followed the arc and watched the paper land on the floor. Only then did she notice there were three others like it already littering the hallway.

Lamplight shifted on the pale linoleum as if the person inside the office was moving around, and Marin flattened herself against the wall, trying to make herself one with it. *Please don't come out. Please don't come out.* The silent prayer whispered through her as she counted the doors between her and the mystery voice, mentally labeling each one. When she realized it was one of the offices they let the Ph.D. students use and not a professor's, she let out a breath.

Either way, she had no intention of alerting her hall mate that he wasn't alone. But at least she could stop worrying she'd gotten all fevered over one of her professors. Now she just had to figure out how to get past the damn door without letting him see her. She'd gotten used to skipping meals to save money since starting college a few months ago. But she wasn't going to make it through the next two hours of data entry and sleep monitoring if she didn't get some caffeine. No wonder none of the upperclassmen had wanted to fill in during break.

Marin's gaze slid over to the stairwell. If she stayed on the other side of the hall in the shadows, she could probably sneak by unnoticed. She moved to the right side wall and crept forward on quiet feet. But as soon as she got within a few steps of the shaft of light coming from the occupied room, a large shadow blotted it into darkness.

She'd been so focused on that beam of light that it took her a moment to register what had happened. She froze and her gaze hopped upward, landing on the guy who filled the doorway. No, not just any guy, a very familiar guy. Tall and lean and effortlessly disheveled. Everything inside her went on alert. *Oh, God, not him.*

He had his hand braced on the doorjamb, and his expression was as surprised as hers probably was. "What the hell?"

"I—" She could already feel her face heating and her throat closing—some bizarre, instant response she seemed to have to this man. She'd spent way too many hours in the back of her Intro to Human Sexuality class memorizing each little detail of Donovan West. Well, his profile, really. And his walk. And the way his shoulders filled out his T-shirts. As a teaching assistant, he usually only stopped in at the beginning of class to bring Professor Paxton papers or something. But each time he walked in now, it was like some bat signal for her body to go haywire.

It'd started with the day he'd had to take over the lecture when Professor Paxton was sick. He'd talked about arousal and the physical mechanics of that process. It was technical. He'd been wearing a T-shirt that read *Sometimes I Feel Like a Total*

Freud. It shouldn't have been sexy. But Lord, it'd been one of the hottest experiences of her life. He'd talked with his hands a lot and had obviously been a little nervous to be in front of the class. But at the same time, he'd been so confident in the information, had answered questions with all this enthusiasm. Marin hadn't heard a word in the rest of her classes that day for all the fantasizing she'd been doing.

But now she was staring. And blushing. And generally looking like an idiot. Yay.

She turned fully toward him and cleared her throat, trying to form some kind of non-weird response. But when her gaze quickly traveled over him again, all semblance of language left her. *Oh, shit.* She tried to drag her focus back to his face and cement it there. His very handsome face—a shadow of stubble, bright blue eyes, hair that fell a little too long around the ears. Lips that she'd thought way too much about. All good. All great.

But despite the nice view, she couldn't ignore the thing in the bottom edge of her vision, the thing that had caught her attention on that quick once-over. The hard outline in his jeans screamed at her to stare—to analyze, to burn the picture into her brain. The need to look warred with embarrassment. The latter finally won and her cheeks flared even hotter. She adjusted her glasses. "Uh, yeah, hi. Sorry. I thought I was alone in the building. Didn't mean to interrupt… whatever."

He stared at her for a second, his brows knitting. "Interrupt?"

Goddammit, her gaze flicked there again. The view was like a siren song she couldn't ignore. *Massive erection, dead ahead!* She glanced away. But not quick enough for him not to notice.

"Ah, shit." He stepped behind the doorway and hid his bottom half. "Sorry. It's uh… not what it looks like."

She snorted, an involuntary, nervous, half-choking noise that seemed to echo in the cavernous hallway. Really smooth. She tried to force some kind of wit past the awkwardness that was overtaking her. "Ohh-kay. If you say so."

He laughed, this deep chuckle that seemed to come straight out of his chest and fill the space between them with warmth. Lord, even his laugh was sexy. So not fair.

"Well, okay, it *is* that. But why it's there is just an occupational hazard."

His laugh and easy tone settled her some. Or maybe it was the fact that he was obviously feeling awkward, too. "Occupational hazard? Must be more interesting than the sleep lab."

He jabbed a thumb toward the office. "It is. Sexuality department. I'm working on my dissertation under Professor Paxton."

She could tell he didn't recognize her from class. Not surprising since she sat in the back of the large stadium-style room and tried to be as invisible as possible. Plus, she was wearing her glasses tonight. "I'm with Professor Roberts. I'm monitoring the sleep study tonight."

"Oh, right on. I didn't realize he'd taken on another grad student. I'm Donovan, by the way."

I know.

"Mari." The nickname rolled off her lips. No one called her that anymore. But she knew he probably graded her papers, and the name Marin wasn't all that common. She forced a small smile, not correcting him that she was about as far from a grad student as she could get. She wanted to be one. Would be one day if she could figure out how to afford it. She'd managed to test out of two semesters of classes, but high IQ or not, that dream was still a long way off—a point of light at the end of a very long, twisting tunnel.

Marin shifted on her feet. "I was heading to get a Coke so that I don't fall asleep from doing data entry and watching people snore. You need anything?"

"A Coke?" He glanced down the hall. "Don't waste a buck fifty on the vending machine. I've got a mini-fridge in here. You can come in and grab whatever you want."

Are you an option? I'd like to grab you. The errant thought made her bite her lips together so none of those words would accidentally slip out. She had no idea where this side of herself was coming from. Not that she'd really know what to do after she grabbed Donovan anyway. This was a twentysomething-year-old man, not one of the few boys she'd awkwardly made out with in high school. This was a guy who'd know how to do all those things she'd only read about in books.

"No, that's okay, I mean..." She shifted her gaze away, willing her face not to go red again.

He caught her meaning and laughed. "Oh, right. Sorry. Yes, you should probably avoid strange men with erections who invite you inside for a drink. Good safety plan, Mari." He lifted his hands and stepped back fully into the doorway, the pronounced outline in his pants gone. "But I promise, you're all good now. You just caught me at an... unfortunate moment. And now I'm going to bribe you with free soda so that you don't tell the other grads in the department about what you saw. I keep these late hours and work through holidays to avoid that kind of torture."

He gave her a tilted smile that made something flutter in her chest. She should probably head straight back to the office she was supposed to be working in. He was older. Kind of her teacher. If he found out she was one of Pax's students, he'd probably freak out that she'd seen him like this. But the chance to spend a few minutes with him was too tempting to pass up.

Plus, the way he was looking at her settled something inside her. Usually she shut down around guys. Being jerked around from school to school on her mom's whims hadn't left her with much time to develop savvy when it came to these things. But something about Donovan made her want to step forward instead of run away. "Yeah, okay. Free is good."

"Cool." His face brightened. Maybe he'd been as lonely and bored tonight as she had been. He bent over and picked up the papers he'd thrown into the hallway and then swept a hand in front of him. "Welcome to my personal hell. The fridge is in the back corner."

Marin stepped in first, finding his office a sharp contrast to the sterile sleep lab. His desk was stacked with photocopied articles and books, a Red Bull sat atop one of the piles, and a microphone was set up in the middle with a line going to the laptop. Along the back wall was a worn couch with a pillow and a blanket. More books were on the floor next to the makeshift napping quarters. Controlled chaos. She carefully made her way to the fridge and grabbed a Dr Pepper.

"Did you want me to get you something?" She peered back over her shoulder.

Donovan was busy gathering a pile of papers off the one other chair in the small office. "No, I'm good. Just opened my third Red Bull. I think my blood has officially been converted to rocket fuel. Don't light any matches."

She smiled and stepped back toward the door. "I hear ya.

Well, thanks for the drink. I'll let you get back to—uh, whatever it was you were doing."

He pointed to the spot he'd cleared. "Or you could stay for a sec and take a break. God knows I need one."

She hesitated for a moment, knowing she was taking the I'm-a-fellow-grad-student charade to far, but then she thought about the endless boredom awaiting her in the sleep lab. She moved her way around the desk and sat. What could a few more minutes hurt? "Yeah, you sounded kind of pissed off when I walked by."

He stilled, and she cringed when she realized what she'd revealed.

He lowered himself to the chair behind his desk. "You can hear me in the hallway?"

"I—sound travels. The hall echoes." She made some ridiculous swirling motion with her finger—as if he needed a visual interpretation of the word *echo*. She dropped her hand to her side and tucked it under her thigh to keep it from going rogue again.

"Good to know. So you heard…"

"Enough."

He laughed, all easy breezy, like they were discussing what they'd had for lunch today instead of X-rated talk and random erections in an institute of higher learning. "Well, then. Guess I should probably explain what I'm doing so I don't look like a total perv."

"It's fine. I mean, whatever." She wasn't sure if she sounded nonchalant or like she'd taken a few sucks off a helium tank. She guessed the latter.

He lifted a crumpled paper off his desk. "This is what you

heard."

She leaned forward, trying to read the crinkled handwriting.

"Scripts," he explained. "I'm doing my dissertation on female sexual arousal in response to auditory stimuli. I'm recording scripts of fantasies that we may use in the study."

"Your study is about *dirty talk*?" she asked, surprised that the university was down with that. And if he was the one doing the dirty talking, where did she sign up to volunteer?

He smirked and there was a hint of mischief in that otherwise affable expression. "Yes, I guess that's one way to put it. If you want to be crass about it, Ms. Sleep Disorders."

"I'm no expert, but I know what I heard."

"Fair enough. But yeah, I'm focusing on the effect of scripted erotic talk on women who have arousal disorder. A lot of times, therapists suggest that these clients watch erotic movies to try to increase their libido. But in general, porn is produced for men. So even though that method can be somewhat effective, the films don't really tap into women's fantasies. They tap into men's. Erotic books have worked pretty well. But I want to test out another method to add to the arsenal—audio. It'd be cost effective to make, wouldn't send more money to the porn industry, and could be customized to a client's needs. Plus, it's easy to test in a lab."

Marin liked that he was talking to her like a peer, and his frankness about the topic saved her some of the weirdness that would normally surface when talking about sex. Academic talk soothed her. Plus, his passion was catching. That's what she loved about this environment. In high school, everyone acted like they were being forced to learn. She'd always been the odd one for actually enjoying school. Books and all that information had been her escape. Schools changed. The people around her changed. Books were one of the few things that stayed constant. But here at the university there were people like Donovan, people who seemed to be mainlining their education and getting high off what they learned. "So what were you so frustrated about?"

He grabbed his can of Red Bull and took a sip, keeping his eyes on her the whole time. "I'm discovering that women are complicated and that I'm having trouble thinking like one."

"Ah. And this is shocking news?"

"Well, no. I knew it was going to be tough, but the fantasies are turning out to be harder than I thought. We did a round of romantic ones in a small trial run, and they were a major fail. Women reported enjoying listening to them but the arousal was..." He gave an arcing thumbs-down. "My friend, Alexis, one of the other grads working under Pax, told me that I needed to go more primal, tap into the forbidden type of fantasies, that sweet romance makes a girl warm and fuzzy but not necessarily hot and bothered."

Marin's neck prickled with awareness, but she tried to keep her expression smooth. "Makes sense."

"Does it?"

"I—uh, I mean..."

"Never mind. I retract the question." He leaned back in his chair and ran a hand through his dark hair, making it even messier. "I met you like five minutes ago, and I'm already asking you if taboo fantasies do it for you. Sorry. Hang out in this department too long, and you lose your filter for what is acceptable in normal conversation. I spent lunch yesterday discussing nocturnal penile tumescence with a sixty-five-year-old female professor, and it wasn't weird. This is my life."

Marin smiled and played with the tab on the top of her soda. "I'm clearly hanging out in the wrong department. My professor just talks about sleep apnea. Though I've been monitoring the sleep lab and can confirm that nocturnal penile tumescence is alive and well."

"Ha. I bet."

She wet her lips and, feeling brave, leaned forward to grab the script he'd left on his desk. He didn't make a move to stop her, and she squinted at the page, trying to decipher his handwriting. The fantasy looked to be one between a boss and subordinate. She saw the parts she'd heard him read aloud. *I'm hard for you. I tug down your panties.*

She crossed her legs. The part he'd gotten hung up on had various crude names for the female anatomy listed and scratched out—like he couldn't decide which one would be most effective. She didn't have input to give him on that, but just seeing the fantasy on the page had her skin tingling with warmth, her blood stirring. She shifted in her chair. Kept reading.

"Okay, well that's a good sign," he said, his voice breaking through the quiet room.

Marin looked up. "What?"

He leaned his forearms against the desk, his blue eyes meeting hers. "You just made a sound."

"I did not."

"Yeah, you did. Like this breathy sound. And your neck is all flushed. That one's working for you."

She tossed the paper on his desk. "Oh my God, you really don't have a filter."

He smiled, something different flaring in his eyes, something that made her feel more flustered than those words on the page. "Sorry. It's all right, though. Seriously. You already saw me with a hard-on. Now we're even. But this is good information. I thought this one may be too geared toward the male side—a fantasy that'd appeal to me but not necessarily to a woman. You're telling me I'm wrong."

"I didn't say anything."

"You didn't have to. You're like..."

She could feel her nipples pushing against her bra, their presence obvious against her T-shirt, and fought the urge to clamp her hands over them, to hid her traitor body. She stood. "Okay, so I'm leaving now."

"No, no, come on, wait," he said, standing. He grabbed her hand before she could escape, and the touch radiated up her arm, trapping her breath in the back of her throat. "You can help. I've got a stack of these. I need to know which ones to test next week and which ones to trash. Or maybe you can offer suggestions? I promise to keep my eyes to myself. And I swear, if you help me, I'm yours for whatever you want. I can take a shift in the sleep lab for you or something."

She stared at him. He was kidding, right? He had to be kidding.

"You want me to read through fantasies and tell you which ones *turn me on*?" His hand was so warm against her cold one. And she'd said the words *turn me on* to him. Out loud. She might just die. "Can't you ask your friend who's in this department to do that?"

"She's a lesbian, so her fantasies don't quite line up with these. I need a straight girl's opinion. Wait—are you straight?"

She blinked. Were they actually having this conversation? "I—yes. But this is beyond embarrassing."

"Why? Because you get turned on by fantasy stuff? It's not embarrassing. It's human. You'd be shocked by how many people struggle to tap into that part of themselves. That kind of responsiveness is a good thing."

Responsiveness. Donovan West was taking about her sexual responsiveness. *Hello, alternate universe.* "Donovan, I don't know…"

He let go of her hand and opened a drawer. "Here. I have an idea. I'll give you some headphones and a thumb drive with the ones I've already recorded. You can take them back to your lab and listen to them while you do data entry. Then you can just tell me which ones you recommend when you're done. You won't have to feel self-conscious sitting with me. Plus, I need to record some more tonight, and I can't do that if someone's in here with me."

He held out the earbuds and a blue thumb drive. She eyed them like they would bite her, but on those files would be Donovan's voice in her ear, saying those explicit things, things she'd never had a guy whisper to her. Things she'd only imagined in the private quiet of her room when she gave her mind leave to go to those secret places. The temptation was a hot, pulsing thing low in her belly.

She needed to say no. Make some excuse. Stop this lie she'd started.

She took the items. "Okay."

His eyebrows lifted. "Yeah?"

"I'm not making any promises, but I'll let you know if I've listened to any before I leave tonight."

His grin was like a physical touch to her skin. "That would be amazing. I'll owe you big-time, Mari."

She got caught up in that smile like a fly in a web and wanted to linger, wanted to stay there all night and listen to him talk about his research, what made him passionate, what else made him smile like that. But if she stayed, she'd only risk embarrassing herself further, or worse—get herself in trouble. Because the thing blooming inside her with him looking at her like that, like her opinion mattered, was intoxicating and potent. She wanted to cling to it, to wrap herself up in that feeling and jump into the unknown without thinking about the consequences. Something she could never do.

She lived her life carefully, always making sure to stay between the lines on the road. No alcohol. No drugs. And definitely no risky behavior with boys. She'd learned from her mother that one foot off the path, one chased whim, could lead to chaos. She knew enough about her mom's disorder to know that those genes probably lingered in her, too, and this pulsing desire to flirt with Donovan, to push this charade further, could be a dangerous one.

She probably shouldn't listen to the tapes at all, shouldn't open that door. Things were safe right now, calm. She needed them to stay that way.

But Marin couldn't bring herself to hand the flash drive back. Not yet. She didn't want to do anything to erase that smile off of Donovan's face.

So she mumbled a quick good-bye and headed down the hall with the thumb drive tucked in her pocket and the soda in her hand. She'd only told Donovan she'd try. She had an out. She needed to take it and focus on her job. Get those little numbers entered into the computer, get lost in the monotony, and forget about the sexy T.A. down the hall.

But it wasn't more than twenty minutes after she stepped back into Professor Roberts's lab that the temptation proved to great. Maybe she'd just listen to one, show Donovan a good faith effort, and be done. She cued up the recordings, and Donovan's voice filtered into her head.

"I spot you first across the bar. You look beautiful and I know you've come here with someone else. I can see him getting you a drink. But I can feel your eyes on me, taste your desire, and I know that tonight, it's going to be my hands on you, my body moving over yours, and my name on your lips..."

Marin didn't get another lick of work done that night.

acknowledgements

Thank you to my husband, Donnie, who never wavers in his cheerleading and who picks up all the household and parenting slack when I'm buried under a deadline. Love you (and your veggie burgers)!

To my parents and family, for always being there and believing in me.

To my kidlet, for always, always making me laugh and for not complaining when mom has to work extra hours. (Even though he may be so accommodating because it means video game time for him, lol.)

To my agent, Sara Megibow for wielding all her agent-y goodness on my behalf and for supporting me in all aspects of my career.

To Dawn Alexander, for the beta reading and for being in the "cubicle" next to me during the day even though we're miles away from each other. This can be a lonely job and it's nice to have a co-worker to chat with and vent to.

To Kelli Collins, for giving this book a fantastic edit and saving Elle from being a super-mega-unlikable bitch, lol.

To the planner peeps group, for being a warm and cozy place on the internet when I need to hide, chat, and look at pretty things.

And finally, to all my readers, you are the best. I get to write stories that I love because you choose to read them. So thank you, truly. I never take your time for granted and will continue to work hard to write stories that you want to read.

about the author

Roni wrote her first romance novel at age fifteen when she discovered writing about boys was way easier than actually talking to them. Since then, her flirting skills haven't improved, but she likes to think her storytelling ability has. If she's not working on her latest sexy story, you can find her cooking, watching reality television, or picking up another hobby she doesn't need—in other words, procrastinating like a boss. She is a RITA Award winner and a *New York Times* and *USA Today* bestselling author.

CPSIA information can be obtained
at www.ICGtesting.com
Printed in the USA
LVHW040906180619
621577LV00002B/110/P